The Novella Nostalgia Collection

Book One

THE NOVELLA NOSTALGIA SERIES

This publishing initiative brings together the uniqueness of the novella and various memorable movies from the history of cinema.

The word 'novella' comes from the Italian for 'novel.' It has been interpreted in various ways including 'a long short story' or a 'short novel'. It can be traced back to the early renaissance in Italy and France. Giovanni Boccaccio wrote 'The Decameron' in 1353. This comprises 100 tales of ten people fleeing the black death. It was not until the 18th and 19th centuries that the novella emerged as a literary genre.

In 1941, the Austrian novelist Stefan Zweig wrote 'The Chess Novella' which was later renamed 'The Royal Game'. This was the inspiration for the 1960 film 'Brainwashed'.

Most modern novellas are published by Penguin Modern Classics. The various novella prizes seem to stipulate a word count of between 7,500 and 40,000. A key feature of the novella is its limited punctuation. There are no chapter headings and no breaks apart from spaces where the author needs to show a scene change.

In 2018 City Fiction created the *Novella Nostalgia* series with the publication of *Lunch with Harry* inspired by the American romantic comedy, *Breakfast at Tiffany's*. More titles followed, new authors were recruited and, in early 2020, the tenth title in the series was launched.

'The Novella Nostalgia Collection: Book One' contains four of the series selected by the publisher.

Full details of the Novella Nostalgia series can be found at www.cityfiction.co.uk.

THE NOVELLA NOSTALGIA COLLECTION: BOOK ONE

CONTENTS

NOVELLA ONE

THE MAN WHO HATED

by

Tony Drury

Inspired by the 1993 film 'Falling Down'

THE MAN WHO HATED

He was trapped, and she was the cause.

There were knobbly joints in Elsie's fingers. The cartilage had become pitted and brittle and she could not straighten them. She had been late that morning in taking her analgesics. The young woman on the supermarket till was patient, sympathetic and told her customer to take all the time she needed. The eighty-year-old had some vouchers which could reduce her bill. She managed to find them in her purse, which was at the bottom of her bag. There were nine, but three were out of date. Frustration flashed across her face because she did not have enough cash to pay for the seven items on the conveyor belt. Elsie looked around. She needed to use the toilet.

Three of the purchases were frozen meals. They were a treat for the weekend ahead. She told the assistant she would have to pay with her credit card which was in her coat pocket, but she could not remember which one. The young woman suggested that she try the right-hand side, and there it was. Slowly, Elsie managed to push the card into the slot. She could not recall the PIN but then she remembered: it was her birthday. 1934. She briefly relived her early years in pre-war Brighton. Agonisingly, she pressed the four digits: 1934. 1 August 1934. The card was rejected. Elsie looked up and apologised for being a silly old woman.

Milton Grant concurred: he was due to have sex at eleven-thirty. He had completed his shopping and selected this particular till because the customer being served only had a few items in her basket. As he laid out his organic purchases, a woman with two children

1

came in behind him and started to add her groceries behind his purchases. The customer at the front of the queue was taking ages to complete her business. Milton was pleased she had such disfigured hands. He hoped her painkillers were not strong enough to provide more than temporary relief.

He made eye contact with the checkout assistant. She immediately looked away. Her hand hovered over the call button as she wondered if he was going to kick off. The situation was frustrating, but her training had emphasised that every customer was important. She was reassured by his shrug and casual glance at his watch. His benign expression concealed his loathing and impatience.

He hated his name: Milton. He had instigated several fights at school when mates tried to shorten it to Milt. His patriotic parents, before they separated, had named him after a new town in Buckinghamshire. This was post-war Britain and people were full of hope and ambition. The government was building hundreds of new homes in a place called Milton Keynes. Stella liked his name. If he satisfied her in the way she relished, she would say, "Milton, that was heaven." It was a pity about the other matter…

The supermarket assistant suggested that her customer tried the PIN one more time. Elsie pressed 1934. It was rejected. Milton felt tension in his stomach. The woman behind him was telling her children how much she loved them. His anger was mounting. The older woman cried out: she remembered she had read an article in the *Daily Mail* about credit card security and she had reversed her birth year for her PIN to make it safer. Elsie entered in 3491 and it was rejected. The assistant suggested that the reverse was 4391. The elderly lady laughed and said, "Silly me, dear." Milton was just about holding his temper. Elsie entered 4391 and the assistant celebrated the completion of the transaction with her. Elsie put the credit card into her pocket, thanked the young woman on the till, picked up her shopping and immediately dropped the bag. Two of the six eggs smashed.

It took around four minutes to clean the floor. By this time, the customer behind Milton was struggling to control her children. The earlier theme of matriarchal love had been replaced by bribes as she opened a packet of chocolate biscuits and reluctantly distributed them. She told Milton she was in a hurry and blinked when she heard his reply. The till cleared and he paid for his purchases, rather abruptly indicating he did not want cash back. He hurried away for his eleven-thirty appointment.

As he drove out of the supermarket car park, he spotted the old lady hobbling towards the bus stop. Elsie was unsteady on her feet, which pleased him. He waited his moment and slowly drove alongside her. As she glanced towards his vehicle, he suddenly pulled over towards her. She threw her arms into the air and fell onto her right side, crashing into a concrete bollard and screaming as her femur shattered.

Milton laughed as he drove away. He knew that his car's registration number was being recorded on the CCTV. That would not help the police in any way. The vehicle had false plates. Tomorrow, he would drive to Shoreditch in East London where he would meet a man he had once arrested for car theft. Milton would buy a replacement vehicle from him for cash.

He'd then drive the forty miles home, garage his vehicle and fit new number plates.

It was eleven twenty-nine when he pulled up in her drive. Their ritual remained unchanged. After he had taken early retirement from his job as a police constable, having convinced the medical authorities that the demands of attending motorway accidents was resulting in stress and loss of sleep, he divorced his wife and told his daughter, Jennifer, that he would send her three hundred pounds every month. His plan was taking shape. At last his life had a point to it. He met Stella on a dating website, having paid five hundred pounds for the introduction. Hers was the twenty-third reply he had received; he had rejected the gold-diggers and one woman he suspected of plotting an entrapment. The site had a feature he liked. People could connect but were not allowed to share photographs. Milton knew exactly how to get around that, but he played by the rules because he liked Stella's candid answers. Stella had been through two divorces and was concerned about becoming involved with another potential husband. She was not prepared to risk the humiliation of a third failed relationship, but let slip that her two former spouses had funded her future needs. Her sons had long since left home, but they stayed in touch from Estonia and the Antarctic.

They met. Milton looked after himself by following a near-vegetarian diet and taking daily six-mile runs. He also went hillwalking regularly, where he relished the solitude of the peaks. Stella worked part-time in a local hospital as a physiotherapist. She knew she was a few pounds overweight, but was fairly secure that her attraction to men remained potent. She was sexually intuitive and, within three meetings, had Milton summed up, ready for the bedroom. Sex was straightforward: he was a normal heterosexual male. He had no special requirements; he loved female flesh and reacted positively when it was revealed, sensitively. During their second meeting, in a coffee shop, he told her that he occasionally watched *Breakfast at Tiffany's* so that he could enjoy the scene in the Manhattan flat where Audrey Hepburn playfully messes around in a white shirt, allowing the revelation of her near-perfect figure.

Stella greeted him at the door with a glass of pinot grigio. They pecked each other's cheek and shared a few minutes together drinking the wine. She made a comment about his punctuality and followed up with her usual mannerism. Milton wished she wouldn't, but let it go. They went into the back room extension, where their privacy was assured. She had prepared the Jacuzzi ready for their time together: she had saved up for it and she loved it.

She was wearing a long pink shirt. They sat down by the Jacuzzi and sipped a second glass of wine. Stella crossed her legs but ensured that the material did not rise up above her thighs. Her skin was smooth, and the undoing of a top button revealed more of it to Milton. They exchanged small talk, discussing politics and the rise of Jeremy Corbyn. Milton suggested that the slogan 'For the many, not the few' brilliantly caught the mood of the country. She teased him by telling him she found the Labour leader rather sexy. She uncrossed her legs, allowing the shirt to rise a little. He wondered what she might reveal next. Stella had chosen black knickers because she had worked out the colour stirred his juices. She lifted her bottom off the seat and pulled the shirt from under her, leaning over to test the temperature of the water. She stood up and encouraged Milton to stand too. She undressed him and led him to the steps. As he submerged himself, she removed her shirt. Two hours later she sighed with pleasure. "Milton," she said, "that was heaven."

Milton left her house around three in the afternoon and went to the cinema to see *American Assassin*, which he found entertaining. He related to the vengeful CIA black ops recruit Mitch Rapp as he helped a Cold War veteran (Michael Keaton) stop the detonation of a nuclear device. The brooding Shiva Negar, playing the mysterious Annika, took his fancy. When she was being tortured in a bath tub it made him wonder about Stella's Jacuzzi and its potential for excitement. He left the cinema, bought a vegetarian pizza, returned home and opened a bottle of chilled white wine which he took into his office. Milton switched on a CD of Chopin études, which added to his contentment. He and his companion met twice weekly and occasionally went out for Sunday lunch. He liked her… but he wished she wouldn't do that one thing.

He had wondered whether to tell her about his mission – especially as she occasionally chided him for having few outside interests – but he decided not to, chastising himself for showing weakness. Secrecy was paramount, and he had no wish to even be interviewed by the police. He looked at his list of eighteen possible corrections and eight situations. This was the result of many weeks of research of people's pet hates. The difference was that he, Milton Grant, would do something about it instead of just moaning. He and Stella would have Sunday lunch together and he would start his mission on Tuesday, in the knowledge that she would be waiting for him in the afternoon.

He had selected 'traffic lights' as his first correction, remembering the case as though it had only happened yesterday. He had been a police officer for five years, on traffic duty, when he was called to a minor collision. The lights had turned from amber to green and the lady driver and her companion, who had turned to face each other, had continued their conversation, ignoring the horns from the two cars behind them. One driver got out and went to remonstrate with the driver, who reacted angrily then accelerated away, not noticing that the lights had changed to red. A van hit her.

Milton had arrived at the scene to see three people shouting at each other. The woman driver then collapsed. A paramedic arrived and she was taken to hospital. The Crown Prosecution Service prosecuted her for driving without due care and attention. She asked for the advice of her husband, who suggested that one of Lincoln's Inn's finest criminal barristers should defend her. Milton was confident about the evidence he would give until, under pressure from the defence counsel, he made a comment about women needing to face each other when they were talking. He was only repeating what the driver behind the defendant's car had told him.

Counsel pounced and managed to discredit his evidence, believing he was prejudiced against women drivers. The case was dismissed, the CPS lawyer called Milton a moron and, as he left the court, the woman came up and thanked him for being a misogynist.

This event had coincided with Milton's growing realisation that his wife and young daughter were establishing an alliance which resulted in an unhealthy accusation of his perceived faults. He decided to have a vasectomy as he wanted no more children. His wife found out when she opened the bill from the hospital – and that, effectively, was that. They struggled on for another few years until her parents died within a few months of each other. She inherited half a house and bought out her brother. Their divorce was business-like and Milton breathed a sigh of relief when he finally gained his independence.

The seeds of his correction programme, in which he had decided to make an example of people guilty of eight of the worst faults he had detected in his fellow human beings, had been sown both by his experiences as a police officer and on receiving the diagnosis from his doctor. He would carry out the first correction next Tuesday. The first on the list, 'traffic lights', was one that annoyed him beyond expression, although several others were equally irritating. After the court case he had found himself becoming obsessed by drivers who were slow to react when traffic lights turned green. With the increasing number of vehicles on the roads, it was selfish for drivers to take too long to accelerate away from traffic lights. He spent Friday travelling down to London to meet his acquaintance, change his car and replace the number plates. Stella joined him for Sunday lunch at a local pub. They discussed his love of classical piano music and her obsession with *Strictly Come Dancing*.

She knew her Chopin, but was annoyed by the results of the voting from the previous evening's programme.

By Tuesday morning Milton had put on two stone in weight, lost his hair and was two inches taller. His inspiration for this disguise was the Clint Eastwood film *In the Line of Fire*. In it, actor John Malkovich played the part of Mitch Leary, the former Secret Service agent who told the President's personal security officer that he was going to kill his boss. He plagued Clint Eastwood by continually disguising himself. Milton had watched the film time and again and revelled in the finale, in which Agent Frank Horrigan (played by Eastwood) dived in front of the President and took the bullet fired by Mitch Leary. He also won the heart of Agent Lily Raines (played by Rene Russo), whose bedroom antics and black underwear left Milton Grant dripping with sweat.

After spending several hours perfecting fitting his range of hairpieces, he swallowed a small piece of cordite which was an army technique to make the skin temporarily go white. He padded out a jacket two sizes too big for him and put on platform shoes. On Monday he travelled to some local woods which he explored to ensure he was familiar with them. After leaving his car at home, he went indoors, changed his clothes and walked half a mile to the garage he rented, carrying a suitcase. This was where he kept the vehicle he had bought in Shoreditch the previous Friday, and which now had false number plates. He stored his disguise in the boot. He went to bed early, slept soundly and woke up early, whereupon he went for a six-mile run followed by a shower and a breakfast of mixed nuts, raisins and fresh fruit.

He wanted to find his victim in the Tuesday morning commuter traffic. At around eight-fifteen there would be a combination of office workers and school-run parents fighting for space at the crossroads he had selected. He was not fussed if his victim was male, female or even transgender, although he abhorred all the modern nonsense about LGBT. He just wanted to find an example of a selfish driver failing to respond to the changing lights in a considerate manner.

He collected his car from the garage and parked in a side street, then walked to the traffic lights and took up position. As he stood there, a youth in a Vauxhall Astra delayed accelerating away due to the fact he was resetting his iPod. He was oblivious to the protests behind him and, having found the music of his choice, sat up and checked his acne in the driver's mirror, brushing away the flecks of dead skin. The van driver behind him gave another angry wake-up blow of his horn. After looking in his mirror, the Astra driver lowered his window and held out his hand, his middle finger pointing in the air. He refocused on the lights, which were changing from amber to red, accelerated away and left several frustrated drivers behind him.

Milton rushed to his car, turned into the main road, spotted the red Astra ahead of him, and was following it when the driver turned into a private car park for employees of the local council. Milton drove on, parked in a side street and waited for an hour before returning to search for the red Astra, using the registration number he had written down. He found it towards the back of the parking area. He was glad the car park had no security. Taking out a portable drill he punctured the four tyres, found his tube of transparent glue and sealed all the locks and handles. He took out a plastic container and smeared oil over the windscreen. Then he stuffed mashed cardboard into the exhaust pipe. After ducking for cover when an employee of the council came to collect her car, he decided that she had not seen him, waited for several minutes and then stood up. Taking out a piece of white paper, he applied some glue and plastered it onto the oily windscreen. When the car driver had returned to his car, recovered from his shock, then removed the adhesive from the locks, changed his tyres, sat down in his seat and looked ahead he would read:

When the lights change to green, it means you drive away as quickly and safely as possible.

The driver would later discover the consequences of a blocked exhaust pipe.

Milton parked in Stella's driveway and immediately accepted the offered glass of champagne, making his way into the hall. The white shirt she was wearing was frustratingly opaque. Her skin glistened. They exchanged small talk, and her mannerism appeared briefly. He just wished she wouldn't do it. In the back room, the lights from the hot tub provided the only illumination. Sniffing the air, he sighed with sensual pleasure. She had strategically placed a series of Hooyei-koh incense sticks around the room. The Japanese 'Eternal Treasure' was giving off a mixture of sandalwood and cinnamon. They would burn for around an hour. Long before that Milton would be submerged in the water. Perhaps two hours later he would be receiving the reassurance that their time together had been "heaven".

Police Constable Lucy Smith threw a peanut at her husband, Detective Sergeant David Smith. He was universally known as Dave, apart from to his mother, to whom he was David. His mother had originally worried about the nine-year age difference between her son and his new wife but, two years on, all seemed to be well. It needed to be. Police marriages were notoriously unstable, but she was reassured when she read in a magazine that statistics revealed that police officers who married another police officer generally experienced more fulfilling relationships than officers who found partners outside the police force.

Dave looked up. "I said no, and I mean no."

"I've a cold bottle of lager in the fridge for you," said Lucy.

"Anything else on offer?" asked her libidinous husband.

"How about a cold bottle of lager from the fridge?" replied Lucy.

He laughed. Dave could not believe his luck: his wife was scrumptious.

"Luce," he said. "We agreed, no work gossip at home."

"You also promised a number of other things at the altar," she laughed.

"That was to impress your mother," he said.

She returned from the kitchen with the bribe.

"I'll give you two sentences," he said.

"OK then," she began. "This one is really strange. A man, who we have on CCTV but can't identify, goes into a car park owned by the council and vandalises a car. He punctures all the tyres, glues the locks, puts oil on the windscreen and stuffs mashed cardboard into the exhaust."

Dave held out his empty glass and gave her a pleading look. She stood up, moved towards the kitchen and returned with another glass of lager. Lucy knew she might appear to be a subservient wife, but to hell with gender equality. She knew that Dave loved her and she was happy with their relationship. And what was to happen within weeks would reveal her inner strength...

"You drink too much," she chided. "You're beginning to get a paunch."

"I know a way to lose that..." he said.

"Later." Lucy smiled. "You said two sentences. Well, having trashed the car he left a message on the windscreen."

"Call Patel Car Valeting Services on...." chuckled Dave.

"It read *When the lights change to green, it means you drive away as quickly and safely as possible.*"

"I can only imagine that the owner was none too pleased," Dave commented.

"You mean 'call me Dowie'," said Lucy. "He was incensed. It didn't stop him trying to look down my blouse." She sipped her glass of elderflower. "When I asked him if anyone had any reason to bear a grudge against him, such as an ex-girlfriend, he gave me fifteen names then stopped."

"So, why are you telling me this in breach of our marital vows?" said Dave.

"It's not one of his exes, Dave."

"Ah. So now we are a detective," Dave said.

Lucy had moved over to sit at his feet.

"I'm in my second month of secondment," she said. "I really do want to be a detective constable."

"No one was hurt. The police don't care about cars any more. It doesn't help the statistics. Move on, Luce," suggested her husband.

Lucy stood up and went to look out of the window. "And if it was your case, Dave, would you move on?"

"No," he replied.

"Ah ha!" cried Lucy. "Why not, Detective Sergeant Smith?"

"Because of the exhaust pipe," he replied.

"The exhaust pipe?" she exclaimed.

"You are saying he stuffed mashed cardboard into the exhaust pipe," he said.

"Yes, Dave. The engineer said—"

"Luce. Trust me. Whoever he is, he's nasty."

Criminally, the engineer had failed to clear all the mashed cardboard out of the exhaust pipe. A section had been pushed further inside and had hardened. Dowie had finally been able to collect his vehicle, and spent a long time returning it to its pristine condition to attract the girls.

He was furious that someone had vandalised his precious car, and needed to assuage his anger. He drove to the motorway feeder road and accelerated away. He checked his hair in the mirror, chuffed with the high fade and textured quiff which his pal in The Razor Sharp Salon had done for free. Dowie turned on the music and began to croon.

Within the car engine, pressure was building as discarded gases built up inside the exhaust system.

Finally, the head gasket blew. The car rapidly lost power and slowed down in the outside lane. Dowie banged his foot down on the accelerator pedal, looked in his mirror and saw a lorry bearing down on him. Panicking, he opened the car door and flung himself out of the stationary vehicle. He landed on the central crash barrier and slumped, screaming, to the ground on the other side. This protected him from the carnage as the lorry, the driver blaring his horn, smashed into his car, demolishing it.

The music filling his office reflected his mood. Milton was elated by the success of his first correction, and relished the thought of the selfish motorist trying to sort out his vandalised car. As Milton absorbed the uncharacteristically cheerful music of Dimitri Shostakovich, who had dedicated his Piano Concerto no. 2 in F major to his son Maxim on his nineteenth birthday, Milton thought about Stella, who had been at her sensual best. Thursday could not come soon enough.

Milton looked down at his list. He had taken an item from the reserve page and added it to his total of eight human faults. It was now at number two. The incident had taken place two hours earlier. The odour had nauseated him. It must have occurred on the grassy area between his driveway and the road. As he entered his hall he looked down and realised that his carpet was smeared with dog mess. Tearing off his shoes, although only the right one was affected, he rushed into the kitchen, took out a plastic bin liner, threw the shoes into it, went outside through the side entrance, soaked his feet and threw the waste into the dustbin. He returned to his kitchen, took off his clothes, prepared a bucket full of soapy water, went back into the hall and scrubbed and scrubbed until the carpet was free of any canine waste. Back in the kitchen, he poured the contents of the bucket down the sink, disinfected the whole area and went upstairs and put on his running kit. He left his house and ran for six miles, returning soaked to the skin. He stripped off and showered. He dried himself, dressed in casual clothes, entered his office, put on his chosen music and began to plan correction number two.

During his years as a police constable human behaviour had often perplexed him. He had been called to a block of twelve flats in a pleasant suburban area. Eleven of the homes were occupied by a mixture of law-abiding citizens (well, relatively – two were involved in tax fiddles and one abused his wife) who wanted to sleep at night. The twelfth, a man in his fifties, played David Bowie's music, rather too loudly, throughout the night. Every night. In the end, at considerable cost to the taxpayer, the council managed to obtain an order against him. The music lover moved half a mile into another block of flats and repeated the same pattern of behaviour.

As far as Milton was concerned, dog shit came into the same category of selfishness. It baffled him that a minority of owners refused to clear up after their pet. How could they desecrate public areas where children played? The law of the land was clear. The Public Spaces Protection Order stipulated that dogs must be kept on a lead, they were not allowed in restricted places (such as farmland), and the owner must clear up after his animal had defecated. Inevitably, a minority decided that they were above the law.

It took him the whole of Wednesday to prepare his corrective campaign. He walked for miles with a plastic scoop and bucket. By the end of the day he was ready. As always, sleep came easily. In the morning, he woke refreshed, ran six miles, showered and ate breakfast. The morning would be spent in the local park, where he might be vulnerable to being caught on CCTV. This was countered with a simple disguise. He wore a hat, put on glasses with clear lenses, carried a walking stick and assumed a limp. Adding an indistinctive raincoat, dark trousers and black shoes, he carried his equipment in a supermarket carrier bag.

By nine o'clock, after the school run was over, he was in the local park. His plan went well – until it went wrong. He kept to the tree line and watched for dog walkers who did not clear up their pet's mess. By ten-thirty he had located and punished three offenders. After each had committed the offence, he followed them until the opportunity came for him to slip into their pocket – or, preferably, the bag they were carrying – a plain envelope. When his first victim returned home, she groomed her cocker spaniel and then discovered the package in her shopping bag. It was not sealed. She undid the flap and put her hand inside, recoiling as she felt the sticky substance into which she had placed her fingers. She pulled it out and felt ill as it dawned on her what it was. The dog owner read the notice she had withdrawn from the envelope:

You selfish person. Clean your dog's mess up. Look at your fingers. A child could have landed in your animal's poo. I'll be watching you.

She ran to the toilet and vomited, then afterwards

vowed never again to fail to collect her pet's mess.

The fourth candidate for correction proved to have a different attitude. There was a car park near the lake. Milton was resting at the water's edge, eating an apple. He saw a middle-aged man get out of his Range Rover, open the rear door and release a bloodhound. It did not go too far before stopping and emptying its bowels in the middle of the path. There seemed to be a mountain of excrement. The owner whistled and walked away in the opposite direction. Milton watched with growing anger. He waited for a few moments as several walkers skirted round the mess, then went over and scooped the whole pile into his bag, having taken out the remaining envelopes. Returning to the dog owner's car, he smeared the shit all over the windscreen. He took out one of the notices and placed it in the centre of the screen, hid in the trees and waited.

The owner returned twenty minutes later, opened the rear door and encouraged the bloodhound to jump into the boot. He went round to the front of his vehicle and looked at the message, lifted it off and read it. He laughed, went back to the rear door and opened it. Taking out some rags and an ice scraper he proceeded to clear the windscreen, whistling as he did so. He put the cleaning items back in the car and then, to Milton's complete surprise, gave a command. Out jumped a small mongrel. The man then closed and locked the vehicle. The second pet ran away, then stopped and defecated on the path. The owner whistled and walked off in the opposite direction again. Milton followed him.

His opportunity came a few minutes later when the dog owner sat down on a park bench and stared across the lake. Milton checked the area and saw there was nobody around. Approaching the dog walker from behind, he hit him across the back of the neck with a fallen branch. He then put his arm around the dazed man and, with his right hand, smeared excrement all over his face, squeezing closed his victim's nostrils. As the dog walker gasped for breath, Milton stuffed shit into his mouth. He whispered into his ear, "Got the message, arsehole?"

Lucy and Dave were reluctant to accept mid-week invitations. Working at different police stations (Dave was attached to Area HQ) gave them problems when trying to co-ordinate their hours. This Wednesday evening, however, they were both off, and they were sitting around a dinner table with Annabel and Amjit. Both were doctors at different local practices. Annabel's friendship with Lucy had originated at high school. As they opened the third bottle of wine (with Lucy on Diet Coke and driving duty), the conversation became more excitable. Annabel and Amjit had been to Glastonbury and were reliving some of the music of Foo Fighters – although Annabel would have preferred Jamie Cullum who, for her, had lit up the weekend. The hosts asked about Lucy and Dave's police work. This often happened on social occasions. Dave was a past master at deflecting the subject. Lucy, who was clear-headed, asked to be excused and returned a few moments later looking ashen. Dave failed to understand the signs. Annabel did, and she put her hand on Lucy's arm and encouraged her friend to talk.

"We're not allowed to talk about what we do," said Lucy.

"So what's happened?" asked Annabel. "I've been your friend for a long time. You're a tough one. Something's upset you. What is it?"

"Luce," said Dave, "shall we go home?"

"It sounds awful," said Lucy. "He stuffed dog poo into his mouth."

She stood up and rushed to the toilet. Amjit followed her. A few minutes later they were all together again around the table. Annabel served coffee. Lucy told the whole story: the emergency call from the park, the taking of the victim into hospital following his violent allergic reaction, the police search of the area, the forensic team working on the notice, and the reaction of the man's wife, who wanted to sue everybody.

"Luce. Tell us again. What did the notice say?"

Lucy was now recovering her poise. "*You selfish person. Clean your dog's mess up. Look at your fingers. A child could have landed in your animal's poo. I'll be watching you.*"

"That's nasty," said Annabel as she kissed her friend.

As they drove home, David had a deep frown on his face.

"Please stop the car, Lucy," he asked.

She did as requested and came to a halt in a lay-by. She turned and faced her husband.

"I'm very sorry, Dave. I'll never do it again. I was totally out of order."

He hugged his wife and suggested they went home.

Lucy began to drive away.

"Dave," she said, "did you hear the word that Annabel used?"

"What word?"

"She said 'nasty'." She slowed and indicated to pass a cyclist, then accelerated away. "Nasty," she said again, rather quietly.

Milton turned up the volume as he prepared to listen to Rachmaninov's Piano Concerto no. 1 in F sharp minor. He slumped at his desk, the list in his hand. Using an orange marker pen, he eliminated 'traffic lights' and 'dog poo'. The 'vivace' came and went and the pianist slowed to begin the 'andante'. He sipped a whisky. With six subjects to go, he knew which would be number eight. It was the one that best summed up the demented – or perhaps tormented – person he was becoming.

He returned to the selection process. There were seven minutes remaining of the 'allegro vivace' in which to make up his mind. The acid mixture was ready. It was no contest. He marked his list with 'No. 3' by the chosen category. He would do it on Tuesday and then he'd see Stella in the afternoon. He was excited by the thought of what was to come. He spent the next four days alone.

On Saturday, Stella phoned Milton to excuse herself from Sunday lunch, explaining she'd decided to run an extra physiotherapy surgery as she had so many patients waiting for an appointment. Easing her patients' symptoms was the easy part of her job. Sorting out the causes of their problems was more of a challenge – and the responsibility of doctors and surgeons. She knew, both as a human being and as a professional, that around half her patients were overweight. In a five-minute examination of a near naked person she would nearly always diagnose the cause of their problems but she would never judge;

that was not her role. Earlier that day she had watched her patient, a man in his fifties, crawl to the weighing scales. He weighed in at twenty-two stones, and told Stella he had been a big baby. Later in the session she asked him about his diet – and how many beers he consumed in an average day. His answers were complete fabrications.

She told Milton about this, and was more than surprised by his reaction.

"Fucking selfish bastards," he suggested. "They know they're fat. They make ludicrous excuses and then expect society to provide for them. Some people are so fat they're stuck in their own houses, and the ambulance service has to get hoists made to get them out." He paused. "Stella, why do we pussyfoot round? Tell them straight. 'You're fat. Lose some fucking weight. If you don't, we'll leave you at the side of the road'."

"And who makes that judgement, Milton?" she asked.

"The ambulance crew. There are enough people who genuinely need their help," he said.

"Yes, I get your drift, but who do you take to hospital and who do you leave by the side of the road?"

"It always the same claptrap, Stella." He sighed. "I'm talking sense and you're going to tell me about their human rights."

"No, I'm bloody not," she said, raising her voice. "Don't you think I feel the same as you? Do you have any idea what it's like physically trying to massage an obese person?"

"Exactly! Throw them out and concentrate on the ones who can be of use to society."

"Milton," she responded angrily, "that's obscene."

"Is it?" he snapped. "Perhaps I'm one of the few people prepared to think the unthinkable."

"You don't get it, do you?" She wiped her eyes. "I'm asking you, who makes the choice? 'Just a moment, Mr Brown, I'll be with you in a moment and we'll sort out your back pain.' 'Sorry, Mr Robinson, you're fat and over twenty stones. We're going to leave you in a field.'"

"So answer me this. Truthfully, please. Are you seeing more and more obese people?"

She put her head in her hands and slumped forward. "I've now got twelve children under ten years old who are more than 70% over their correct weight." She sighed. "The truth is, Milton, we don't know what to do about it."

"You know that everybody has a view about the NHS, Stella?" he asked.

"Oh yes." She laughed.

"Do you know what the NHS's real problem is?"

"Money," she answered. "We are low down the European scale for spending per patient as a percentage of GDP." She looked pleased with her reply.

"No," responded Milton.

"All right, then, tell me," she said.

"The NHS has created its own problem."

"Problem?" she repeated.

"It's too successful at keeping people alive. Whereas they used to nurse people in their seventies, patients today are mostly in their eighties."

"Good point," said Stella.

"That's not the challenge," he continued.

"So what is?" Stella asked, increasingly frustrated.

"People in their eighties are more fragile and vulnerable. The NHS is taking care of an increasingly demanding age group. They fill hospital beds, they need many more prescriptions, they need surgery, and their relatives laugh all the way to their sun-filled beaches as the taxpayer picks up all the bills."

"Yes and no," said Stella.

Milton stared at her.

"Some of the relatives I meet are saints. Without their commitment to their relatives – usually their elderly parents – hospitals would collapse." She hesitated. "But you're right. We have whole wards full of people needing full-time care, and their children have simply walked away."

"Blocking A&E departments," he added.

"Milton. I can solve this," said Stella.

"Go for it," he encouraged.

"Pass a new law. When UK residents reach eighty years of age, they are exiled to a Pacific island."

Milton stared at her. "Brilliant!" he exclaimed. "Just my style."

She noticed that he wasn't laughing.

He looked at her, thoughtfully. "Of course, a neater solution would be to shoot them."

Milton always slept soundly now he had a bed to himself. Two days later he woke at 6am, put on his running shorts and shirt, shuddered as he opened the side door and felt the chill autumn wind, and began his six-mile run which would take him round the local park. He returned within his forty-seven-minute target, showered and put on his tracksuit, omitting breakfast because he could not risk any stomach upset. After sipping some water, he left the house carrying a green bag. He went into his garage, where he had assembled his equipment. He stripped off and took out the clothes he had bought in several London stores. The bra strap caught his skin and he winced as he adjusted it. The silk knickers might have suggested a bizarre sexual desire. Their purpose was rather different: it was necessary to think like a woman. He knew he would be picked up by CCTV and possible witnesses, and he needed to convey the image and personality of a female. It had taken him over three hours in Oxford Street to achieve the appearance he wanted. He had bought the coat from a charity shop. He checked himself in the full-length mirror he had smuggled into the garage. He wore flat sandals, knowing he'd have to change the way he walked and take shorter strides to pass for a woman. The weather forecast predicted a chilly but dry day. It was a thirty-two-mile journey to the centre of the nearby town. At seven forty-five he was in place – and ready to select his first victim.

And there she was. He disliked her the moment he set eyes on her, because she epitomised the selfishness of the modern phone user. She had come out of the railway station and was walking towards the office block at the end of the road. "You bitch," he said quietly to himself as he watched other commuters skirt around her as she strolled, eyes down, glued to her mobile phone. She was immaculately dressed and she seemed to be sending a text message. An older man stepped out of her path into the road, and a cyclist shouted at him.

Milton made a quick calculation. He realised that if he cut through the shopping mall he could possibly overtake her and then turn back. His manoeuvres worked well and within three minutes he was walking towards her down a quieter street. He froze as he saw that she still had her fucking mobile held out in front of her – and now she was laughing. The woman passed close to him, fully occupied by her phone. She never noticed the plastic barrel protruding out of the side of his coat. She didn't notice him squeeze the plastic bulb in his hand. She did not immediately register the acid as it smeared over the inner side of her left thigh. The mixture Milton had prepared contained a slow-acting constituent to give him a few moments to leave the scene.

She stumbled and dropped her phone. Her leg went from beneath her and she fell to the pavement. She started to scream, writhing in agony. A man rushed over to her.

"Are you OK?" he asked. "What happened?"

"My leg! My leg!" she yelled as the tears poured down her face.

He moved her coat and gasped as he saw the mess the acid had made of her limb. He pulled out his phone to call the emergency services. Her phone lay on the pavement.

The paramedics arrived within minutes and immediately listed the case as urgent. She was rushed to hospital. In the coming two years she was to undergo thirteen operations – and would wear jeans for the rest of her life, to avoid the stares of other people.

Three hours later Milton had attacked five more people. It was proving more difficult than he had anticipated, partly because of increased police activity and because he was careful to select deserving victims. When he finally returned to his car he had assaulted another four women and a man. He drove towards the motorway, stopped at the pre-selected section of the woods, walked for a mile, changed his clothes and buried the bag containing his female disguise deep in the undergrowth. Milton walked back to his car and drove to Shoreditch, where he sold his car and bought a van. Then he returned to his garage and changed the number plates. He reached Stella a little after four o'clock. She did not ask why he was later than usual. Their routine remained unchanged, although she found him tense and taut. The wine, the hot tub and scented water, the striptease and the caressing were delivered in their usual way and he responded with his usual vigour, but then found he couldn't reach orgasm.

She laughed and he hated the sound.

He finally achieved climax, then quickly dressed and reassured her that he was well satisfied. He just wished she wouldn't do it.

Lucy was running around the lounge of their modest home, waving a yellow card in the air.

"Yellow card," she said, laughing. "Dave Smith is awarded a yellow card for trying to begin shop talk, contrary to our marriage vows."

"Luce," he pleaded, "not tonight, love. Please, not tonight. I've had a terrible day."

She entered the kitchen and poured him a glass of lager, quickly returning and putting it into his hand. He nodded his appreciation of her understanding as she sat opposite him.

"I'm sorry, love. What's happened?" she asked.

"Didn't you hear it on the news?"

"I've been studying all afternoon," she responded.

"Want to talk about it?"

"No."

She pulled her legs underneath her and sat very still.

"Some bastard's been spraying acid on innocent people," he said.

"Shit," said Lucy.

"Six attacks in three hours, Luce." He drank deeply. "In the centre of town," he continued. "Two badly injured, four others hurt."

"CCTV?" asked Lucy.

"We've got her," he said. "A middle-aged woman carrying a tube which she hid inside her coat. She sprayed people as she went past them."

"So arrest her," suggested Lucy.

"We can't find her," Dave responded. "We've had every single available officer out today. You couldn't drop a sweet paper without being arrested. She just disappeared." He paused. "Luce?"

She stood up and went over to her husband, sat on his lap and kissed him.

"Go on, tell me, Dave," she said. "You'll feel better if you get it off your chest."

"Luce," he said and then choked. "There's nothing I haven't seen in my career. Abused babies, motorway carnage and the rest." He wiped his eyes. "The first victim. She's nineteen, absolutely beautiful and, until this morning, had her whole life ahead of her. But her thigh was eaten away by the acid down to the bone. It was hideous."

"She'll still have a life ahead of her, Dave," she said. "An abused baby usually has nothing."

"Yes, you're right." He sighed. "I suppose it's because I can hide my emotions with a battered child:

there's usually nothing I can do. This woman, today... it was awful to see a life with such potential destroyed."

"Dave," said Lucy, "I want you to go upstairs and shower. When you come down I will have prepared some nibbles and opened another bottle of lager. I want you to tell me everything." As he stood up, she hugged him.

An hour later Dave had told her everything. Lucy listened attentively. She was staggered by the amount of information the police had obtained. In each of the six attacks, the victims were minding their own business, thinking about their lives, taking calls, in one case catching a train, or planning to stop for coffee. The man was going for a job interview. The attacks were clearly random and, beyond hurting the individuals, seemingly inexplicable. The acid had already been analysed and an initial report suggested a professional attacker was at large. A team was watching hours of CCTV for clues, and the woman had been captured no less than seventeen times. Unfortunately, she apparently knew the system and had tried hard to ensure her face was not visible so she could not be identified. They talked until nearly eleven-thirty. Then they went to bed and held each other closely. Dave was soon snoring. At two-thirty Lucy was shaking her husband, trying to wake him.

"Dave!" she was shouting. "Wake up!"

Slowly, he focused.

"What is it?"

"Dave," she cried. "They were all using mobile phones. That's what they had in common!"

He shot up in bed.

"We need to talk about this. I'll make a pot of tea,"

he said.

He was back within four minutes and poured himself a cup in his Arsenal mug. He wore a deep frown.

"Luce. You're inspirational. And you're right. All of them were using mobiles. The two sisters were texting each other: crazy."

"So their heads were down," said Lucy.

"And so they didn't see the attacker approach them," he continued. "That was clear from the CCTV."

"But she saw them," said Lucy.

Dave frowned. "That's where we drew a blank," he said.

"Dave," said Lucy, but she did not wait for a response. "I'm not yet a detective." She paused as her husband went to say something. "No. Let me finish. Criminal work is for you men, while we PCs help old ladies across the street."

"Don't be too hard on yourself, Luce," he said and chuckled. "So?"

"So, what if I tried some detective work?"

"You were saying about helping old ladies across the street," he laughed.

"Nasty," she said.

"Sorry, Luce. Just trying to be funny."

"That's what you said when I asked you about the man who stuffed mashed cardboard into the exhaust..."

Dave was becoming increasingly interested.

"And what word did Annabel use?" She paused. "Hey, Dave. What word?" She did not wait for his response. "Nasty." She stared at him. "Quite a coincidence, huh?"

Detective Sergeant David Smith leapt out of bed.

"He's disguising himself," he shouted. "It wasn't a woman today, Luce. It was a man – for some reason targeting people who annoyed him by looking at their mobile phones."

"Or being slow at traffic lights," said Lucy.

"Or objecting to people who don't clear up after their dogs," he said.

He was searching for his clothes.

"Oh, fuck me, Luce. We've got a nutter loose," he shouted.

"He hasn't killed anyone yet, Dave," Lucy exclaimed.

"He will, Luce. He will. It's just a matter of time."

"What are you doing?"

Dave was getting dressed. "Going in."

"What, at three in the morning?" she asked.

"He's at it now, Luce. He's planning his next attack."

Milton Grant knew exactly what the police would be doing. They depended on repetition for much of their detective work. He wanted to avoid them, and also needed to clear his head. He had now completed three corrections, and worried that someone might connect the elderly woman in the supermarket car park to the other attacks. Stella never pressured him and so, when he called round to tell her he couldn't make Sunday lunch, she reacted with equanimity.

He just wished she wouldn't do that thing.

After confirming that she would see him the following Tuesday afternoon, they said their farewells.

Early on Friday morning he joined the M1, stopped on the M6 for breakfast, took the toll road round Birmingham, re-joined the M6 and sped past Manchester and Preston. After passing Kendal he took a left towards the eastern section of the Lake District. He reached his destination of Brothers Water, north of Windermere and south of Ullswater, around eleven o'clock. He found a comfortable hotel in the village of Hartsop, which meant 'the valley of the deer', booked in, showered, changed into his walking kit, ate three bananas and left to complete a twelve-mile hike in the four hours of daylight that remained.

He had found the small lake, once called Broad Water, some years earlier after he and his ex-wife had argued. He had walked out and disappeared for a week. The lake is best seen from the northern end of the Kirkstone Pass, but Milton discovered that its real wealth was to be discovered by walking and sliding over the rocky fells surrounding the shallow waters. At the peak, the path is precariously close to the edge of a sheer drop down the scree-laden slope.

He arrived back, exhilarated by the exercise. He rested in his room for a while then went down to the lounge bar, where he ordered suet pudding. He was reading a Lee Child novel: he relished the violence as Jack Reacher demolished a group of five Los Angeles thugs. Later, another guest came over. "My name's Ray," he said. They chatted for about an hour and Milton let slip that, in the morning, he planned to go for a twenty-mile walk. The man invited himself to join him. Milton was displeased, but said nothing.

They left on time, after breakfast, on a stunning autumn morning. Milton's companion said little for the first hour. When they reached the start of the climb up the side of the mountain, Milton was interested when Ray volunteered that he was the chief executive of a private logistics business. He then told him that he was gay and his partner was in New Zealand on business.

They stopped to consume packed lunches, provided by the hotel, and drink some water. They decided that they had seen no more than perhaps twenty hillwalkers during the morning. Milton was beginning to warm to the other man: Ray was informed and interesting. They talked about politics and Brexit. They were enjoying themselves. His companion described the British taxation system as the biggest con trick ever levied by any government anywhere in the world.

As far as Milton was concerned, Ray's opinion was compelling. Ray explained that the majority of British workers were trapped in the PAYE system. Their pay-as-you-earn remuneration suffered deductions at source of national insurance and income tax. That was for starters. HM Revenue & Customs had draconian powers to pry: pensions were taxed at source, capital gains were taxed following disclosure on the annual return (and a fine levied if the return is submitted one day late), and then virtually all free money spent was subject to value added tax at 20%.

"Then there is the ultimate abuse of us all: fuel tax." Ray continued without hesitation. "A litre of petrol is around £1.16. Excise duty is 57p. On top of that there is VAT at 20%." He laughed. "The cost of a litre of petrol is 40p. Fuel duty is 57p. VAT is 19p." He stood up and walked a few paces before turning back. "I've done the maths, Milt. The tax rate on a litre of petrol is 190%. Fucking 190%, Milt."

He had only just started. "The Chancellor of the

bleedin' Exchequer collects all this money so that six hundred and fifty MPs can have fabulous salaries, unlimited expenses, housing allowances, mouthwatering pensions, knighthoods, peerages and chairmanships of government quangos, most of which achieve fuck all." He paused for breath. "They have numerous outside jobs and sit in parliament for three days a week, for less than twenty-two weeks of the year."

They were now picking up their pace.

"One more fact about tax," Ray said, slightly out of breath. "If you survive all the deductions." He gasped as he stumbled on a rocky outcrop. "When you die, the taxman takes most of your money in inheritance tax. The Conservatives came up with the plan that, when you go to heaven, any remaining assets should pay for your health care. As you're dead, you're paying for something that has rather let you down. It's crackers, Milt."

"It's called democracy," said Milton, assessing the storm clouds on the horizon.

Ray stopped and looked at his hillwalking friend.

"Paying tax is for lemmings," he said.

Milton grimaced. He had difficulty in understanding the taxation rules and codes he was forced to follow, and he was baffled by the deductions made following his divorce and the split of assets. "So, you don't pay tax?" he asked his companion.

"Oh yes, I do," was the immediate response. "There's a well-known code amongst us high earners. The best accountants will be able to keep your personal tax below 5% of total income." He walked ahead of Milton and then allowed his companion to catch him up. They passed three hikers who were heading towards Kirkstone Pass.

"Below 5%," mused Ray. "I earn around half a million a year." He hesitated. "That's between you and me, mate. I don't even pay 190% fuel tax. My car, when my driver is not around, is filled up from the pool pumps. HMRC call it 'benefits in kind' and try and tax you." He looked at Milton. "They'll get you, Milt, but not me." He puffed out his chest. "I'm smarter than those pricks," he said.

He had yet more to say on the subject. "If a worker is earning perhaps £40,000 annually, he will be paying around 55% in tax when all deductions, VAT and so on, are taken into account."

They walked on, and began to descend into the valley. The sun had disappeared behind the clouds coming in from the west. Milton was lost in thought. Eventually, without reducing his pace, he posed a question. "What about the morality of your position?"

"What the fuck's that to do with it?" snapped Ray. "You sound like a religious type. I employ over seven hundred people. They depend on me. That's my fucking moralistic position. I go to work and give all I have because I earn big money. I have a luxurious pad on a secure housing estate. I travel first class and stay in top hotels. I have my wealth managed for me, overseas. My driver brought me up here because I wanted a break. He'll collect me tomorrow afternoon. I get tickets to any sporting event in the world. I go to the O2 arena whenever I want. I have a private doctor and a personal dentist. Everything is paid for by the business. And Mr HMRC knows better than to come near me. I employ particularly nasty and expensive tax lawyers and accountants." He laughed.

"Last year they got me a tax rebate."

They walked on. Suddenly, Ray stopped and turned to face Milton. "You know what's best about my life, Milton?" He laughed. "I'll tell you. I haven't a worry in the world." He laughed and tripped over a fallen branch.

They returned to the hotel and agreed to have dinner in their rooms. They met early the next morning for breakfast, and Milton found he was looking forward to their second walk together. He had tossed and turned as he recalled their discussion on tax and money. But Ray was proving good company. They shared an interest in politics and he knew his stuff about global warming. Milton made a note to go and see *An Inconvenient Sequel*, Al Gore's latest work on climate change. Ray asked few questions about Milton.

They set off in slightly chillier conditions and calculated that they would eat an early packed lunch at the top of High Hartsop Dodd. They walked for two hours without speaking, and then revisited the previous day's discussion about wealth creation.

"Milt," said Ray, as his new friend recoiled at the use of his shortened Christian name, "Maggie got it right. Labour is very good at spending other people's money."

Milton decided he was warming to Ray – a lovely man, he thought. His companion was uncomplicated, which Milton liked. He would remember these two days for some time. They finished their lunch and Ray moved to the edge of the precipice, stared down at Brothers Water far beneath them, and breathed the fresh air deep into his lungs.

"My father used to bring me here," he said.

Then Milton came up behind him and gave him a ferocious shove in the back. Ray didn't make a sound as he fell. His body bounced off the outcrops of rock and into the water below. There was a splash. Over the next hour his body began to sink. The thunder began later that afternoon, and it would be three days before the corpse resurfaced at the southern edge of Brothers Water.

"Should have paid your taxes," said Milton.

He returned to the hotel and settled his bill using a false credit card. The name of Monty Underhill would later mean nothing to the police. He made a point of asking the whereabouts of the man he had breakfasted with and who had not kept their lunchtime rendezvous in the hills. He left the hotel and stopped the car after about ten miles, where he dumped his walking clothes and changed the car number plates as he wanted to avoid being caught on the automatic number plate recognition system used by the police. The following day he would drive to Shoreditch, sell the vehicle for cash and buy a saloon, also for cash, take it back to his garage and change the number plates.

He got home late on Sunday night, showered, changed and settled into his office. He was exhilarated by the past three days, decided it was time for Chopin, and put on the appropriate CD. He took out his list and added *No. 4: paying taxes*. He would go into London the next day and see the Al Gore documentary. He would see Stella on Tuesday and Thursday and prepare for correction number five on the list. This would take place on Friday. He looked forward to the challenge.

At this stage he could not afford to attract

attention. Later, it would not matter. But, for now, the adrenalin rush of being in charge and hitting back was exhilarating. His wife and daughter had tried to order him around, suggesting his police boots should be kept in the garage. But it was his inability to convict the bad guys that he hated. There had been the driving case that had ended with the CPS lawyer calling him a moron and the woman thanking him for being a misogynist. He was a police officer who had been prevented from controlling people's bad behaviour – due to their fucking human rights. But Milton Grant was made of sterner stuff. He was getting revenge, making a difference – and he was loving it.

By unspoken consent, Lucy and Dave had ditched their post-marriage vow. Shop talk was now the order of the day. It was Sunday evening and they were seated at their dining room table, which was in an extension of the kitchen.

Lucy looked at her husband, nodded, bowed her head and closed her eyes. Dave opened the Bible and began to speak. "Saint Paul taught about tolerance. This is from Romans 14, verse 13." He coughed. "Therefore let us not judge one another anymore, but rather resolve this, not to put a stumbling block or a cause to fall in our brother's way."

Lucy mouthed "Amen" and stood up.

"Come on, Luce, what is it?"

"Hah," she laughed. "You know the choice of four. If you get it right you will receive a special reward later."

Dave groaned with anticipation. "Hell, Luce, one out of four. The odds are weighted in your favour."

"Your choice, Dave. By the way, I went shopping yesterday."

He moaned inside and wondered if they could skip the meal – but he was hungry.

"Beef, pork, lamb or gammon," he said.

"Correct," she acknowledged. She hated chicken so never cooked it.

As he had looked in the oven an hour earlier, he knew the answer but decided to play up to his wife.

"Gammon," he chose.

"Lucy's the champion," she sang as she danced around the kitchen. She returned with a serving dish containing a rack of Welsh lamb, and took the lids off serving bowls full of roasted parsnip, carrot and cheese-covered cauliflower. Finally, blowing an imaginary trumpet, she revealed her pièce de résistance. Her roast potatoes were in a class of their own because her mother had taught her to sprinkle sugar over them every thirty minutes.

One of Lucy and Dave's relationship 'rules' was that, when their duty rosters allowed, they would have Sunday dinner together at seven in the evening. This went back to Lucy's childhood. As a child, Lucy and her brother had always sat down for dinner with their parents. Her father always read a passage from the Bible before they ate, and her mother always served a roast dinner. They talked together during and after the meal, and this family time was important to Lucy.

She was working hard to make her marriage a success: she had too many colleagues whose relationships were in trouble. She was determined that her marriage would not wither because of the lack of communication she detected in others. The other danger area was not a risk for them due to Dave's insatiable appetite for her.

Four months after their wedding they had gone to her parents' home for Sunday dinner. Dave started off well by giving her mother a bouquet of flowers, her father the latest Wilbur Smith novel and her brother a ticket for the next home game. They talked until after ten. On their way home, Lucy had suggested that they should adopt her parents' tradition of having Sunday dinner together. Much to her surprise Dave agreed, and said he wanted to start by reading from the scriptures. She had thought that the only God her husband worshipped was Arsene Wenger, closely followed by St Paul (aka Patrick Vieira).

Sunday dinner together became embedded into their lives. After Dave had read from the Bible, Lucy served the meal and Dave poured wine. Both police officers were on early shift the following morning, so they were limiting their alcohol intake.

"Dave?" asked Lucy.

"Yes, honey?" he replied before adding a further roast potato to his plate.

"You never do anything without there being a purpose to it," she said.

"Am I that obvious?" he laughed.

"The scripture reading you chose. About tolerance. Are you trying to tell me something?"

He put his knife and fork down and drank some wine. "We can't find the acid attacker. He's still out there, and my boss says it is only a matter of time before he kills someone. He's made the case a priority. We're under pressure to find him."

"Clues?" she asked. "I'm trying to think about tolerance."

"Well done, Luce. That's the path I'm treading." He drank some more wine.

"Could I have a herbal tea?" she requested.

He returned with their drinks.

"Right. This shit we're looking for objects to drivers who are slow to pull away from traffic lights, attacks people who fail to clear up after their pets, and sprays acid on people with mobile phones."

"So far. But this last week has been trouble-free," she said.

"Yes. So, he's a male around forty or fifty, he's about five foot eleven inches tall, he weighs around twelve stones, he's dark-haired and he's fit. That's what the clever lot tell me from their studying of the CCTV images."

"He's violent and he hates," said Lucy.

"Yes. He's intolerant of people's habits. Mobile phone users piss me off but I don't go around spraying acid on them."

"There's a sequence, Dave. Traffic lights, but no immediate physical assault, dog poo – and you saw what he did to the man in the park, and mobile phones, and he ruined a young woman's life. All we have to do is work out what he might do next."

"That's where I am, Luce. I'm preparing a list of what annoys other people."

"Can I help?" she asked.

"Shoot," ordered Dave.

"Where do I start?" She laughed. "Men who order me about."

"Interesting. There are four of us working on the case and both my female colleagues have come up with that one." He drank his coffee.

"Middle-lane hoggers," she said.

41

"Don't say that to traffic." Dave laughed. "They're sensitive to what they take as personal criticism."

There was no stopping Lucy. "People who eat with their mouth open," she suggested.

"People who eat in the street," said Dave. "My mum never let me do it."

"People who don't put their dustbins back after the council have emptied them," continued Lucy.

"Cyclists who use the pavement," suggested Dave.

They started to clear away the dinner plates.

"You know Alice, who I work with?" asked Dave.

"You mean the one with the big—"

"Yes, her," said Dave, as he pretended to smack his wife. "She came up with an interesting one."

"Men who don't have an erection when she enters the room," said Lucy, hiding playfully.

Dave began to wash up. Lucy grabbed a tea towel.

"She said that the thing that annoys her more than anything is elderly people who fumble at the supermarket till and take ages to pay their bill. They really—"

Lucy dropped a plate on the kitchen floor.

"Dave!" she cried. "Three weeks ago. An OAP who had delayed people at the checkout at the supermarket was assaulted – a hit and run – and we've got it on CCTV."

Stella lay back in the bath and allowed the warm water to ease the bruising between her legs. Milton had been quite loving on Tuesday but two days later he had acted like a man possessed. She smiled in satisfaction as she recalled the effect her suspenders and stockings had on him. He never spoke when they made love, but was always caring and attentive to her.

She relished the simplicity of their relationship. The rules were clear and acceptable to both parties. She wondered if it would ever end. If it did, she would move on. One of her ex-husbands was hounding her for money. The pretty assistant ten years his junior with whom he had set up home had run off with all his assets. "Hard fucking luck," had been Stella's unsympathetic response. The hot water was cooling, so she turned on the tap to top up the bath. She had milked her ex for all he had. Stella laughed. "Tee, hee, ha," was the sound that emerged from her mouth. "Tee, hee, ha." She always laughed in the same way. To Milton, it sounded like a cross between a five-year-old and a Chinese stand-up comedian. He wished she wouldn't laugh like that.

Milton was alone in his office at the end of an enjoyable Thursday. He was playing a Beethoven CD and preparing for correction number five. Tomorrow, in the evening, teenagers and twenty-somethings would descend on the town centre, where they would consume so much alcohol that a number would have to be taken to hospital. They would puke on the streets, they would fight each other, they would assault innocent pedestrians, they would throw bricks at cars, and the local press would photograph girls lying in the gutter with their mini-skirts up to their unmentionables. A few offenders would reach the magistrate's court where they would get a slap on the wrist.

Milton became interested in the behaviour of the young people. One fact he did discern was that 'binge drinking' was affected by the fact that the young people did not drink alcohol during the week. Many did not have the money. By the time Friday night came around, they were worked up in the expectation of escaping their dreary lives. They inflicted on their bodies an avalanche of alcoholic drinks. They would drink too much, they would be ill, some would take drugs and many would need medical help. The next week they would return for more.

Milton despised them. He thought they represented a decadent decline in society. They created havoc and damage. They didn't vote. They had never fought a war. They expected other people to look after their grandparents. They had no respect for authority.

In his early years as a police constable, it had been different. Some of his colleagues relished the fights and made sure that the bad guys were sorted out. Over a period of time, with the increasing use of CCTV and ambitious chief constables trying to make a name for themselves by favouring society against policing, things had changed. He hated it, and did all he could to avoid Friday night duties. When his efforts failed he resented the hours he spent in hospital corridors watching people fight and vomit.

Before his marriage ended he had a brief affair with a female officer. It was his usual style: pure sex. After an argument, she had stormed out of their hotel bedroom, leaving behind her uniform. She and Milton were a similar height. Even though the uniform was a few years old, it was perfect for his needs.

He stripped off and showered, then he shaved his legs. He needed to think like a woman. Last week, he had bought white underwear, which he now put on. The blonde wig was perfect. He shaved his eyebrows, and he would shave his face an hour before going out.

He put on the rest of the clothes and added the equipment carried by front-line officers, including pepper spray. He had rebuilt the boots and lowered them by an inch, and added deeper pockets at the top of the trousers to hold everything he needed. He spent four hours preparing for his evening out. Mitch Leary would have admired his performance. Milton was not going to try to kill the President – but he was intent on causing some serious damage.

The next day, he left his home by the side door. He had not eaten since lunchtime because of the need to be physically alert. He had surveyed the area many times and decided his chances of being seen were remote. In any case, no one was going to challenge a police officer. He covered the mile and a quarter into town in around forty minutes, ducking in and out of the shadows. He checked his watch, which he had bought in Poundland. It was clear faced with a pink strap. It was eleven fifty-two. His plan was to keep to the back streets until he reached the town centre, where the northern side of the square housed the war memorial and led into the park.

A number of blue lights flashed. There was an increased police presence following an unusually nasty fight. Milton was unaware that a small group of travellers had descended on a school playground and planned to stay there until council officials moved them on. Three of the travellers left their caravans and decided to drink in the town. The locals then decided to sort them out. This was a situation in which the police operated effectively. They arrived in force, made some arrests and restored order. Milton was frustrated. He would have preferred to handle the travellers himself.

45

The town centre was settling back to normal, with drinkers everywhere. He decided to keep to his plan and select three men and two women for correction. He kept to the shadows of the war memorial and watched two girls trying to light a cigarette. They were drunk, their clothing awry, and one had slumped over a concrete wall and seemed to be unconscious. Her friend was giggling and attempting to pull her upright.

Milton went behind her, put one hand over her mouth and pulled her away and into the entrance to the woods. His strategy was dependent on speed of action. Once the police realised there were multiple attacks taking place, they would close the area down. The woman was utterly confused, although she tried to fight off her attacker. She was on her back. She opened her mouth and gasped for air as he poured a mixture of washing-up liquid and bleach down her throat. He whispered in her ear, "Think before you drink, cretin."

He left her lying in the grass. After he had run about a hundred yards and exited the trees, he spotted two youths trying to fight each other but they were so drunk, it was a farce. Neither knew what had hit them when Milton repeated his corrective actions. He left them moaning in the undergrowth, kicking one on the head to give him a few more precious minutes to escape, then put his mouth to his ear. "Think before you drink, cretin."

He was pleasantly surprised to find, on re-entering the square, a young man on his own. Milton overpowered him and poured the liquid down his throat. The young man heard the same message.

Milton needed just one more victim. Then he spotted her. She was trying to hail a cab, but the driver drove straight past her. She shouted abuse after him. Before long Milton was dragging her behind a parade of shops. She heard a dog bark and somebody play loud music.

He squeezed her nose and held the last bottle of liquid over her mouth. He was worried about the time that had elapsed since his first attack, and wanted to complete the correction as quickly as possible. He was totally unprepared when she fought back. She scraped her nails down his face – and knew that she was fighting a man. Unusually, Milton was slow to react. When she grabbed his testicles and squeezed, his agony was enhanced by the shock of her resistance. He was slow and dulled by shock. He hit her on the side of the head. She lost consciousness, so she did not feel the kick he added for good measure.

Forty minutes later he was home. He entered by the side door, locked up, went into the kitchen and undressed, putting every item of clothing into two black bin liners. He showered, put on a tracksuit and went into his office. He had pre-selected a CD, which was ready to play. As a Mozart piano concerto filled the room, he slowly sank his head into his hands and shook with anger.

Stella spent some of Saturday evening in her hot tub, drinking too much wine. She was listening to Neil Diamond, who wanted to tell her about 'summer love'. Milton's telephone call had surprised her, and the prospect of no sex for a week was disappointing. She kept to her self-imposed discipline of never asking questions: she would see him again a week on Tuesday. Perhaps her boss might give her a week's break. Then she remembered the patients who depended on her healing powers and decided against it. She would go to the cinema and see *Goodbye Christopher Robin*. She wiped a tear away as she recalled her mother reading Winnie the Pooh stories to her. She laughed as she remembered Tigger's antics. "Tee, hee, ha."

Lucy bowed her head as Dave read from the Bible.

"Matthew 6, verses 14 and 15," he began. "For if you forgive other people when they sin against you, your heavenly father will also forgive you. But if you do not forgive others their sins, your father will not forgive your sins."

She opened her eyes, went to the oven and took out a side of pork which she had already partly sliced. She then took out the potatoes and vegetables and a sauce. He poured the wine and they began to eat.

They were tired. The hunt for the mysterious attacker was proving abortive. Dave and Lucy had both had to work overtime, partly to reassure the public. The press naming the attacker 'The policewoman attacker' had not helped to calm things down.

All five victims were seriously ill after they had been forced to drink the mixture of liquid soap and bleach. Two recovered relatively quickly, as they had managed to spit much of the substance out. The girl who had been attacked first was the worst affected, and remained in intensive care.

"So," said Lucy. "You are suggesting we forgive this bastard?"

"I was reading from the gospel according to St Matthew," replied her husband.

"How near are you to getting him?" she asked.

"We know a lot about him," replied Dave. "The image from the supermarket CCTV, thanks to you, was constructive. We have a pretty good idea now about his appearance. The girl who fought back saw him close up, and her Identikit picture has been helpful. We've plastered it everywhere and visited most homes in the area but nobody can identify him."

"He's gone to ground, hasn't he?" she asked.

"She also managed to scratch him. She got some skin – and his DNA – but we haven't been able to find a match. He's hiding."

"What does the profiler say?" she asked.

"What you would expect: the attacks are escalating, but he's following a pattern. The profiler thinks he will kill before very long. He needs to be found, but he also wants to make it as difficult for us as he can." Dave paused. "We call him 'the man who hates' in the office. The profiler has cautioned us about that. He says that everybody has hang-ups, especially motorists. We are all annoyed by the selfishness of mobile phone users." He stopped to spoon another roast potato onto his plate. "He suggests we concentrate on what has triggered his campaign. It doesn't seem to be sexual in any way, though. All his women victims have confirmed that there was absolutely no sign of that. You know, Luce – no ripping of clothing, or hands on breasts. And he had the opportunity."

"So," said Lucy, "he's not a sexual pervert."

"We've checked everyone with a record of sexual deviance, rapists and paedophiles to a radius of twenty miles. We've arrested two people as a result, but neither is the man we want."

"If he's not a sexual predator, that suggests he's

sexually satisfied," she said.

"Yes," he said cautiously, "it's generally accepted that rapists are on a power trip – that raping is not sexually motivated."

"Let me finish, Dave, and stop interrupting me," she said.

"Go on," encouraged Dave, enjoying his wife being on her own power trip.

"So, I think he's happily married."

"Unlikely, Luce." Dave poured them each another glass of wine. "Can you see him managing to perfect his disguises and arrive back with scratches on his face without a wife or partner noticing?"

"Oh yes. Time to rethink. So maybe he's a loner. I still think you might be missing something."

Dave frowned but said nothing.

"OK, Dave, sorry," she said. "I'll leave the detective work to you."

"Go on, Luce," said Dave. "Sorry, honey. I was out of order."

"You're tired, Dave." She went round to him and sat by his side.

"One piece of Lucy detection and then you're going to bed." She kissed him and then poured him a whisky. He grabbed the glass.

"He knows too much, Dave." She sipped her glass of elderflower. "He's here in our midst. I just don't believe he's coming in and out of town. Anyway, he was at the supermarket shopping. I think he's local."

"OK," said Dave.

"We've had no success on the ANPR system, so we think he's changing his number plates. He's disguising himself. That's not easy, but he knows what features matter. His skin is different each time, according to the witnesses. That's smart." She marshalled her thoughts. "He seems to know too much. Take the Friday night bleach attacks. He knew where we would be. But there's not one police officer who can recall seeing him. No CCTV caught him. He was wearing a policewoman's outfit and would have stood out a mile at around six foot. Nobody saw him. And where did he get the uniform? We've visited the fancy dress shops and nobody has handled one for months." Lucy laughed. "We did find a strip-o-gram who does a policewoman act, but she starts off wearing so little in the first place."

The introduction of levity lifted their discussion. Dave yawned.

"So," said Lucy, "do you want me to solve the case?"

"What's keeping you, Luce?" laughed her husband.

"He's a former police officer," said Lucy.

"Say that again?"

Thirty minutes earlier Milton had looked down into the toilet bowl at the black blood. He knew that the end was not too far away.

Now, he lay back in his office chair and absorbed the preludes of his favourite French composer. He and Claude Debussy had one thing in common: rectal cancer. The maestro had chosen to have a colostomy which had failed to prolong his life, and he had succumbed at the age of fifty-five. Milton had ignored the bleeding until, eventually, he had no choice but to see a doctor. He did not even consider the operation he was offered. He had no one to look after him and, in truth, nobody to live for. His ex-wife had moved away and his daughter Jennifer rarely contacted him, not even to acknowledge receipt of her monthly allowance. This year, for the first time, she had missed his birthday.

After his diagnosis, he had spent nearly three weeks walking in the Pyrenees deciding his future. A combination of suppositories, and a drug prescribed by the surgeon, held the cancer temporarily at bay. He even managed to bed a hotel guest, like Edward Fox in *The Day of the Jackal* when he seduced the countess, later murdering her, but Milton had simply moved on. He found it frustrating that the oncologist couldn't give a definitive answer to his obvious question. Instead he gave a rather bland reply: "Let's say between seven and twelve months."

Milton reflected on his parting of the ways with the police force. He recognised that he had been lucky to have an Assistant Chief Constable who understood the circumstances of the event that had resulted in his disciplinary hearing. It was, in his mind, ludicrous. He had been called to a dispute in a charity shop. Two people were arguing over purchasing rights to a dress: neither would give way. Each claimed to have been the first to want to buy it. The elderly assistant panicked and called the police. When Milton arrived, the two aggressors were squaring up to each other. The sight of Milton propelled them into violence. As he attempted to part them, one, whose hair was dyed orange, deliberately (in his opinion) poked Milton in the eye. He should never have said what he did, but he did.

"You fat lump of lard," he had cried out.

The two pugilists stopped in mid-fight.

"Did you hear what he said?" one asked the other. "Who's he calling fat?" She then shouted at her two children, who were spreading jigsaws over the floor.

Milton had got on his radio to ask for assistance. His eye was now closed and rather painful. From there on, the situation escalated out of his control. Both ladies were obese. Their years of eating burgers, chips and chocolate were reflected in their dress size – which was the cause of the fracas. Neither would admit it, but they found it hard to buy clothes that fitted.

Milton was taken to hospital. The two women both put in formal complaints, the shop assistant said that she couldn't remember what had happened, and the more heavily built complainant accused Milton of inflicting his eye injury himself to deflect attention from the words he had used. They were both after money – and that is what they received. Milton was appalled at the amount they were paid. The Assistant Commissioner told him to accept a formal reprimand. When Milton hinted at taking early retirement, the senior officer made it straightforward for him. Milton was out of the force three months later.

Initially, he was lost. He enrolled at the local college to study music, but did not mix well with the younger students. He maintained his fitness regime but noticed that he was struggling to finish his six-mile runs. His diagnosis changed everything. He had a short-term purpose in life. He found Stella and settled down to plan his list. Before he died, he would apply correction to eight groups of people he hated.

The supermarket incident was a bonus. He had now completed five of the eight actions, and he knew what the last would be. He could hardly wait. After the girl in the market square had fought back, he knew the police would find him. But first, he had three tasks to complete. He completed the sixth with relative ease. Milton hated Irish travellers. To him, they were scum. When he watched the news item about three caravans in a school car park and the disruption to the school, after a day tending his face, he went out late at night and placed an incendiary device under the first mobile home. The bomb exploded. Of the seventeen people on the site, three received serious burns, one broke a leg jumping out of her caravan doorway, and two suffered smoke inhalation. Other travellers arrived to take them all away to a new site. A council officer arrived and pinned an eviction notice to the last remaining caravan.

Milton was pleased that correction number seven was under way. He had selected the retail outlet. He recoiled at modern eating habits, because, in his opinion, wherever he went, people were pigging themselves. In the cinema they spoilt his enjoyment by munching noisily through huge boxes of popcorn and slurping giant cups of coke. Some managed to spread the cheese covering their nachos all over the seats. In the streets he watched as they ate burgers, chips, chicken nuggets, ice cream, crisps and more. They would then expect the medical world to sort out their polluted insides and wrecked joints. They were the first to complain when they could not get a doctor's appointment. They blamed immigrants, and argued that their own benefits payments were too low.

He had found a food outlet where the meat was delivered early in the morning in a secure refrigerated van. He had followed the delivery van several weeks earlier and now knew when the driver would stop for his morning coffee. He took from the back of the unlocked vehicle a parcel of meat which he took home and refrigerated. Last night he had injected the meat with a poison he had bought on the internet. He calculated it would be enough to poison about twenty people – they would experience an agonising intestinal disorder. Early that morning he had waited until the driver went in for his coffee and slipped the package into the back of his van. Two days later, the local A&E was overwhelmed with patients, all of whom were vomiting blood.

Milton Grant was left with one final correction. He could not wait to begin.

Lucy read the text message she'd just received from Dave. She was on enquiries and had been dealing with a mother whose daughter had been missing overnight. Lucy had been baffled that, when the mother handed her a photograph of her daughter, she had apologised that her daughter was rather overweight.

Dave's text read:

He's Milton Grant. He lives on the north side. We're going in. Luv u x

Lucy decided not to return the text. "Please remember, Dave," she said to herself, "he's dangerous."

To hell with protocol, she thought next. *Luv u 2*, she texted.

The police cordoned off the area and the armed unit went in. Another group raided Milton's garage. Inside the house they found everything they needed. There was enough evidence to send him to prison for life. They discovered his disguises. They read his medical notes and letters. They had all they required to close down the man who hated. There was just one problem. Milton Grant was nowhere to be seen.

Pinned to the kitchen wall was a note.

Late again, lads. Hope the fatties did not delay you.

He had rented the flat as a potential bolthole three months earlier. He calculated the police would find him within forty-eight hours. That gave him enough time to do what he had planned. He lay low for a day and then went to see Stella for the last time.

She had purchased a fresh set of underwear and cleaned the Jacuzzi. She did not ask any questions, although she noticed the marks on his skin. She watched his face as he savoured the incense and watched as she slowly slid her skirt up her thighs. When he saw her black knickers, he exploded with passion. He took her to bed. He was brutal during sex, and hurt her.

When he was preparing to leave, Stella noticed a grey hair in his head and pulled it out. "Tee, hee, ha," she laughed.

He circled behind her, took out a knife and pulled it savagely across her throat. Blood spurted from her carotid artery. He let her body slump to the floor.

"I wish you didn't do that," he said.

Lucy knew that Dave was tired. The message Milton Grant had left in the kitchen had upset him. She mused over his words: *Hope the fatties did not delay you.* They went to bed early as they were both on early duty the next day. The next morning an elderly man came into the police station to report his wife missing. She was diabetic. Her husband was worried because she had not returned home the previous evening from a walk in the park. Lucy blinked when she looked at the photograph he had brought with him.

Milton began the final stage of his corrective campaign by completing a two-mile run, showering, enjoying a bowl of bananas and peaches, and putting on a casual outfit. He left the flat with a handkerchief and chloroform in his pocket, reached the disused warehouse and entered through the back door. He switched on the lights and checked his two prisoners.

The first was the girl of nineteen. She was naked and her hands were tied behind her back. The rope was attached to a bracket Milton had previously hammered into the wall. She had a gag around her mouth. Her eyes reflected her fear. Urine and excrement dribbled down the inside of her legs. She was heavy, with rolls of fat around her stomach, a large bottom, and breasts hanging painfully without the support of a bra.

The other victim was the elderly diabetic woman. She was semi-conscious. She was also heavy, but not as heavy as the young woman. She was tied up in exactly the same way and was also naked. Milton prodded them both and pinched the young woman's stomach. Her screams were muffled by the gag.

"Now, ladies," said Milton, "You are both very fat. You are selfish – because you expect me and my fellow taxpayers to cough up for all the medical treatment you require." He stood up and hit them with a stick. He was loving this moment of fulfilment. "You drink to excess and you stuff processed foods into your mouth all day long. You block our buses because your arse is too large to fit into a seat. We can't get appointments at the doctors because you are there needing pills to treat a multitude of illnesses as a result of your self-inflicted obesity. The chemists are overworked because you need so many pills." He wiped his mouth. "It's because all you do is push food into your huge mouth all day."

He then took out a whip. He turned the women around so they were facing the wall and gave them each five lashes on their buttocks, which wobbled under the impact.

"When you leave here, I want you both to turn over a new leaf: You will stop eating to excess. Right, I'm going out now. When I return, I'll talk to you some more."

He turned them round, ignoring the stench. He was enjoying himself. He left the building and went out into the park. He spotted her within five minutes. A woman in her twenties was running and then stopping to do push-ups. Her colour offset her white kit. She was perfect for his needs. He went up to her to congratulate her on her fitness. Initially, the athlete was suspicious, but he seemed a pleasant man and quite fit himself. When she briefly turned her back on him, he put one arm round her throat and with the other held the handkerchief, which he had soaked in chloroform, to her mouth and nose. After fifteen seconds, she had stopped struggling.

He dragged her to the warehouse, where he stripped off her clothes and tied her to the bracket by his other two prisoners. The gag prevented her from screaming. She was fit – an athlete, a javelin thrower. Her coach thought she had a chance of making the Olympics in Japan in 2020. Her black skin glowed with health. Despite her punishing training regime, however, she was overeating. Her coach had warned her that she was jeopardising her future in the team. Milton looked at her naked body. Because of her relative youth, it was tantalising.

Lucy looked up from reading Dave's latest text message.

We can't find him x

Inspector Sanderson was passing through reception when he spotted DC Avril Wren.

"Avril," he shouted. "I've lost my bloody javelin thrower. She was due here forty-five minutes ago."

Lucy knew that in his spare time the inspector ran the local athletics club.

"She's probably having a burger, guv," said DC Wren. "You need to get her to lose some weight."

"She'll be in the park. Pop down and find her, will you? The coach leaves in an hour."

Lucy ignored this misuse of police time and concentrated on what she had just heard. She pulled out a local map and studied the area around the park. She was thinking through what she knew. There was a missing girl aged nineteen who lived on the north side. There was a missing diabetic woman who lived on the south side. There was an athlete who had been in the park but who was now potentially missing. Lucy sidled over to Inspector Sanderson.

"Have you seen a rather strongly built javelin thrower?" he asked, laughing.

"No, guv," replied Lucy. "You know this area pretty well. Can you think of a building that's secluded where you could hold people?"

"You mean like my missing athlete?" he said

"No, guv," she said. "Just something I'm following up on."

He thought carefully.

"There's the parade of shops on the east side before the motorway link. The area is derelict – the owner is trying to get rid of all the tenants then knock the block down and sell the land for redevelopment. Fifty flats, I think. There's a disused store room behind the building which he also wants to demolish. Must go. Bloody javelin throwers," he added.

It was almost time for Lucy's lunch break. She collected her hat and decided to walk down to the area the inspector had identified. Twenty minutes later, she arrived. There was a side entrance which was locked. She went round to the front and managed to push open the door. She peeped through the crack and saw the three women. Lucy gasped, but knew what she had to do. She stepped back and used her radio to call the duty sergeant. She then ignored the instructions she was given, went back to the front door, paused, took a deep breath and then put her shoulder to the door. Much to her surprise, it opened quite easily and she stumbled into the warehouse. Milton was talking to the bound and gagged prisoners. The smell was overpowering. He turned and started to walk towards her.

"Sent a child, have they?" he sneered.

"It's over, Milton," said Lucy. "I'm going to help these three ladies and you can wait for the cavalry. They'll be here in a few moments."

He reached into his back pocket and pulled out a gun. He pointed it at Lucy.

"I can't allow that," he said. "You take another step and I'll fire."

"If you must," said Lucy. She was clenching every muscle in an attempt to disguise her trembling.

She then heard the sirens of police cars and ambulances growing louder. Three officers, followed by a plain clothes detective, burst through the front door.

"Armed police!" came a cry.

A shot rang out.

The bullet penetrated his jaw and smashed his brain into smithereens. He was dead before he hit the ground. Lucy stepped up and kicked the gun away. She then rushed to the three victims and spotted a pile of blankets which she grabbed. She hugged the young woman. She covered her in a blanket and whispered words of comfort into her ear. The diabetic lady was semi-conscious. The javelin thrower shrugged off her experience, saying she still had time to reach the coach and take part in the athletics tournament.

Lucy was covered in dirt. She looked up. Three armed policemen were staring at her. There was also a plain clothes officer.

"Dave," said Lucy. "We need to have a chat about your time-keeping."

Quickly, the paramedics took over. The young woman was in a bad condition and was quickly taken away for treatment. The elderly lady was delirious. Despite a huge effort by the medical team, she never regained consciousness. The athlete was back to normal within minutes and, after wrapping several blankets around her, managed to persuade an officer to take her home. She said that after she had changed she'd go to the police station.

"Luce," said Dave. "Are you all right? By the way, you smell awful."

"Take me home, Dave," she said. "I need a long, hot shower."

The elderly lady died seven hours later. Her family was by her bedside, including two of her four grandchildren. Her husband never recovered and passed on three months later.

Milton Grant's body was taken to the mortuary. On the gurney next to him was the body of a middle-aged woman who had had her throat cut.

A day later, during a squally shower of rain, a letter was delivered to Milton Grant's house. The postman rarely visited. Because of the police tape, he threw the letter into the porch. The on-duty officer, who had been checking the back of the house, trod on the letter. It somehow became part of the rubbish which was eventually cleared away by council workers. Had Milton opened his post, he would have read the following:

Dear Dad,

Yes, sorry and all that. I should have written. Happy birthday.

THANK YOU, THANK YOU, THANK YOU for the money. I can't exist without it.

Mum has started talking about you again. She's fine. She's seeing a new bloke. He's OK. She says I should try to rebuild our relationship. She keeps bringing up how good-looking you were (sorry, whoops, are) and how she loved the hillwalking you did together. She was proud of you and your career as a copper.

I didn't want to tell you this, but I'd better. I had a bit of bother with the police. Only soft stuff, but I got dragged in front of the court. I was let off, thank God. I've enrolled at a local college to do media studies. I'd like to be a Sky News presenter.

Dad, can we be friends?

Love you.

Jenny

"Please take a seat, Police Constable Smith," instructed Inspector Sanderson.

Lucy sat down opposite her boss.

"You disobeyed orders," he said.

"Yes, guv."

"You were told to await the arrival of the armed unit."

"Yes, guv."

"You went in, against orders," he continued.

"Yes," said Lucy.

"You risked your life."

"Yes, guv," she replied. "That was my choice."

Inspector Sanderson looked askance at her. "He had a gun."

"I didn't know that," said Lucy.

"You risked your life," repeated the inspector.

"I saw the three victims. They were in real trouble. I had to reach them." She hesitated. "May I have some water?"

The senior officer poured her water.

"If officers go around making up the rules, the force collapses, PC Smith. I can't allow it to happen."

"No, guv. I understand that."

"You are off on a week's holiday, I understand."

"Yes. Dave and I have got the press all over us. We're flying out tonight to Spain."

"Lucy, make me a promise," said Inspector Sanderson. "In future, you'll obey orders."

"No, guv," Lucy replied. "If I see someone needing a copper, I'll respond."

"Yes." He smiled. "I knew it was pointless asking." He stood up. "Go and enjoy your break."

Lucy stood up and walked towards the door.

"Detective Constable Smith," said her boss.

She stopped in her tracks and turned.

"There will also be a citation, Lucy. You saved two lives. We think that the pile of blankets were for wrapping up the bodies. We're pretty certain he was going to kill them. The elderly lady was gone anyway."

"Thank you, sir."

She turned and began again to head out of his office.

"Lucy," he said. "The javelin thrower made it to the competition."

She looked back. Her face was a picture of professional fulfilment. "That's great, sir."

"She came third." He smiled.

Their plane was late leaving and they arrived on the Costa Brava at well past midnight. At their hotel, they went straight to bed. The following morning they woke early and decided to go for a walk along the beach. The morning was still cool, but it was better than being at home – and there was not a reporter in sight.

"Detective Constable Smith," said her husband.

"You're still superior to me," laughed Lucy.

"Was that in any doubt?" replied Dave as he pinched her bottom.

She giggled.

"But Lucy," he chided. "Inspector Sanderson was right. You shouldn't have gone in there by yourself. I was worried about you."

"I like to live dangerously," teased Lucy.

"Oh, since when?" he asked.

"I married you, didn't I?"

On a bitterly cold November afternoon in a North London cemetery, Milton Grant was buried in a grave with a plain headstone. There was a brief inscription recording his name and dates. The only additional words were *Father of Jenny*. Jennifer and her mother held hands. Detective Constable Lucy Smith was also there. The minister read a few verses from the Bible and then hurried away.

Milton would have approved of that. He hated fuss.

THE END

FALLING DOWN: THE FILM

The 1993 film starred Michael Douglas as William Foster, a divorced, unemployed engineer. His car vanity plate read 'D-Fens', suggesting an angry white male. His wife had a restraining order to keep him away from their daughter.

In a heatwave, Foster is caught in a Los Angeles traffic jam on his way to his daughter's birthday party. He starts to walk, and commences a rampage across the city. He trashes a convenience store and seizes a knife from two thugs. They chase him with a gun, which he secures for himself together with other weapons. He shoots into a ceiling in a restaurant.

The disintegration of Douglas's character reflects the racial tensions in 1990s LA. He is chased by Sergeant Prendergast, who is working his last day as a law enforcement officer. The film climaxes at Venice Pier where Prendergast confronts Foster, who pretends to draw a weapon. It is, in fact, a plastic water pistol. However, Prendergast shoots him dead.

Towards the end of the film there is one of the great lines in American cinema. William Foster does not comprehend what he has done. He asks: "I'm the bad guy?"

This sentence defines the movie and its meaning.

Falling Down was filmed with the backdrop of the 1992 Los Angeles riots, following the police shooting of Rodney King.

The film was a box office success. The distinguished American screenwriter, John Truby, called it 'an anti-Odyssey story about the lie of the American dream'. On the twenty-fifth anniversary of its release, April Wolfe wrote in *LA Weekly:* 'It remains one of Hollywood's most overt yet morally complex depictions of the modern white victimisation narrative.'

The director Joel Schumacher, now 78, is a US cinema great. His films include *The Client* (1994), *A Time to Kill* (1996), *Phone Booth* (2002) and *Blood Creek* (2009).

Michael Douglas is an all-time acting legend whose life reflects many of the characters he has played.

ABOUT THE AUTHOR

Tony Drury

Tony is the author of five DCI Sarah Rudd City thrillers. In each, he draws upon his career as a London financier to expose the underworld of dark practices and shadowy characters. None, however, are able to withstand the bravery and incisive detective methods of one of the police force's bravest officers. Her juggling of career demands, husband, children and her own demons, make riveting reading.

He has now written two more novels which trace

the early career of probationary police constable Sarah Whitson. In 'On Scene and Dealing' she meets her future husband Nick. In 'Journey to the Crown' she has a devastating affair with Dr Martin Redding. The final chapter jumps ahead to sample her future life as a private detective.

Tony has created an innovative series as a novella writer. Reflecting iconic cinema classics, his first was 'Lunch with Harry', which is inspired by 'Breakfast at Tiffany's' followed by four more. City Fiction (www.cityfiction.co.uk) has attracted new authors and the series now has ten titles.

Aged seventy-three, Tony is a follower of the wisdom of Albert Einstein: "When a man stops learning, he starts dying." He lives in Bedford with his wife Judy. They value every trip down the M1 to Watford to be with Grandson Henry.

Email: tonydrury39@btinternet.com
Website: www.tonydrury.com
Twitter: @mrtonydrury

NOVELLA TWO

THE COURAGEOUS WITNESS

by

Oliver Richbell

Inspired by the 1988 film 'The Accused'

THE COURAGEOUS WITNESS

It was a size too big for her. That was why she was wearing it.

Amanda wrapped the pink-flowered cheongsam around her naked body. In the privacy of her Clerkenwell flat, in the hour past midnight, she felt secure in the protective 'long shirt'. She was sipping hot water which, according to ancient Chinese medicine, stimulated blood flow around the body and had restorative healing qualities. She had a throbbing headache and was ready to try anything to shift it.

Amanda curled up on her sofa which was far too big for her flat. She was not comfortable but staying in the foetal position seemed to ease her stress. She was reading a policy document produced by the Crown Prosecution Service. After yawning, she stood up and stretched her aching limbs. She walked into her kitchen to check that Rumpole's water bowl was full. As she did so, she glanced at the digital clock on her oven. With a sigh, Amanda knew she had to go to bed if she was to function in the morning, but she was acutely aware that the last hour or so of reading had been mostly ineffectual – unless by some sheer miracle she had retained information through osmosis.

Filling Rumpole's water bowl and sprinkling a perfect dozen cat biscuits into his favourite bowl, Amanda focused her mind on the CPS document about the prosecution of rape cases:

Rape is one of the most serious of all criminal offences. It can inflict lasting trauma on victims and their families.

and

The majority of rape victims are women and most know

73

their rapist.

Sarah Tomkins certainly knew the two men charged with her assault. She knew them extremely well.

Rape also has a devastating effect on families of the victims.

Amanda returned to the sofa, lost in memories that sent a shiver through her. She shook her head to try to push them deep back inside. With a groan of discomfort as her headache refused to ease, she returned to the papers.

The CPS realises that victims of rape have difficult decisions to make that will affect their lives and the lives of those close to them.

Amanda had read all of the evidence several times previously and she was still unsure as to why Sarah was refusing anonymity and was focusing on her day in court. Amanda concluded that Sarah was after revenge – and public revenge at that.

The law does not require the victim to have resisted physically in order to prove lack of consent. The question of whether the victim consented is a matter for the jury to decide.

Amanda looked up from her laptop and stared straight ahead as she recited the provisions of The Sexual Offences Act 2003;

The defendant must show that his belief in consent was reasonable.

Amanda was thinking hard and had almost forgotten about her headache. She turned back to the CPS document and decided to reread what she felt certain was the most important passage of all:

Proving the absence of consent is usually the most difficult part of a rape prosecution and is the most common reason for a rape case to fail. Prosecutors will look for evidence such as injury, struggle or immediate distress to help them.

Amanda's immediate challenge was clear, unlike her head that was now beset with a thick fog because of the absolute refusal of her headache to ease. She was simply unable to shake her belief that it was going to be difficult – very difficult – to convince a jury that Sarah Tomkins was the victim of a sexual assault by two men and, in the case of one of them, rape. Amanda was racked by tormented memories that she could no longer repress. Despite her sub-conscious efforts, these were racing around her pulsating head like fireflies and she was struggling to concentrate.

You'll feel better after a good night's sleep was always the advice from her Aunt Eileen. There was no chance of a good night's sleep and Amanda knew it. Her brain was aching as it leapt from thought to thought but, with each passing moment, she started to lose the last remnants of focus as she began to muddle the facts of Sarah Tomkins' case with her own bitter memories.

Amanda fell onto her bed and underwent the fight with the duvet and the scatter cushions as she struggled to get comfortable. Eventually, after a considerable and over-elaborate effort, she was able to wiggle herself down and under the covers. Following two meaningful punches to her pillows, she finally closed her eyes.

A second or so after doing so, a thought came to her. Had she fed Rumpole? She couldn't remember but she knew that if she hadn't, he'd be walking all over her and purring into her ear in just a few minutes.

Amanda kicked the covers off. With a loud cry of "Diu!" (Cantonese for "fuck!"), she stomped into the kitchen. In the half-light of the London night she could see her pet with his face in his food bowl, scoffing his late evening meal.

Amanda spun on her heels and went back to bed but was not quite as comfortable as before. She was giving in to exhaustion – but then the events that haunted her earlier began to replay in her mind.

He had come up behind her, totally unexpectedly. Despite her judo training from Fat Freddie in Kowloon, she was helpless as he forced her over.

Rumpole came and joined Amanda on the bed, curling up between her knees and elbows. She, though half asleep, placed a hand over his stomach. She failed to realise from his breathing patterns that not all was well with her fat cat.

A few weeks earlier, Sarah Tomkins had been lying prostrate on her back on the boardroom table. She could feel the hard surface irritating the skin of her buttocks. Eddie was penetrating her as Ivan, watching from the side, was gathering his breath and pulling up his trousers.

"She likes it rough," he gasped. "Have your fill, Eddie."

Sarah was numb; her mind had switched off and she was unable to register anything. She lay powerless with Eddie – sweaty, odious and panting – on top of her. Around the boardroom were cheap, non-matching chairs that had been upturned around the room a few minutes earlier.

The table and chairs belonged to a vehicle distribution company. It dealt in sales and its management meetings focused on sales figures. It didn't matter that the room lacked warmth and nothing matched or showed a co-ordinated brand identity. Craig Heaton, the company's founder and chairman, didn't care. He only cared about profit and he had a fierce reputation for sacking staff for not reaching their often almost impossible targets.

Ivan was a senior salesman at Heaton Van Sales. He had brought in a significant order – worth close to a half million pounds – for supplying a fleet of custom transit vans. His success had been announced in the very room he was now getting dressed in, and which resulted in an impromptu party that had started three hours earlier in the staff kitchen on the ground floor of Heaton House.

Eddie, Ivan's devoted subordinate, had supported him faithfully like a lap-dog throughout the four months of endless negotiations up to the contract being signed. The order invoiced out at £488,887. Ivan's bonus was 5% of the total, so a smidgen under £24,500 of which he gave £4,000 to Eddie, £1,500 to Luca, an assistant salesman (who played a key role in securing the deal), £400 to Sarah and £200 each to her three colleagues on reception. Ivan still cleared almost £18,000 on one order and this was on top of his basic pay.

When Craig, who was at his beachside apartment in the Canary Islands, heard that the customer had paid in full, he walked round the swimming pool with a bottle of champagne, making sure that everyone knew he had landed another deal. It was, of course, down to him as usual, he boasted, but in reality he didn't even know the names of some of his staff, let alone the precise details of the deals they were doing. It was always about the bottom line with him; about the money in the bank, nothing else. His reply to London was short but exultant:

'Brilliant performance. It's party time: no limits. C.'

Craig liked to sign off every internal email, message or memorandum with a capital C. However, it didn't stand for Craig but for chairman. It was important that everyone knew he was in charge even though he was rarely in the office. As he sat down on one of the empty loungers around his beachfront apartment he cast a disinterested look over the beach. A semi-naked bathing beauty turned over on her sunbed and he found himself wondering if Sarah would hang around for the party he'd just authorised. He liked Sarah; he even recalled her name. Mind you, most men who met her didn't quickly forget her.

His thoughts about Sarah slowly disappeared. After all, he'd never make it back in time for the party. As he turned back away from the splendid sea view, his gold signet ring sparkled in the late afternoon sun. People always assumed that the jewel-encrusted C stood for Craig. It didn't, of course; it stood for chairman.

Back at Heaton Van Sales, alcohol and food had been delivered by the same high-end grocery business that had just agreed their order for a fleet of transit vans. Ivan told everyone who would listen that it was his order. Luca didn't mind; after all, no-one in the office would believe him over Ivan anyway, and it was better to be with Ivan than against him.

As is traditional at office parties, there was far more booze than food. It was not clear who brought in the 'powder'. The repair shop was the likely source although, with the appearance of a number of 'guests' including blonds, brunettes and redheads, their later protests of innocence were accepted. As it was, a few of the staff spent more time in the toilets than they did dancing in the foyer and on the kitchen tables.

The women on reception sorted the music by setting up a playlist on a smart phone.

Their office celebrations were quite regular events but Ivan was keen to make this, one to remember. He wanted everyone to know that he was a dynamic salesman and his parties were the best, especially as Craig was not there to steal his thunder.

There was booze, some food, music, drugs and girls: the party had begun.

Sarah was the head receptionist. She had helped to transform her team into an efficient, professional 'front-facing' part of the Heaton Van Sales machine. She always paid close attention to her appearance and she insisted that all 'her girls' did likewise. Her mantra was: "We are the first people customers see. We must greet them with courtesy and politeness, and always look professional". It would never be the catchphrase of the year, but she really did believe it.

It helped that she and 'her girls' regarded themselves as good-looking. In her case, that was not in question.

Sarah was enjoying the party; she always did. She stayed away from the coke – it wasn't her thing, and never had been, but she accepted that others partook. She had joined in the dancing with enthusiasm, eating little of what was on offer but drinking a lot of vodka and tonic. She was currently without a serious partner. She was happy to wait for one and to date casually in the interim.

Everyone knew that Sarah liked Ivan and Ivan liked Sarah. The flirtatious banter that passed between them over the receptionists' desk was devoid of subtlety most of the time and occasionally was downright lascivious. Neither seemed too fussed that Ivan was married with a child.

As the early evening celebrations began to unravel into the usual drunken shenanigans, Sarah, who had danced with Ivan a lot, at times very closely indeed, suggested to him that they have a more private party. She had surveyed her colleagues who were either wobbly, playing tonsil hockey or hurrying back and forth to the toilets, and had decided that it was time for a bit of fun. He was not exactly a 'newbie' to adultery and did not need any encouragement.

They slipped away from the mayhem and headed for the stairs that led to the boardroom. Ivan gestured for Eddie to come with him.

The fourth of their little group was the ever-present Luca. Apart from running around getting them drinks and taking away their empties, he'd never been more than six feet away from Ivan from the moment the music started. Ivan caught Luca's eye and mouthed "Piss off" to him, gesturing back towards the party.

Ivan and Sarah were giggling like teenagers as they stumbled and fumbled up the stairs. Eddie was half a dozen steps behind them, trying to catch a glimpse of forbidden flesh up Sarah's skirt. Against the wall by the boardroom door, Ivan and Sarah began to embrace. There was no element of sensitivity or subtlety; it was simply animalistic desire.

Eddie walked past them both and into the boardroom.

Sarah and Ivan stopped. Wiping her mouth with the back of her hand Sarah gasped,

"Get rid of him, Ivan, now!"

"We're a team, Sarah, me and Eddie. You've had

your bonus – now it's our turn."

He pushed her into the boardroom, grabbing her backside as he did so.

"That's a fine bit of ass you've got there," he crowed, kicking the door behind him.

As it banged shut, Eddie slurred,

"Remember the porn we watched the other night? Those two blokes and the nurse."

"It wasn't as good as that Japanese lot in the sauna," roared Ivan, high-fiving Eddie.

Sarah was sobering up – and was becoming concerned. She went for the door but, before she could escape, found herself being dragged back across the room and held down on the table. Eddie and Ivan pulled at her clothes. She cried out as her bra was ripped off.

"Please, no," she pleaded.

"I'll go first," growled Ivan as he pulled down her knickers.

Eddie held her as his colleague wiggled down his trousers. Sarah could not understand how Ivan, who she had really fancied, could be metamorphosing into the hefty, panting lump now forcing himself on top of her. She didn't try to resist. She couldn't, as every ounce of fight she thought she had vanished in the sheer terror of the moment. Ivan then had sex with her and slid off the table.

Sarah felt Eddie's grip on her arms relax. She opened her eyes. Eddie loomed up in front of her. Sarah feared that he was going to rape her. Desperately, she tried to climb away but he pushed her down on to the wooden surface. Her head crashed against the frame.

"No!" she screamed aloud.

When she tried to scream again, one of the men shoved his hand into her face. She struggled, but he was too strong for her. Sarah fought back and managed a split second of freedom which was just long enough for her to gasp for air. The next thing she felt was a fist hitting the side of her head. She winced in pain and momentarily lost consciousness. Then the hand returned to her mouth more brutally than before. The tears were uncontrollable as she felt herself being penetrated.

Summoning all her strength she made one final effort to escape but the two men just shoved her back down with the same care they'd treat an overfull wheelie bin.

Panicking, she opened her eyes and saw Ivan watching her, leering, his face sweaty and red.

"Fuck her good, Eddie," he screeched.

Sarah began to shake with revulsion.

Eddie withdrew. He then ran both his hands up her legs and pinched her inner thighs. Sarah's eyes bulged and she yelled out in pain. Eddie laughed and squeezed her flesh again.

Sarah turned her head to one side and tried to retch. Ivan grabbed Eddie and said, "Nice one, mate. You head back down, I'll be down in five."

Ivan moved back to Sarah and tried to re-arrange her blouse. Wild-eyed, Sarah fended him off with frantic hands. She slid off the table, so she was leaning against it, and pulled down her skirt. One of her bra straps had broken, but she managed to fasten the buttons on her blouse. Her shoes were a few feet in front of her.

Ivan suggested, "Let's get back to the party."

Sarah stopped dead in her tracks with one hand on

the back of a poorly-veneered wooden chair. She stared at him in utter disbelief as her contempt began to show.

"You do what you want, but I'm calling the police," she said.

Ivan laughed.

"Will you tell them you were first up the stairs?" he mocked.

"You and your fucking sidekick attacked me," she said.

Ivan laughed again. With more than just a hint of disdain in his voice, he told her that he was going for a drink and, when she came to her senses, she was welcome to join him.

Sarah watched with her hand on the chair as she tried to regain her balance. He sauntered out of the room without another word to her. The sound of that metallic click as the door closed would be one she would never forget.

She slumped onto the seat and grimaced from an internal pain. She had been gripping the chair for what seemed like an age. Her hands were shaking and she felt cold. The pain was beginning to ease. After a few moments, that felt like hours, she slowly rose to her feet. She tried to straighten her hair and wipe away her smeared lipstick. She pulled down her blouse and tried to remove some of the creases. She then turned and, with a deliberate but feigned poise, she took a few steps to the door.

She stepped out into the landing and inched her way to the top of the stairs and stopped. There was more pain and a lot of spasms were hitting her. They seemed to wash over her like a boat swallowed by a gigantic wave. It was then that she realised there was blood running down her inner thighs.

She gripped the banister with her left hand but was feeling light-headed. She wobbled at the top of the staircase and started to fall. In a flash, Luca caught her without a second to spare.

"Oh, mother of mercy," he cried, as Sarah collapsed into his protective arms.

Thirty-five minutes later, Sarah was admitted to the Accident and Emergency Department of Nailton Hospital, having been assessed by a Police Examiner. The doctor inserted three stitches into her perineum, which was ripped, and prescribed a course of antibiotics. When her blood pressure dropped back to an acceptable level, she was discharged with orders to return the next day for further checks to be made. Her mother and step-father had responded to a call from the hospital admissions desk and were together in the waiting room wanting to take her home. As the maternal arms wrapped around her, Sarah whispered into her mother's ear: "Mum, they fucking raped me!"

Back at Heaton Van Sales, the party had come to abrupt end after the ambulance had taken Sarah to hospital. The gossip-mill was turning fast. The police questioned everyone present and recorded their full names and contact details before they were allowed to leave.

The Detective Inspector had arrived and his team had surveyed and catalogued the chaotic remnants of the party: food trodden into the floor; bins overflowing with empty beer cans, wine and spirit bottles; and the pungent smell of stale alcohol that hung in the air like an odious fog. Those who had partaken in other party accessories were paranoid beyond belief and probably brought more unwanted attention upon themselves by their furtive, twitching faces. The police were not interested in that aspect. They concentrated their investigations on the initial questioning of Ivan, Eddie and Luca. All the members of the reception desk were keen to make statements. At around eleven o'clock the Detective Inspector cautioned Ivan and Eddie and arrested them on suspicion of aggravated assault and rape.

There was only one topic of conversation throughout the office on Monday. Sarah did not report for work and Ivan and Eddie were missing. Craig was furious in having to have spent a lot of time dealing with Yvette, the personnel director, over the weekend. She laid out the factual and legal position to the chairman and notified Ivan and Eddie that they were suspended, pending the outcome of the police inquiry together with an internal company investigation. Craig was mainly concerned with the costs involved and whether the incident could depress sales.

Some weeks later, Amanda Buckingham was feeling the lump in Rumpole's belly. She felt awful. She'd always been diligent about getting him checked out when he had been ill but, this time, engrossed in her work and thoughts, she kept forgetting to book an appointment.

An hour later, the on-duty vet was ruffling Rumpole's head. Amanda's stomach turned; *one phone call was all I needed to have made so why did it take me so long to do it!* Her pet licked the vet's hand.

"I've been so irresponsible," said Amanda.

"No, not at all, don't be too hard on yourself," replied the vet, Ben Lister. Ben smiled at her reassuringly and made eye contact. Amanda held his gaze for several moments and then he broke away with an over-elaborate, "Anyway...back to Rumpole."

She had met him on several occasions when taking the cat for his injections and regular check-ups. Ben often teased Amanda with the suggestion that she should receive a loyalty card for the number of visits she accumulated in a year. Rumpole was nine years old which, in human terms, was around sixty-five years.

The vet's good looks were not lost on Amanda – and nor were hers on him. He had, at one of their earlier encounters, nodded with respect and interest when Amanda dropped into conversation that she was a barrister. Since then he teased her about her profession and told her the name for the cat was cute but a little obvious.

Amanda seldom missed signals. She was trained to read people and was blessed with an above average gift of intuition. For once, she merely took Ben's interest as part of the bedside manner. She later made a conscious effort to pay more attention to Ben's non-cat chat.

The vet was studying a scan of the lump in Rumpole's stomach. Amanda caught his gaze. He looked up.

"Yes, it's as I thought," and, with a slight pause for dramatic effect as Amanda held her breath, continued, "it's a cat."

He smiled and Amanda laughed.

"It's not too critical," he diagnosed, after a

moment or so of careful deliberation.

"Too?" was the word that Amanda heard and repeated.

Perhaps, somewhat unprofessionally, he walked over to her and put his arm around her shoulders; it seemed, somehow, acceptable. She felt him squeeze her.

"You say he's had no food since late last night so we'll take the lump out later today," he said, "and then, I'm afraid, it's in the hands of Saint Gertrude." He smiled at Amanda who seemed bemused. "Saint Gertrude is the patron saint of cats," he added.

"If it's cancer?" she asked.

"We'll send the lump for biopsy, and we'll find that out later. The first priority is to remove the growth and get him stable and comfortable," said Ben.

"What are his chances?" she asked.

"If Ben Lister is operating, better than most," quipped the vet.

Amanda appreciated the further effort at light-heartedness. Ben put Rumpole into his cage and he buzzed for a nurse to take him away.

"You go off and win your case and I'll fight on here," he suggested. "I'll text you when I have some news." He stared at her. "We'll do our best for him," he said.

"You and Saint Gertrude," said Amanda.

From her early days as a barrister, the Head of Hartington Chambers, located in Lincoln's Inn in central London, had taken a special interest in the niece of his friend, Anthony Buckingham.

As Amanda was sitting directly in front of Rufus

Hetherington-Jones QC, she was being circumspect in reflecting her annoyance.

"Firstly, Rufus, I defend – so why have I received a prosecution brief?" she asked.

"We take what we're given," responded the Head of Chambers. "You know that is the way it works." He then repeated his favourite adage. "You know what I always say, Amanda: 'It is better to have your hand up than out'."

Nodding impatiently, Amanda continued her objections.

"Secondly, and after my review of the papers, I understand why the CPS is bringing this case to court but I've got some concerns. I am not sure how I can convince a jury that she did not consent. She led the way to the boardroom. She allowed sex to take place with the first man and, although she claims she said "No", she still had sex with the second one. She cannot explain why she allowed this man to remain in the room at the beginning or why she did not protest when the door was locked. She must have realised that they intended to have sex with her." She raised her eyebrows as she awaited Rufus' reply.

Amanda was taking out her frustration, at the brief she had been presented with, on her Head of Chambers. This was not usually a wise course of action for any barrister at Hartington to follow. However, given the nature of their relationship, she was allowed a certain degree of latitude which was not afforded to any of her peers – and most certainly not to her colleague, with whom she shared a room, Mr Trevor Hamper-Houghton.

As the two barristers continued to debate the case, the usual hum of activity, in and around the Clerk's room, was beginning to wane as other members of Chambers and staff were passively listening to the conversation while trying to appear, and in the most failing, to look busy. They were enjoying the verbal back and forth as the barristers traded shots in a game of intellectual tennis.

Rufus, noting that they were becoming a distraction, waved Amanda into one of empty conference rooms. As he did so he caught the eye of Hartington Chambers' practice manager, a seasoned clerk by the name of David Blyth. David was a 'Dave' from Essex who had clerked his way up the ranks and, whilst he called himself Dave, Rufus always referred to him as David.

Rufus had no problem talking through any issue with anyone at chambers and he liked the paternal persona he thought he cultivated. Not all, if any, agreed that he generated this very well. However, no-one ever told him and so Rufus's belief in his own 'father-figure' status remained a constant source of amusement within chambers and no more so than to Dave and the rest of the support staff.

Amanda dutifully followed him into the conference room. Rufus closed the door. She sat down without waiting to be asked as she could feel her inner tension mounting. She decided to speak first.

"Rufus, let me summarise the position." She lingered for a second or so, allowing Rufus to take a seat opposite her, and so she could re-gather her momentum lost by the change of scenery. "Sarah Tomkins was one of the leaders in organising the office party. She had, by her own admission, drunk a lot of alcohol. There were drugs on hand but there is no suggestion that she used them. She went willingly with Ivan, and his associate Eddie Delaney, to the boardroom away from the party. She, in her own statement, claimed she protested that Eddie was there but, nevertheless, had consensual intercourse with Ivan. Her clothes were ripped but there is nothing to suggest she resisted at that point."

Rufus leant into the middle of the table and opened a bottle of expensive bottled water. He poured himself and Amanda a glass each. He then sat back, awaiting the next volley.

Amanda nodded her thanks. Moving the glass in front of her, she didn't wait for a coaster – much to the annoyance of Rufus. She carried on.

"Now, this is where matters get even more complicated. Eddie alleges he was encouraged by Sarah to have sex with her; she says she said "No". Sarah then claimed that someone hit her on the side of her head, but the Police Examiner reported no bruising. Sex occurred, the accused say, with consent, Sarah says the opposite."

Rufus, having had little to say so far, finished his glass of water with an audible smack of his lips. Sarah moved on, ignoring the noise.

"The two men then abandoned her and return to the party. Sarah found her own way out of the room, discovered she was bleeding, and collapsed. Luckily, Luca Toskas caught her. She was taken to hospital where she had three stitches to her perineum and was prescribed antibiotics."

She hesitated momentarily and looked down at her notes.

"Ivan was charged with sexual assault and Eddie with sexual assault and rape. I gather that the CPS considered charging Ivan with rape as well but they subsequently dropped that charge against him because there was not sufficient evidence."

Amanda drained her glass, this time placing it neatly in the centre of her coaster. She looked at Rufus. He returned eye contact and Amanda concluded with, "They are both, without a doubt, guilty."

"So, prove it and get a conviction," said the Head of Hartington Chambers in a rather matter-of-fact tone.

"I can't prove either of the charges and the defence counsel will slaughter Sarah in the witness box."

"And you lose a case," interjected Rufus.

"I can live with that, Rufus, but I don't want the see the woman destroyed."

Carefully, and with a degree of sensitivity, he responded.

"Right, Amanda, let's take a step back and focus on what you have in your favour?"

Amanda snapped, "You mean in Sarah's favour, surely!"

Rufus recoiled back in his chair, with his arms out in front of him, in surrender.

He did not understand what Amanda said next because it was mumbled and certainly not in English.

With a slight air of apology, she smiled.

"Sorry, Rufus. Cantonese."

It broke the tension. Laughing in reply, Rufus added, "I can speak French."

"Eh bien," countered Amanda.

The two barristers sat silently for a moment until Amanda declared, "I can certainly present enough evidence, but it is about how the jury view Ivan and Edward. Ivan is a father and has a pregnant partner. Eddie, from the statements on file, is the more aggressive personality but they both maintain that sex with Sarah was consensual."

"The CPS is bringing the case, not you, Amanda," declared Rufus, "and you cannot get emotionally involved." He wondered if he was being too cold-hearted and tried to back-track. "The CPS is to lead and prepare the evidence and your job is to present it in the best way and then allow the jury to decide the outcome."

That was the end of the conversation, Amanda was not really sure if the discussion had been of any use but she was grateful Rufus had at least listened to her. She followed him to the door and, as he politely ushered her out of the conference room, her mobile phone vibrated.

She walked a few paces and then read the message. *'Op in 30 mins. R is peaceful. B.'*

Amanda sat with the CPS officer and went through the police files, the evidence and the charges. They had a lot of work to do. Inwardly, Amanda lacked confidence in the case but the CPS was optimistically bullish. While they waited for Sarah Tomkins to arrive, Amanda decided to express her reservations. The CPS solicitor was indifferent. "We have passed the threshold test," was the 'stock' response. Amanda raised her concerns from a professional standpoint; personally, she felt a sense of unease and impending defeat.

Sarah Tomkins arrived and was ushered into the meeting room by a male caseworker, perhaps in his early twenties who, incredibly, 'checked out' Sarah's behind as he closed the door. Amanda noticed this with a sense of utter incredulity that she only just managed to keep to herself. It was with a heavy heart that she smiled at Sarah as she sat down at the table.

She was wearing a blue top, pressed jeans, sandals and her hair was cut short.

"I'm here, Sarah, to understand your position and to prepare the Crown's case," she began.

"Thank you," interjected Sarah, "but, please, no legal niceties; there is no need."

" OK," she replied. She waited as Sarah rummaged in her bag. She put two pieces of menthol chewing gum into her mouth and began to chew. Amanda understood that this was her signal to press on and go to work.

The meeting lasted for several hours. Sarah was composed throughout and responded honestly to Amanda's detailed questions. The CPS solicitor added much to the conversation about how Sarah would give her evidence at the forthcoming trial. Sarah and the CPS solicitor had discussed and agreed that she would not seek any special measures in relation to the giving of evidence. Amanda was impressed with the courageous approach being taken by Sarah.

After the meeting ended, and on her journey back to Chambers, she reflected on what Sarah had said. The conclusion was the same as it had been earlier in the day: this case was going to test the barrister to the limits of her abilities.

Later that afternoon, Amanda was in her office, poring over the case file and her notes from the meeting. Papers were strewn across the table, on the floor and on the windowsill behind her. Post-it notes of all shapes, sizes and colours protruded from all angles making, to the untrained eye, her desk seem like a primary school art collage. Amanda felt comforted by the effort she was putting in and she gained some reassurance that, at the very least, she was going to be well prepared for trial.

She sensed her mobile phone vibrate on her desk. Searching through papers and bundles and text books she finally located it hidden between the pages of her notepad.

She read the message received:

'Op over. R rather poorly. Sorry. B.'

She read the message again. She drafted a response but didn't send it. She placed her mobile into her bag and returned to her paperwork.

Amanda spent Sunday afternoon with Trevor Hamper-Houghton. He was courteous, funny and well-informed. He asked her for another 'pre-date date' as he liked to call their irregular gatherings. She agreed to meet him again the following Saturday and he suggested taking the Eurostar to Brussels for a day trip. She wondered if she had shown him sufficient enthusiasm as he clumsily back-tracked in fear of being rejected.

The truth of the matter was that Amanda's mind was preoccupied with the upcoming case. Her pre-occupation with Sarah's innocence continued to invade her rather cramped brain. The preliminary hearing was set for Monday. If the defendants didn't have a Road to Damascus bout of conscience, the matter would be listed for trial at Crown Court.

Monday came and went. The two defendants

confirmed their respective names and their pleas of 'not guilty'. Sarah was not present. This entire episode lasted a matter of minutes and was, at best, perfunctory.

Amanda had her routines as well as her quirks. On the morning of each new trial she did two things. She rose early and went to the gym. Her personal trainer, Zach, was quite amenable to this routine as Amanda was paying well over the odds. Although he kept his thoughts to himself, he relished the look of Amanda in Lycra kit. She liked to box before a trial; pad work, mainly, but she found it far more rewarding than a normal gym session. The second of her pre-trial rituals was a real indulgence. It was a full-fat cappuccino with chocolate sprinkles from her favourite coffee shop just off Lincoln's Inn Square.

She sat in her room at Chambers, a dank, mouldy old pump room in the bowels of the Old Square. The clerks had told her it was only a temporary office but that had been several years ago. Energised by her gym work-out and a warm feeling inside as she devoured her cappuccino extravaganza, Amanda was ready.

With a clenched fist of delight as she three-pointed her immaculately drained take-away cup into the waste paper bin, Amanda picked up her trolley bag that she had carefully packed. The handle was grabbed and, with a hefty tug, given the weight of the paper inside, she strode away. Amanda walked assertively passed the other 'temporary' residents of her floor. Her office door had closed with a thud and inside it was now almost completely dark, save for the neon glow of the phone that had been left on her desk.

A few moments later, Amanda re-entered her office and grabbed her mobile, stuffing it into her coat pocket. She then left for a second time, with a renewed determination to win the case.

Nailton Crown Court was as inspiring as a Stalinist gulag in the depths of winter. It lacked warmth, charm and architectural appeal. "Buildings can be warm and inviting," thought Amanda, but this court edifice was neither, especially as the heating was unreliable.

In the robing room, Amanda donned her black gown and short wig. It wasn't a flattering look for anyone but she quite liked the history and the tradition behind it. Walking into court, with a bow of the head as she entered, she took her place next to her trolley bag. Meticulously she laid out her papers, notes and pens. She poured herself a beaker full of tepid tap water that had been placed in a plastic jug by the court clerk.

There was nothing else she needed to do. She was ready. She was Amanda Buckingham, prosecution counsel.

Unlike scenes from Hollywood movies, British jury selection consists of a series of random ballots. First you are summoned, then you are allocated an alpha-numeric reference and placed into a pool. Fifteen of your pool colleagues then attend before the judge and the court where a final lottery takes place. If your number comes up you take one of the twelve seats. It's like a bizarre game of musical chairs, without music, levity or a prize, pondered Amanda. She, even as a junior member of Chambers, had seen too many jury formations to easily recall each in detail but, every time, the sheer randomness never disappointed her. She was not a football fan but, as she watched the jurors-in-waiting being called as jurors, and taking their seats in two banks of six, Amanda likened the process to those halcyon days of cup draws with stiff, crusty old farts pulling numbered balls out of silk bags.

Assessing the final twelve members of the jury was an essential element of the criminal legal process, whether you are defending or prosecuting. Amanda hoped that she would be fortunate with the final make-up. Inwardly, she prayed for more women than men to be on the jury. She reasoned that women would be more empathetic towards Sarah.

The final composition of the jury was six men and six women.

"It could have been worse," she said to herself.

Judge Clarke went through his usual repartee. He was a solid and well-respected man but he had certain peccadilloes. Amanda had been before him on several previous occasions. While he would never tolerate questioning off the beaten path, he had always allowed her some degree of latitude. Judge Clarke reminded the jury of their serious and civic duties in painstaking detail. Some of the jury were already lost; others took frantic notes; one looked half-asleep. When he had finished with the jury he turned to public gallery.

Amanda sat watching the jury, looking for eye contact. She caught two or three sets of eyes and smiled back – not a teeth flasher, but a professional smile with a slight nod.

Sarah's mother and step-father sat quietly together

in the gallery. They were surrounded by friends of the defendants and a few unknowns who were looking for some enthralling courtroom jousting. There was a law student present – he was obviously a student as his legal text books were by his side together with a cheap-looking packet sandwich.

The only other person left in the room was Archie Morton, an experienced bulldog of a defence counsel. He had made a good living in defending criminal cases; his motto (and that of Waitland Chambers where he had practised and honed his craft for two decades) was, *'If they pay, we'll plead nay'*.

Amanda really didn't like him at all, even on a professional level. He was fixated by money and the 'Holy Grail' of becoming a QC. There was no altruism, no public interest, no soul to Archie Morton; this did, however, make him a formidable opponent and Amanda knew she would have to be at the top of her game from the off.

During a long and tedious narrative from Judge Clarke, Archie did nothing other than assess and scan the jury. He was slick, like slow-moving oil, and just as toxic, but for some reason, he often managed to get jury members on his side. He nodded to some, smiled at others and stared others out.

All of this administration and ground rules meant that Judge Clarke decided on an early lunch; the jury looked relieved and funnelled out of the courtroom. The two defendants seemed confused at this unexpected halt in proceedings. Eventually, the court room emptied save for Archie and Amanda.

"Well then, Buckers," sneered Morton, "I see you are playing with the other side of the bat on this one."

He continued the cricket analogies. "The wicket's no good for you, I'm afraid, and there's no chance of this going five days."

Amanda didn't follow cricket and so Morton's words were lost on her. She had to respond, albeit ineffectively.

"I'm happy to take this one on," she stammered.

She finished packing away her papers into her trolley bag and left the courtroom.

After an uninspiring lunch with the CPS solicitor, Amanda opened the Crown's case against Mr Ivan Derbyshire and Mr Edward Delaney. Every single word had been revised, reviewed, amended, modified and triple-checked. Amanda delivered her speech perfectly. Her tone was spot on and the tempo was even better. Silence is such a powerful tool in any successful advocate's arsenal and Amanda let every detail of the events that had taken place in the Heaton Van Sales boardroom hang in the air like poisoned arrows. There was a deathly silence as they landed on the jury.

Archie, however, had seen this coming. By the time he'd dissected Amanda's opening comments, the visitor in the gallery was perplexed. What would the verdict be? At the end of day one, the law student summarised his notes with two words: Not Guilty.

Day two saw the start of witness evidence. The first person called took the oath and confirmed that his name was Luca Gabor Toskas. He stated that his parents had brought him and his sister to live in the United Kingdom in the 1990s. He said that he had joined Heaton Van Sales three years ago and was part of Ivan's team. Luca made it clear that he liked his job very much.

He then went through the events of the Friday evening, when the alleged assault took place, and confirmed that he had followed Ivan, Eddie and Sarah up the stairs. Ivan had told him to go back to the party. He said that he did not mind because a pretty blonde girl was waiting for him.

He categorically denied taking any drugs but confirmed that they were available but the source of such were unknown to him.

"So, Mr Toskas, how far up the stairs did you climb?" asked Amanda.

"To the first floor," he replied.

"And that was the point when Mr Derbyshire told you to return to the party."

"Yes."

"What did he say?" asked Amanda.

"He made it clear that I was not welcome," replied Luca.

"What words did he use, Mr Toskas?"

The assistant salesman looked around him, unsure if he was allowed to swear an oath and in court. Amanda read the situation and placated the witness with a smile.

"He told me to piss off," he stuttered.

There was a snigger around the court room. Judge Clarke raised one of his bushy eyebrows in annoyance and gently tapped his bench with his left-hand knuckles to let everyone know he had heard the laughter and that it was not permitted in *his* court.

Amanda repeated, "'Piss off'...do you think that is a friendly way to be spoken to, Mr Toskas?"

"It's the way he always speaks to me," he replied.

"I can imagine," she acknowledged, glancing at Judge Clarke. He'd heard her comment, but, thankfully, let it slide. Archie was texting under the table, so he missed her unprofessional remark.

Amanda noticed that two of the six women who made up the jury were fidgeting and exchanging nods of agreement.

"Did you immediately return to the party?" enquired Amanda.

"Yes. You can be sure. I'm olive-skinned. The girls love us Europeans."

There was at least one laugh from the gallery. The student looked around but all heads had dropped like a mass prayer had been called. Judge Clarke imperiously scowled at where the noise had come from. Waiting for the nod from the judge, Amanda stood still. The approval came and she began again.

"So, you returned to the party?"

"Yes."

"Therefore, you have no idea what happened to Mr Derbyshire, Mr Delaney and Miss Tomkins," countered Amanda.

"We all know what happened," said Luca.

"How do you know?" pounced Amanda.

"Well...I don't. I wasn't there," stammered Luca.

"Thank you, Mr Toskas," interrupted Amanda, "we have your evidence that you were not there. Now, I want to ask you about the events that happened later. This was when Miss Tomkins collapsed into your arms. This took place on the third floor?"

"At the bottom of the stairs leading up to the boardroom," Luca said.

"On the third floor," said Amanda.

"Yes."

"What were you doing there?" she asked.

"I have explained. Ivan and Eddie are my friends. I wanted to make sure they were having fun."

The courtroom fell into a brief period of silence as Amanda waited for Luca to keep talking. After a few moments it was apparent that he would not; Amanda then rallied.

"So, what about the girl at the party?" asked Amanda.

"I don't understand you," said Luca.

Amanda debated explaining the point but she hesitated.

"You went up the stairs and you caught Miss Tomkins."

"Yes. There was blood on her hand."

"Yes, thank you, Mr Toskas. We will come to that shortly," declared Amanda. She paused and wrote that down on her notepad.

"You must have passed Mr Derbyshire and Mr Delaney on their way down the stairs then?" Amanda asked.

"Just Ivan," he said. "We passed as he went back into the party."

Luca ran his hand through his hair and fiddled with his tie. He went for the water and gulped down a large cup full.

"Mr Delaney was upstairs," stated Amanda.

Morton had finished his texting and he rose to his feet.

"It would seem, Your Honour, that this is a statement of conjecture rather than a question," said the defence counsel.

"Miss Buckingham?" queried Judge Clarke. He had that judicial knack of saying the same words on multiple occasions but each time they sounded and meant something entirely different.

Amanda turned back to the witness box. Smiling, she said, "You owe a lot to your two friends, don't you, Mr Toskas?"

"I have a great job, thanks to Ivan and Eddie," said Luca.

"Would I be right in thinking you'd do anything for them?" asked Amanda.

Archie was up like a rocket. "Your Honour!" he screeched.

Amanda said flatly, "No further questions" and sat down.

The defence counsel stared at Amanda. He shuffled his feet, pulled on the lapels of his gown and began his questioning.

"Mr Toskas, hello. I'm Mr Archie Morton and I want to ask you just one question."

Luca smiled as he hoped he'd soon to be out of the witness box.

"When you left Mr Derbyshire, Mr Delaney and Miss Tomkins to go further up the stairs, at the point when Mr Derbyshire told you to go back to the party, what was your impression about Miss Tomkins' attitude?"

"I do not understand the question," said Luca.

"Was it your impression that Miss Tomkins was going willingly with the two men?" rephrased the defence counsel.

"She was laughing and touching Ivan," he answered. "She was going up the stairs quite quickly; I know that because I was taking two steps at a time myself."

"No further questions," declared Archie as he sat down with a smugness that some barristers possess.

Amanda's re-examination was cursory. She knew that she had misjudged Luca and had, naively, not seen Archie's single question coming until it was too late.

Judge Clarke decided on an early finish. The jury were delighted until he kept everyone another ten minutes to explain that the members of the jury must not talk to anyone about the case or undertake any research in relation to the facts or the law.

As Amanda watched the two defendants depart, she was repulsed by the thumbs up Eddie Delaney gave to Archie. She spoke to the CPS solicitor outside the courtroom and, after a few perfunctory comments, they agreed that it was early days. She left the building through a side exit and switched on her mobile phone.

There were three messages and several emails, but she knew the one she would open first. She read the words carefully:

'R *has an infection. On antibiotics. Not good. Lump was benign. B.*'

Tuesday was a damp, mild June day. It started badly for the prosecution team and never recovered. Edward Delaney entered the witness box and promised to tell the truth. He radiated self-confidence. He agreed with everything that Amanda asked him.

Yes, he had gone up to the boardroom to have sex with Sarah. None of them had taken drugs although all three had consumed rather a lot of alcohol: in his case, he estimated seven cans of lager.

He confirmed that he was in awe of Ivan and would do anything for him. He liked Luca, and he thought that Sarah was "sensational". He did not deny that he had made a rather crude suggestion involving the two males but said that Sarah had applauded his idea. Amanda glanced to her left; Sarah was shaking her head in silent outrage.

She had chosen to attend the trial, and, at the pre-trial conference with the CPS, she agreed that she would not opt for any of the evidential special measures that were afforded to victims of sexual assaults. Sarah had also waived her right to give evidence by video-link even though the CPS solicitor had delicately explained that she might find being questioned in the witness box incredibly harrowing. Ultimately the CPS made the ruling, but Sarah confirmed it was the right thing to do. It was a courageous decision.

Amanda continued with her questioning of Eddie.

"Mr Delaney, I regret that I need to raise an unpleasant matter with you."

Eddie Delaney remained impassive.

"Do you deny that, at the end of your assault on..."

"If I may, Your Honour," cried out Archie Morton, "counsel is prejudging the decision of the jury. Her statement is grossly misleading."

Judge Clarke was displeased. He decided to reassert his authority.

"Miss Buckingham! I will not allow you any further leeway in this case. You will not again, in my court, make such a distorted statement." He turned to the jury and ordered them to disregard the question.

Amanda was stung by the judicial rebuke.

"I apologise, Your Honour," she said, sensing that she might have lost the momentum that she was carefully trying to build.

"Mr Delaney," she continued. "Did you, towards the end of the events in question, touch Miss Tomkins' inner thighs?"

"No," Delaney replied.

"No, Mr Delaney?" exclaimed Amanda incredulously. "May I remind you that you are under oath and you are required to tell the truth."

"I did not force myself on Sarah. She was gagging for it and she encouraged me." He paused and added, "She was laughing. She loved it."

There was total silence in the courtroom. Sarah Tomkins collapsed in tears into her mothers' arms. The judge allowed a few moments to elapse before indicating to Amanda that she should continue.

"What happened next?"

"I was wondering whether we might do other things," responded the witness.

"Other things?" asked Amanda.

"Well, she was having fun."

Sarah Tomkins put her hands over her face and wept silently.

Judge Clarke was not an uncaring or insensitive man. Realising that the emotions inside his courtroom had ratcheted up, and the increased tension had engulfed everyone like a noxious gas, he called a halt to proceedings and ordered that everyone would take an early lunch. He then asked both barristers into his Chambers. This style of judicial conference used to be quite commonplace but, with the various changes to legal processes, they now occur less often. When they do take place, what is said is added to the Digital Audio Recording Transcription and Storage court recording system – DARTS. Judge Clarke was careful in what he said to both barristers but he made it abundantly clear that he was growing displeased with their conduct. Both Amanda and Archie left, chastened, like two naughty schoolchildren exiting the headmaster's office.

When the court resumed, Archie Morton revisited all the previous evidence and managed to convey to Amanda and, in her view, the jury as well, Eddie Delaney's disbelief that Sarah was suggesting she had not participated willingly. By the end of the day's proceedings, the body language of several of the jury appeared to suggest that they were satisfied that the accused might be innocent.

The records of the police examiner were admitted without objection from either barrister so the third witness to take the stand was Dr Rebecca Atkinson.

Amanda took a line of questioning that proved to be a little too casual. She established that Dr Atkinson had been on duty at the Accident and Emergency Department of Nailton Hospital on the Friday night when the Heaton party had taken place. Dr Atkinson confirmed that she had examined the patient identified as Sarah Tomkins and had inserted three stitches inside her perineum. She had prescribed a course of antibiotics and later discharged the patient as they were desperately short of beds.

When asked the direct and final question, Dr Atkinson said that, in her medical opinion, the injuries, which included redness on the inner thighs, were consistent with a physical sexual assault.

Amanda left the last phrase hanging in the air and invited her professional adversary to cross-examine the witness.

Archie Morton rose to his feet slowly and with

deliberate purpose.

"Dr Atkinson," he began. "How long was it between Sarah Tomkins arriving at the Accident and Emergency Department and your examination taking place?"

"I can't be certain," replied the doctor. "We were very busy that evening. There had been a fire in the town centre and we had some patients needing help with breathing difficulties due to smoke inhalation."

"Quite," observed the weasel-like barrister. "Thank you for your helpful answer, Dr Atkinson. We accept the pressures you must face in your work. I will repeat my question. How long was it between Sarah Tomkins…?"

"I understand the question," snapped the doctor. "I think from memory it was about three hours which is within the government's target timings."

"Three hours," repeated the defence counsel. "Can we therefore conclude that the injuries sustained by Sarah Tomkins were not considered to be an emergency?"

"No," responded the doctor. "I work in the Emergency Department."

"You work, Dr Atkinson, in the Accident and Emergency Department. I put it to you that the injuries sustained by Sarah Tomkins were not an emergency. They were an accident, which you correctly and efficiently treated."

"She needed stitches," said the doctor. "She had been assaulted."

"We'll come on to that," said Archie. "If you had not seen Sarah Tomkins for four hours, what would have been the medical consequences?"

"She needed stitches," replied Rebecca. "She had

been assaulted."

"Dr Atkinson, it is not for you to say she had been assaulted." Archie paused to allow the jury to consider his words. "Shall we agree," he continued "that your patient was not an emergency? She needed hospital treatment which was non-urgent?"

"You're putting words in my mouth," replied Dr Atkinson.

Amanda was now realising that she had erred badly in not taking the doctor's evidence more seriously and that there should have been a lot more direct questioning as to the nature and extent of Sarah's injuries. On several occasions she went to challenge Archie Morton's questions but decided to wait.

"You have said that you inserted three stitches, Dr Atkinson. Where was that?"

"The perineum, at the entry of the vagina."

"How long is the vagina?" asked Archie Morton.

"It varies but shall we say about four inches in this patient's case."

"And where, Dr Atkinson, were the stitches inserted. How deep in did you have to go?" asked Archie.

"I inserted the injuries at the opening," replied the doctor.

"The opening," mused the defence counsel. "And why did you insert three stitches?"

"Your Honour," pleaded Amanda "There is simply no purpose in this line of questioning. We have accepted that Sarah Tomkins required three stitches."

"I'll permit the question," said Judge Clarke.

"Thank you, Your Honour." Archie Morton took

a pace back and stared at the witness.

"Could Sarah Tomkins have managed with two stitches?" he asked.

"In my medical opinion..."

"Did the injury need stitches at all?" he said. "Was there internal bleeding?"

"There was no bleeding. There was a tear which, in my medical opinion, required stitches."

"Would you have endangered the patient if you had inserted two stitches?" asked Archie.

"In my medical opinion..."

"Thank you, Doctor Atkinson. How often do you come across this type of injury?"

"More often than you might imagine," said Dr Atkinson.

"Are you able to explain to the court the usual cause?" asked Archie.

"Oh. That's easy. The vagina is quite delicate and nearly always it's the result of physical intercourse taking place. It looks worse..."

The defence counsel was quite happy for the doctor to continue talking.

"...because injuries in what is a very sensitive area can bleed a lot during and after sex, due to the heart working harder."

"The result of sexual intercourse, Dr Atkinson. Between a man and a woman."

"Well, there are a number of variations but yes, heterosexual sex."

"Dr Atkinson. You have referred to Sarah Tomkins being assaulted. You witnessed the alleged assault, did you?"

"Of course not. The paramedics told us. It was written on her triage notes. It's also what the patient had told them."

"The injury you treated. Can you say with any certainty how it was caused?"

"It was consistent with a physical assault."

"Or was it consistent with normal consensual sexual intercourse?" asked Archie.

"Well, I suppose it could have been."

"Can you say, Dr Atkinson, with any degree of certainty, that, in your opinion, there was clear evidence that your patient had been physically assaulted?"

The witness hesitated.

Archie Morton stood, his eyes fixed on the witness stand and counted to ten in his head.

"Dr Atkinson," he continued. "Did your patient, Sarah Tomkins, tell you that she had been assaulted?"

"She didn't say very much at all and I had a heavy workload."

"I want to repeat your words, Dr Atkinson," said Archie. "'She didn't say very much'." Does that tell you anything?"

"Women who have been sexually assaulted usually react in one of two ways," replied the doctor. "Some, quite evidently, are distressed and traumatised. Others say absolutely nothing."

"And what does the reaction tell you?" asked Archie.

"Usually I'm afraid that I'm too busy tending to the medical needs of my patients to get too involved in their mental state." She paused. "If I feel a patient needs psychiatric support I will call in a colleague."

"Thank you, Dr Atkinson," smiled Archie. "What you are telling the ladies and gentlemen of the jury is that you were otherwise engaged with your medical duties and, in truth, you had little idea about Sarah Tomkins' emotional state."

"I wouldn't put it like that," replied the doctor.

"I want to ask you about the alleged damaged skin on her inner thighs," continued Archie. "What treatment did you administer? How many marks were there?" he asked.

"The skin was inflamed and red," said the doctor.

"And how many marks were there?"

"There were several impressions on the skin. They did not need treating although I did rub some cream into her body to help the healing."

Archie continued his questioning.

"Dr Atkinson. I only have two more questions for you. The redness, as you call it, on Sarah Tomkins's thighs. If that had been her only injury, how would you have treated it?"

"I have no way of knowing that," replied the witness. "She would never have reached me. A nurse would have seen her."

"Thank you," said Archie. "My final question. Can you please describe the condition of Sarah Tomkins when you first examined her?"

"She was lying on the bed. She was half asleep."

"When you talked to her, was she rational?"

"She asked if she could still have children."

"What was your answer, Dr Atkinson?"

"I was able to tell her that, as far as I could be certain, she was physically fine but she should see her own doctor if she wanted further reassurance."

"And you judged that physically, and emotionally, she was ready to be discharged after you had treated her?"

"Yes. We needed the bed."

"No further questions, Your Honour," said Archie Morton.

Amanda knew that it was too late to undo the damage inflicted by Archie Morton's incisive cross examination. She was personally affronted, but professional impressed, by Archie's skilful approach.

She watched again as Eddie Delaney put up his thumb towards Archie and the visitor's gallery. She vaguely heard Judge Clarke closing the day's proceedings and again advising the jury that they were not to talk to any third party about the case.

Amanda put her papers in her case and sat down to think. She had the option of re-examining Dr Atkinson in the morning but she could see no advantage in doing this: there was little she could do now Archie had won the day. As she left the building she turned on her mobile phone. There were seven messages and three missed calls. Not one of them was from Ben.

The law student's tally chart, with marks out of ten, from the back of the public gallery, now read: *Not Guilty 6. Guilty 3.* He needed to work on his mathematics.

Amanda left the court building in need of carbs. Arriving back at her flat via the local pizza takeaway, her mobile phone vibrated.

'So sorry. R is struggling. We're fighting for him. B.'

Amanda went into her bedroom, stripped off her clothes and put on her cheongsam. She returned to the kitchen and ate a thin and crispy Hawaiian pizza with extra pineapple as if she had not eaten for days. She managed all but a few crusts and one solitary slice which she threw into the bin. She collected a bottle of chilled mineral water from the fridge, and walked to the sofa, where she had discarded her case notes minutes earlier.

Later she went to bed before midnight but didn't fall sleep until after two in the morning. She then had a dream. She was back in Kowloon with Fat Freddie or, rather, Fat Son Sue. He was telling her to work harder.

She made her first misjudgement on Wednesday morning by texting Trevor Hamper-Houghton to confirm their Saturday trip to Brussels. His curt reply of "Agreed" left her feeling a little emotionally empty.

Ivan Derbyshire proved to be a more challenging witness. He had clearly decided to say as little as possible and his repetition of "Yes" and "No" unsettled Amanda. He even prevaricated when giving the details of the deal he had secured for Heaton Van Sales and the commissions he had paid out of his bonus. In answer to the question "So you gave £200 to Sarah Tomkins?" he replied "Yes". When asked why he had done so, he said, "I wanted to".

Amanda took him through the events of the Friday evening: the party, the atmosphere, Sarah's disclosure that she suggested a more private party, the climb up the stairs, Eddie's role, his physicality, his shock at Sarah's injuries about which he had known nothing, and his concern for her well-being.

Amanda played her trump card.

"Mr Derbyshire. You have a partner and you live together."

"Yes."

"You have a son?"

"Yes. Billy."

"I understand that your partner is pregnant."

"Yes."

"How many weeks?"

"Twenty something, I think."

"Was it difficult for you to explain to your partner that you had been unfaithful?"

Archie Morton went to object and then sat down again.

"No," said Derbyshire.

"No!" repeated Amanda. "What is her name?"

"Debbie."

"Debbie," said Amanda. "What does Debbie think about what's happened? How does she feel about you standing here before this court?"

Archie Morton again went to protest at the question but sat down.

"Nothing," said Ivan.

"Nothing," said Amanda.

Ivan remained quiet.

"You are asking the jury to believe that your pregnant partner was relaxed about you having sex with a work colleague."

"She told me to."

"I beg your pardon, Mr. Derbyshire. Are you saying that Debbie encouraged you to have sex with another woman?"

"Yes," he said. "With Sarah."

Amanda turned to Judge Clarke.

"Your Honour, this witness simply cannot be trusted with this evidence."

"Continue with your questions, please, Miss Buckingham," was the terse reply.

"Let me understand this exactly," said Amanda. "You are telling this court that your pregnant partner encouraged you to have sex with Sarah Tomkins?"

"Yes."

"Why?" asked Amanda.

"Debs is struggling. She's got high blood pressure. She understands that I need regular sex. She can't do it. She told me to shag Sarah. She worked at Heaton and said all the girls thought that Sarah was gagging for it."

The law student marked down another point for Not Guilty and then closed his note book.

Amanda lay on her sofa in complete silence. There was no music, no background sound and no cat. She went over and over the evidence she had heard during the last three days. There was no doubt in her mind that Ivan and Eddie had assaulted Sarah Tomkins. Sarah's behaviour had muddied the waters by dancing with Ivan and wanting to have sex with Ivan. However, Sarah had never expected Eddie to become involved and immediately she made it clear that she was not consenting, the two salesmen had broken the law.

Sarah had been determined so far, but tomorrow she would give her testimony, and Archie would tear her to pieces.

Amanda was worried. She had never lost a case before but she felt that might change tomorrow. She tried to sleep, she wanted it, she needed it but, as she drifted in and out of consciousness, she went back to her disagreement with the officer from the CPS.

"The decision to prosecute is quite straightforward, Miss Buckingham," she had said. "It's a clear case of assault and rape. The girl said "No". There was no consent. There were her injuries.

There was the damage to her body. She collapsed down the stairs and was lucky that the man caught her. All you have to do is persuade the jury that Sarah is telling the truth, not the defendants."

Amanda tossed and turned from side to side. She put her arm out to rub Rumpole's head but he was fighting for his life in the animal hospital.

In the early hours, Amanda woke from a fitful sleep and went over to the window. She looked at the lights of the twenty-four hour city beneath her. She turned back to the divan and sat down with a glass of water in her hand.

Her memory went back to her abortion. The five-star treatment at the private hospital and Eileen's love and care, which partly mitigated the pain and humiliation. She relived the event. Even Fat Freddie's judo training had not prepared her for a man of fifteen stones grabbing her from behind. He had seemed so caring and friendly. She accepted that they were moving towards the start of a relationship and she had arranged a doctor's appointment to ask for a prescription for birth control pills.

It was a sunny day and she drank too much wine. When his hand strayed too far up her thigh she told him to stop and he complied. She relaxed and a few moments later stood up and removed her skirt and blouse to reveal her bikini. That was naively provocative. Five minutes later he came on her from behind. She collapsed under the pressure of his weight and was unable to stop him penetrating her. As they stood up and faced each other she suddenly executed a perfect *harai goshi*. The sweeping hip throw resulted in her assailant landing on his back with

Amanda holding his arm which she was twisting against the joint.

"I am two inches away from breaking your shoulder," she said, before she released him and fled the scene.

What she did not do was to see the doctor and obtain a morning-after pill. It never occurred to her that she might be pregnant. She fought the increase in her weight until she started being sick in the mornings. Eileen knew immediately and booked an appointment for her to see a doctor at her own private clinic. Her uncle was not involved. She looked after her niece and rarely left her side. Her recovery from the termination was medically satisfactory and complete. Her aunt never once preached to her. She just hugged her.

The day before she was discharged from the hospital, she received a visitor. Anthony Buckingham, as always, looked immaculate. They discussed Tony Blair and the Conservative Party's inability to dislodge him. He moaned that his wife did not understand him and then winked at his niece.

He stood up to leave. As he reached the door he turned back.

"The chairman of a company," he began, "where I was marketing manager once saved my skin. I had dropped a huge clanger and he covered up for me. As I left his office after the biggest reprimand I had ever faced, he said to me, "Buckingham. Your gross incompetence is history. You judged the supplier on face value. You did not think things through. You did not check the facts. You can now only make one more error. If you fail to learn from your mistake you'll leave us." He paused before choosing his words, "I did learn and I prospered," he added.

As she stared at the closing door, Amanda made a vow to herself. She would learn from her mistakes. It was a lesson she was never to forget.

After she returned to her bed, she continued to slumber into the early hours. She inevitably thought further about Sarah Tomkins. She went over and over the events of the Heaton party. She wanted to be sure that she was not judging things on face value. At five-fifteen in the morning she received a text message and immediately pictured Rumpole alone in the animal hospital. She got out of bed and went into the lounge. She then read the brief request:

'Is it too early to chat? THH.'

She pressed his number and immediately heard his voice.

"Just wondered how your case was going?" he asked.

Amanda lay back on her bed and tried to avoid an adverse reaction from her friend because she was trying to look forward to their planned Saturday trip into Europe. It was not too long before Trevor was testing her. He explained that he had been in Chambers the previous afternoon (and he did not fail to mention that he had won a case against the Inland Revenue for one of their clients who had become involved in a dubious film financing scheme) and picked up comments that she was not handling the sexual assault too well. He then added to Amanda's angst by suggesting he might be able to advise her on her courtroom strategy.

Amanda proceeded to go through the key points of the case with him and was reassured that he did not interrupt or make any comment apart from the occasional "oh boy". When she had completed her summation, she admitted that she was nervous about putting Sarah Tomkins in the witness box.

"That's your big chance. Tell me about the jury," said Trevor.

Amanda went through the make-up: the six men and the six women.

"Pity," he concluded. "You need at least eight or nine women," he said.

"I know," admitted Amanda.

"Well, good luck. What approach will you be taking later?" he asked.

"I will try to show that she is a lovely woman who was assaulted. I shall focus on her evidence that she said "No"."

He interrupted her.

"Hang on, I want to top up my coffee."

Amanda used the interval to decide if their call was positive.

"Right. Back on duty," she heard him say. "Did you know that they call you 'AB' in the office? I'm going to call you 'AB'," he said. "Not very original I grant you, but it suits."

Did she just feel her heart race? For THH it was a rare moment of flirtatious banter.

"Well, BB," she said, "how would you handle Sarah?"

"BB?" he asked.

"Brilliant Barrister," she laughed.

"AB meets BB. Read all about it," he chuckled.

Amanda was enjoying their exchange. She really did wonder if THH might develop into something more real. Their similar legal backgrounds were a good start. She just wished he'd ask her more questions about herself.

"I would keep it short," he said. "You want the jury to be left with just one memory: she said "No"."

"And what about what Edward Delaney did to her?"

"I leave justice to the kingdom of heaven," said Trevor. "Good luck and let me know," and with that he terminated the call.

She went into the shower and turned the water to its hottest level. He was right. She realised that she was siding with Sarah and ignoring the facts. She knew that she only had one real opportunity to influence the jury. Sarah had said "No" and that is rape.

She dried herself and put on a tracksuit. She cycled on her machine for twenty minutes and felt awful. Her breakfast consisted of half a cup of filter coffee. Thursday was starting badly.

She re-read the message on her mobile phone:

'R very poorly. Trying different treatment. We're fighting for him. B.'

As she reached the court she ran into Judge Clarke. He nodded and hurried on into his Chambers.

Later that morning, Sarah Tomkins strode confidently to the witness box, Amanda silently applauded her. She was wearing a demure grey suit, no make-up, a hair band and low heels.

At first, Amanda concentrated on her early career at Heaton Van Sales and her success in becoming head receptionist. When Sarah let slip that, last year, the company had allowed her time off to nurse her dying grandmother, Amanda was in like an Exocet missile. By the time she was finished, she had portrayed Sarah as a humane, selfless and caring person.

They covered the events of the Friday party, her willingness to have sex with Ivan and her initial enthusiasm as they climbed the stairs to the boardroom.

Amanda was heading for the key moment if she was to convince the jury of the defendants' guilt. She enabled Sarah to exhibit her utter horror when she realised that she was expected to have sex with a second man, her punitive treatment on the boardroom table and her repugnancy at the physical pain inflicted by Eddie.

"Miss Tomkins," said Amanda as she faced the jury. "Did you, or did you not, agree to have sex with Edward Delaney?"

"No, I did not," replied Sarah in a clear and confident voice.

"Did you use that word, 'No'? Is that what you said?"

"That is what I said both to Ivan and to Eddie. I said "No" and I meant no."

"No further questions," said Amanda, as she returned to her seat. She studied the faces of the jury members. She was convinced that she had sowed the seeds of doubt in several of their minds.

Whereupon Archie Morton rose to his feet with the deliberation of a man convinced of his own importance and he proceeded to attack the creditability of Sarah Tomkins.

"Your Honour, members of the jury, I must start my cross examination of this witness with an apology. My job is to defend my clients to the best of my humble abilities and is to prevent a possible miscarriage of justice. My two clients, Ivan Derbyshire and Edward Delaney, are two hard-working and successful businessmen who were seduced by a colleague at an office party. We, here today, are all worldly-wise and this type of liaison occurs up and down this great country of ours. So, all that is needed, members of the jury, is to deal with just one matter."

Amanda's instinct was telling her that the mother of all bombs was about to be detonated in the courtroom.

"Miss Tomkins," he exploded, "I wish I did not have to ask you this question." He paused with superb timing. "Do you regularly have sex with married men, or men who have longer-term partners?"

Sarah tried desperately to retain her dignity.

"I consider that an unfair question," she replied.

"Miss Tomkins," continued Archie Morton. "Do you have sex with men who effectively are cheating on another person?"

Amanda was on her feet but Judge Clarke took no notice and so she sat down.

"Eddie forced himself on me," she pleaded.

"Miss Tomkins, how many times have you had sex with a married or committed man?"

"Amanda was up on her feet. "Your Honour, this has nothing to do with this…" Her words were lost as Judge Clarke intervened

"The witness will please answer the question. Continue with your questions, Mr Morton."

"I'm obliged, Your Honour," he said. "Miss Tomkins. Let's take this step by step." He smiled at the witness. "Can we assume that you usually know the marital status of the men with whom you have sex?"

"Yes," said Sarah in a hushed voice. "One or two pull the wool, but you usually know."

"And do you perform vigorous sexual acts in your relationships with the men with whom you choose to have a relationship?"

"Some men make demands, yes," said Sarah.

"And can we assume that you perform these acts willingly?"

"It is part of love-making," she said, as Amanda wanted the floor to open up and swallow her whole.

"Do men ever force themselves on you?" asked the defence counsel.

Amanda rose and held out her hands in exasperation.

Judge Clarke took off his glasses.

"Mr Morton. I must admit I am wondering if you are beginning to push my patience and that of this court."

"Thank you, Your Honour," he said as he nodded. He then paused with magnificent effect. "If Your Honour will allow me to reach my crucial question?"

"As quickly as you can, please Mr Morton," replied the judge.

"I am most grateful, Your Honour."

"Miss Tomkins," he barked. "How many times have you had sex with a married man?"

"I honestly don't know," she said. Amanda looked at her feet.

"You don't know," repeated Archie Morton. "Let me try to help you, Miss Tomkins. "Shall we agree more than ten times?"

"I can't remember. Possibly."

"Twenty times," said Archie.

"You are trying to show me in a way that is not me," said Sarah.

"I am trying to show you as a woman who enjoys casual sex," said Archie.

"No," shouted Sarah. "Never. The partners I chose are all..."

"Are all what?" asked the defence counsel.

Amanda remained seated.

"Eddie raped me," said Sarah.

"No, Miss Tomkins. That is not true. You consented to the events that took place by admitting you wanted sex, by rushing up the stairs, by leading the way with two men into the boardroom, by having intercourse with Ivan while Eddie watched, and then having sex with Eddie." He paused and turned to the jury. "That is what happened, isn't it, Miss Tomkins?" He didn't wait for an answer.

"Just one more question, Miss Tomkins. And this puzzles me. You have told this court that you willingly went up to the boardroom to have sex with Ivan Derbyshire. As you reached the room you realised that Edward Delaney was to be involved." He paused. "Why, Miss Tomkins, why did you not simply walk away and none of the subsequent events would have taken place?"

Amanda knew the answer to the question. Sarah was aroused and wanted sex with Ivan. "Say nothing," Amanda thought to herself.

"I wish I had," shouted Sarah.

"Had what, Miss Tomkins?" asked Archie.

""Walked away", as you put it," she said.

"So, the members of the jury can base their

decision on your evidence that you were in that boardroom willingly?"

"I said "No"!" shouted Sarah, defiantly.

Amanda decided to leave it at this point. She felt there would be no purpose served by re-examining the witness. She wanted the last thing ringing in the jurors' ears to be the word 'no'.

Not Guilty 8. Guilty 2. The law student considered not bothering to waste the bus fare again tomorrow as this case was all but over.

She returned to her flat alone and lonely. There were no messages from Ben and Trevor had not phoned her. The night hours seemed endless as she sat in court imagining the summary that Judge Clarke would deliver later the next morning. The two rapists would walk away laughing with their families and friends and go to the pub to celebrate their acquittal. Sarah would sneak away to a humiliating return to the reception desk at Heaton Van Sales, her reputation in tatters.

Her eyes were closing and she was drifting. She simply had no further stamina left to review the four days of evidence. She found herself dreaming about being in the Sung Wong Toi Park in Kowloon and there was Fat Freddie – both of them. They were each holding her hand. They sat down and Freddie Wing Wey turned to her and smiled.

"Ben niao xian fei zao ru lin," he said.

A clumsy bird that flies first will get to the forest earlier.

She woke up and was immediately alert.

"What, Fat Freddie. What is it? What am I missing?" she cried out.

She ran her hand through her hair and then she

remembered something. She leaped out of bed, catching her foot in the duvet. She hit the floor with a shudder. It only momentarily impeded her progress. She dashed to her desk where she opened her papers and searched for Monday's notes. She then re-read several police files. She was becoming animated as she sensed a lead. She turned over each page, skim-reading the contents, and then she went back to one particular section. She found the passage she was looking for and then she located the later testimony. She checked and re-checked. She went on to where Sarah had fallen. It was all there and she had failed to realise its significance.

She rushed to the bathroom and threw cold water over her face.

"It's the hair. It's the colour of her bloody hair," she shouted out.

As his driver weaved his way through the Friday morning commuter traffic, Judge Maynard Clarke relaxed back into the cushioned rear seat of his judicial car and reflected on the readings which his monitor had recorded earlier in the morning. "147/85," he pondered. During a recent annual medical examination, his doctor had noted raised blood pressure. Before starting prescriptive treatment, he suggested that his patient, in order to eliminate 'white coat syndrome' (the stress of the doctor's surgery resulting in misleading results), buy a home monitor and record his BP each morning and again at the end of the day (but before the evening consumption of malt whisky).

His Honour knew that the systolic value (the reading showing the pressure as the blood leaves the heart through the arteries) was too high. He was pleased that the diastolic figure at '85', showing the pressure as the blood returns to the heart through the veins, was at a healthier level.

An hour later, in his room at the Nailton Crown Court, as he stared at Amanda Buckingham, had his blood pressure been taken, both readings would almost certainly have been considerably raised.

Archie Morton was frustrated and concerned. He had been caught completely off guard with the CPS's application to recall an earlier witness. Archie had tried to say 'no' but he had no idea what he was saying 'no' to or why he wanted to say 'no'. After a lot of multi-syllable verbosity his main reason for objecting was because the CPS had asked.

"I grant the application Miss Buckingham," declared Judge Clarke, "but be under no misapprehension: I can give you no latitude with your questions."

The CPS and Amanda had achieved the requisite permission from Judge Clarke but it took several hours for the court officials and the police to locate the individual and bring him back to court.

At 11.59 on Friday morning of the trial of Ivan Derbyshire and Edward Delaney, the man stared out of the witness box looking bewildered and anxious. He confirmed his name and that he understood he was still under oath. He watched as Amanda Buckingham approached him.

"Mr Toskas," she said.

Despite all the events of the last five days, Judge Clarke secretly admired the prosecuting counsel. In his assessment, she had that special quality that marked her down as a barrister with a future.

"Mr Toskas," she repeated. "I want to revisit some of the evidence you gave to this court last Monday."

"I told the truth," he spluttered.

"Mr Toskas," she continued. "During the events of the Friday night party at Heaton Van Sales you told this court that you followed Ivan Derbyshire, Edward Delaney and Sarah Tomkins out of the staff canteen and up the stairs."

"I told the truth. Ivan told me to piss off and so I went back to the party."

"Yes. I am satisfied that you have correctly confirmed what you said."

"Your Honour," interrupted Archie Morton. "Where is this meaningless line of questions taking us?" he said.

"Sit down, Mr Morton," ruled the judge "Miss Buckingham. Please speed up your questioning."

"Thank you, Your Honour," said Amanda.

She looked down at her notes.

"Mr Toskas," she continued. "Did you tell this court that you returned to a particular girl."

Luca Toskas put his hands to his face.

"Yes," he said.

"What is her name?"

"Chaudra," he replied.

"And what colour hair does she have?" asked Amanda.

"Your Honour," angered Archie Morton, "this is a farce. We'll be told the name of her hairdresser if prosecuting counsel continues this approach."

"Miss Buckingham, I really can't permit your line of questioning much longer."

"Thank you, Your Honour," said Amanda.

She turned and faced the witness box.

"Mr Toskas. You have said that you returned to the party to be with a special girl. Yes or no?"

"Yes, Chaudra. She's dark-haired," he answered. "She is beautiful."

"Can I confirm that, please Mr Toskas? Chaudra is dark-haired. A brunette."

"Yes," said the witness.

"Yes," repeated the prosecution counsel. "That is what you said to the police officer who interviewed you on the evening of the party. He specifically recorded her name and that she was dark-skinned and a brunette." Amanda paused.

"So why did you tell this court that she was blonde?"

Luca reddened in his face. He looked down and started to fidget.

"I don't remember," he spluttered. "Chaudra is dark. She is what I told you. I can't have said that."

"Shall I have the recording of your evidence given last Monday played back to the members of the jury?" asked Amanda.

"P-perhaps I said she was blonde," muttered an increasingly desperate Luca.

But the wheels were coming off. He tried to argue that he could not tell the difference between the two colours, that Chaudra often changed the colour of her hair and that he had been confused.

Finally, Amanda pounced.

"Mr Toskas. I put it to you that, in fact, you did not go down the stairs, but you waited and, after a few moments in time, you went up the stairs?"

Tears filled his eyes.

"Please. I'm so sorry. I'm going to church every day to ask for forgiveness. I am so sorry".

"Why are you so sorry?" asked Amanda. "Why, Mr Toskas?" she repeated.

He looked across the court room towards the two defendants.

"I can't tell you. Eddie will beat me up," he said.

She now took the terrified witness, step by step, thought the events of the Friday evening. He had waited for several minutes before following the three participants up the stairs. He said that he wanted to know what happened. When he reached the third floor the door was closed but the window blind had not been fully lowered. He had watched the events with a clear view. He said he could see and hear everything.

When Eddie had left the room, he had hidden along the corridor and then, moments later, watched Ivan leave. He looked into the room and saw that Sarah was sitting in a chair. He went down the stairs and then heard her open the door. As he turned around and looked up the stairs he found her collapsing into his arms. He said that there was blood on her hand.

"Mr Toskas," said Amanda. "I want you please to think carefully about my next question. When Sarah was struggling on the table, and being held down, did you hear her say anything?"

"She was fighting to get free. Ivan was holding her down."

"Did she say anything?" asked Amanda.

"She shouted out "No!"," said the witness.

"Are you sure? Could she have said 'oh'?" asked Amanda.

"No. She said "No" and then Eddie hit her. He and Ivan were like animals. She was in terrible trouble."

Eddie leaped up and threw himself at the protection screen that guarded the defendants from the open courtroom.

"Luca. You're a fucking dead man walking," he bellowed. Amanda stood in horror as the real Edward Delaney presented himself to the world. He looked deranged. His eyes bulged; the veins in his neck looked like they were trying to force their way out of his skin. Several of the jury recoiled.

Eddie thumped the screen and spittle dripped down like rain on a windscreen.

Eventually he was restrained by the court officials. When sense returned he slumped down into seat with the heaviness of a man who knows he's in serious trouble.

After that, events moved quickly. The defendants changed their plea and admitted to the offences with which they were charged in order to try and mitigate their custodial sentences.

Their families and friends emptied from the visitor's gallery and never returned.

The law student sat, open mouthed, his eyes flitting back and forth in disbelief at what he had just witnessed. He never updated his tally score. He was glad he had made a late decision to return to the courtroom.

Judge Clarke thanked and dismissed the jury, remanded the prisoners in custody and deferred sentencing until two weeks' time. He warned Ivan Derbyshire and Edward Delaney that they faced custodial sentences.

As the court rose, Amanda caught the eye of the

Judge. There was hardly a flicker of recognition but there was, perhaps, an imperceptible nod of his head. Archie Morton refused to acknowledge his peer and stormed out of the building.

Amanda later spoke to her Chambers. She was told that there was a bundle of papers being couriered to her home detailing a case of death by dangerous driving starting at the magistrate's court on Monday morning. To her relief she was defending the motorist. As she headed for her car she checked again and felt disappointed that there was no message about her cat.

There was, however, a text from Sarah Tomkins asking if they could meet. Reluctantly, Amanda decided to agree. She felt that the receptionist had been through so much over the last few weeks. It was an ill-advised move but she said she would see her in the park later in the afternoon. She knew that the fresh air would do her good in the light of another text message she had received:

'Well done AB. Sorry, but u're not my type. Let's move on. THH.'

She spoke just one word: "Diu."

As they later came together in the open spaces Amanda felt a sense of admiration for her.

"Thank you for agreeing to meet with me," said Sarah. "I'm a bit tearful but at least it's all over."

"Briefly, Sarah," said Amanda "and then you must never contact me again."

They walked together along a tree-lined path. They watched as two dogs chased each other.

"Did you hear that Debbie Derbyshire lost her baby last night?" she asked.

Amanda said nothing. She allowed a period of silence to continue.

"You know I can't find the words," said Sarah.

"I did my job," said Amanda.

"I wanted to tell you my news," said Sarah. She ignored the silence. "I'm going to train as a social worker. When I nursed my Gran last year I found something I wanted to do. I'm going to study to be a manager of a care home."

"Sounds good," said Amanda. "The cut in pay will hurt."

"I have all the money I need, I'm to receive a decent pay-off,'" said Sarah. "Mr Heaton, the chairman, phoned me from his holiday home." He had listened carefully to the advice given to him by Yvette, the personnel director.

Amanda paused. She wanted to know something.

"Sarah, what will happen to Luca?" she asked.

"Unbelievable. The lads from the office collected him and took him back to the depot. He was kissed by all the girls." She paused. "A particular brunette took charge of him."

"Chaudra," said Amanda.

Sarah laughed.

"Justice has won the day. Isn't that right, Amanda?" Before the barrister could reply she went on, "Did you know that a clerk from accounts has gone to the police? She's claiming she was also raped by Ivan and Eddie."

Amanda winced. She took Sarah's left hand and squeezed it.

They shared a fond, almost sisterly, embrace and, as Sarah walked away, Amanda watched her go.

As she turned towards the Tube station her phone

vibrated. She looked down at the message:

'*He's better. He's has had small meal. One more night to be sure. Collect him tomorrow mid-morning. B.*'

She stood still, beaming, and then skipped down the stairs into the underground station. As she neared her Clerkenwell flat there was a further text message from Ben.

Ivan Derbyshire and Edward Delaney were sentenced to five and seven years in prison. Eddie took to the brutal regime like a duck to water and began to make several questionable associates. Ivan became reclusive and needed medical help for depression. He was not helped by the disappearance of Debbie who, once she had been discharged from hospital following the loss of her baby, relocated to the Lake District with her son. She found work in a Windermere restaurant and, within a year, she had begun a new relationship and became pregnant. She never saw Ivan again.

During the investigation at Heaton Van Sales, the police uncovered a discrepancy in the sales invoice for the van transaction, which had triggered the party. It was later revealed that the money due to be paid was being collected by a Guernsey-based associated company and HMRC tax inspectors were undertaking a comprehensive audit and review. Not long after, the chairman was back in the country facing prosecution for VAT-related fraud. The business subsequently went into liquidation and was bought out by a competitor. The girls on reception all survived but, by now, Luca had left. He and Chaudra emigrated to Italy to begin a new life together.

Sarah Tomkins decided to fly to Portugal for a week in the sun. She was soon talking to the man sitting in the window seat and they arrived at Faro in a decidedly relaxed manner. He was into property sales and Sarah accepted his invitation for her to visit him at his villa. After a repeat trip several weeks later, this became a more permanent arrangement. She remained in close contact with her mother and tried to persuade her to join her and her new partner in the Iberian sunshine.

Archie Morton reacted petulantly to the loss of the case but quickly recovered and was soon back in court. Judge Maynard Clarke overcame his blood pressure problems by adopting a vegetarian diet and losing two stone in weight.

Early on the Saturday morning following the end of the trial, Zach put Amanda through her paces in the boxing ring and insisted she swam forty lengths of the pool. She feasted on bowls of fresh fruit and figs. She returned home and decided to wear her hair loose, a white shirt and jeans.

She arrived at the vets late in the morning. Ben brought Rumpole out to her in his cage. He immediately tried to lick her fingers which she had pushed through the wire cover.

She turned to the vet.

"I received your text message," she said.

Ben looked at her.

"You've a spare ticket for the theatre, tonight," she laughed.

Ben said nothing.

"I think I can consent to that," she smiled.

As she put her cat in the back of her car, she realised that she had no idea what they were going to see.

THE END

NOTE: THE STORY OF 'THE ACCUSED'

This 1988 American drama was one of the first Hollywood films to include a rape incident of unimaginable graphic realism.

The storyline for *The Accused* was loosely based on the 1983 gang rape of Cheryl Araujo in New Bedford, Massachusetts and the resulting trial. This film is set in Washington State but was filmed in Vancouver, Canada.

Sarah Tobias (played by Jodie Foster) is gang raped in a bar.

Assistant District Attorney Kathryn Murphy (played by Kelly McGillis), agrees a plea bargain with the legal representatives of the three men accused. They plead guilty to a charge of 'reckless endangerment' which carries a lesser prison sentence and the chance of parole. Sarah is incensed, not least because she was denied the opportunity to testify in court.

Kathryn opts to prosecute three witnesses identified by a friend of Sarah. They are charged with criminal solicitation. The evidence in court is partly overlaid with a visual reproduction of the whole of the rape scene. Another bystander gives evidence and the three men are convicted. One consequence is that the perpetrators, now in prison, will serve longer sentences and not be eligible for parole.

The final scene is a display, by Sarah and Kathryn, of mutual respect as they go their separate ways.

+

The French-born director, Jonathan Kaplan, was a

protégé of Martin Scorsese and made *Truck Tuner* in 1974. He continued actively although it was his 1988 film 'The Accused' that was one of his most critically acclaimed works. He now concentrates mostly on TV films.

Kelly McGillis's distinguished career includes *Witness* (1985) with Harrison Ford and *Top Gun* (1986) with Tom Cruise. In 1982, she and her live-in girlfriend were assaulted and raped by two men in her New York apartment. For this reason, she turned down the part of Sarah Tobias in *The Accused* but agreed to play the Assistant District Attorney, Kathryn Murphy. She lives in North Carolina and teaches acting.

Jodie Foster is considered to be one of the best actresses of her generation. Her breakthrough came with Martin Scorsese's *Taxi Driver*. She was not an immediate choice for the role of Sarah Tobias in *The Accused* but went on to win an Academy Award. She then played Clarice Starling in *The Silence of the Lambs*. She now concentrates on film directing.

AMANDA BUCKINGHAM: AN EARLY HISTORY

Amanda was born on 3 June 1983 on Kowloon Island, Hong Kong. She was an only child and registered as being British. Her father, Arthur Grosvenor Marin Buckingham, was deputy head of the civil service in the Territory. He played a pivotal role in negotiating the handover from Britain to China.

These were turbulent times, with anti-British riots and bombings which were encouraged by the Chinese authorities. There was an influx of Vietnamese refugees of whom, by 1988, there were 50,000 on the island. There were continuing fears that the Chinese would abandon their commitment to their 'one country, two systems' pledge. The transfer of sovereignty eventually took place in 1997 when Amanda was fourteen years old.

Her early years were dominated by her father's descent into heavy drinking and libidinous behaviour. She was the product of a brief dalliance with a hotel receptionist, Julie Neo, a Hong Kong citizen. Her father died the day after the transfer of Hong Kong to China by the British government.

Amanda was educated at the Diocesan School for Girls in Hong Kong learning Cantonese and later French much to the annoyance of her father. After his death it was decided, in conjunction with the British authorities, that Amanda should move to London.

She arrived with a dual passport and a trust fund of several million pounds. Her uncle, and a firm of London solicitors, were the trustees. She knew that she would be eligible for half the money when she reached twenty-one years of age and the balance when she was thirty.

She took her time and spent the early days with her aunt, Eileen and her step-brother, Jonathan, who both amused and irritated her in equal measure. Her uncle was rarely at home.

Her academic record, including twelve GCSE's and four A-Levels including Law, resulted in her achieving entrance to Lady Margaret Hall, Oxford, including a year at Pantheon-Assas, in Paris. In 2005, she graduated with a First Class, Oxon in Law (Jurisprudence). She included European Constitutional Law in her areas of expertise.

After coming down from Oxford University Amanda sailed through the Bar Vocational Course. A pupillage was secured for her at Hartington Chambers, a leading London criminal law set, Amanda was called to the Bar in 2007.

ABOUT THE AUTHOR

Oliver Richbell

After spending over a decade as a lawyer Oliver runs a dispute resolution consultancy that helps businesses resolve their commercial disputes through dialogue and negotiation. He is Chairman of Bedfordshire's region of Wooden Spoon, a charity that helps socially, mentally and physically disadvantaged children and he is also a volunteer at a local homeless outreach organisation. He lives in Bedford with his wife and daughter. Oliver published his first novella, *Gloriana*, which is inspired by the Tom Cruise film, *Valkyrie*, in September 2018. Using the background of 'Brexit', *Gloriana* is a thunderous political thriller with an unexpected twist in the tale and it has received critical acclaim with many four and five star reviews on Amazon.

The Courageous Witness is his second novella and launches the career of mesmeric barrister Amanda

Buckingham. She next appears in *The Star Witness* which is being published summer 2020.

Contact Oliver:

Instagram	@oliverrichbell
Facebook	oliverjamesrichbell
Twitter	@richbelloliver

NOVELLA THREE

THE WHITE HOUSE, HOLYHEAD

by

R. M. CARTMEL

Inspired by the 1942 film 'Casablanca'

THE WHITE HOUSE, HOLYHEAD

The year is 2039 and the United Kingdom is a distant memory. Scotland achieved its dream of independence and the European Union (the 'EU') welcomed them back. Ireland (and Northern Ireland) held a referendum and, by a large majority, united: there was a little pointless bloodshed, but power passed to Dublin. They were already members of the EU.

British politics (meaning England and Wales) disintegrated as the Conservatives were never forgiven by the populus for their betrayal over Brexit. Labour's period in minority government, following its period of vacillation, led to a financial crisis as they borrowed and borrowed and wrecked the once vibrant economy. New, smaller political parties were created and government became a matter of coalitions.

As time moved on, global warming became an ever-worrying challenge. The sea level was rising, despite the profusion of windmills and solar panels proliferating especially in Wales and East Anglia. A sea wall was built around London. Throughout the world, aeroplanes were phased out in favour of huge nuclear fusion powered airships whose waste product, the inert gas helium, was reused to fill their gasbags. Electric helicopters filled the skies, lifting passengers and cargo from the ground up to the giant airships.

Pods, as electric runabouts became known, appeared everywhere followed by similarly powered vans and buses.

However, political strife was never far away and after a number of years of Westminster inertia, in

145

2029, Anglia took global warming seriously and declared independence. It did not help that Yarmouth, Wisbech, Holbeach and Harwich were now under water. Anglia developed a pyramid meritocracy allowing all to vote in local elections so creating an Anglian National Government, jokingly nicknamed all over the Island an 'Academic junta'. Its leader was called the 'senior lecturer'.

Wales already was ready for independence and rose up, painlessly. There was rejoicing in the hills and valleys. The West Country followed, renaming itself Wessex, and, modelling itself on the Anglian system, set up its Witan in Winchester.

For nearly ten years all went to plan. Anglia, Wales and Wessex started to negotiate firstly with Scotland, then Ireland and finally with the EU asking to re-join the now totally federalist movement.

In 2038 England created an army out of its fractious unemployed and invaded Anglia. Tensions developed elsewhere but England was hindered by its dire financial situation. The politicians were, however, desperate to maintain its borders including some control over its immediate island neighbours.

Holyhead, off the western coast of Anglesey on a small island of its own called Holy Island, is a small port where ferries ply the waters between North Wales and Dublin in Ireland. It has, however, been made very clear by their English 'advisors' that the only passengers on those ferries should have Welsh or European passports. Even the English passports must have a Welsh or Irish visa attached. That is unless they have a special pass issued by what the English still insist on calling the British Government. One source of Welsh travel visas is the police headquarters in Holyhead, and holders of English passports have to have persuasive reasons to liberate one of those precious Welsh visas.

These restrictions haven't stopped refugees in their thousands making for Holyhead in the hope of finding a way onto a ferry to Ireland, and from there, to catch an Airship to America or Europe. However getting a Welsh or Irish pass is extremely expensive or extremely difficult or both. And if you don't have the money or influence, all that is left for you is to sit in Holyhead, and wait, and wait, and wait.

§§§§

G'day. I'm Shane, and I'm from God's own Country, down under. So what, I hear you cry, is a true blue Aussie doing, running a bar on the edge of North Wales? Not an unreasonable question, which you might be able to work out yourself from what I've already told you. "I'm Shane" should have given you a big clue. An even bigger clue is to tell you that it was the name my parents gave me when I was born; I haven't relabelled myself in any way. Yes, you've got it; both my parents were cricket mad drongos. Shane has always been a good name for an Aussie cricketer to wear; we've had a Shane Warne, who was the best leg spinner the world has ever seen. Then there was Shane Lee, who played Shield cricket, and whose brother Brett was an internationally swift bowler, and finally there was Shane Watson who opened the batting in a baggy green cap for a while. I don't think my parentals would have minded what I did with my life long term, as long as it included playing cricket for Australia.

The problem was that while I do enjoy playing cricket, it rapidly became clear that, contrary to popular belief, you do need something else apart from a cricket name to be a great cricketer; you need a thing called talent. I know Colin Cowdrey's parents might tell you differently, and that he became a great player because of the initials they gave him at birth, but I reckon the old pommie batter was a good player because he knew which end to hold a bat. There must be so many others who have given their kids strange initials like SCG, in the hope of them playing for Australia at the Sydney Cricket Ground, and nobody ever heard of them again. As I was saying, to create a successful career in cricket, you need ability, but the talent gods passed me by. Mind you, I was found to be quite clever at other stuff and so I went to University in Adelaide. My parents were still disappointed in me. I didn't get into any college teams at any level, but I did earn a half decent degree, and, on the back of that, I was offered a place to do a Masters in Cambridge in England. Well the old dears were really thrilled by that, so I really didn't have any choice in the matter. Even if I had wanted to stay in Oz, I was on my way to the heart of England quicker than any Lillian Thomson bouncer. I was going to do a Masters in European History, but as far as my parentals were concerned, I was going there to learn how to bowl a proper Bosie like Benaud and get the pommie batters in a tangle at Lord's.

It's a strange thing looking at it, how cricket has blithely refused to accept any of the changes that have happened to the old country recently. Despite it having voted to have a Brexit, and effectively blowing itself to pieces as a result; the island still gets to put out an 'English' Championship from which it selects an 'England' team, which includes Somerset players from Independent Wessex, Glamorgan players from Powys in Wales, and even Essex players from an Anglia which is currently under military rule from Westminster. They still play the odd test as well as the usual high-speed stuff. After all, Great Britain may be a single island but it is currently made up of five fiercely independent little countries, so I suppose it's a bit like the West Indies, all those funny little islands that don't seem to talk to each other much, and yet clubbing together to form one "national" team.

And of course, being in Cambridge, I was right in the middle of it when the balloon went up. Walking into Anglia was easy for the English army, especially as there wasn't much resistance to speak of. At the same time they hoped to discourage any other province who might be watching from a cautious distance thinking how much better the small independent countries were doing without any interference from Westminster. They were probably fairly twitchy about the Ridings of Yorkshire declaring independence. If it did, and decided that it also wanted an independent cricket team as well, like Pakistan when it separated from India in '48, the Poms would be completely up the creek. The last thing Westminster wanted from those other provinces was a movement of their own planning their own exit.

Somehow for me, staying in Anglia really wasn't an option. I'm not going to go into details right now. Suffice it to say, I had about twenty-four hours notice to get out of Cambridge before the tanks arrived. A chum of mine from Cambridge called Ali and I caught a silly o'clock in the morning train to Birmingham, from where we caught a rather slower train that seemed to stop at every station from there to Shrewsbury, hoping that people weren't already on the lookout for me. But the stations remained deserted. Once we were in Shrewsbury however, it was easy enough to cross the border into Wales, where we rented a pod. Even if the Welsh were aware at that point what was going on the other side of the island, they certainly didn't seem interested in an Australian and an Asian tourist doing a spot of rock climbing in Wales. So Ali and I pottered along the coast road to the Menai Bridge and on into Anglesey, and from there along the road to Holyhead. The main road into Holyhead is so impressive I didn't immediately spot that it was a bridge onto another Island. Once in Holyhead, we stopped for a night in a friendly little gastro-pub called The White House to get our bearings, and find out what exactly we needed to do to get passes to get over the water to Ireland. The answer was 'lots,' and it was going to cost a load more than I had ever owned in my life, so we had to find jobs, and start saving up.

The White House was a bit short staffed, at that point in time, as the Polish couple that ran the kitchen had up-sticks and left on the boat for Dublin as soon as any sign of trouble started. I stayed on to help out, and to give myself a little time to get earning the money needed to bribe the appropriate person to get that pass. To cut a long story short, it's a year later, and I now just about run the place. I'm told locals even call us 'Shane's Aussie Eatery,' which is a bit daft, as I haven't seen a 'roo' steak anywhere in my time on the Big Island. But I guess we get by.

Ali and I had first met in a pub in Cambridge

where I used to hang out when I wasn't working on my dissertation. I guess we got to know each other pretty well over time. He was the pub's house musician, playing god knows how many different instruments, and when the balloon went up, it appeared he needed to get out of Cambridge in a hurry as well; I never did ask why. If he ever feels one day I need to know, I'm sure he'll tell me, and I might tell him my story in return.

We took on the kitchens, which started as a ping and ding. You know, take it out the freezer, bung it in the nuke, press 'ping' and five minutes later 'ding' you've got something warm to swallow with your pint. Ali did potwash to start with, but I knew what he really wanted to do was get behind that tatty ancient piano in the bar, or even get out his old guitar, and sing the blues a bit. As I took over, I guess I changed the place. I found a couple of welsh speakers who could really cook mutton and leeks from the ground upwards, while I became the face of the place. Ali and I even turned out in the occasional cricket match. Neither of us was anywhere near as good as the locals, but our team presented this Asian feller and me as if we were their international stars. Ali used to toss the ball high in the air, and when it didn't spin he would grin, knowingly at the batter up the other end. Used to worry the wombats out of the opposition and it usually took them a little while to work out exactly how good we really weren't.

§§§§

Joey McGregor was more weasel than man. I know he had a Scottish name, but he didn't resemble any Scot that I've ever met. He was forever coming to me with some little knick-knack, which I suspected he had effectively stolen from someone waiting just outside the docks, willing to sell any possession, even their bodies, to find the money to get one of those elusive passes to Ireland. He would bring whatever he had got and ask me to look after it for a few days. He was at least true to his word in that sense, as he never left his trivia very long in my place, and he always came by with an 'I've found a buyer' and he would often leave me a bit of cash for my trouble. You just know that it's an under the counter sort of business, the way that cash is still used in Holyhead. Cash is so much more anonymous than the electronic money you wear on your wristy. You know, wristies are funny things; back in my father's day, Dad wore a device on his wrist that told him what time it was, period. These things we call wristies are rather smaller than his old watch, but carry my identity 'papers', access to various bank accounts, access to services like summoning a pod if I needed one anywhere on the Big Island, and it still tells the time. The device probably tells the powers that be where I am too, so that's why everyone's so cautious about when they use them, and when they still use cash. There was never anything trustworthy about doing deals with the Poms, there never has been.

Why did people like Joey go about involving me in their business? To be honest I don't really care. The place is teeming with Welsh Police and English soldiers, but then when they're in my place, they all seem to be off duty, and sometimes they even ask me to store some booty for them as well. Okay, I can cope with that, it's none of my business. I'm neutral, I don't rattle their cages, and they don't rattle mine. I suppose that's what they mean by 'hiding stuff in plain sight.'

'Shane, can I leave something with you for a few days?' was his usual opening gambit.

'Aren't you running out of little old ladies to prey on?' was my usual contemptuous reply. It was no different this time.

'I think you're going to be impressed with me this time.' That was a change; Joey knew he never impressed me. He reached into his inner jacket pocket and pulled out an envelope. It was the wrong sort of envelope to be carrying money, and wasn't thick enough to be carrying a lot of it anyway.

'So what is it this time?'

'They're English Royal Travel Documents,' he said proudly.

That was different anyway. He'd nicked some rare souvenirs from his little old victim this time. They might be quite valuable to a collector if he could find the right one. 'Okay,' I said, 'I am a little more impressed, I'll give you that. Just don't leave them here too long. If there's a hue and cry about the theft, I'll burn them.'

'Oh, don't worry about that, Shane, I already have a bidding war about these. I'm afraid that they will be stolen off me if I'm found walking about with them. A couple of days, top whack.' He passed me the envelope, and walked out of the room.

I have a number of secret places in my office, including a couple of safes. I chose the safe where I keep the booty where I store the stuff the English soldiers have left for my safe keeping, and tossed it in there behind the silver menorah, which had surely been 'borrowed' from a synagogue, somewhere. I was kind of hoping that once this was all over, I might return the menorah to the place where it belonged. I'm not the slightest bit religious, but I know some people are, and it upsets them when their religious artefacts get stolen. I can remember watching a whole download once about some invading army nicking the Arc of the Covenant. It was a great bit of hokum.

I shut the safe and locked it.

I walked out of my office out into the bar. Ali stopped playing whatever it was he was playing, and started on something else completely. 'Were you playing it?' I asked as I strode in his direction.

'Of course I wasn't,' he replied awkwardly. Ali had one real difficulty with me, he couldn't tell a lie convincingly.

I looked down my nose at him. I didn't need to say anything.

'Oh okay, I was, but why is that so wrong?'

'Its taboo in here,' I snarled. Most people would have shut up at that, but I guess Ali knew me too well to be intimidated.

'But why? I like it, and back in Cambridge it was your favourite number.'

'Back in Cambridge, it was *her* favourite number, and I never want to hear it again.' I turned on my heels, at least half looking for someone else I might mistake for the woman from Cambridge, that happened often enough, but she wasn't here today. Instead I came face-to-face with the local Police Chief. I have usually found Rhys Evans to be an amiable man, but then I didn't have to do business with him; not yet anyway. I supposed that when the time came and I did end up doing business with him on my own behalf, it would be to my own benefit if we understood each other in advance. We certainly knew that there are things that each of us doesn't want the other to know and, like sensible men, we avoid those subjects.

'Fancy a drink?' he said, 'I'm buying.'

Evans? Putting his hand in his own pocket? We both knew that when his bar tab gets too high, I give him a bill. He then looks me right in the eye, and tears the bill up and we both smile. I think we know that one day in the future I will collect on that debt. However, if he was going to pour something expensive down my throat, I think I wanted his contribution up front. We walked over to the bar. Behind the bar Myfanwy James was serving; pretty girl, nice eyes, and a good set of pipes when she gets up to sing on a busy night. We all call her Miff for short, 'I'll have what he's having,' Evans said.

'Do you really want a glass of water?' Miff asked with the slightly coy smile that would probably get her in a lot of trouble if it wasn't widely known that she was one of my employees. I think some people think she and I have a thing going.

Evans looked quizzically at me, 'You mean it's really true that you don't drink with customers?'

'It really is,' I replied.

'On this occasion, I think you ought to change your mind,' he replied, quite firmly.

This was becoming interesting. I raised an eyebrow and told Miff, 'I'll have what he usually has.'

'Do you want it in a glass, or would you like the whole bottle?' she asked.

What on earth does Evans drink? I wondered. 'There's a table over there,' she said, 'I'll get Paul to bring it over to you.' She pointed at an empty booth along one wall. It was early in the evening, and the place hadn't really started to fill up yet. And yes he pointed his wristy at her reader, and paid whatever it was worth on the spot.

'So what's this all about then?' I asked as we were both sitting in the booth.

'What do you know about Andrew Ryan?'

'He's the most wanted man on the whole of the Island. The locals call him the head of the Resistance, the English just call him a terrorist. It depends whose side you're on.' I replied dryly.

'And which side are you on, Shane?' he asked gently, but his eyes flickered with interest. We both knew that I had just been asked the most important question I had been asked since I left Cambridge.

'Neither,' I replied, 'This bar is the most neutral place on the whole of the Big Island, and I intend to keep it that way. Look,' I waved a hand at the bar that was still far from full. There were a few locals in one corner, a few English soldiers in another corner, and coming towards us was a little old man carrying a tray with a bottle and two glasses on it. I remarked to Evans as he got there, 'You come in here, you drink, you have fun, and you leave your civil war outside on the street.' The bottle was put on the table. It had a screw cap like many wine bottles do nowadays, but I was seriously impressed with the one he had chosen. Maybe it wasn't desperately expensive as wine goes, but a red German Dornfelder from Boppard is difficult enough to find anywhere in Britain at the moment, and I was aware that the previous owner of the bar had acquired our current stock by finagling a complex deal which involved several strange people in Dublin, Cork and Cherbourg.

'Your very good health,' he toasted me.

'Chug-a-Lug,' I replied and we both drank. I was quite impressed, the wine had indeed aged quite well in our little beer cellar. I looked up at him, and asked, 'you were going to tell me something about this Ryan bloke,' I said.

He nodded, 'Well he caused all sorts of trouble in Anglia after the invasion.'

'For which they executed him,' I replied, finishing his story; I thought.

'It appears that they didn't,' Evans replied, 'they only said they did.'

'Really? I heard it said the bastard was slippery, but I had no idea he was that slippery. So what does the Anglian eel have to do with us out here?'

'His last reported sighting was in Chepstow, a few days ago,' he began.

'He's in Wales?'

'He is, and they say he's heading for Ireland. If that's true, he's either going to Haverford West, or he's coming here, and if he wants to get to Dublin Airport to catch an airship,' he continued slowing down, expecting me to complete the sentence.

'He'd come here,' I duly did.

'Exactly. Now there's something else, a courier was knocked off his motorbike near Bangor yesterday, and his bag was stolen.'

'Go on,' I said. This was becoming more interesting by the minute.

'He was carrying among other things, two English Royal passes to Ireland. I'm not sure I believe in that sort of coincidence.'

'Why would he need two passes? Has he put on weight or something?'

Evans looked at me, 'No, He's travelling with a woman, and rumour has it that she's very good-looking.'

'You look impressed Rhys,' I replied.

'To be honest, I am. I'm getting a lot of pressure from the English to the tune that Ryan must not get out of Wales. Nobody would dare being found with those documents on their person. The English can be quite ruthless about these things, even on Welsh soil. So they have to have been hidden somewhere. And the fact that the courier was killed in Bangor, makes Holyhead the most likely place they will be hiding.'

'Killed?' I asked, with a sense of foreboding. Joey McGregor had been right a few minutes ago. I was becoming more impressed by the minute.

'Oh yes, there was a length of wire stretched across the road, I'm told. The pathologist said it took his head clean off. Anyway Shane, that's all I have to say. I'm supposed to be keeping a close eye on you.'

'I hope you'll be keeping your other eye on our old friend Tubba down at the Green Shamrock as well,' I replied.

'We have police watching the Shamrock too.'

I think I needed to have eyes at the back of my head sometimes, there seemed to be some sort of kerfuffle going on by the bar. 'Excuse me,' I said, and got up and walked over.

There was an English soldier with his paws all over Miff, and she obviously wasn't enjoying the experience. Mind you she had a large glass of something interestingly coloured in the hand that wasn't exactly fighting the soldier off as such, so perhaps he was feeling he had already paid for what he was claiming.

'I'm afraid I don't allow people to manhandle the staff,' I said fairly gently, in the hope that he would understand what I was saying without making an issue out of it. We shared momentary eye contact, and he backed down. However I did feel that that wasn't going to be the end of it.

'My hero,' slurred Miff as she slung both her arms round my neck. Her breath smelled inflammable. What was in that mixture? I must make a note that bar staff will not mix Mickey Finns to be drunk by other bar staff.

'I think it's about time you went home to bed,' I said fairly gently.

'Can I stay with you again tonight?'

'Not tonight, kiddo,' I replied. On the one side was that foxy little body that had been most enjoyable on occasions. On the other side there was that breath, and the distinct possibility of her throwing up all over me during the night. I looked around for Paul. 'Can you get her a taxi home, and pour her into it?' I asked him.

'Sure thing Boss,' the old Pole replied, 'come along honey,' he said to her. 'You'll feel much better in the morning.'

She let him guide her out, but as she went through the door she howled despairingly at me, 'But we love each other.' I ignored her.

I watched the English soldier to make sure he wasn't going to follow them out, but he wasn't. He was already engaged in conversation with a group of soldiers dealing a pack of cards.

I went back to my table with Evans who had been watching the whole incident with interest. 'You're a very generous soul, Shane,' he said. 'I can't think of many men who would have turned an offer like that down.'

I looked at him without saying anything. There wasn't any point. I knew how Evans's mind worked, certainly as far as the female of the species was concerned, and it wasn't going to be worth my while to openly disagree with him. I took another mouthful from the contents of my glass.

We have a quasi-legal casino in the back of the bar. They play Roulette, a little Baccarat, a few craps, you know the sort of low skill stuff which gives the bar a slight edge. Evans lets us get away with it provided he's allowed to occasionally frequent it, and win a little. He probably has quite a reasonable second income if you add up all the bars in Holyhead all allowing him to 'win a little' in their back room casinos. I'm not quite sure what the actual law states, but then I'm not stupid enough to ask. Raoul is a Frenchman we took on to run the casino to give it a bit of that Monte Carlo glitz, though I suspect he comes from a part of France that is nearer to Holyhead than it is to Monte Carlo. He has this skill of not being anywhere in sight, and suddenly being right there at your elbow.

'Boss,' he said apologetically, 'It won't happen again, but we've had a winner, Boss, and he wants the money in cash.'

I asked him how much, and he told me. Well, Raoul was right, we don't carry twenty thousand Euros at the tables, it's asking to be robbed. We don't have that sort of cash in Welsh pounds either, but people tend not to gamble in Welsh, as we don't exchange currency at the bar. The exchange rates are too unstable. I nodded at Evans, 'Stay there a moment Rhys, I've just got to go and sort this out.' I walked up the stairs into my office. I suppose it was really the front room of my flat over the business, with a kitchen, an ablution department and a bedroom off it. But in reality I saw the whole bar as my living area. I walked over to the smaller less obvious safe and let myself into it. I took out the pistol, and slipped it into my jacket pocket, there was no point in my being mugged for carrying that sort of money, even for a few yards. That sort of money could get you out of urban Holyhead and planted in patches of newly created swamp where they'd never find you again, if you weren't very careful. I took out the pile of cash I kept for just this purpose, and peeled off twenty thousand. I put the rest back. Not to worry, we'd replenish the stock over the coming days.

I slipped the cash into an envelope and stuck it into the inner pocket of my jacket, closed the safe and spun the wheel. I cast an eye around as I walked to the door, switched off the lights, and set off back down the stairs. I walked straight through to the casino where Raoul was talking to a tall thin man who was not disguising his impatience very well.

'Congratulations sir,' I said shaking his hand with the envelope. 'You've been very lucky. I don't suppose we'll see you again.'

He shook his head, and I added, 'best of luck with the rest of your life.' The man scuttled out indecently quickly with his hand in his pocket, presumably still holding my envelope.

I went back to the bar to re-join Evans. He was looking at his wristy. Presumably he was checking the time. 'I must go soon,' he said, 'something's coming up.' I couldn't imagine what that could be. Could it have anything to do with a man walking swiftly out of my bar with his hand in his pocket? More than likely.

§§§§

He hadn't even reached the door when four figures in bottle green uniforms walked in. They came in adopting a 'missing man' formation, and it was obvious who the leader was. He had scrambled eggs on the peak of his cap and far heavier epaulettes than the others. He also had that air about him. Evans twitched, almost as if he was about to bow, and then caught himself in the nick of time. 'Colonel,' he said, and turned on his heels, and hurried back into the bar. He found Paul, and grabbed him by the shoulder.

'Paul,' he said urgently. 'Colonel Willoughby's here. Can you get him the best seat in the house?'

Paul gave him a beatific smile, 'I've already arranged it, knowing he would take it anyway.' He waved at a table in the corner facing into the room, with the backs of all its chairs facing to the wall. The Colonel and his entourage were already sitting down at it.

Evans nodded at them. 'Can you get them a bottle of Champagne and some glasses?' he told Paul.

Paul bustled off, and the policeman walked over to the Colonel's table. 'Colonel, I've ordered you a bottle of Champagne, on the house, and I've laid on a little entertainment for you this evening.'

'On the house?'

'The Landlord and I have, shall I say, a little understanding.'

The Colonel smiled knowingly and went on, 'and

the entertainment?'

'Oh yes, I've arranged for the man who killed your courier to be arrested here in this bar this evening.'

'I would expect nothing less,' he replied acidly, as Paul arrived with a tray carrying an obviously cold glistening bottle of Champagne and some glasses. The waiter picked up the bottle, and put his hand round the cork and with a deft twisting movement, noiselessly removed it.

'We don't want to attract unwanted attention, or to waste any of the nectar,' Paul said to the surrounding English. 'We have not just won a motor race or launched a ship.' You could tell the English were not amused by his Polish accent, which got much more Polish in the presence of soldiers in uniform.

'Quite,' said the Colonel accepting the first glass.

Paul had only just left the table and its occupants had hardly started talking among themselves, when it all started to go down. I did tell you the excitement never stops at The White House, didn't I? Joey McGregor was at the till buying some gambling chips, when he felt a huge paw grab his left shoulder, and a voice snarling in his ear that he was under arrest, or some such platitude. McGregor was a wriggly weasel, and he wriggled out of the officer's grip. The next moment he was trying to hide behind me. 'Shane, you've got to help me.' he wheedled up at me.

I looked down my nose at McGregor, 'I haven't "got" to do anything,' I replied, 'you have to sell it to me, just like everyone else. What's going on?'

'They're going to arrest me,' he said.

I stepped smartly to my left, leaving him in full view of the Welsh policeman, and a huge English Army sergeant. 'As I was saying, boyo,' said the policeman, 'you're under arrest.'

'Shane,' McGregor positively squealed.

The Sergeant looked at me, and I shrugged, as if to say, 'Nothing to do with me.'

They manhandled McGregor to the main entrance of the bar, and as they opened the front door, McGregor whirled round with a pistol in his hand and fired without aiming, behind him and rushed out. The huge Englishman swore, and grabbed his left arm. The Welshman turned and looked at his colleague for a moment, and then rushed off out after McGregor. I patted my jacket just checking that McGregor hadn't picked my pocket and taken my pistol a few moments before, but it was still there. A moment or so later, you could hear a fusillade of shots from the outside.

I raised my voice. 'It's all over, nothing to worry about. Carry on enjoying yourselves.' However I was aware that there was something to worry about, and I made my way back up to the office. My pistol needed to be not in my pocket any longer, and that envelope had to be someplace safer than the British Booty safe, though, for the moment I couldn't think of one. I opened the safe, put my pistol in it, and got the envelope out, and sat down at my desk and thought about it.

Meanwhile, what was going on next down in the bar, Paul told me about later. The front door opened and in walked a couple. The man caught Paul's eye, obviously the correct eye to catch, as there was no-one else wandering around with a tea towel over his left arm. 'I have a table booked,' said the man to Paul, and he continued, 'ideally as far away from the English Army as possible.'

'The name?' Paul asked.

'Andrew Ryan,' he replied.

'This way,' said Paul, and led them away from the area that was beginning to fill up with increasingly boisterous men in uniforms of varying persuasions. As they walked to their table, Ali and the woman's eyes met, and there was a flash of recognition between them. As the two sat down, Ryan ordered drinks for the pair of them.

'Darling,' she said, 'I think we ought to go. I have a definitely uneasy feeling about this place.'

'Nonsense,' he replied. 'It looks a delightful place. It's absolutely teeming with the English, and they only go to the best places.'

'Yes, but they're the English.'

'You worry too much, the English can't do a damn thing to me in Wales. This isn't an occupied country, they're simply here as advisors. And besides;' he paused, 'I arranged to meet Joey McGregor here in The White House.'

'What does he look like?'

'I haven't the faintest idea, I've never met him. But he will know me, my picture's everywhere.'

'You two look you might be heading to Ireland,' said a voice with an Irish lilt behind Ryan's shoulder. 'Can I be of assistance?'

'Joey McGregor?' Ryan asked.

'Er no,' replied the man, but he sat down anyway. 'The unfortunate Mr. McGregor got himself arrested a little while ago.'

'So what do we do now?' asked the woman.

'Can I borrow you for a moment,' the man said to Ryan, 'It may not be a complete disaster, well, not for you anyway. Though I wouldn't be holding out a lot of hope for poor Joey McGregor himself.' The man gave an official looking pass with a green cover to Ryan.

Ryan flipped through it and gave it back, 'That isn't a lot of use to me,' he said, it's got your picture in it, and we don't look anything like each other.'

'Just establishing my credentials,' the Irishman replied, 'Mickey Riley at your service. If you wouldn't mind hanging on here,' he said to the woman, 'I would recommend you enjoy the music for a moment. The musician over there has quite a reputation round here. Ryan followed Riley off to a corner where there were various other people sitting in a huddle. She looked back at Ali, then got up and walked over to him.

'Hello Ali,' she said, 'Long time no see.'

'What are you doing here, Jenny? Please make yourself scarce before he sees you. You're bad news as far as Shane's concerned.'

'Is he here?'

Ali paused and looked awkward. 'No, he went home,' he said after a moment.

'When will he be back?'

'Probably tomorrow, but we don't know so much nowadays. Umm, he's got a girlfriend over at the Green Shamrock, you see, and they say she's quite hot, so sometimes we don't see him for days at a time.'

Jenny looked at him gently. He could tell already that she didn't believe a word that he'd said. 'Play it Ali,' she said.

'What?'

'Play Layla, Ali.'

'Don't know if I can remember it, Jenny.'

'Nobody who worked out an arrangement of a

song that originally involved two lead guitars and a bass for a single piano would ever forget it. It wasn't just Eric Clapton's masterpiece, it was yours too. Play it Ali.'

Ali turned round and played that rolling opening on the piano and went into the song itself. He didn't often sing the words, they weren't that important, just the melody.

Up in my study, I was aware there was something going on down in the bar, and, pushing the envelope into my jacket breast pocket, I got up and went to the door. When I got as far as the landing, I knew exactly what was going on, Ali was playing that bloody tune. I was down those stairs in a flash. 'Ali, I thought I told you, never to play that,...' He'd stopped playing already as he was aware I was heading his way like a charging rhino. However he wasn't looking at me, but somewhere to my left. I stopped and looked at where he was looking. He was gawping at someone else who looked like Jenny. Everywhere I look there are people who look like Jenny. I've seen pictures on billboards that look like Jenny. Damn it I've even seen zoo animals I had to look at twice to persuade myself they weren't Jenny. When I look again, of course I can tell that they're koalas or something, but seeing fake-Jenny Laings has become so much a part of my life, a trick my mind plays on me. I hated it, but it was something I'd got used to it since leaving Cambridge.

I looked back at Ali, and then back at the woman. Oh crap, it still looked like Jenny. She had the same lustrous raven hair. Funny, many Welsh women, and Irish women for that matter, have black hair, but somehow theirs is a more matt black than hers. Jenny's is lustrous, and shiny, almost as if she'd put some product into it, which of course she never did. I knew, I had run my fingers through that hair often enough in Cambridge. It is naturally shiny, and if you get closer you could see they aren't coloured highlights, just lights. The same way as I knew what her shape was like inside those clothes, I had seen her naked often enough. I had held that body so close, I had even been inside that body. And here she was, what the hell was she doing in Holyhead?

'Play something soft,' I said to Ali, 'just not that.' And I walked over to her.

'Shane? Is that really you?'

I recognised that voice too. It really was her this time.

'Shane,' said a voice behind me. That one I recognised as belonging to Rhys Evans. 'May I introduce you to someone, who I think you may have heard of?'

I turned and there was a man possibly approaching middle age, but wearing a face that had obviously known many difficulties on its journey to Holyhead. 'This is Andrew Ryan.'

'One hears a lot about Shane in Holyhead,' said the man as he shook my hand.

'One hears a lot about Andrew Ryan everywhere,' I replied.

'They said he was travelling with a beautiful woman,' Evans continued, 'but I can see they were guilty of an outrageous understatement.' He paused to allow her to pretend to simper embarrassedly before he continued, 'this is Miss....'

'Jenny,' I replied, almost catching her eye.

'Shane,' she said, looking away.

'Oh,' said Evans, 'You two know each other.'

'Come and join us for a drink Mister Shane,' said Ryan.

'Shane never drinks with customers,' said the policeman apologetically.

'I'd be delighted,' I replied ignoring him completely.

'Well I never,' said Evans, 'This evening is full of surprises.'

We went back to Ryan's table and we sat down. Evans retrieved his bottle of Dornfelder, which still had a bit in the bottom, and he emptied it into a glass. I was just about to pour a splash of water into the Islay malt Paul had brought me together with a tiny jug of room temperature tap water. He knew how I liked to drink it if I was drinking to be pleasant company.

'Missster Ryan,' hissed a serpent like voice above and behind me.

Rhys Evans was up like he had sat on a hot coal. 'Colonel Willoughby, won't you join us?'

'Must he?' remarked Ryan drily. 'I would really not share air with a member of the English Army, if it's all the same to you, Inspector Evans.'

'It's Superintendent Evans,' Rhys replied, slightly stiffly.

'Really?' came out of both the Colonel and Ryan's mouths simultaneously with an equal amount of surprise. Under other circumstances they might both have laughed.

'This is a pleasure I have been waiting for a long time,' said the Colonel.

'May I say that the pleasure is all yours,' Ryan replied drily, 'Personally, it was one I would just has soon have done without.'

'I agree, this is neither the time nor the place for us to have the discussions that we need to have. May I suggest the Superintendent's office at nine o'clock tomorrow morning?'

'You can wait outside it if you like,' replied Evans, 'I'm normally expected in about ten. I would hate to unsettle my constables.'

'Ten o'clock it is then,' snapped the Colonel.

'Superintendent, I am under your jurisdiction here,' said Ryan, 'Is this your wish?'

'Take it as a polite request,' he replied. 'And do rest assured, you will be perfectly safe. Especially if you bring the exquisite Miss Laing with you.'

'We'll be there,' she replied, 'and we will have breakfasted, so you won't need to feed or water us at all.' There was an edge to her voice that I didn't remember from before.

'Good day,' said the Colonel standing up and saluting, 'till tomorrow.' He walked off, back to the group of men in green, chatting to Evans who was following him like an obedient puppy dog.

'I don't trust that man an inch,' Jenny remarked across me to Ryan.

'He's dressed in an English army uniform,' I said, perhaps to remind everyone I was still there. 'That level of trust's a no-brainer.'

'They really mean to get you this time,' Jenny said, ignoring me.

'Well I've been caught in London, Cambridge, and in Bristol, twice, but they haven't managed to hang on to me yet,' he replied with a grin.

'Ladies and Gentlemen,' said a rather stentorian voice into the microphone by Ali's piano. 'May I remind you that it's five minutes to closing time.

Drink up please.'

'And at the moment we do have a curfew to enforce,' said Evans, returning to our table. 'I would hate to catch myself out after hours, and be forced to fine myself. I would find that one of the more difficult bills to tear up. May I recommend you return to your hotel?' That last remark he addressed to Ryan and Jenny.

They tossed back the last of their drinks and walked to the door. As they did, Jenny looked over and caught my eye, hers narrowing slightly. I had managed to avoid catching her eye up till that moment, but when it had finally happened, it was like a thousand volts of electricity passing through me. Then the couple was lost to view.

I walked through the throng as it made its way to the door. I made my way to the bar, where Paul was cashing up. 'Any more of that bottle of Ardbeg you gave me a shot of?' I asked.

'Water, Shane?' he asked.

'No thanks, just the bottle.

He passed it to me. I picked up a glass, and walked across to a table near the piano where Raoul was waiting with the evening's takings from the casino.

'I'm sorry Shane,' said Raoul, 'I haven't yet made up for the loss we had earlier.'

'Don't worry,' I replied, 'You will.' I put the takings in an envelope, and wrote *Casino* and the date on it, and added *minus twenty thousand from the safe*. 'See you tomorrow Shane,' said Raoul, and he joined the crowd squeezing through the door into the street.

I poured myself a scotch from the bottle, as Paul came up to me with the bar takings. They weren't cash takings, but dockets from peoples' wristies, which would need counting and checking against our machine. The Taxman would need to know all that, but at least the Taxman in Holyhead speaks English, not always the case in North Wales nowadays. The dockets also went into a brown envelope, on which I wrote, *Bar* and the date. I looked at the bottle, it was about half full, so I added on to the envelope *minus half a bottle of Ardbeg, but includes a contribution from Evans.*

'Good evening Shane,' said Paul and he headed for the door.

I took another couple of mouthfuls of whisky. I looked at Ali.

'Play it Ali,' I said.

'What?' he asked, as if he didn't know.

'Play Layla, if she can stand it, so can I.'

'Hadn't you best go up to bed now mate,' he said. 'You've got a lot of bureaucracy to do in the morning, to bring those accounts up to date.'

'Play it Ali. She's coming back.'

'How do you know that? Oh please, don't go there. She fucks with your head that woman. Go up to bed and forget about her.'

'Just you play that sodding piano,' I snarled, and refilled my glass.

He played Layla. He played Layla like he had never played it before, and when he got to the chorus, he sang, 'Layla, you've got me on my knees.'

I think when he got to the slower piano bit, I must have nodded off.

§§§§

Flashback; Cambridge the year before
The sight that greeted my eyes as I walked in was

somewhat disconcerting, especially to a young man newly arrived from down under. The room was almost completely dark apart from the odd coloured light in the darkest of corners. Those bulbs were mainly red, and the whole ambience rather reminded me of certain streets of ill repute I had heard about in Sydney. There were little pockets of girls dancing together, out of self-protection round the pillars, and boys prowling the empty spaces between the pillars like wolves. I didn't know who looked more frightened, the girls or the boys. The only thing that was possible to do over that noise was to sign to a girl you were looking at if she wanted to dance.

"C'mon," said Will, my mate, standing by the door, where I could just about hear him, 'What do you think of those two?' he asked, and tugged at my sleeve. We took a deep breath and dived into the maelstrom. Before I had properly orientated myself, I had danced a slightly built raven-haired girl towards the bar, and Will had manoeuvred her companion in a similar direction. The door to the bar was open but the hubbub from the meat market, was reduced enough to allow some form of conversation. The bar was marginally better lit too, so having selected ones victim, it gave a girl, or a boy, the opportunity to see exactly the nature of the trophy that had been won in the darkness next door. Even in the market itself, I could see that the girl fate had selected for me was quite pretty. Under marginally better light, she was even prettier.

"Thank god we're out of that," said the girl whom Will had danced into the bar, "I was beginning to feel self-conscious."

"Really?" said the dark-haired girl, "I was really

rather enjoying it."

"Drinks?" asked Will.

"Coke," said the girl Will had rescued from the Maelstrom, "Cinzano Bianco," said the one who'd followed me. I escorted them to a table, where they parked, and I went to help Will with the drinks. While we were collecting the drinks, we worked out between us which girl we were each going to try to charm. Disgraceful things young men aren't they? Will said he would like to talk to 'Coke', which left me with 'Cinzano', which suited me just fine. I liked the look of her dark hair and her smile. They obviously liked the look of us enough to stick around, as they were still at the table when we got back.

"I'm Jenny Laing," said the dark girl who drank Cinzano, "I'm studying English at Girton."

"And I'm Liz Powell," said the fair haired girl, "studying Philosophy and Psychology at the same place."

'Jennifer?' I asked.

'Genevieve, like the car,' Jenny replied.

We introduced ourselves too, in the same way, name rank and serial number; or in Cambridge's case, name, subject and college.

I was about to move the conversation on when Jenny beat me to it. 'I think this Fresher's Ball is such a good idea, don't you? Especially if you want to meet people, and at University, it's so important to meet people, don't you think?'

'Perhaps,' said Liz, 'but I was beginning to wonder what sort of people we were going to meet at a place like this. There were some nasty looking prowlers in there.'

'You're not necessarily out of the wood yet,' Will said and leered at her.

'What, sounding like you do?' asked Jenny, in a fairly accent free voice of her own. 'There is no way you could be the sort of animal Liz is after. She likes them rough and ready. So if you're rough, she's ready!'

'What!' spluttered Liz; I think it was an in-joke that Liz thought was still 'work in progress' between themselves, I don't think Liz was ready for it to be given a public performance quite yet. It was rather like the ramp-shot, there always has to be a first time when you try it out in a game. In my case, I had been quite lucky to hang on to my teeth.

From thereon in the conversation drifted into the usual pleasantries, who's your father, how's your mother, what did your brother die of, when did you last see your uncle, you know the sort of tedious thing, and all the time Jenny Laing laughed gaily, quite often at comments that really weren't in the least bit funny, flashing her brilliant blue eyes from beneath her wavy dark fringe. Her skin was lightly tanned, presumably from a summer in the sun. She didn't appear to be wearing much make up, on her face, but then again she could just have been better trained in its use, than I was in its detection. And yes, I could tell I was attracted to her. In fact I would go so far as to say that I couldn't take my eyes off her, even then. Was this what people talked about when they talked of love at first sight? Complete stuff and nonsense, of course, how could anyone fall in love with someone you don't even know?

Despite her initial excitement with the meat market, even Jenny tired off it fairly quickly, so we all went off to Will's room in college in a pod. Yes, the first thing I had done on arriving in Anglia, was make sure my Australian permit worked here, and I had got myself a pod pass tapped into my wristy.

Will produced a pot of really rather good coffee, and we settled down to try out a 'serious conversation'. But the conversation soon made its probably inevitable turn to one of the three 'forbiddens', sex, religion or politics. Politics, it was in our case, and Anglia's independence cropped up, and as far as I understood it, Jenny was in favour of it, the other two rather less so, Liz was quite emphatically in favour of re-unification at the next possible moment, with no obvious explanation on how that might be achieved.

The conversation eventually switched to lighter topics, and finally the girls announced they needed their beauty sleep, and Jenny summoned a pod of her own, but not until after we had all agreed to meet up on Parker's Piece the following day at two. It was only when I went to bed with a warm smiling feeling inside, that I realised I hadn't thought about Kylie all evening.

"Come in!" and in I went. Jenny was dressed, and how! "We're going to a party," she said, "There's one in Magdalen this evening, and I feel like waving a leg," and to demonstrate the point she waved a particularly lissom one at me.

I have to say that the idea of a dance rather appealed to me. I hadn't really seen Jenny dance before, despite the fact we had met at an event that was billed as a dance, but for one reason or another, we hadn't actually got round to dancing; and I was fascinated to see how she made out. The walk to Magdalen took us some twenty minutes during which we bored each other silly about how we had spent our first few academic days in Cambridge.

She had gone to a lecture by her professor and apparently it was as awful as his English, despite the fact it purported to be his subject. He had apparently delivered the whole lecture in Chaucerian English, complete with pronunciation. She had found it difficult to keep her eyes open, especially as her brother had kept her up talking well into the night. I wished I had been her brother; he seemed to be an all round good guy with whom she was willing to sit up talking for hours. Mind you if I had been, then my thoughts about how she looked in that little dark blue skirt would have been singularly inappropriate. He was articled at the Bar in London, and she assured me that we would all know his name in the future. As an aside, I hoped that it would not be for spending the night in his sister's room in Cambridge.

She was dressed in a light, fluffy, Oxford blue sweater, which followed the curves of her body at the same time making them look as if they were in soft focus, and moving south, that short skirt of contrasting midnight blue almost denim material. Her legs were sheathed in tights that made them look as if they had had good exposure to last summer's sun before they disappeared into her boots, which laced up to two thirds of the way up her shins. But the spectacular addition to her whole outfit was a thick black shiny patent leather belt, which, buckled loosely in front of her navel, just rested on her hips, leaving an obvious gap between the buckle and her fluffy sweater. Oh, and yes, one other thing, she could dance too. As she moved, her hair flew everywhere, and yet she appeared in complete control of it, so that at the end of each number, it was just exactly where she wanted it to be. And this spectacular young woman was here with me. I could not believe my good fortune. I had been in Cambridge for precisely one day, and I had met up with a goddess and we had made contact. I realised I was falling for her as wildly and uncontrollably as I had done for Kylie some three years before down under. I thought hearing my earlier warning to myself, at least she seems to like me enough. One other thing I had spotted on a more positive note, any thought of Kylie was not now filled with pangs of anguish. I was learning more about this man called Shane, when he falls, he falls hard, but it is curable! I looked at the small dark girl in front of me with the flashing eyes she was firing right back at me. "You're gorgeous," I shouted at her over the racket.

"I know, sickening isn't it," she shouted back with a dazzling smile that would be worth a million bucks a week in Hollywood. She mouthed something else, which might have been funny, if I could hear anything over the din coming out of the speakers.

With the next song the DJ played straight into my hands; it was a slow sweet number drenched in Hammond organ. She snuggled up close to me hanging round my neck with her slender arms. She looked up into my eyes, and kissed me. The various aromas from her, and her hair especially, were an intoxicating mixture. Behind the, not overpowering, smell she had acquired from a bottle, there was a much more fascinating scent which was obviously natural. By now I should have realised I was in desperate need of help. If her natural musk was having this effect on me, I was a lost cause. Still, the signals I was receiving from those brilliant eyes, and the light filigree kisses were all positive. "You're sweet," she said as she nuzzled my left ear, just as the music ended.

Maybe I could play vain too, "You know, you're the thirteenth girl who's said that to me today."

"That's unlucky. You poor boy having to get your kicks from counting how many girls say you're sweet. Haven't you got anything better to do?" She cocked her head on one side, and still ravaged me with her smile, but I was aware that I had not achieved any points with that one. I smiled weakly back and kissed her, but I was aware how much power I was under.

"Drink?" she said to me, and I nodded. We made our way out of the dance floor into a quieter room with a makeshift bar at the far end. We could at least hear ourselves think here. She asked for a brandy, which I thought was quite a strange choice to have when you were thirsty. Me, I had a pint of the local 'gnats', because, however odd it tasted, it was a cool watery liquid.

One had to be deaf dumb or blind to be unaware of the undercurrent. It had been obvious to me that it wasn't just her feelings for me that had led her to moving out of college where she had lived with her erstwhile friend, Liz, whom I had met on that first night what seemed like a lifetime ago. Jenny came from Norwich, and was Anglian through and through, and Liz was a Londoner and very English.

I looked across the bed at the sleeping form, which glowed at me in its nakedness. She didn't sweat, exactly; she just shone as if there was a light source deep inside her. She opened one eye; once again she had caught me looking at her. Guilty as charged, how could I not look at such beauty when it was there before my eyes? I wasn't just in love, I was addicted to this woman.

'Penny for your thoughts,' she whispered.

I thought for a moment and said, 'I was wondering what the odds were, that someone like you should be there and available when someone like me turned up. How come nobody had snaffled you up before I arrived?'

She gave me a look of infinite sadness for a moment, 'There was,' she said, 'but he died.' She paused for a moment, before throwing her arms round my neck and saying gently, 'and now I've got you,' and snuggled herself into me and kissed my ear.

When we woke again, you could tell there was something going on outside. There was a pod with a loudspeaker on its roof, explaining exactly how the locals should behave when the English Army arrived the following morning, and that from then on there would be a curfew from 6pm every evening, the breach of which would lead to immediate arrest.

That evening we spent in the pub down the road. Nobody felt much like live music, so the ambience was of the canned variety, while Ali joined us at our table. Jenny was quiet, almost disconcertingly so, while Ali and I discussed the plans we had for crack of dawn the following morning. He had already bought tickets for us to catch the milk train in the morning to Birmingham, where we would change for Shrewsbury, and points west. He passed me two tickets, one of which I slid into my pocket.

'I have to pick up one or two things before we go,' said Jenny popping the other ticket into her bag. 'If I don't see you both before, I'll see you at the train.' I could see she was tapping her wristy, summoning a pod.

The following morning was wet. The sky knew what was going to happen to its beloved Cambridge, and it couldn't control its tears. I looked at my wristy, and it was counting down to our departure time. I was standing by the Birmingham train, and people were rushing around me trying to get on board, while I jumped up and down to see over the top of them. It was at moments like this that I wished she was taller.

Ali pulled on my sleeve, 'Come on mate, it's time to go. If she was coming she would be here by now.'

My face was wet, whether it was the rain or my tears, I had no idea, she was coming, she had to be coming, we loved each other didn't we? She's been delayed, perhaps that's it. She'll be here any moment.

A man stood at the end of the platform and blew his whistle.

'Come on mate, time to go,' said Ali as he pulled me onto the train. As it pulled out of the station, I was still hanging out of the window, looking down the platform for the person who was nowhere to be seen.

§§§§

Flash forward to present day
I felt a tug at my shoulder, 'Shane ... Shane.'

I opened my eyes, and there she stood.

'Pull up a chair,' I said pushing the bottle and a glass towards her. 'Help yourself,' I slurred, 'I kept it for you.'

She ignored them. 'Shane,' she said, 'we need to talk.'

'What about?'

'Cambridge; I have a story to tell you.'

'Is it a good one, starting off with once a polly-tight-oh, like all good fairy stories should? Has it got any jokes in it? Right now I'm in need of a good joke.'

'Shane, stop it.' Her voice sounded cross. I looked at her face, and I knew she could take total control if I gave her an inch.

'Okay,' I said, 'tell me your story, and I'll tell you if I like it.'

'It's the story of a girl who met a rather wonderful older man, whom she first met at a meeting in Norwich. He was telling the audience about Anglia's newly won independence, and he fascinated her with his thoughts and philosophy on life. She was very young at that time, maybe ten or eleven, but she became infatuated with that man and over time, following him round to other places she thought she was in love with him. He helped the people of Wales and Wessex achieve their freedom too. Many people became, how do you put it, disenfranchised when the two main English political parties disintegrated and the ruins re-coalesced together to form a single party of government, to drive through Brexit and all the little bits of legislation that would be required to be discussed and passed in the minimal amount of time they had before B-day. That at least was how it should have been if there had been an opposition. But as there wasn't such a thing, those laws just passed themselves tick, tick, tick, and Bob's your uncle. They had a snap election immediately afterwards, far too quickly for any other new party of opposition to get itself together, and the land still voted Conservative or Labour, mostly blissfully unaware they were voting for the same thing, and that was the last election they ever had in England.

'Andrew helped set up pressure groups in local areas, and became something of a name. I suppose the first time I knew he had been arrested was in Maidstone when he was talking to a Home Counties group. He escaped from there and the next time they caught him was in Leeds, also preaching at a meeting, this time they accused him of inflaming the people of the Ridings of Yorkshire. I last heard of him being caught in Cheltenham in Arden, and I heard he was shot resisting arrest.'

'Good story, perhaps if one was to be picky, it could have done with a few more jokes here and there. Tell me what you think of my story, which also starts, "it's the story about a girl, who met a man," who thought she was rather wonderful, and then one day she simply wasn't there anymore and he was left on a train station dripping wet with a stupid expression on his face, because his guts had been ripped out. Not many laughs in my story, either I suppose.' I refilled my glass from the now nearly empty bottle.

'You don't understand. I became his muse, his icon of disenfranchised youth. I married him when we were in Scotland.'

'So you married him when you were in Scotland, and he got potted while he was running around upsetting the English. How many times did you tell that tale between his getting potted and your meeting me in Cambridge?'

She looked at me sadly. 'I could have told my story to the Shane I knew in Cambridge, and he would have understood. I haven't got a chance with the drunken photocopy sitting in front of me now, so I don't think I'll bother. Tell you something Shane; if I had known you were going to be in Holyhead, I would have done my level best not to come here. But actually, now that I have, I'm sort of relieved that I did. Just think what would have happened to me if you'd turned into this nasty vicious drunk sitting in front of me, while we were still together.' She stood up and walked away saying, 'Goodbye Shane, it was wonderful while it lasted.' And, without looking over her shoulder, even once, she eased out of the bar and into the night.

I watched her go. I picked up the two envelopes off the table, and while sliding them into my jacket breast pocket, I realised there was already an envelope in there. I pulled it out. It was those travel documents. They needed hiding properly, as Evans would be hunting for them high and low once he realised that McGregor no longer had them.

I was looking at the piano, and the piano looked back at me. I flipped up the top of the piano and slid the envelope in behind the strings. Nobody would think there was anything there, even if Ali was playing a Beethoven Sonata. Did Ali play any Beethoven? I had no idea. They might be difficult even for me to get them out again, and I knew they were there, but they were safe, and they might come in useful for Ali and me in the fullness of time.

I closed the top of the piano, and picked up the other two envelopes, and made my slightly unsteady way up the stairs to my flat to put them in a safe, and me into bed. I had enough whisky on board to guarantee that I fell asleep again.

§§§§

The following day was bright. Surprisingly I felt quite bouncy, considering how much I had put away the previous evening.

'Morning Shane,' said Geraint, our storekeeper from behind the bar.

'Morning G,' I replied.

'I was wondering whether our supply of Scotch has arrived at the Green Shamrock yet,' he said. 'Our stock level's running down.' He glanced at the nearly empty bottle of Ardbeg and the glasses, which had somehow made their way from the table by the piano back onto the bar. He didn't make any comment, but his thoughts were obvious enough.

'I'm in the mood for a walk this morning,' I said. 'I'll wander over. Oh and if the police want to look over the place, give them every assistance you can.'

He smiled at me, 'I always do,' he replied, 'but they never find anything. Anything in particular that you want them not to find today?'

I shrugged, 'Not that I can think of, but they arrested McGregor here last night so I expect they'll be looking for something.'

'Joey McGregor?' he asked and I nodded, 'Poor bastard,' he said after which there was little more that needed saying.

§§§§

The Green Shamrock isn't very far from the docks either. It is owned and run by a huge Irishman, called "Tubba" O'Laorie. I've no idea what his real name is, but he's known as "Tubba" to one and all in Holyhead, and believe me it's a respectful nickname. Nobody disrespects "Tubba" and gets away with it.

'Shane, you old bastard,' he shouted across the bar at me as I walked in.

'Tubba, you apology for a Leprechaun,' I replied, 'how you doing?'

'Come and sit with me,' he waved a huge paw at an empty table. 'Drink?'

'At this time in the morning, it's too early for anything other than coffee.'

He flicked his fingers at his barman, and called out, 'Coffee for one.' The barman stopped whatever it was he was doing, and went over to his barista machine. Any friend of Tubba's, you know the rest. The speed it took for the cup of coffee to arrive at my table was simply breath taking. If there had been a camera trained on that barman, he'd have got a ticket.

'So what can I do for you today?'

'I wondered if my supply of whisky had arrived yet?'

'You're in luck; it arrived yesterday. Straight off the boat from the islands.'

'Good, I'm told by my stock controller that my levels need replenishing. And, by the way, when I pay you for a dozen bottles, I really do expect to get a real dozen, and not a Tubba's dozen which is usually eleven, but it's not unknown to be even fewer.'

He shrugged, 'you know, we do have expenses to cover, people need bribing to turn blind eyes. You do know the Ardbeg you buy from me is real Ardbeg, not that knock off Islay Mist stuff, relabelled.' We both glared at each other for a moment, and then his voice became almost chirpy, 'I hear you had a little excitement last night at your place,' he said, 'an arrest or something.'

'Ah yes, poor old Joey,' I sighed. I tried to sound sad, but I'm really not that good an actor.

'And they said he was responsible for that courier being knocked off his bike and killed for some travel documents he was carrying.'

'Is that was what it was about,' I said lazily, 'I did wonder.'

He grinned at me. 'I don't think for a moment you don't know exactly what's going on in your bar. I imagine you're also aware of who he had intended to get those documents to?'

'Oh?'

'There's a fellow in town called Andrew Ryan who I understand is desperate to get to Ireland PDQ, and I understand that Joey had got those documents for him.'

'Really? If they turn up I'll let you know.'

'If he turns up in your bar, you'll be a very rich man,' he said. 'Stop me if you've heard this before, but I don't suppose you'd like to come into partnership with me, would you?'

'And why would I want to do a thing like that? I'm scared enough of where I might end up every time I walk into your bar. They say that the last person who disagreed with you was found underneath the Menai Bridge wearing concrete wellies. At least they think it was him, the body was unrecognisable, but he was still identified by the expensive gold wristy he was wearing. Now I'm no detective, but I can't help thinking that a wristy like that would have been the first thing that anybody would steal if it was the straight robbery and murder they claimed it was. We both know you're a gangster Tubba.'

'True, true,' he nodded sagely, 'but isn't it better to be on the side of the devils and feel safe, than on the side of the angels and feel threatened?'

'I'm not on anybody's side,' I replied.

I finished my coffee, wiped my mouth, and grinned at him. 'That should do,' I remarked, standing

R.M. CARTMEL

up.

'What for?'

'I think Evans has much the same feeling that you do, that McGregor's mythical documents have somehow ended up in my bar. I needed to give them time to search the place. See you later with the whisky,' I said, and stood up. As I reached the door, who should I meet coming the other way, but Ryan and Jenny?

'The guy you're looking for is the fat drongo sitting over there,' I said to Ryan, and tossed a thumb at Tubba as I made my way out. I ignored Jenny completely.

§§§§

The first person I came face to face with when I got back was, you'll never guess, Rhys Evans. I was pleasantly surprised to see the police helping my staff reassemble the bar, and getting all the tables back in some sort of order. They had been thorough.

'Hello Shane, I saw you weren't here, been anywhere interesting?'

'You know I can't standing watching you and your goons go through my bar like a spinner through a batting side on a drying pitch. I went over to the Green Shamrock to have a coffee with my mate Tubba.'

'And, no doubt to check on the status of your illegal orders?' I raised an eyebrow. This was another of those things that we both knew, but as long as we didn't admit it, it didn't actually exist. I think the phrase was plausible deniability. 'Time for another cuppa?' he added.

'Why not? Somehow I always prefer the stuff we serve here than the stuff he serves at the Shamrock. I think it's how we grind the beans. We crush the beans whereas he cuts through them with what is in effect an electric scythe. Our cell walls are still intact, but his are blasted to smithereens, which makes his coffee far more bitter.'

'I did wonder. I always assumed you get the beans from the same place; and yet somehow the result is quite different.'

'I have a deal with a man in Dublin; I think he gets the beans from Germany. Where they come from before then, I have no idea. It doesn't pay to ask, and if I buy enough for the Shamrock as well, it's cheaper that way for both of us.'

'It all got rather exciting here last night, didn't it, one way or the other, don't you think?'

'It had its moments. Just as a matter of interest, what's going to happen to McGregor?'

'Oh poor Joey. I'm afraid he didn't make it, poor lamb.'

'What does it say on his death certificate?'

'I haven't decided yet. It may say suicide, or it may say shot while resisting arrest. It might even say diabetic ketoacidosis.'

'I didn't know he was diabetic.'

'They say these things can come on awfully quickly. Anyway I suspect the Colonel will probably have the final say on that one.'

'As you say, very sad.'

'One thing, a propos of nothing in particular,' the policeman's tone changed quite sharply, 'they say he was carrying some travel documents that were stolen from the courier who was murdered in Bangor.'

'Joey? Did that? I never knew he had it in him.'

'So you don't know anything about those documents? And the reason that I ask, is that shortly after we apprehended Mister McGregor, who should walk into your bar but the famously indestructible Andrew Ryan. What do you think he might have been looking for in here do you think?'

'A drink? This is a bar you know.'

'Now I just know you're being flippant. No, he would have been coming in here to find McGregor to get those documents from him. Those Royal travel documents are the only ones for leaving Holyhead which don't have to be signed and rubber stamped by me.'

'Really? Do tell.'

'When they shipped the Queen and the other Royals off to Canada after Brexit, ostensibly to keep them safe during the period of unrest...'

'Was there unrest? I was a kid in Adelaide, down under, at the time. So I wasn't interested in the newspapers apart from the sport and the funny pages.'

'The army was out and about, much as they are today, and there was a curfew, but not a lot else. Anyway, as things calmed down, the Royals were allowed back into the country. They're harmless enough, and they're good for business as far as the English are concerned. They even have royal castles in Anglia and Scotland, and every bit of Royalty brings money into the island from outside. The Western folks like us, the Irish and the Wessexmen, don't have a lot to do with them, but we do allow them to travel in and out of our countries without rocking any apple carts, and they have their own official travel documents.'

'Fascinating, so that's what it was all about. And our favourite Mister Ryan is pretending to get to Ireland on a Royal pass?'

'Got it in one.'

'Does he look like a Royal? You know receding chin, jug ears and the rest? And Jenny, which Royal would she pass for, for Gods sake?'

'Ah well, they don't have pictures on or anything like that, merely a statement that it requires all whom it may concern to allow the bearer to pass freely without let or hindrance, and to afford their bearer such assistance and protection as may be necessary.'

'Ah.'

'The bottom line is this. I would really rather that Ryan never gets to Ireland.'

'He's a slippery bastard isn't he? I've lost count of the number of times he's been reported dead, and then up he bobs still alive somewhere else.'

'Oh, I'm not planning on killing him. I want him to become a permanent resident here in Holyhead. How would you like that? Ryan and that lovely girl a permanent fixture in your bar? I thought you'd enjoy that. You run a casino, they tell me. How would you fancy a little wager?'

'I run a casino, so I know exactly how they work. You don't think I'd be stupid enough to gamble in one do you?'

'You'll like this one. I'll bet you that Ryan will get out of Holyhead into Ireland.'

'Huh?'

'I bet you that he will, so if he fails to get to Ireland, you win.'

'How much are we talking here Rhys?'

'Ten thousand a year?'

'Wow! You are serious; make it twenty and you're on.'

'You drive a hard bargain. You do know I'm only a poor corrupt policeman don't you?'

'Most of that, apart from the "poor" bit.'

'We have a deal?'

'We have a deal.' And with that, we shook hands, and he followed his policemen out of my bar.

§§§§

I took the empty cups over to the bar, and I was just about to go upstairs, and how do you say it, powder my nose, when I heard, 'Are you Mister Shane?'

She was small, blonde and pretty in a way that was far too young to be in a bar. 'How did you get in here?' I asked, 'There is a minimum age limit to be allowed into bars in Wales you know.'

'I came in to find Inspector Evans,' she replied. 'I was told to meet him here.'

Oh, that's how it was, was it? 'Go on.' I said encouraging her to continue.

'How trustworthy do you think the Inspector is?' she asked.

'I think if he has promised to do something, you can pretty much count on his doing it.'

She thought for a moment, and then continued. 'I thought that might be the case.' She paused and then looked at me directly with eyes that were far too big for her best interests. 'You're a man of the world Mr Shane, aren't you?' This was getting awkward, and I sort of half guessed where this was heading.

'Go on,' I said.

'If you did something really bad but for all the right reasons, and nobody knew, then that would be all right wouldn't it?'

'And you're trying to get to Ireland…'

'…to catch the Airship to America yes. And it's so difficult to get two tickets.'

'Two?' I asked, looking at her, there was scarcely enough in that package to merit one ticket, let alone two.

'I'm going with my boyfriend. He has relations in Cleveland Ohio. I'm told it's safe there. But in some ways, he's terribly young, and very possessive, but he's so sweet. And he'd never know. I mean, who would tell him? There's nobody we'll meet here we'll ever meet in Cleveland, and over there, who's ever heard of Holyhead?'

'And you want my permission?'

'No, yes, oh I don't know.' She looked on the verge of tears.

'Have you any idea what it is you're being asked to do?'

'Yes, no. But I'm told it's very nice, you know, the best thing that two people can do together.'

Oh for crying out loud! 'Where have you two come from?'

'Ilford, in Essex.'

'And you want my advice?'

'Yes.'

'Go back to Ilford.'

'But I can't. Joshy's in your casino trying to win the money to pay Inspector Evans for the passes, but you and I know how casinos work, don't we? He hasn't got a snowball's chance in hell of winning that sort of money has he?'

'He's in my casino, you say?'

'Yes,'

'Follow me.'

It was impossible not to tell who 'Joshy' was. He was by some ten years the youngest person in the room. He still had some acne, and was still several years short of growing a half acceptable moustache, although he was trying. He was sitting by the roulette table, looking seriously anxious. You really should never gamble with money you can't afford to lose.

I walked up behind him, catching Raoul's eye. 'Have you tried Number 10 yet? I have a gut feeling that it's going to come up shortly.' I said into his ear.

'But I...' he stammered.

'Number 10.' I said sharply, and he pushed his chips onto number 10.

'*Les jeux sont faits. Rien ne va plus,*' said Raoul instantly, telling the one or two other players dithering round the table that no further bets would be accepted for that spin of the wheel. He then gave it a good spin with his right hand, while his left hand went out of sight beneath the table's rim. When the wheel stopped, there was the little white ball, nestling in number 10. '*Numéro Dix,*' he said, '*noir et pair.*'

The boy was about to grab the chips off the table, still not understanding his 'luck.' 'Leave them,' I snapped, and Raoul had already started spinning the wheel. The boy looked at me, and looked at Raoul, and obviously still hadn't the faintest idea what was going on.

'*Numéro Dix,* said Raoul again, '*noir et pair.*'

'Now,' I said to the boy, 'take those chips to the cashier and cash them out. Don't come back. Hopefully you will have a wonderful rest of your life in America.' He grabbed at his chips and rushed up to the till.

The tiny blonde sidled up to me, 'Thank you Mr Shane, thank you, I don't know how to thank you.'

'Don't mention it,' I thought for a moment and then added, 'ever.'

She rushed over to where Evans was sitting looking at the menu and contemplating what he was going to have for lunch. 'Inspector Evans,' she bounced at him, 'I've got your money. I'll be round by your office, promptly at eight o'clock tomorrow morning.'

'And I shall be there at ten,' he replied acidly, getting up and wandering over to where I was standing. 'You know you can be irritatingly ethical when you really put your mind to it,' he said. 'I've got a spectacularly athletic redhead coming in tomorrow, and if you interfere with her too, I might persuade myself not to overlook some of the discrepancies I have a habit of overlooking, if you see what I mean?'

Oh yes, I saw what he meant, Grown-ups can look after themselves, but really; those kids really were little more than children.

Raoul tapped on my shoulder, 'Shane, can I have a word?'

I looked at Raoul, 'How are we doing mate?' I asked grimly.

'Not as well as I would have predicted at the beginning of this week,' was his dry reply. 'Have you still got that envelope I gave you last night?'

'Sure, I haven't banked it yet.'

'Good, even a trivial win by Inspector Evans would embarrass our float right now.'

'Say no more, I'll go and fetch it right away,' and I

did just that. I went up to my office, opened the safe and got the envelope marked 'casino' out of it. I scribbled on the envelope, 'Takings zero', opened the envelope and put the cash in my pocket. The envelope went back into my safe to remind me what had happened and when, as a memento for my next meeting with the taxman.

I walked back down the stairs again and the place was beginning to fill up with lunchtime customers. Evans was already wrapping himself round the choicest cut of the day. We couldn't keep our promise to give him the best meal in the house if somebody had already eaten it, so he did meet us half way and come in early. I wandered back into the casino, and passed the contents of my pocket to Raoul, and he went straight into the place we jokingly called 'The Chip Shop,' and stowed it safely.

Another reason for the bar feeling full was that Tubba was there, complete with an even more massive sidekick, only this sidekick wasn't constructed from lipids, but from several tons of mineral and protein. He was carrying a crate of whisky on each shoulder. 'Ere, Guv, where d'you wann'um?' the stevedore asked Geraint behind the bar, suggesting that most of his electrical tissue was used for power rather than problem solving, and they both disappeared down, out of sight into the cellar.

'Shane, look, I'm as good as my word. Four cases of the finest Ardbeg.'

'And you wonder why everyone's terrified of you Tubba? The size of that man, it's more terrifying than Mitchell Starc steaming in at you at full chat.'

'I take it that that's one of your cricket metaphors,' he replied. I don't really get them you know.'

'But you play cricket in Ireland. Right now you've got a damn good team, far better than that shower the Poms fielded the other day. Absolutely wrecked by the Yanks they were.'

'I did always say that when the United States did finally start playing cricket properly instead of claiming that their Baseball tournament was a World Series, they'd probably get quite good at it. Oh very good! I see what you did there, very clever. Of course I follow cricket, who doesn't?' He looked around us, giving me a big fat hint that he was in the process of changing the subject. 'To be sure this is a nice place. Tell you something, I'll give you double what you paid for the place, right now cash in hand.'

'Not difficult Tubba, I never paid for it.'

'You mean old Aunty Eluned just gave you the place? I never knew. Why would she do a thing like that?'

'I don't think she liked you very much Tubba, and she did know Ali and I had some really good plans for it.'

'And so you did, and here they are for the whole world to see. If you won't sell me the place, how about me putting in a bid for Ali's services instead? He adds a touch of class to a place with all that ivory work. Do you think he'd come and work for me?'

'Why don't we ask him?'

We walked over to the piano where Ali was sitting doodling something to himself. 'Ali,' I said, 'Tubba is asking whether you'd like to go and work at the Green Shamrock.'

'Must I Shane? I'd much rather work here.'

'He'll pay you three times as much as I do you know,' I grinned at the look of surprise on Tubba's jowls.

'I don't get to spend all the money I earn here anyway,' he said, 'and besides I'd still get to play on Aunt Shazia if I stayed here.' He caressed the piano.

'I'll buy you that piano,' said Tubba.

'Aunt Shazia's an old lady, man. She'd never survive being wheeled round to the Shamrock without falling to pieces.

Tubba and I shrugged at each other. 'Well you can't blame a man for trying,' he said. The Stevedore was coming up from the cellar again. 'Weww, vat's ve whisky sorted boss,' he said through the relatively few teeth he'd got left.

'Did the coffee arrive?' Tubba asked.

'It's in the kitchen,' I said. 'Follow me.'

'Go along, follow him,' Tubba said crossly to the man-mountain who hadn't moved. We walked through the door, and I subconsciously checked that the frame was still in one piece after he had passed through it. It was, but it was a close thing. I pointed to three large hessian bags on the counter. He picked them all up at once, to the amazement of the chef, and walked out again.

'Handy to have one of those,' remarked the chef.

'Can't think when I'd ever use one,' I replied, 'apart from once a month at delivery time, and I always know where I can borrow it if it's needed.'

'Once again it's been a pleasure doing business with you,' said Tubba, tapping his wristy, and showing me the numbers on its face. 'That's what it looks like altogether.' I checked, and was tempted to knock off a nought, just to see what he would do. But then I could see the stevedore was watching us, and thought better of it. Those numbers were acceptable, and so I accessed my wristy and transferred the money across.

Tubba followed his man, loaded with bags of coffee, but not laden with them, if you see what I mean, out of the front door. He passed a man coming in, 'That's him over there,' he said pointing at me, 'by the piano.'

He had met Ryan at the door.

I pointed at a choice of tables, but he said, 'I'm not here for lunch. Is there anywhere we can go and talk, which isn't so overlooked?'

'My office, if you like. Follow me,' and we walked up the stairs and into my holy of holies. It really was private. It had a camera that looked straight down the stairs, and there was a monitor over the door. There was also a sensor under the third step which made a fairly polite noise through the monitor to tell me that someone was on the way up. Up until now, I had always managed to get the other half of an illicit tryst into my bedroom before the main door opened. 'What can I do for you?'

'I'll get straight to the point, I came to your bar yesterday to meet a man called McGregor.'

'Ah yes, poor Joey, so sad.'

'Quite,' he said not swallowing my sympathy for a moment. 'And this fellow McGregor had a couple of Royal Transport documents for me.'

'Uhuh.'

'They weren't on him when, um whatever happened to him happened to him.'

'When they killed him, you mean?'

'I wasn't sure you knew.'

'I think that you can safely count on the fact that I know about most things that happen here in Holyhead.'

'So I'm led to understand. So, to cut a long story

short; you've got those documents and I want them. How much?'

'You think I've got the documents? Joey McGregor came in here yesterday, and got arrested. They killed him, but didn't find those documents on him, and now everybody assumes that I've got them. Why is that?'

'Haven't you? How does half a million sound to you?'

Whoa! Talk about starting low and working up until a mid point is met that's acceptable to both parties. How far was this joker going to get to? He had that sort of backing behind him? He was now considerably scarier than Tubba with all his hired muscle.

I looked at him quizzically and didn't say anything, partly because an image of Jenny was flitting before my eyes, and somehow I couldn't help wanting to see her again, and again. 'You do know who I am?' he asked rather petulantly like an over-educated toff who felt whatever he wanted was his by right.

'Yes,' I said, 'I know who you are. Do you know who I am?'

'You're the Australian, who, right now, holds the fate of the free world in his hands.' This drongo really did have a high opinion of himself didn't he? Probably higher than anyone else, bearing in mind that to most people, myself included, he was some sort of hero. Mind you, given the fact that he had pulled Genevieve Laing before I had, maybe he did have some right to that opinion. However my opinion of him as a person was dropping fast.

'With the best will in the world,' I said slowly, 'and if, of course, just as a matter of argument, let's say I do have those documents, or at least know where they are; why would I not be saving them for my own personal use? In the fullness of time I might need to get out of North Wales in a hurry? From your own perspective, you can tell it's not an inconceivable question.'

He looked me straight in the eye, and replied, 'a million.'

'My final answer remains no.' I snapped, aware I was losing my temper.

'For God's sake, you could buy one of the Welsh Police's documents for a hundredth of that price.'

'So could you.'

'No I can't. It was made abundantly clear to me by both the Inspector and the British Colonel this morning, that I have absolutely no chance of getting one of those Welsh travel documents. So why won't you sell me yours?'

My stack just blew, 'May I suggest you ask your wife,' I said.

'My wife?' He looked puzzled.

'Your wife,' I replied and explained to him how the door to my flat worked.

§§§§

The bar had well filled up by the time I followed him out of the front door to my flat. He had got perhaps two steps down my stairs when a large man in an English Army uniform started singing 'Land of Hope and Glory' at his table. Ryan had barely descended two more steps when the whole table caught in on the act. I had rather hoped they might pull him into some semblance of tune, but hope like that rarely happens. It was just a louder bunch of crows cawing.

My brain was sensitive to the atmosphere in my

bar, and I could already feel an uncertainty about it, maybe a sort of instability. I tried to catch Ali's eye to hint that he might play that thumping syncopated version of 'Waltzing Matilda' that he had once come up with to amuse me. We had found that ever since we took over the place it was an excellent peacemaker, as it was generally considered that Ali was taking the mick out of me, and somehow the Welsh thought that was funny.

I was also aware that Ryan was accelerating towards Ali, and that Ali was aware he was coming. Ryan bent down and said something to him, and then walked over to a group of Welsh Policeman standing near the bar. He raised his hand and started singing;

'Wele'n, sefyll rhwng y myrtwydd
Wrthrych teilwng o fy myrd,
Er o'r braidd 'rwy'n Ei adnabod
Ef uwchlaw gwrthychau'r byd:
Henffych fore! Hennfych fore!
Caf ei weled fel y mae.
Caf ei weled fel y mae.'

§§

Lo between the myrtles standing,
One who merits well my love,
Though His worth I guess but dimly,
High all Earthly things above.
Happy Morning! Happy Morning!
When at last I see him clear!
When at last I see him clear!

William Williams Pantycelyn (1762) Translated Peter Williams (1722-96)

§§

By the time the verse was finished, the whole room was ablaze with the sound of a Welsh Male Voice Choir at full throttle, with the full four parts and more heard on the '*caf ei weled*' bits. I could even see young Myfanwy singing at the top of her voice behind the bar. I had no idea what any of them were singing about, but it was stirring stuff, and I was really impressed, at least I was until a shot rang out, and the bar was bathed in instant silence.

Not far from the table where the English soldiers who started the sing song stood Colonel Willoughby. He was purple with rage, and he held a pistol from whose barrel a curl of smoke was visible.

I was down the rest of my stairs in a flash. I didn't care who he was, or which government he claimed to represent. Nobody was going to fire guns in my bar and get away with it; certainly not for the second day on the bounce.

Rhys Evans beat me to him.

'Don't worry,' said the Colonel. 'I only fired a blank.' That was probably aimed at me, as I was half looking for holes in my ceiling. 'I wanted to get your attention.'

'You've got it boyo,' said Evans. 'I have to say, I really rather enjoyed the singing. I didn't know we had so many people here in Holyhead who know the words to the Cwm Rhondda.'

'It would be an interesting test to see if they know the words of the second or subsequent verses,' I remarked cheerfully. 'Same with the Poms, they all know the words to the first verse of God Save the King, but the rest of them, not a chance, not even the 'knavish tricks' bit.'

I had no idea I was making things worse, but

Evans obviously did, as he said sharply, 'When you're already in a hole, you idiot, stop digging!'

'I think we must reconsider our plans about Ryan,' said the still purple Willoughby. I don't think we can afford to keep him here in Holyhead indefinitely. If he can wind up your police in a single day, just think what he might achieve if he's still here in a month.'

'But..' Evans started to say.

'And I want this bar shut now. It's a hive of dissidence and revolutionary fever.'

'Now look here,' I began.

Evans looked at me, and then the Colonel, and then his face changed. 'What!' he said very loudly, 'It appears that gambling is going on in this place. That's against the law! I declare this bar closed forthwith.'

'Your winnings, Inspector Evans,' said Raoul, sidling up to the policeman and putting a bulging fist into his pocket. It was less bulging when it was removed.

'Thank you Raoul,' said the Inspector. 'Now clear the bar. Everybody out.' He looked at the English Soldiers, 'You too. This place is now closed by order of the Welsh Police by order of...' blah blah bliddy blah. Evans had the bollocracy off pat.

And suddenly the place was empty apart from me and my rather stunned looking staff.

I said to the assembled company. 'Sorry about that.'

'I don't see how any of that was your fault,' said Raoul, all trace of any French accent now missing from his speech.

'How much food have you got ready?' I looked at the chef, 'that won't go back into storage?' I asked.

'About a dozen plates,' said his wife. 'We can put the rest back in the fridge for later. It'll need eating soon though.'

'I hope you can all face a spot of lunch over the next few days,' I said to everybody. 'It's on the house.'

There was a hubbub of 'thank you very muches' and the like; they sounded like a chorus of Elvises. I turned to Paul. 'How's it looking financially?'

'We're okay at the moment,' he said and grinned, 'despite some strange occurrences in the Casino over the past twenty-four hours.

'Good,' I replied. 'In which case, you're all still on salary, unless you want to go somewhere else, until I can work out exactly who needs bribing, and how much.'

'Surely it's Rhys Evans you've got to bribe,' Ali started.

'It's not quite so simple. He put on the show just now, true, but he was told to shut us down by that English Colonel chope. It's becoming clearer by the day who really rules the roost here on Holy Island, and I'm fairly sure they're not based in Caerdydd.'

The lunch settled down to being a group of friends quietly licking their wounds together, and talking about anything but the elephant in the room, as friends do. Once the eating had been done and the bar had been tidied, everybody quietly and sheepishly left the building, leaving just me and old Paul kicking the can down the road and drinking one final cup of coffee, before he too set off to wherever he was planning to go. I insisted that I shouldn't know where that might be in case my discussion with Rhys Evans or with whoever it was I would need to transfer funds to, didn't go quite according to plan. Plausible

205

deniability, and any other clichés you can pull off the top of your head.

He was leaving by the main door, when I heard him say, 'he's over by the piano.'

I didn't need to look at the person coming in to know who it was. It was a little earlier than I had anticipated, true, but I had known this conversation was going to take place as soon as I saw her yesterday. And I knew it was her simply because of the aura of magic she always carried with her. She didn't need a scent, as an early warning siren. She just had 'it'. I can't remember when I first became aware of it, maybe the second time we met, maybe the third, but once I had been bitten, there was never going to be anyone else, ever.

'Hello Shane,' she said in a soft voice like silk as she walked over to where I was sitting. I hadn't stood up. I know that was impolite of me, but I was still trying to maintain some sort of control.

'Hello, my precious,' I said trying to sound like Smeagol. 'Do you want a coffee or anything stronger?' I offered.

'I don't think so, I just wanted to see you.'

'And here I am. What do you want to see me about?'

'I want those travel documents, Shane.'

I laughed drily. 'The travel documents, the travel documents. It's always the bloody travel documents. It seems that as long as people think I have those travel documents, I'll never be on my own.'

'You know that's not fair Shane. I only want one for Andrew, and I'll give you anything for that. Just tell me what you want. Anything,' she repeated slowly.

'I don't know that I want anything right now. I've

got everything I need. Look.' And I waved an expansive paw all around the bar. 'All mine.'

'I don't see any customers Shane.'

'That's a rather a cheap shot, but it's only a temporary glitch, nothing to worry your head about.'

'You're going to have to come up with a big bribe to reopen your pub, and that might be a little difficult while Andrew is still around. You know we can sort that out between us now.'

'What, you give me loads of money, I give you the tickets, you both disappear, and my pub gets reopened, simple as that!'

'Just one ticket will be enough.'

'You mean, you're going to take a powder, and you're leaving poor old Ryan here to face the music. That's a side to you I wasn't previously aware of. You really are some kind of mercenary Mata Hari, aren't you? I supposed it was always going to be this way. In every relationship there's always someone who does the loving, and there's the other one who just lets it happen.'

It sounded like a sob that turned into a snarl. 'Just give me those fucking tickets,' she spat at me. And then I realised she was holding a revolver, and it was pointed straight at me.

'Dingo's kidneys.' I said, 'You've learned some new cuss words since we were together.' I walked slowly towards her. 'Now bring your hand up a little,' I said. Her hand shook slightly, as I lifted the business end of the revolver a touch. 'There,' I said, 'that's it. Now all you need to do is squeeze the trigger, gently, and you'll be putting me out of my misery.'

She was still shaking and said, 'Go and get those documents.'

I put my hand over my jacket pocket. 'I don't have to go anywhere, they're right here. I suppose you'd have to miss them when you shoot me, I don't know how valid they would be covered in blood, with a bullet hole through them. Some Customs officers might think there was something, shall we say, not quite bonzer about them in that condition.'

'Stop it Shane....' she blurted.

'Just pull the bloody trigger, woman!' We were so close at that point that one of only two things could possibly have happened, and the fact that I'm here telling you all this will tell you what actually did. She dropped the gun, and threw herself into my arms and kissed me.

You think I could resist that? This was the one woman I loved most in my entire life, and she was kissing me? She pulled away for a moment and gave me both barrels with those fabulous eyes, and then rushed back in. After a moment, she said. 'I think we should go up to your flat. Someone might come in, and I don't think either of us would be able to stop.'

I followed her up the stairs and opened my flat. It took me a moment, but when we got up there, I sank down in the chair behind my desk and pulling the envelope out of my pocket, I slapped it on my desk. 'I've got to hand it to you kid,' I said acidly, 'you're good.'

'What? You think that was a payment for those tickets do you?'

'Wasn't it?'

She smiled at me softly. 'You silly old pillock. Of course it wasn't. Don't you realise that it's you I'm in love with; it's only ever been you, right since that first day at the meat market? Come here.'

A spot more kissing took place, and then I pulled back. 'So what about Ryan?' I asked, 'I still don't understand.'

'As I said, I was very young when I met him. It was terribly exciting being involved with a dangerous, revolutionary figure. Do you remember all those posters students at university had on their walls, the one of Che Guevara? I was a kid who had got herself a real live Che Guevara. And then he got caught, and I heard he had died resisting arrest, and much to my relief, I grew up and went to university. On my first day there, I met you. And the rest is history.'

'So everything we had in Cambridge was genuine?'

'Yes,' she looked worried for a moment, 'Wasn't it for you too?'

I smiled, 'and then some,' I replied. 'I couldn't think of anything else. So what happened?'

'You know that day when you, Ali and I were planning to come west the following morning, I met Liz in the street for the first time in a long time. She told me that Andrew had escaped, but only just, and was hiding somewhere near Lincoln gravely ill, and he needed me. She made it sound like he was on the way out, and he wanted to say, you know, goodbye. I left that afternoon. I think it had still been my intention to join you and Ali at the station the following morning.'

'So, what happened?'

'As you can see, the one thing he never actually did was die. I ended up nursing him back to health. Travelling secretly through Lincolnshire, I realised how desperate the rest of the country was. We were comfortable and warm in Norwich and Cambridge. It wasn't until I saw the real England that I realised how poor and downright dangerous the place was. There were scruffy kids starving, and begging in the streets. There weren't any police, just the Army wandering about in squads, amusing themselves by abusing the locals. The only vehicles about weren't those dinky little electric pods we had in Anglia, and we have here in Wales, they were big smelly armoured cars that belch black fumes, and usually with a massive gun mounted on the front of a turret. Those people needed a hero, someone to believe in, someone to rescue them, and that person was lying, feverish in the bed in front of me. Do you think I could abandon him then?'

I saw her point. Certainly the Jenny I thought I knew couldn't do that. I looked at her and adored her even more at that moment than I ever really thought I had done before. Was that possible?

'But he's well now,' she continued, 'and he doesn't need me anymore, and you and I found each other again. Oh Shane, just hold me, as if it's the last opportunity we'll ever have.' And she started unbuttoning my shirt.

§§§§

I looked at her, just as I had done before. Her body was still the most beautiful thing I had ever seen, and it still shone like it had some strange internal light source. I am probably exaggerating a bit here; it was probably the moonlight coming through the open window that was reflecting off her perfect skin.

While I was just gently gaping, I became aware of some activity on the monitor in the next room. I slipped out of bed without disturbing her, and walked into my office, pulling on the dressing gown I had hanging on the back of the bedroom door.

I sat down at my desk and watched the screen carefully. The old chap pouring the drinks was Paul, anyone could see that, but who as the other guy? At one moment he glanced up at the camera. He probably wasn't even aware it was there, but at that point I knew exactly who it was. I went back into the bedroom and touched Jenny softly on her wonderful shoulder.

'Mmm?' She mumbled.

'You've got to get up,' I said softly.

She took that as an invitation and threw a sleepy arm round my neck, 'Tiger man!' she grinned, 'you have no idea how much I love you right now.'

You have no idea how tempted I was at that moment just to throw caution to the winds. But I said, 'you've got to get up. Something's come up. Get dressed.' And she could see I was serious. I got dressed myself, intentionally not watching her. I still wasn't sure whether I could keep my hands off her if I saw her actually covering herself up.

'What?' she said after fully reassembling herself.

I led her to the office and pointed at the monitor. She saw immediately what I was looking at and said, 'Oh shit.'

'Quite,' I agreed suddenly thinking ridiculously quickly for someone who was asleep a few moments ago. 'Go back to the bedroom, I'll see if I can attract Paul's attention.'

She went back into the room and I threw open the office door. 'Paul,' I bellowed, 'Can I see you up here for a moment.'

They both made a move for the stairs. 'No just

Paul, I'll be down to join you in a moment.'

Paul made his way up the stairs and into the office, shutting the door behind him. 'Yes Shane?' he said quizzically, suddenly becoming aware of the figure standing behind me. His mouth formed a perfect circle in surprise, but he didn't say anything.

'Paul, you know all the alleyways and byways of this town by heart don't you?'

'I would think so Shane, yes.'

'Can you get Miss Laing back to her hotel without getting either of you caught?'

'Piece of cake.'

'Right, I'll see you when you get back.'

Our parting kiss was rather a tame affair after what had gone on before, but what was probably more lingering was the 'See you tomorrows,' we both said. And through the back door, they were gone.

I opened the front door of my office and went down the stairs. Ryan was down by the bar trying to single handedly put a plaster on his left wrist.

'Here, let me help,' I said.

'Thank you very much.'

'That looked nasty.'

'I had to climb through a window. I think they were waiting for us.'

'The Police?'

'The Police, the Army, Uncle Tom Cobbleigh and all. Suddenly they were everywhere. Somebody had grassed us up.'

'Aren't there times like this when you really wonder whether it's all worth it, doing this thing that you do?'

He looked at me and smiled, 'It's what I do. It's my reason for getting up every morning.' He looked at me silently for a moment and then added, 'Can I tell you a story?'

'Why not? Everybody else seems to want to tell me stories.'

'Not very long ago I was passing through a midland town, and I saw an aging Asian man, sitting outside a chip shop with his family. At least I assumed they were his family. They were sitting with him, their faces covered in the full niqab, so you couldn't see their faces. But the rest of them wasn't covered by very much. Some of those kids were paler than others. While I was passing, a man in uniform walked up and gave him some money. The soldier looked at the kids for a moment, and selected one, who immediately trotted off behind him. The Asian then gave the money to one of the other kids, who rushed into the chip shop to buy some chips. Can't you see what sort of country this place has become where a man is forced to sell the bodies of his children to get food for the others?'

'Nasty,' I said.

'And you ask why I bother? It's not as if you're entirely innocent of caring either, Shane,' he remarked drily.

'What do you mean by that?'

'I was watching your performance with that little blonde kid today. That wasn't the action of a man who doesn't give a damn about the state of the world.'

'We all have occasional lapses. She was a pretty little thing, after all.'

'Oh right, and you want me to believe that's why you did it?' I shrugged. 'I know quite a lot of things about you, Shane,' he continued.

'You do?'

'I knew for a fact that you are in love with a woman, who means the world to you, and that interestingly enough, she's the same woman I'm in love with. I don't actually have a problem with that. In fact, every day I'm secretly surprised that there aren't more people out there who feel the same way about her that I do. Now I realise you're not going to let *me* have those travel documents, but seriously are you going to keep her here just because of me? Give her one of those documents and at least let her get off this godforsaken island.'

'You love her that much?'

'You may see me as just a warrior standing for a cause. Well I'm a human being too, and, yes, I love her that much.'

The conversation might have gone on forever, but that wasn't to be. The front doors flew open, and in walked three rather burly men wearing the uniform of the Welsh border police. 'Mister Ryan? You're under arrest,' said the one in front.

'On what charge?'

'Take your pick,' replied the NCO, 'Shall we say being an enemy of the people, for now?'

Ryan looked at me, and I shrugged. What else was there to say?

§§§§

'Shane, Listen. There's no point in going on about it,' Rhys Evans could look quite cross when he wanted to. 'Why are you getting so agitated anyway? We both know you've got a thing about his woman? Surely everything would be better without him being around and in the way?'

'But that's just it. He will still be around. What evidence have you actually got? Probably enough to

214

keep him behind bars for a week or so top whack, and then he'll be out again, glaring balefully at us across some bar or another. That won't be good enough for anybody, for you, me or anybody else for that matter.'

'You've piqued my interest, what have you got in mind?'

'Let him go now, and we'll see if we can't come up with something better, shall we say, a rather more permanent solution to our problem?'

'I think Colonel Willoughby would have an apoplectic fit if we released him right now.'

'Really? I thought he was going to have one yesterday to be honest, and I was quite looking forward to seeing what happened when his head exploded. Oh, come on Rhys, you can't say that that thought doesn't amuse you? Oh come on, don't tell me you like the chope?'

'Nothing could be further from the truth, I can't stand the man.'

'There you go then. Explain to the drongo, that you have a plan to stitch Ryan up permanently, but the only way you can do that is to let him back on the streets for the moment.'

'Go on.'

'You've probably guessed the least well kept secret in Holyhead at the moment.'

'What? You mean that you've got those travel documents? Yes, I must ask you about them sometime.'

'What you really need is for them to be found in Ryan's possession when you next arrest him. You might even make it stick that he was responsible for killing that unfortunate courier. Accessory to murder would probably cook his goose.'

'You know you really are a tricky customer, Shane. Tell me, you'd do all that for a woman?'

'Come on Rhys, you've seen her, and it's me she wants, not him. This will help everybody. Just let it fly, what have you got to lose? Now he's a tricky bloke, so you've got to be careful. We don't want him smelling a rat before we catch him.'

'So what have you got in mind?'

'Get someone not wearing a uniform to tell him to meet me at the docks at five o'clock this evening, just before the high tide sailing, and I'll have the documents ready for him when he gets there. Meanwhile, while we're round and about today, keep your goons off the street. It won't do the plan any good if I'm arrested with the documents in my possession before the handover, will it?'

'But if Ryan leaves Holyhead for any reason, you'll lose our bet. You do realise that don't you?'

'You've seen Jenny Laing. Don't you think that a lifetime with that wouldn't trump any stupid little bet that you and I might have? Oh and one other thing, perhaps you might also see your way clear to allowing my bar to reopen its doors, as a little extra thank you for helping you over this.'

'You're really quite a nasty piece of work, under that veneer of Australian cultivation, aren't you Shane.' He looked at me, and shrugged, 'Very well, let's get on with it.'

§§§§

My next port of call was the Green Shamrock. Tubba was there slurping a mug of coffee as I walked in. 'Is that offer still open?' I asked, offering him the use of my hand.

'I hope you're not expecting me to have that kind of cash on my person,' he replied, acknowledging both my question and me.

'To be honest, I'd be surprised if you didn't somewhere, but as long as your wristy is as trustworthy as mine, I can cope with it just being an electronic credit transfer.'

We held our wrists together in a moment that would have looked very camp in times other than our own. 'By the way, you do know that Ali gets twenty-five per cent of the net profits don't you?'

'I happen to know it's only ten per cent. But whatever you say is all right with me. You know something Shane; it's going to be an emptier place without having you around. I really hope she's worth it.'

I looked at him, possibly slightly wistfully for a moment, and then said, 'So do I Tubba, so do I.'

§§§§

It was one of those drizzling afternoons that the British Isles are so famous for as I walked back to the bar. It was strange walking in there and seeing nothing going on. I walked up the stairs to my office and sat down at the desk for a moment. I have to say I was feeling kind of wistful when I looked round for the last time. As I did, something caught my eye. It was Jenny's revolver, still on the side stand where she had put it down last night and after one thing or another we had both forgotten all about it. I picked it up, and flipped it open. I wasn't actually expecting it to be loaded, but it was, all six chambers, and as I flicked them out I realised they weren't blanks. It was

217

a chilling experience just looking at them. She had been prepared to shoot me when she came round last night. You don't carry around a loaded gun unless you're prepared to use it; right? I thought about it for a moment, flipped it back together, and dropped it into my pocket. Well if she had come loaded for bear, then perhaps I ought to too. At the very least I could return it to her. She might have use for it further down the line.

The documents I slipped into the inside pocket of my jacket, and turning slowly on my heel, muttering a slightly sad farewell to the place, I made my way down the back staircase and wandered off towards the docks.

I ambled into the departure lounge, certainly aware that there didn't appear to be even a minimal police presence about. Rhys appeared to have been as good as his word, at least until I entered the rather scruffy departure lounge itself. When I walked in, there was Rhys Evans, sitting in a chair facing the door.

'Oh there you are Shane,' he said. 'For a moment I was beginning to think you had stood me up.'

I looked at him for a moment, and asked lazily, why he thought I might do something stupid like that?

'You've got the documents?' he asked. I looked at him for a moment and then looked around the room. Well, I suppose this was the moment of truth. If it was all about those travel documents, then I was stuffed. I had to just hope that it really was Ryan he was after. I tapped my left breast, and he looked up at me. 'All safe and sound?'

'All safe and sound,' I replied.

He smiled and then asked, 'satisfy my curiosity. When we searched the place, we couldn't find those documents anywhere; where did you hide them?'

'In Ali's piano,' I replied.

'Serves me right for not being musical,' he said with a chuckle. He looked up at the door behind me, 'And here they are, bang on time.'

And there indeed they were. They both looked slightly alarmed by Evans's presence. 'You've got the documents?' Ryan asked.

'Sure have,' I replied.

'Good, just a moment, got one or two things to sort out' and he went to the small door with a drawing of a pair of trousers on the front.

Jenny pulled me aside, 'Shane, haven't you told him yet? He thinks I'm going with him.'

'Ssh,' I replied, 'I'll tell him just before the boat departs. That way he'll have less time to think about it. Trust me.'

'Mr Shane,' said Ryan coming out of the little boys' room, 'Can I say thank you so much for all your help.'

'Don't mention it.'

He pulled up his sleeve and displayed his wristy. It was quite a nice one actually, not one of those standard black plastic things, this one was stainless steel. 'Now I'll need your details,' he said.

'Save the money until you get to America, you'll need it over there.'

'Thank you very much,' He looked at Jenny as if he was trying to work out what was going on. 'Are you sure that's what you want?'

I put my hand inside my jacket, I said, 'Quite sure,' and pulled out the envelope, and passed it to him. He took it and looked at it. Suspiciously for a moment, and then put it in his own jacket.

It was at that moment that Rhys Evans said,

stentoriously, 'Andrew Ryan, you are under arrest, for the possession of stolen travel documents, and for the murder of the English courier who was carrying them.'

Ryan looked around first at Jenny, who edged slightly closer to me, and then at me with a look of utter loathing and contempt. 'What?' he said, 'You were both in this together?'

Rhys Evans walked towards him, holding out a pair of handcuffs. 'You're surprised at them?' he said drily, 'It appears that they thought about things in general and lust won.' He turned round and was about to thank me when he realised I was holding Jenny's revolver and it was pointing straight at him.

'Not so fast, Rhys,' I said. 'I don't think anybody's getting arrested for the moment.'

'What? Shane have you taken leave of your senses?'

'Probably, but this is the decision I have decided to take.'

'You do realise what this means for everybody don't you?'

'I imagine so, but in the meantime, those documents may not need any official stamp, but they still need validating by the police. So I'm asking you to do that. Right now.' I passed him a ballpoint from the top of the departure desk. He looked down at the gun and my hand, which was remarkably steady considering I'd never fired a gun in anger at anyone in my life.

'And what would you like me to put?'

'The names on those documents should be Mister and Mrs. Andrew Ryan.' I said.

'And that's what you want me to put?'

'That's what I want you to put.'

'And if I don't?'

'I shall put a bullet right through your heart.'

He started signing the documents, muttering, 'I can think of other places I might find more painful.' He passed the documents back to Ryan, and I called a baggage handler, and asked him to escort their bags to the boat. For a moment Ryan followed them while Evans still watched the gun I still had pointed at him.

'What?' That one came from Jenny. 'What about us? Last night we said..'

I interrupted her. 'Last night we said a great many things, not all of which were true. What is true is that right now we are sitting on a nasty little shit storm of an island that is drifting out into the middle of the Atlantic where it won't bother anybody, least of all, itself. On this island you will find corrupt officials and starving kids, and nothing else to recommend it either. Now that man,' I jerked a thumb at Ryan, 'may just have the answers to some of those problems.' While keeping a weather eye on Evans, I added, 'and that man loves you. You are the reason he gets up in the morning, and fights the battles he fights. I don't know how he does it, but I do know what might stop him, and I don't want to do that. So you're getting on that boat with him, because if you don't, you'll regret it soon, and maybe for the rest of your life.' I looked across at Rhys, 'Isn't that right Rhys?'

'I don't know,' he replied, 'it started getting soppy and I switched off.'

'Go and get that boat moving,' I said, waving him across to the communicator on the departures desk.

He picked up the rather old fashioned desk-communicator, 'Superintendent Rhys Evans here. Those travel documents in the name of Andrew Ryan are genuine, I repeat, genuine. Prepare for departure with the tide.' He looked at me, 'how was that?' he asked.

'That should do,' I replied.

'Andrew,' I said calling out to the man at the back of the room, trying to look inconspicuous. 'Just so as you know, Jenny was round my place last night.'

'I don't have to know this,' he said.

'No. But I'd just as soon you did. She tried everything to persuade me to give up those tickets. She even tried to persuade me she was still in love with me. Me, shitty little turd that I am. I might have even led her on a bit, but she was there batting for your team the whole time. I *am* still in love with her, and my request to you is that wherever you go, whatever you do, you look after that woman as if your life depends on it. It probably did here today, and it may yet do so again.' I offered him my hand.

'Look after yourself, Shane,' he replied, 'and welcome back to the war. This time I know which is going to be the winning side.'

He put his hand on Jenny's and steered her through the gate.

§§§§

They had hardly disappeared, when there was a loud squealing of brakes outside. Somebody was driving something other than an official pod. There was a crash through the waiting room door, and Colonel Willoughby stood in front of us, obviously fuming. When was he ever not fuming?

'What was the meaning of that?' he howled at Evans with breath that was in desperate need of assistance from a good mouthwash, which probably hadn't been available in Holyhead for a considerable period of time. 'Is Ryan on that boat going to Ireland? That must not be allowed to happen. Do something about it.'

Evans looked down at the pistol in my hand. 'I would,' he replied drily, 'but Shane has different views on the matter.

Willoughby looked down at the pistol and up to me. He walked over to the communicator on the desk. 'Hello, Is that the Captain?'

'Put it down.' I snapped, 'now.'

He looked at me, and then said into the mouthpiece, 'and you're preparing to sail on the tide?' He was drawing a pistol of his own from his webbing belt when I shot him. He looked surprised for a moment, dropped the communicator and collapsed on the floor.

The room was suddenly swarming with police.

Evans was suddenly everywhere directing traffic. 'Colonel Willoughby has just been shot,' he said. 'Round up the usual suspects.'

After a moment, he eased me through into the departure lounge. 'Come on mate,' he said, 'I really do think there are better places for you to be than here right now.'

'What do you mean?' I asked.

He put his hand into his pocket and drew out an envelope. 'I've got a couple of travel documents of my own here. I think that right now, you could really use one.' He paused. 'You know something? I'm getting pretty browned off with Holyhead too. right now; I've got all those winnings of our bet sitting in your wristy. Provided we live reasonably frugally for a while, I'm sure we can make ends meet. Why don't I come along with you for the ride?'

'Where are we going?'

'That boat is going to Dublin, and from there we can go anywhere. I'm told that Sydney can be quite a pleasant place to be at this time of the year, all that cricket and the Sydney opera house. They say there's going to be a really good cricket Tri-Series coming up. India and the Americans are going to tour Australia together.'

'You know something, watching India play the States in a Test Match would be superb. Have the Americans got that pair of Comanche quick bowlers touring with them?'

'Yes, and that mad Mohawk wicket keeper.'

'Getting better by the minute, this exile idea.'

We walked out into the drizzle and up the steps onto the ship. He waved his documents at the woman at the embarkation point, but she didn't take a lot of notice of them, just waving us to 'Go to deck six.'

'One thing,' he said, 'While we're on this boat, please give Jenny Laing a wide berth. I would hate to be a third wheel.'

'You know something, cobber,' I said. 'This may be the beginning of a beautiful relationship.'

THE END

CASABLANCA DIRECTED BY MICHAEL CURTIZ

Casablanca released in early 1943 has remained one of the most popular Hollywood films ever since. It was just one of many films made at the time, and while it was known that it had a reputable cast of good actors, and had a good crew behind it, it was not expected to do any more than entertain the masses until the next good film came along, probably within the next few weeks. In fact the makers were still faintly surprised that it was still in mind when the Oscars came along at the end of the year. They were even more surprised when it won three: Best Film, Best Director and Best Screenplay! But even those accolades don't explain its lasting popularity.

Its stars, Humphrey Bogart, Ingrid Bergman, Claude Rains, Conrad Veidt, Sydney Greenstreet, Peter Lorre, and Paul Henreid, were all popular journeyman in Hollywood at the time. Bogart, Lorre and Greenstreet were often seen in Warner Brothers films together, such as The Maltese Falcon, and Across the Pacific. They seemed to come as a package. Ingrid Bergman, a Swedish actress, was under contract to David O. Selznick, who swapped her with Warner Brothers who had Olivia de Havilland under contract, and Selznick wanted de Havilland for a picture of his own. William Wyler, the producer's first choice for director was unavailable, so Curtiz, an ex-Hungarian Jew, brought over to Hollywood as a cinematographer in the 1920s, and who spent the rest of the silent pictures period learning to speak English and making silent pictures, was selected as he wasn't doing anything in particular at the time, and with Curtiz came Claude Rains an English actor who played the Sheriff of Nottingham in Curtiz's The Adventures of Robin Hood. How Paul Henreid, an Austrian who came over in 1935, got the gig is lost in the mists of time, but he didn't get on with the rest of the cast, even Conrad Veidt, a well-known actor in Germany who escaped from the Nazis to Hollywood, and spent most of the rest of his film career playing Nazis. He wouldn't complain though, as he was the highest paid member of the cast.

The Screenplay was written in lumps by Howard Koch and the Epstein Brothers, all of whom had other [?bigger] projects they were working on at the time, and certainly when filming was started in May 1942, the script was unfinished. It was based on a play called *Everybody Comes to Rick's*, by Murray Burnett and Joan Alison. It hadn't been produced in a theatre anywhere, but it had got itself into Warner Brothers library, and Hal B. Wallis bought the rights to make the movie in 1942, The story went that according to Bergman, she was regularly asking which of the two men, Bogart or Henreid she was supposed to be in love with, she was told to play both men the same, as they weren't quite sure of the ending yet, and the original stage play was ambiguous too.

After its release it was a solid if unspectacular success. It made a profit, but at a little over a $1m cost to make, it didn't have to be an enormous hit to break even. However it became a conversation piece. There was a competition in the 1950s about the 100 most memorable lines from Hollywood Movies and Casablanca won it hands down over classics like Gone With The Wind and Citizen Kane, even after all the misquotes were cut out, like 'Play it *again* Sam' which never appeared in the picture. One of the favourite quotes was 'Here's looking at you kid' which apparently Bogart ad-libbed during a down-time card game with Bergman, and Koch who was also playing, liked it and wrote it in.

It never garners the Number 1 accolade in 'best picture of all time' lists, but in all of them it features. With its combination of wartime drama, romance, dry comedy, tension, and twists, it was probably the most generally complete picture of all, and it remains one of the most popular films ever with the man in the street. Nobody dislikes it, and if it appears on the TV, as it does often, it never gathers a 'not that old chestnut again' comment.

To describe the plot to someone who doesn't know the film would be a spoiler. Who doesn't know it anyway? It is available on Netflix or a Sky library near you. It is also available on DVD for next to nothing. Settle down and watch it. It's an hour and three quarters of sheer unadulterated pleasure.

The play, *Everyone Comes to Rick's*, has been performed in theatres occasionally since, without much success. They have talked about making a film sequel, but it never got off the ground. Someone tried to recirculate the screenplay around various production companies under the title of *Everyone Comes to Rick's* and changing Sam's name to Dooley. It was universally rejected, and only one or two people even recognised Casablanca in the script. One wag suggested that perhaps it would do better as a novel.

As a film it is living proof of the old adage that you can't create magic, it just requires all the different ingredients to crystallise and magic happens, and in

Casablanca it did so, spectacularly.

Incidentally it is my favourite picture too, from a very eclectic list, and when this idea was put to me, I couldn't resist it.

ABOUT THE AUTHOR

Richard Cartmel

Richard (Dick) Cartmel is a retired General Practitioner and lives in Peterborough, United Kingdom.

He has combined his love of fine wines, politics and human nature when writing a series of six novels.

A French police officer features in three - *The Inspector Truchaud Mystery* series - which takes him into the vineyards of Burgundy.

His well-reviewed book, *North Sea Rising*, envisages a post-Brexit Britain in 2039.

Dick Cartmel cleverly picks up this theme in his novella *The White House: Holyhead*. This is his first publication for City Fiction Limited.

Full details and contact can be found on:

Email   dick.cartmel@gmail.com
WWW   rmcartmelauthor.com
Twitter   @cartmelDr

NOVELLA FOUR

TIME OF DEATH

by

B. J. SANDIFORD

Inspired by the 1945 film 'Mildred Pierce'

TIME OF DEATH

The blade, large, sharp and ugly had dried blood on its edges. All the man had to do was to press deeply and draw the knife from left to right and Detective Constable Hudson would be decapitated, just like the other two victims. Moonlight glinted off another thinner blade as the second assailant sliced the buttons from the detective's suit jacket.

Detective Sergeant Laura Hollis sat in a grey van with blacked-out windows opposite Hudson, beads of sweat were covering her face. Speaking into a microphone she said, "Wilkins and Collins, move in." The command was aimed at the two plain clothed police loitering in the shadows, smoking cigarettes.

Hollis observed the two men crouched beside Hudson. The pair wearing suits, were indistinguishable from any other businessman who worked in the area. It was only the knives they held that gave a clue to the fact that their work was not conducted behind a desk. The plain clothed officers were not going to reach Hudson in time. Laura Hollis looked at the knives and switched her gaze back to the distance the officers had to cover. The officers needed to run if they were to save Hudson. It was the one thing that the two officers could not do. Should she jump out of the van and assist Hudson? What if her sudden movement made the assailants either attack Hudson or run off? Weeks of painstaking planning would be ruined, or her colleague would be dead. Which was the best option to choose?

A tall lean man walked along the pavement towards the small group. He was yet another suit wearing man, intent on reading a text on his phone, rather than watching where he was stepping. He appeared to be oblivious of the three men crouched together on the ground. As he moved forward, he tripped over the assailant holding the knife to Hudson's throat. The phone fell to the ground. In the act of bending to pick it up, the man hit the assailant's wrist. The knife was dropped. The man kicked it away.

The drunkard, Hudson sprang into action at the same moment. He kicked his other assailant in the groin. The man groaned, dropped his knife and clutched his groin. Both attackers reeled from the unexpected violence. Detective Sergeant Lee Hudson aimed a punch at the solar plexus of the man who had sliced off his buttons. Hudson's saviour, Detective Chief Inspector Chappell hauled the other knife man to his feet and placed cuffs on him.

The plain clothed officers grabbed the recipient of Hudson's vicious punch and held his arms behind his back as Detective Sergeant Laura Hollis handcuffed him. She had sprinted from the van the moment Chief Inspector Chappell had appeared. Never had she been so happy to see him. Both assailants were escorted to a waiting police vehicle by the plain clothed officers, as Chappell, Hollis and Hudson walked over to the van.

Hollis turned to Chappell, "Where did you come from, sir? I didn't think that you were going to be here. You said that you were going to leave it up to me."

Chappell gave a wry smile, "And I did. I was however, in the area. I thought I'd help out. I did say I'd be watching." The Detective Inspector noticed Laura's flushed expression and the slight tightening of her lips. "Laura, I am not raining on your parade. You set this up. This was your operation. Well done. It was a success. You deserve all the credit for going out on a limb and making it work. Hudson, you equally deserve the credit for being prepared to act as a would-be victim."

"Thank you, sir. Thank you." Hudson appreciated the praise from his senior officer. He nodded and smiled at Chappell.

Chappell spoke to the rest of the team through their earpieces by using a microphone attached to the van's dashboard. The officers heard the congratulatory voice of their boss, "Well done everyone. A job well done. Process them and rest up in the office. Well done, commendations all round. You've stuck with this one. Hudson almost took one for the team. Good work, I'm proud of you all."

Chappell exited the van and sauntered away. Hollis' brown eyes bore resentfully into the back of his retreating head. She repeated her question, this time to Hudson.

"What was he doing here?" She needed an answer. "This was my operation. I handled it."

Hudson shrugged, "Forgive me Hollis, if I say I was pretty glad he was around. Anyway, you know what he's like. Our Detective Chief Inspector Chappell likes to be in at the kill. You didn't expect him to stay away did you? Just remember he trusted you, he let you run this operation. You're new to this team, this was your first test. I'd say you passed it."

The ringing of the telephone broke Detective Chief Inspector Mike Chappell's concentration. He had been intent on writing up a report.

"Chappell."

"Chief Inspector, it's Officer Barnes. There's a man here... he says..." Officer Barnes' voice trailed off.

"Yes, what did he say?" Chappell became alert, "come on, what do you want to tell me?"

"Sir, he says that he was out jogging this morning and, well, he found the body of a woman. He's come in to report it. He says that she is floating in a lake on his land."

"Thank you Officer Barnes. I'll deal with it." Chappell replaced the receiver, sipped at the cold coffee that had sat for some time on his desk and grimaced. He sighed deeply as he got to his feet and stepped out of his office into the large team room.

"Everyone, I need your attention."

"A drowning has been reported. We need to investigate the circumstances."

Detective Dave Sampson spoke up, "But we've only just finished…"

"Yes, and now you are back on duty," Chappell said. "I'm going to the scene. I'll expect you all back here within the hour."

Tarn Lake was a neat rectangle. It was part of an old quarry that had since filled with water and wildlife. With the sun shining and no breeze to ripple the water the lake resembled a mirror. The branches of a weeping willow hung low almost kissing the water. A family of ducks had settled on a bank watching the activity happening opposite them.

When Chappell reached the lake, the body of a woman; Jennifer Lindsay, had already been pulled from the water. The man who reported the drowning, Frederick Southpool, had been able to supply the name and details of the dead woman. Southpool had recognised her as one of the employees in his computing firm.

Jennifer lay on her back. Her hair had been pushed away from her pale face. Her eyes were closed, and her skin had developed a green tinge. Her clothes were sodden and covered in mud and weeds.

In the midst of the activity on the bank, Hazel Wilks crouched beside the body, the frame of her glasses glinted in the bright sunlight.

"Mike, there is bruising around the throat, and the eyes show petechiae; evidence of strangulation. There is a large dent, actually a hole on the back of the skull. It is doubtful that she fell into the water accidently. I do not think that this is the primary crime scene."

The coroner stood up, pulling off her rubber gloves. Chappell nodded, resisting the temptation to ask for further information. It would not be supplied if he asked.

The coroner walked away, indicating to a nearby white suited officer that the body be taken to one of the nearby ambulances.

"Mike." Hazel called out, "One thing you might need to know right now, is that this woman has a black eye."

"Oh?"

"Yes, it was healing. You just need to know that she had a black eye for at least a week. I don't know if it gives you a start but, there you go." She shrugged and got into a waiting car.

Chappell walked to where the body had been found. The lake was on private land, but it was beside a local footpath. Even though there were several 'No Trespass' signs on posts beside the path, there were any number of people who regularly broke down the wire fences and had picnics or sunbathed on the grass bank.

It would appear that the dead woman had also been having a meal beside the lake. He looked down at the remains of the picnic. There were two empty bottles of wine, packets of sandwiches, small pies and sausage rolls. One fact that struck him immediately was the absence of any drinking glasses. He would be interested in the forensic evidence from the bottles. Had the young woman, Jennifer Lindsay, and her companion each drunk from their own bottle?

Chappell bent down and put a hand on the grass. Just as he suspected, the grass was damp. It was not the weather for an al fresco meal, so where was the ground covering? His initial impression of the scene was that it was staged. Where was the sharp instrument that caused the hole in her skull? There was no blood on the ground or on the bank. Where had the body come from, more importantly who had brought the woman to the lake? He looked up and viewed the large but narrow and deep expanse of water. Another set of warning signs explained the fact to trespassers foolhardy enough to want to go for a swim.

He stood up and looked at the trees and grasses bordering the lake on all sides. At the far end of the lake was a car park which belonged to a local pub. There were a few cars present in it. He made a note to have the grounds around the pub looked at by the forensic team. Heading back to his own car, Mike had the distinct feeling that he was being watched. He scanned the lake and its surroundings once more. Chappell's car was the only one left on the grass bank.

He looked at the trees, bushes and grasses on either side of his position. Everything was still. He stared at a clump of long grass and trees to his left. The feeling that he was being observed intensified. A movement caught his eye. A duck waddled out of the grass, into the water and set sail. Chappell breathed a sigh of relief. Just a duck. He had been so sure it was a person that had been watching him.

"Come."

Chappell put down the file he was reading and stared expectantly at his office door. His office was a neat square beige room with one window. He was fastidious about the organisation of his working space. The only personal memento in the room was the large framed photograph hanging on a wall. It showed Mike and two friends climbing the Matterhorn.

When it became clear that the person on the other side of the door was not going to respond to the single barked command, Chappell stood, rounded his desk and glanced at the picture. Just looking at the image brought back a rush of exhilaration and a jolt of adrenaline. He grinned to himself. Adrenaline and caffeine were two things he craved. Chappell was at the door in three long strides and opened it.

"Ah, you asked to see me Detective Chief Inspector?"

"Yes, I did. Come in Officer Barnes, Toby isn't it? Come in, sit down."

Officer Barnes walked in, swallowed visibly and sat down in one of the two visitor chairs Chappell indicated. "Did I do something wrong, sir? I mean I don't think..."

Chappell softened his normally severe expression. "No, not at all Officer Barnes. I just want to know about your impression of Mr Southpool. You were the first person he spoke to when he came to make his report. What was he like? What was his demeanour? "

"Well, it's funny you should ask."

"Why?"

"He was calm, very cold and controlled. I thought him to be..." Toby Barnes paused and then said "I can't think of the words. He was wrong. Something about him was wrong. Not normal." Barnes gesticulated randomly with his hands and shook his head.

"Chief Inspector, Mr Southpool did not panic. He seemed like he had all the time in the world. That struck me as not being right."

Chappell nodded and attempted to put the officer at his ease, "Let's look at it a different way. Describe the people you saw yesterday."

"Well, I came on duty at three in the afternoon. A few people were waiting, there were two tourists from America who thought they'd lost a passport. They were panicking. They hadn't, it was in the bottom of a bag of shopping. Then, there was someone who came in to report a car accident, a few other people wanted directions, and someone wanted to collect a form for something and then there was him, Southpool. I mean he came in, sat down and waited patiently to speak to me. He must have sat there for at least forty minutes, then he drops this bombshell. I mean, he hadn't made a fuss or pushed into the queue. He just waited patiently and announced that he'd found a dead body. Who does that?"

Chappell nodded thoughtfully. "Why did he come here?"

"He said that he'd been jogging when he saw the woman in the water. So, he ran back to his house, collected his car and drove over here. Why didn't he just ring the police? Just too controlled. If you ask me I think …"

Chappell stood up and said, "Thank you Officer Barnes you have been very helpful. I mustn't keep you." Chappell walked over to the door and held it open.

Chappell spoke to his team, "So to recap, we have the body of a woman found floating in a lake. The owner of the lake, Mr Frederick Southpool drives over here to inform us. As of yet we have no suspects." He looked around the incident room, noting the expressions of his assembled team. Preliminary investigations into the suspicious death of Jennifer Lindsay had begun.

Detective Sergeant Laura Hollis said, "Sir, do we really need to do this? We have a suspect; we know where to find him. Why drive over twenty minutes to a police station when you could just pick up a phone and ring? He's practically given us a confession."

Chappell raised the coffee cup he had been holding to his mouth, thought better of it and put the cup down on a table.

He replied, in a calm conversational tone, "Hollis, I am not aware that he confessed to anything. Mr Southpool is a civic minded man who came to the police station to report the death of a woman on his land. That's a report, not a confession. As to what he reported, let's have a look. What exactly did he say?"

Hollis' pale brown cheeks burned with embarrassment. The eyes of her colleagues were upon her. She knew that she needed to just shut up and listen but sometimes she spoke first and thought later.

Chappell had turned to a white noticeboard already covered by photographs of the drowning incident and photocopies of Mr Southpool's report. He summed up the situation, "Yesterday, Frederick Southpool reported the death of Jennifer Lindsay. The coroner, from her observation at the scene, tells me that death by drowning is highly unlikely, but she had yet to carry out the formal autopsy. Jennifer Lindsay's eyes showed evidence of strangulation. Why is Mr Southpool saying that he knows nothing about how this young woman ended up in the lake on his land? Did he strangle her? What was this young woman doing by the lake anyway? I want answers to these questions. I want to know if she was murdered and if so, who ended her life?"

The team turned back to their computers and began sifting through the information they had already found. Jennifer Lindsay was a twenty-four year old female. Southpool had been able to provide information about her address and place of work. Jennifer worked for Southpool Computing and lived in a shared house on the edge of Bristol. Her body had been found in Tarn Lake which was near the village of Forge Tarn.

The result of questioning the villagers had revealed that although Jennifer Lindsay did not live in the area she was known to spend a lot of time in the village pub. Southpool had told the police that he had given Jennifer permission to visit the lake whenever she wished. Her presence by the lake had not surprised him although her death had. No-one in the village could swear to the fact that they had seen Jennifer in the area over the last few days. She had not visited the pub, nor any of the local shops.

Chappell walked over to Hollis' desk, picked up and read the research she had so far collected. He said, "I want you to have look at that lake, see if you can spot anything that may have been missed."

When Hollis did not immediately speak, he looked at her expectantly, raising his eyebrows.

Hollis uttered, "What, me? On my own?"

Chappell nodded, "Yes. I don't think it needs two people. Besides which, I'd like your impression of the place."

"Well, I ..."

Chappell carried on, not allowing Hollis to speak, "You are pretty astute at picking up on atmosphere and identifying things that are out of place."

Hollis' response was one of genuine surprise, "You really think so?"

"Yes, yes I do. Besides you need to get more involved in the investigations. You've been here three months and you've only helped to plan one operation. It's time to see what you can do with this one.

"When you get back, I want both of us to visit the place where Jennifer Lindsay lived. We also need to visit Mr Southpool at his home."

Detective Constable Dave Sampson who was seated nearby interrupted Chappell, "Sorry to but in, but Mr Southpool is staying in the hotel down the road. He said that he had a few business meetings in town, and he didn't feel comfortable living in his house at this time. I've got his details here." Sampson proffered a sheet of paper which was covered in his distinctive scrawl.

"Thanks, Dave."

Chappell walked away. As soon as he was out of earshot, Sampson said, "No pressure Hollis. No pressure." He grinned at her, winked and returned his attention to his work.

Hollis gave him a tight smile, hung her head and allowed her long golden brown curly hair to hide her face. No pressure indeed. Chappell had asked her to take a hand in the last operation. No doubt this was another one of Chappell's tests. She reached out for her bottle of water and took a swig.

The surface of Tarn Lake reflected the overcast sky above it. Police warning tape billowed in the wind. Yellow incident signs had been placed by the area where the body had been found in the water and were dotted along the footpath. The cold breeze rippled the surface and ruffled her hair. Hollis shivered, whether it because of the temperature or because she was standing in a desolate crime scene she could not tell. She pulled her suit jacket around her slim frame and crossed her arms.

Hollis had studied the crime scene photos before arriving at the lake. The body had been found by one of the short sides of the lake. At the other end there was the car park behind the local pub. If she could see the pub and the few cars parked beside it, then the opposite was true. How was the body placed in the lake without the assailant being seen?

Could it have been done by using a boat? Hollis began to walk around the perimeter of the lake. From the photos she had seen a clump of bushes beside a tree. She headed towards it. Hollis missed it at first, but she stubbed her toe on a rusted mossy pole lying flat in the grass. She knelt to look at it. Connected to it was a chain that was fastened on its other end to an old rowing boat. It lay low in the water, weeds and slime were in the bottom. She inspected it and then looked at the chain that fastened it to the bank. "Why use a new chain to connect a rotting boat to the bank? This boat doesn't look like it is worth keeping." Hollis had a habit of speaking to herself. It allowed her to marshal her thoughts.

She looked at the boat again, picked up a long twig that lay on the ground and dipped it into the slime that coated the inside of the bottom of the boat. The twig went through the boat into the water beneath it. She looked around the area beside the boat. In the mud near the water's edge was a set of footprints and some ash from a cigarette. The ash looked fresh. She bent down to take photographs and took a sample of the ash. Standing up, she looked towards where her car was parked. If someone had stood in this position, they would have had a clear view of what the police had been doing when Jennifer Lindsay's body had been recovered. Had that person been the killer?

The drive back to the police station allowed Hollis to shape her ideas about the possible murder of Jennifer Lindsay. The fact that bothered her the most was the picnic. The way the picnic was laid out did not seem like a realistic thing to do. Was someone pointing the police in a particular direction? Why? The attacker would have been better served by not leaving any clues whatsoever. "Why?" She spoke the question out loud.

Hollis met with Chappell as soon as she returned

to the station. She told him of her uneasiness of the staged picnic.

Chappell said, "You have that feeling too? I sensed it when I was there. I wanted to know if you would pick up on it. I'm glad it wasn't just me."

Hollis smiled. "It was obvious if you think about it."

Chappell tilted his head, regarded her for a few seconds and asked, "If it was that obvious, why did the killer do it?"

Hollis opened and then closed her mouth. She shrugged, unhappy that she did not know the answer.

Chappell said, "When we know the answer to that, we will know the answer to everything. I think that the picnic is the key to us solving this murder."

Hollis had been the first to return to the incident room and the rest soon gathered bearing further information. Chappell sensed their nervous energy. His team were alert and had information. As always, he had ordered coffee and pastries from the canteen to be delivered. Once they had eaten, Chappell asked for the results of their research.

"Sampson you start."

Dave Sampson said, "Jennifer Lindsay, as we know is, or rather was, female, Caucasian and twenty-four years old. She was a computer whizz kid with a glittering future in front of her. She lived in a shared house with people she knew from school who were now studying at Bristol University or had just graduated. I interviewed her fellow housemates." He paused to look down at his notes, "none of the housemates had a bad thing to say about her. She kept herself to herself and mainly kept to her room. They said that you would never know if she was in unless you knocked on her door. I had a look at her room, it was tidy and clean. Everything was well ordered. Her pride and joy was her computing equipment. I've had that brought in so that it can be looked at. On the surface though she does not look like she has anything to hide.

"Everyone in the house knows each other from school or study but it appears that they have separate social lives."

Chappell nodding, looked around at the rest of the team and asked, "Does anyone have anything else to add?"

"Yes sir," Detective Sergeant Lee Hudson answered. "I've been trying to track down her social life. She didn't have much of one. She used to frequent the Mountlee Pub near Frederick Southpool's house, not recently though. We took a photo of Jennifer Lindsay from her room and took it to the village with us. The staff at the pub recognised her picture and said that she used to be in there at different times of the day. Sometimes on her own and sometimes with different people. Her companions seemed quite young; all they did was just have a few drinks and chat. She did not argue with any of them."

Chappell nodded. "Why the pub there? She lives in Bristol and the business is in Bristol. What would she be doing drinking close to her employer's home? There is still a lot we need to find out. One thing I am certain of is that Jennifer Lindsay did not accidentally drown. That's my personal opinion for now, we'll see when the pathology report comes in."

Chappell asked Sampson to set up meetings with the housemates. "I also think that we need to investigate the background of Mr Southpool a little more." He said. "That man interests me; I'm suspicious and surprised that he drove over here to report the death instead of using the nearest phone. That one fact in itself, stands out."

Jennifer Lindsay's lodgings were much as Chappell suspected the house would be. It was a red brick terraced house that had seen generations of tenants passing through its rooms. There was nothing to distinguish it from any house along that street. From the outside the house was clean and tidy. Hollis stood across the road from the house and took a few moments to look at the house. There were no twitching curtains or ghostly shadows hiding behind the windows. Crossing over the road, she joined Chappell as he knocked on the front door. After a few minutes the door was opened by a young expensively dressed woman clothed entirely in black.

The woman asked, "Yes, may I help you?"

Chappell's attention was caught by the pile of packing crates he saw in the hall behind her.

He asked, "Is someone moving out or in?"

A smile played around the woman's mouth, "My, my aren't you observant? You must be a policeman. I'm Elle Latimer." She held out a hand, "You are?"

Chappell looked directly at Elle, did not take her hand and said, "Sorry, I'm Detective Chief Inspector Chappell and this is Detective Sergeant Hollis. May we come in?"

"Certainly. I've been expecting you." Elle stood aside to let Chappell and Hollis enter. "I'm glad you were prompt; I have to go out soon."

Hollis who was slightly taller than average height for a woman at five feet and seven inches towered over the diminutive Elle Latimer.

The interior of the house matched the outside. It was equally well kept. As Hollis and Chappell walked deeper into the hallway, they had to navigate past even more boxes and crates. Elle led the way to a large communal lounge and sat down on a red velvet sofa. Chappell sat down on a chair opposite her while Hollis walked over to the picture window that dominated the far wall. As she did so she made a cursory inspection of the room.

"Now tell me, Detective Chief Inspector Chappell what is it that we can help you with? The other policeman came and told us about what had happened to poor Jennifer. I thought that it was an accident?"

"That is what we are investigating Ms Latimer."

"Is that so?" Elle Latimer looked Chappell directly in the eyes and smiled. Chappell did not return the smile. Instead, he narrowed his eyes and followed Hollis' movements around the room. He let a few seconds elapse before he spoke.

"Ms Latimer..", he said.

"Elle. Please do call me Elle."

Chappell cleared his throat, "Ms Latimer, please can you give us some background information about Jennifer Lindsay?"

Elle smiled and asked, "Background information such as what?"

Chappell did not smile back. He asked, "Were you friends? Did you socialise with each other? Do you know who her friends were?"

Elle still smiling said, "I see. In short, no. Jennifer and I had very little in common other than the fact that we shared a house and some mutual friends. Jennifer just wasn't my kind of person." Elle shrugged her thin shoulders and crossed her arms.

Chappell asked, "Who were your mutual friends? Is there anything you can tell us about her other friends?"

Elle said, "Everyone in this house. We either met at university or we knew of each other through people that we knew. Jennifer was a...Jennifer was gay. I'm not, so I really didn't associate too much with that circle of people. When she was at home she was quiet, but she wasn't at home that often. She spent a fair amount of time with her girlfriend, I seem to recall."

Chappell asked, "Can you tell us the name of Jennifer's girlfriend?"

Elle shook her head. "No. I didn't take the time to find out. I wasn't interested in Jennifer; who she saw or what she did. Peter or Jack might be able to help you."

"Do you know if she was at home over the last few days. We need to build up a picture of her last movements."

Elle frowned, thought about the question and then shook her head once again. She stared at Chappell, opened her mouth, closed it, then said, "Chief Inspector Chappell. That is such a mouthful. Don't you have something else I can call you by?"

"Chief Inspector is just fine. You were about to say?"

Elle pouted and replied, "I'm an architect and I've been working some long hours to finish a project. I've been travelling for the past few days. I only got back on Thursday, no sorry, Friday." She blushed and began to pluck at a loose thread on a nearby cushion. "The first I knew about anything was when the other policeman knocked on the door. I did not see Jennifer when I came back on Friday and I have not seen her since."

Elle stared at her feet, "Look, I wasn't keen on Jennifer, but I am sorry that she's dead." She stopped plucking at the cushion and held her hands in her lap.

Chappell asked, "Is there anyone she was particularly close to in this house?"

"She was close to Jack and Peter. Mind you she had a fight with Jack. Those boxes in the hall belong to him."

Chappell asked, "When you say fight, what was it about? Was it physical?"

Elle thought for a moment and said, "I'm not sure what it was about, but I did see Jennifer slap Jack and he punched her in return. He gave her a black eye. Jack is normally a gentle giant but, I've got to say, I think that she probably deserved it. She split up from her girlfriend recently and she had been totally unbearable to live with. Like I said, I barely had anything to do with her, but people were complaining about her all the time."

"Where can we find Jack? What's his surname?"

"Jack Danvers. He's in the process of moving out. Those are his boxes in the hall. I think his new address is on the board in the hallway too."

Chappell narrowed his eyes as he looked at Elle and asked "Elle, does Jack's moving out have anything to do with this fight with Jennifer? Was there anything else behind his moving out?"

"Possibly. I don't know for sure. I do know that Jennifer had really pissed him off about something and he had said that enough was enough. To be honest though, I suspect he probably just wanted to move closer to the hospital."

Chappell queried, "The hospital?"

Elle said, "Yes, Jack is a junior doctor. He works incredibly long hours and comes back at all hours of the day and night."

"So, at this stage is there nothing else you could tell us about Jennifer?"

Elle gave Chappell a flirtatious smile and said, "No, but if you give me your card I'll ring you if I remember anything."

Chappell attempted to look apologetic and lied, "I'm sorry I don't have any cards, but Detective Sergeant Hollis will give you one of hers. Please do not hesitate to ring if you remember anything. It could be important. We'll be upstairs looking at Ms Lindsay's room."

Chappell turned and headed for the stairs located to one side of the hallway. Hollis walked back from her position at the end of the room and handed a card to Elle Latimer. Elle took the card but did not take her eyes away from looking at Chappell.

Jennifer's room was exactly as it had been described. It was immaculate. The room was painted the same off-white as the rest of the rooms they had seen. The only colour in the room came from the turquoise duvet cover and bright green pillows. There were no clothes draped over chairs or on the bed; all were folded on shelves or hanging up in the wardrobe or on hooks on the back of the door.

Chappell and Hollis searched methodically looking for anything that would provide a clue to her character and why she had been killed.

Hollis muttered softly to herself.

Chappell looked over at her, "Did you say

something?"

"Yes," she replied. "I just wanted to know who Jennifer was."

Chappell looked around him, "That's what we are here to find out."

A door closed softly. Chappell heard footsteps walking along the pavement.

Hollis pointed to the collection of make-up organised in a number of small decorative baskets. "Jennifer Lindsay used a fair amount of make-up. Some of that stuff is really expensive. I should know, I use some of the same products. She took care of herself." Hollis carried on with her search.

There was a cork board on one wall, it was covered with receipts, tickets to gigs, concerts and a few shows, some of them bore dates for the coming few months. On the front of the wardrobe was a collage of photographs.

Hollis studied some of them and shouted "Bingo."

Chappell was startled by Hollis' shout. "What, what was that?"

"Jennifer Lindsay's girlfriend. Look at these." She pointed to the photographs; Jennifer had her arms around the same woman in a few of them. In others the same woman had her arms around Jennifer and in the last few Jennifer and the mystery woman were kissing. The pictures showed Jennifer Lindsay in happier times. Her blonde hair was cut into an asymmetric bob, short on one side and long on the other. Jennifer was grinning at the camera as she waved a bottle of beer in front of her.

Chappell said, "I wonder how recent these are." He pulled the photos from the board turned them over and checked for date stamps. There weren't any.

Chappell and Hollis searched through everything they could find; books, folders, drawers and the wardrobe looking for more photographs or anything else that could give them some idea of how Jennifer Lindsay had lived. There was no evidence of any hidden life or anything that she would not want anyone to see.

Chappell who was looking through a chest of drawers asked, "Hollis, what did you make of Ms Latimer?"

"She really did not care for Jennifer. Beyond that, I felt that she was hiding something."

"Why do you think that?" Chappell queried her as she crouched down to look under the bed.

"Elle Latimer said nothing to explain her movements over the last few days. I would have expected her to say what she had been doing."

"You expected her to volunteer the information? Some people don't Hollis. Remember you will need to be as objective as possible when you investigate. Do you think that you can do that?"

"Yes, certainly." She paused, "It's just that..." Hollis would have continued but a door slammed below. There was a heavy tread on the stairs. A face appeared at the open door of the bedroom.

"Who are you? What are you doing?" A young sandy haired, freckle faced man asked. His face and eyes were red as if he had been crying.

Chappell said, "I'm Detective Chief Inspector Chappell and this is Detective Sergeant Hollis. Who are you?"

"Oh, I see. Peter Riggs. I've come back to see you. I live here. Jennifer was my best friend. We went to school together. I can't.... can't..." Peter's face crumpled as he burst into tears.

Chappell reached out a hand and guided the boy to a chair. "No, I can't sit in here, let's go to my room." Chappell and Hollis followed him up a short flight of stairs to another landing. Peter opened the door of his room. The room was messy. There were piles of clothes and books on every surface. The small bin was overflowing with takeaway food containers. The room smelt of stale food and body odour. Chappell was tempted to open the window, but it had begun to rain, large raindrops were hammering against the glass.

Peter stopped sobbing long enough to say, "Sorry about the mess. Sit down." He pointed to two chairs, "I mean just shove some stuff on the floor and sit down."

Chappell and Hollis did as instructed while Peter sat on his bed. He wiped his eyes and runny nose on the arm of his grey sweatshirt. "Is there anything you can tell me? The policemen who came yesterday said it was an accidental drowning, but if you are here today that means that you are not sure, right?" Peter directed his question to Chappell.

Chappell replied, "We need to be sure."

Peter said, "She's dead and someone was with her. What do you need to be sure about?"

Chappell spoke with a calm patient tone, "Life is not always so clear cut. We need to know that we have come to the correct conclusion. To do that we need to gather as much evidence as possible. Her death may well have been accidental but then again it may not have been."

Peter hung his head; his sobbing subsided and instead became a series of hiccups. His shoulders rose and fell convulsively. "Is there anything I can help you with?"

"Yes, was Jennifer seeing anyone? Is there anyone in particular that she was dating?"

"Jennifer had been seeing Lisa Blaine." Peter paused, swallowed loudly and continued, "They broke up not that long ago."

Chappell said, "It was quite recent…"

Hollis interrupted Chappell and asked, "Do you know why?" It was not in her nature to be silent during an interview. Chappell turned his head sharply and looked at her.

Peter nodded and said, "Lisa cheated on her. It broke Jennifer's heart, it really did. She thought that Lisa was special, but Lisa didn't feel that way."

Hollis looked at Chappell. He waved his hand, motioning at her to continue with her questioning. She asked, "How long had they been together?"

"Three years, I think. It was definitely a while. Then Lisa started seeing someone else and didn't make a point of hiding her new relationship."

"What do you mean not hiding it?"

"Jennifer and I regularly went out for dinner. On this occasion we had gone to a local restaurant and there was Lisa with her new girlfriend. They were just leaving, holding hands and staring into each other's eyes. It was sickening."

Hollis asked, "What did Jennifer do?"

"She had a bit of a cry. Once she came to terms with what she'd seen she started looking for a new job. She said that there was no way that she was living in Bristol where she would be constantly bumping into Lisa and her new partner."

Chappell resumed his questioning, "Did she follow through with her plans?"

Peter nodded and replied, "Oh yes, she wrote out a new CV and applied for as many jobs as she could. She went to quite a few job interviews and collected quite a few offers for jobs. She was making up her mind when this happened. I know that she told her boss Frederick Whatshisname and he bit her head off."

Chappell's eyes narrowed. He watched Peter intently as he asked his next question, "Frederick Southpool. Do you have any idea what he said exactly?"

Peter's face began to crumple. He started crying. Chappell looked around the room while he waited for Peter to stop sobbing.

Eventually Peter said, "Jennifer said that he swore at her and called her all the names under the sun. She really hated that guy. She really liked Samuel though, he's the assistant."

Hollis asked, "What did she say about him?"

Peter sniffed, "She said that Samuel was the one who spoke sense in that business. Samuel really looked out for the employees while Southpool just thought the employees were robots. He expected them to work, never take holidays and hardly ever gave them pay rises. I think that she was working on some program for Southpool, something different to her normal job."

Chappell asked, "Do you know what it was?"

"No, he wanted her to work on it at his home. She borrowed Jack's motorbike to get there. Southpool lives way out in the back of beyond and Jennifer said that she needed to make sure she could get home. She certainly wasn't staying under his roof."

"When she said that, did you get the impression

that there was something between them or that Mr Southpool wanted there to be?" asked Hollis.

Peter thought for a moment. "I don't think so." Peter spoke slowly, voicing his thoughts as they came to him. "Jennifer is...I mean was..." Peter stopped and sniffed loudly. Hollis handed him a tissue from one of her pockets. "Thank you." Peter blew his nose and blinked back his tears. "Attractive. Men and women were attracted to her. Her preference is...I mean was girls. I don't know what Mr Southpool was after, but Jennifer was only interested in the project. She could be single minded like that. She believed in this project and that was the only thing on her mind."

Chappell asked, "Was the project successful? Were they developing what Mr Southpool wanted?"

Peter shrugged and said, "No idea. I'm a Psychology graduate. All I need to know about a computer is that it works when I turn it on. Jennifer seemed happy about the progress they had been making."

Hollis asked, "Peter, we've been trying to account for Jennifer's movements over the past few days. Is there anything you can tell us about that?"

Peter replied, "I...er...no, not really." Peter paused and got up. He walked over to the window and looked out over the street. The rain had stopped. He opened the window and took a gulp of fresh air, "I've been pretty busy myself. I just assumed that she was around." Peter sniffed loudly.

Hollis asked "Was there any reason for Jennifer to go to Forge Tarn Lake? Did she go on her own?"

Peter nodded, "Yes, she went all the time. She found it peaceful there."

Chappell asked, "How did she normally get

there?"

"By bus, there are two buses you need to get there and then you have to walk. Some of us from the house and our other friends went with her a few times. It was such a trek that we would go to the pub and pay for a taxi to come back. We felt sorry for her after she split up with Lisa, so we kept her company." Peter smiled fondly at the memory. "Jennifer said that she got some of her best ideas for her work when sitting by the lake."

Chappell asked "Who is we? We've spoken to Ms Latimer and she really did not care for Jennifer and I understand that Jack Danvers and Jennifer had a fight."

Peter said "Me, Jack and a few other people who still live around here. A big contingent of us came down to Bristol and we meet up from time to time. Jennifer was in a pretty bad way after her break up, so we tried to check in on her when time allowed."

Hollis asked, "Peter, would Elle know who Jennifer's girlfriend was?"

"Of course! Lisa Blaine is Elle's boss. Elle knew exactly what was going on with Jennifer."

Chappell and Hollis looked at each other. Chappell shook his head at Hollis.

Chappell got up and smiled sympathetically at Peter. "We'll be off now. I'll give you my card. If you think of anything, no matter how small just ring me."

Hollis and Chappell nodded their thanks and made their way down the stairs. She took down the details of Jack Danvers' new address, while Chappell left the house and walked over to the police car. The engine was running by the time Hollis reached the car a few seconds later.

"Sir, Elle Latimer just lied to us."

"Yes, she did, didn't she? What would you do about that?"

"Well, I'd go back in there and ask her. Sir, I don't know why we aren't talking to her right now."

"Because she left soon after we started searching Jennifer's room."

"We can't let her get away with lying to the police."

Chappell smiled, "I think she'll keep Hollis. What did you make of Peter Riggs?"

"Peter's answer about not knowing if Jennifer was home over the weekend seemed vague. Come to think of it he was pretty vague about his own movements. I just wish we could get some idea of why she was killed."

"Hey, you there. I think you've overcharged me." The man waved his hotel bill under the manager's nose and glared at him.

"No sir, I do not think so."

"Read it, go on read it. That charge there for £500. What's that for? There's a mistake on this bill. I want you to fix it."

The manager smiled pleasantly at the outraged man. "Please let me have the receipt." He raised his hand to take the paper.

The customer dropped the receipt onto the counter and jabbed a finger into the manager's chest. The manager did not react to the show of rudeness.

The customer said, "No-one and I mean no-one makes a fool out of me. So, you can take that charge you have just slipped on to my bill off."

The manager read the receipt carefully and looked at the hotel guest.

"Ah, yes, I see a mistake has been made. This hotel bill is for a Mr and Mrs Brown, whereas you sir, are Mr Henry Spires and the lady who has been keeping you company is Mrs Helen Ronson. Do you wish me to take further action with this payment? Who exactly is making this payment? Is it Mr Spires or Mr Brown? I see that this is a corporate card. I would have to ring and enquire how Mr and Mrs Brown happen to be using this card and staying at the hotel for a romantic break. Do you want me to investigate this issue further?"

The manager stared into Mr Spires's eyes and watching with detached interest as the guest's cheeks turned from a suffused red to bloodless white. Henry Spires began to tremble and looked about the hotel reception for an escape route.

Henry Spires said, "I...I...No, no that's fine. Take the payment."

The manager said, "Very good sir. I will process the bill as it stands. Have a very good day. Would you like the porter to carry your bags?"

"No, no that's ok." Henry Spires hurried away from the reception area.

If he had not been working, the manager would cheerfully have wrung Mr Henry Spires' neck. As it was, he retained his professional manner, smiled and waited to serve the next guest.

It did not take long to reach Jack Danvers' flat. Hollis had called ahead. Danvers had said that he would be in. He had taken a few days off work in order to move and sort out his new flat. It was not hard to identify him, for he was carrying a packing crate from a rental van and heading towards the address that they had been given. Jack Danvers was a well-built man who stood well over six feet tall. It was unusual for Chappell to meet someone who was as tall as himself.

"Mr Danvers?" he asked.

"Yes, who are you?" Danvers stopped in his tracks and stared at Hollis and Chappell.

Hollis spoke up, "Detective Sergeant Hollis and this is Detective Chief Inspector Chappell. We're hoping that you can answer some questions about Jennifer Lindsay for us Mr Danvers."

"So, has that stupid bitch decided to press charges? Let me tell you, she hit me first. I just retaliated. Why doesn't she do everyone a favour and end everything like she keeps saying?"

Hollis blushed and Chappell coughed gently. He cleared his throat and spoke, "No Mr Danvers, Jennifer Lindsay is not pressing charges. She is dead. We understand that you had an altercation with her last week which resulted in you punching her. May we come in?"

Danvers paled, nodded, kicked open his front door and led the way to a lounge filled with boxes, piles of books, potted plants and hi-fi equipment.

"Sit down, if you can find a space."

Hollis sat on a leather stool while Chappell decided to stand. Danvers put his box down and looked thoughtfully at the police officers.

"So, she's dead. I know what I just said sounds bad, but she really did provoke me."

Chappell nodded understandingly, "Why don't you explain."

"Jennifer was normally alright to get along with,

but after she split up with Lisa, her girlfriend, she became really moody and unpredictable. I used to let her borrow my motorbike. I'm a doctor so I really need it to get about. If I wasn't using it, of course I would let her borrow it. Then she started behaving really strangely, she started going out at all hours of the day and night on my bike. She had an accident. Oh, she paid to get the damage fixed but at that point I said enough was enough. I told her that I did not want her using my bike again, she agreed. The next thing I know she is riding my bloody bike, without my permission and I have to go to work. I had to take public transport to the hospital and a taxi back home when I'd finished. When I did get back she wasn't even home, and my bike was nowhere to be seen.

"When she finally got back I shouted at her. She screamed back something about guys bothering her and taking advantage and slapped me round the face. I just lost it and punched her. After that I made sure that I took my keys off her and the next morning started looking for somewhere else to live."

Hollis asked, "Mr Danvers, what did she mean about being bothered?"

"Look, all I know is that once or twice she complained about guys trying to pick her up when she was out socialising.

Jack looked around the room taking care not to look at the police officers. He sighed, "What I just said about her earlier, I'm sorry. Normally, she was fine but after she found out about Lisa cheating on her she just became really erratic. Speak to her one minute she'd be fine, the next minute she'd bite your head off. It was like she deliberately wanted to start a fight with someone, anyone. She was just so unreasonable."

Jack wrapped his arms around himself and asked, "Have you spoken to Peter yet?" Jack did not wait for an answer, but continued, "He's turned into one creepy guy. That's another reason for me moving out. The atmosphere in that place was getting to me. Elle, Jennifer and Peter were just starting to annoy me. To be honest I had decided to leave long ago but I just needed to get my act together. But anyway, Jennifer and Peter went to school together, then the same university but different subjects and then they ended up sharing a house. Peter is…was in love with Jennifer. He adored her."

Hollis interrupted, "But she was seeing someone else?"

"Yes, she was. This thing with Lisa really shook her up and affected her. Peter tried to support her as best he could for a while. He was a good friend to her and then … I don't know…" Jack shrugged and became lost in thought for a moment, "I don't know, maybe he realised that he did not stand a chance with Jennifer. He actively started to sabotage her."

Chappell frowned, "How do you mean?"

Jack said, "She'd ask him to do things for her, things he would have done before, but now he would say no or just not do them."

Chappell said, "I still don't understand."

"They used to do their shopping together or one would do it and the other would give the money for their bit. Now though, Peter wouldn't do her shopping. He'd say that he didn't have enough money, or he'd left his money behind at home. He would agree to pick her up from somewhere and not do it. He's got a small car and before he was happy to be her chauffeur. Now though, he wouldn't offer to give her a lift or anything. I remember a few weeks ago he was supposed to be meeting her by that lake in Forge Tarn. She had already headed out there and Peter told me that he couldn't be bothered to go. She used to go there all the time with her girlfriend. I think she was supposed to be meeting some new person there. Peter said that Jennifer would have to sort herself out. He said that he was fed up with acting like Jennifer's doormat and she could start wiping her feet on someone else.

"I mean, it was clear that Peter was in love with Jennifer and she never acknowledged him. He would go out of his way for her. When I needed my bike, he would go out of his way to collect her. Then his attitude changed. I guess if you have to listen to someone crying on your shoulder about how much they love someone else and how no one else will do, you will get fed up. I lived at the top of the house on the other side of Peter's room. There were times when Jennifer's door was open, and I would see Peter in Jennifer's room sitting on her bed or looking at her things."

Chappell asked, "Was Jennifer in the room?"

Jack shook his head, "No and that's what I mean by creepy. He was becoming a bit obsessive about her. I just thought it was high time I got out of there and after the fight with Jennifer and Peter's behaviour I just felt it was time to leave."

Chappell asked, "What were your movements over the last few days?"

"Oh, I'm a suspect am I?" Jack chuckled dryly. "Sorry didn't mean to laugh. Well I've been moving in here. Loads of colleagues either helped me to build my furniture or drink my beer. I don't think I've been on my own until just before you arrived."

"One last question; did Elle and Jennifer get on?"

Jack waved his hands in an unsure manner and said, "They did to begin with but then some guy that Elle was dating or working with, I'm not sure, started taking more of an interest in Jennifer. Elle didn't like it. Jennifer could be a real live wire and she got on with everyone. Elle just objected to the fact that Jennifer started flirting with this guy. Jennifer could be a real flirt at times. It didn't go down well with Elle at all."

Chappell nodded and raised his eyebrows encouragingly at Jack, willing him to expand his answer.

Jack obliged, "I mean take the week just gone, Tuesday I think it was. One of Elle's colleagues was at the house asking for some drawings that Elle had left behind. He was still there being entertained by Jennifer by the time Elle got back later that evening."

Hollis asked, "Are you sure it was Tuesday?" She checked the notes she had made on Elle Latimer's interview.

Jack replied, "Yes definitely. I had started my packing and the guy was there, so I put him to work. Elle was fuming. I'm amazed they didn't come to blows but then maybe Jennifer had learnt that if you slap people they might hit you back."

Hollis asked, "Do you know his name?"

Jack nodded, "Yeah, Andy something. He was a friendly enough guy. I just asked him to lift a few heavy things for me into the back of the van. Well, if that's all, I have to get on. I have to return the van this afternoon or I get charged a penalty fee."

Chappell turned to leave, "I hope you enjoy your new home Mr Danvers." He and Hollis left and made their way to the car.

"You drive Hollis, I need to think."

Chappell was silent throughout the drive. Hollis had parked in the car park of the police station when Chappell roused himself and said, "No, let's go to Southpool Computing. So far we are getting conflicting information. Elle knew who Jennifer's girlfriend was, Peter was obsessive and actively sabotaged Jennifer."

"Sir, do you think Jack was telling the truth?"

"It would appear so but I'm not taking anything at face value. Make sure you get the names of the people who helped Jack move into his flat. Right, let's go to Southpool Computing."

As Hollis drove Chappell said, "Hollis I want you to start asking more questions when we carry out interviews. Don't feel that you have to wait for me. You've been good, jumping in when paths need to be followed. I want you to do more of that."

Hollis nodded, "Yes sir, I will." She shifted in her seat, made a show of looking in her wing mirror and smiled.

Another victim, another complaint.

Miranda Holland screamed at the man, "You can't do that! I can't afford it. I don't have the money."

The blackmailer responded, "Would you rather I tell what I know?"

Miranda shook her head and said "No."

The man smiled at her and said in a calm conversational tone, "Then, you need to pay up. I'm not asking for much just £250, same as always."

Miranda wailed at him, "I can't keep paying you. I'm not made of money."

"Your husband is though." The man continued speaking in a pleasant tone, "Your husband clearly gives you a generous allowance. You just need to spend less on clothes, shoes and lovers."

Tears sprang to the woman's eyes, her hands trembled as she dug into her bag and produced a wad of notes.

Her blackmailer, threw his cigarette on the ground, viciously grinding it underfoot. Triumph glittered in his eyes as he took the cash. He took his time counting through the money slowly, rearranging some of the notes, so that the different denominations were together.

Miranda's voice was full of rage as she said, "It's all there."

Her blackmailer nodded and said, "Yes, it always is. I look forward to next month's payment."

"There won't be another payment." The woman thrust her face forward, that's the last payment you're getting from me. I don't know what I'll do but, I'm not paying you anymore. You've been warned."

The man chuckled, shoved the money into the back pocket of his jeans and walked away.

Southpool Computing was based in a business centre. The park was landscaped with well-kept green lawns and young saplings. All the office blocks were identical low glass fronted units. In the bright sunshine and blue sky, the buildings gave the appearance of mirrored cubes reflecting the grass and trees. Southpool Computing consisted of a set of these interconnected structures. A low sign set in the grass proclaimed the fact that you had reached Southpool Computing. Outside the main building the car park was filled with several expensive looking cars. It was full except for one space which was reserved for the Company President.

Chappell pointed to the empty space and said, "Since he's sitting in a hotel conducting his meetings, I think that you can park right there Hollis."

Hollis parked. Both police officers got out to walk the short distance to the entrance.

"You can't park there." A voice called out from an open window. It was hard to see through the window since it was mirrored.

"Police." Hollis called out. The window immediately closed.

The reception area had a large console where a receptionist and security guard sat. Behind them were two workmen who were taking down a 'Southpool Computing' sign. Dust floated down as it was moved causing the receptionist to cough. A door to the left of the reception opened and six people came in.

"End of an era", commented one person. Another said "Thank God! Hated the lying cheating bastard." Four of the people nodded at this last statement.

"What's going on here?" Chappell asked.

The second speaker answered, "The takeover, that's what's happening. The high and mighty Frederick Southpool gambled and lost. Who are you?"

"I'm Detective Chief Inspector Chappell and this is Detective Sergeant Hollis. I'd like to speak to the person in charge. Who is that?"

"That would be me." A deep bass voice came from behind Chappell, as a squat dark haired man walked through a doorway on the other side of the reception. He approached Chappell holding out his hand. "I am the Vice-President of Southpool Computing. I am Samuel Adesinsi. How may I help you?" He smiled at Hollis and waited for the police officers to reply.

Chappell shook Samuel's hand. "Is there somewhere a little more private that we can go?"

"Of course, follow me." Samuel retraced his steps with the police officers following him and made his way to a functional looking grey cube of an office. There was a window in one wall that let in little light due to the tree planted right outside the building. Samuel sat behind the imitation wooden desk and indicated that Chappell and Hollis sit in the two visitors' chairs arranged on the other side of it.

Chappell looked appraisingly at Samuel. The man was in his forties, wearing a blue shirt, navy tie and navy trousers. He had intelligent large brown eyes and a quick smile.

Samuel gave the police officers a warm smile and asked, "How can I help you? Is this anything to do with the fact that Fred hasn't come into work today?"

Chappell nodded, "Yes, very much so. Can I ask you for your impression of Frederick Southpool?"

Samuel asked, "Why, is he in some sort of trouble?" Chappell noted Samuel's evasion.

Hollis spoke up, "If you could just answer the question please."

Samuel smiled. There was a vindictive curl to his lips, he gave a short laugh which sounded more like a snort of disgust. "Frederick Southpool is probably the least likeable person you could ever hope to meet. He will offer you the world, anything to get you to do what he wants or to get what he wants. He will never keep his promises. To be honest I would not trust Frederick Southpool to tell me the time. The trouble is, he pays so well."

Hollis wrote in her notebook, "What is he like to work with?"

Samuel let out a sigh, "Dreadful. Frederick Southpool thinks that he is an inspired genius and that he is an inspirational leader. Working here is not easy. He believes that he could be the English Bill Gates or Steve Jobs. He cannot understand that those glory days have passed. Southpool Computing creates bespoke software packages for companies and Fred hates it. He loves the money but hates the fact that the company is just another small to medium sized business."

Hollis changed the direction of her questioning, "What's going on outside, in reception?"

Chappell was happy to let Hollis lead the interview while he sat and watched Samuel. It was clear that Samuel did not like his employer.

Samuel shifted in his chair and said, "Southpool Computing no longer exists in its present form. There has been a change of ownership. Fred Southpool sold shares in this business as a way of raising capital and he was unable to stop a takeover. The shares in this business have been snapped up. Fred Southpool has lost control of his company."

Hollis leant forward in her seat and asked, "When did he find out? How did he take it?"

Samuel gave a short laugh, "We found out last week, five days ago. How did he take it? He was livid. Crazy with anger. He couldn't believe it. It was like he couldn't believe that someone would dare to buy his company out from under him. He was in shock for a while and then just started throwing things around his office."

Hollis nodded and asked, "Does he normally lose his temper?"

Samuel shook his head, "No, no he doesn't. He is normally controlled, too controlled. I would call Frederick Southpool a cool character. You can tell that he is angry by the way he clenches his jaw or narrows his eyes at people. I call it cold fury. I've had enough meetings with him to know."

Chappell asked, "How come?"

Samuel turned to look at Chappell. He said, "Staff normally come to me with bad news and I seem to be the one to pass it on. There has been a lot of bad news recently. The takeover caused a lot of uncertainty and some of our main clients left us for other suppliers. Frederick tried hard to hang onto them. There has not been a good atmosphere over last few months.

Chappell commented, "Judging from what we heard outside, the staff seem happy with the takeover."

Samuel smiled, "The staff are very happy. Frederick Southpool is universally disliked by the staff at this company. He made staff work long hours and at weekends when he wanted them to. People were always one step away from being fired. Frederick reminded at least four people a day about their job contracts. He would make people cancel their holidays and then take off on holidays with his son, Robert at a moment's notice. Frederick trapped people with big salaries, some of the amounts are eye-wateringly big. Once you have that level of money coming in, it is hard to walk away."

Chappell asked, "What about you? Do you like him?"

Samuel Adesinsi raised his eyebrows, "I don't like him, but I got on with him. I am going to be the Managing Director of the new business. See that's another thing, Frederick called himself the President of the company. How can you be the president when you only have 150 staff? Delusions of grandeur. Let's just say I got on with Frederick, but his goal has always been making a fortune and spoiling his precious son."

Hollis asked, "What's Frederick Southpool like with women in general and the female staff at this business in particular?"

"He's very good looking but he just turns people off. The female staff don't like him. He has humiliated most of them at one time or another. I've been to a few conventions and exhibitions with him and yes, some women threw themselves at Frederick. He avoided them like the plague. I've only been aware of him having one or two girlfriends and they didn't stay with him for long. He is not very sympathetic. He is not comfortable showing any kind of emotion and he doesn't like spending money on people unless of course it's on his son."

Hollis was about to speak, Chappell interrupted her, "You've mentioned Frederick's Southpool's son three times now. Why?"

"Robert Southpool is, as the saying goes the apple of his father's eye. Another saying says that the apple doesn't fall far from the tree. Robert Southpool has been spoilt by his father. That young man can do no wrong. If he wants money, his father gives it to him.

Robert is trying to set up his own marketing business. His father expected all staff to work for Robert as well as doing their primary jobs. Honestly, neither the father nor son is well liked around here."

Hollis said, "What can you tell us about Jennifer Lindsay?"

"Ah, Jennifer, the beautiful Jennifer." Samuel gave them a beaming smile. "Jennifer is the future. She is definitely a world-class programmer. I am not exaggerating. When you see her work, it's not difficult to imagine her doing the same as Bill Gates and setting up her own business. She just possesses a kind of inspiration that I have not seen in anyone else. Her creativity and passion are, well, just amazing, absolutely amazing. I tell you she is like the Mozart of the computing world. She's a visionary. She came to us straight from university; Frederick was lucky to get her. I think that he must have promised her the moon, stars and the next universe to get her to come here. May I ask, why are you asking about her?"

Chappell coughed and answered, "Jennifer Lindsay was found drowned yesterday afternoon. She had gone out to the lake at Forge Tarn."

Silence filled the room. Samuel Adesinsi's mouth opened and closed, but no words came out. Chappell waited for Samuel to speak. Hollis observed Samuel. The smooth Mr Adesinsi had nothing to say. The veneer of sophistication vanished from Samuel's face. He started to look haggard and drained of all cheer.

At last when Samuel did speak it was to ask, "Is she really dead? I mean you don't, you haven't mixed up her identity with someone else?"

Hollis repeated the information. "No, sadly, Jennifer Lindsay is now deceased."

"But then this company is dead too. Without her, this company is not worth having." Samuel put his elbows on his desk, closed his eyes and held his head. "This company is screwed. I am the Managing Director of nothing, nothing at all. I was about to set up a special projects department and she was to be one of the leaders of it."

Hollis questioned him further. "Surely you must have other staff who are just as good? How can you run a business with just one good employee?"

"You don't understand. Were you not listening? We have good programmers, excellent ones even, but I'm talking Mozart, Michelangelo, Da Vinci. She is, or rather was, one of a kind. Had she lived long enough she would have become a household name and she would have taken this company with her." Samuel raised his head and shrugged.

Chappell and Hollis exchanged looks. Chappell used his head to motion towards the door. Samuel Adesini was being over-dramatic. People did behave strangely when faced with unwelcome and shocking information.

Chappell said, "We have to go now sir. We will come back in due course."

"Yes, but what was she doing out there? There was no reason for her to be. I would have thought that she didn't want to be there."

"Why do you ask?"

"Because, because he fired her last week." Samuel sat up straight and stared at Chappell, his previous theatricality was forgotten. "Jennifer was getting ready to leave and had two or three job offers. She went to Frederick, asked for more money and the option to pick and choose the projects that she worked on. Not

275

the best time to ask but she did anyway. He started shouting at her calling her a devious, underhanded backstabber. She was quite cheeky really. She didn't say anything while he was shouting at her and then she said, "So that's no then?" Frederick was so angry that he fired her on the spot. She just walked out, left all her stuff and walked out the door."

Hollis said, "If he fired her last week, how was it that she was going to be working for you?"

Samuel replied, "He fired her, I hired her. And now, well, that dream is over." Samuel shook his head. "I guess I'll have to start the search for another wonderkid. It will not be easy."

Hollis asked, "Would it have been possible for Southpool to have apologised to her and taken her out for a picnic to talk to her?"

Samuel shook his head, "I doubt it. I was there, at the meeting. It was ugly. Frederick's bad side came out. He used swear words that I'm not going to repeat, I didn't know that one person could fit so many swear words into one sentence. To paraphrase, he accused her of having no soul and no loyalty. That was rich coming from him. He could have been talking about himself. If you stand in his way or stand up to him, he will destroy you. There is no coming back. After what he said to her there was no way either one of them would go anywhere near each other. He was as mad as hell. Jennifer may have joked around but what he said to her to must have hurt. She was a kind soul. She would joke around but what he said to her that day was terrible."

Chappell raised an eyebrow, "How have you managed to survive working for him and stay on working for the new owners?"

Samuel grinned. "My role has included a lot of firefighting and keeping the peace. I am also the company accountant and I spent a lot of time telling him what we did have money for and what we didn't. Oh, there were arguments, but you can't argue with a lack of cash flow. Frederick cares about two things; the pursuit of riches and his precious son."

"You said that before."

"It's true. Frederick Southpool likes expensive things, the more expensive the better. One of the reasons that this company was in such a financial hole is because its owner used it as his personal piggy bank. I warned him so many times and still he took money out."

"Wasn't he committing criminal activity?" Hollis, who was keen to move into investigating white collar crime was interested.

Samuel shook his head, "No, Frederick was careful to stay on the right side of the law. That and the fact that I threatened him that I would report him if I thought he was embezzling from the company. What his love of money did, was to put pressure on the business. Every single contract mattered. Jennifer was the key to the business's success. She was not the only one, but she was able to come at a problem in a unique way. She was able to write programs that were so successful and efficient. Frederick wanted to work on a special project with her. He thought that it could put the company on the map after the share issue. That's probably another reason why he was so angry. She knew what his idea was for the new software. She could probably have written it herself and sold it. If it was as good as he kept saying it was, it would have made her a lot of money."

Chappell said, "And Mr Southpool couldn't have written this software himself?"

Samuel said, "Frederick Southpool just isn't that good. The bottom line is that he was, and always will be a computer salesman. His programming skills are basic. Even the most junior programmer in this business is streaks ahead of him."

Chappell changed his mind about leaving. "Samuel, was there anyone here who was close to Jennifer? I'd like to speak to them if possible."

Samuel pulled a face and said, "Let's see, there is Marie Clarke. She and Jennifer have worked together on a few projects. Let me take you to the boardroom which is bigger and then I'll get her for you."

Chappell and Hollis were led along a short corridor which ended in a set of double doors. The room beyond them was painted white with a wall of large windows. A long black table was placed in the middle of the room and was surrounded by black leather chairs.

"Please wait here. Sit down if you wish." Samuel indicated the chairs and turned to leave.

Chappell called out, "Samuel, please don't tell her about the nature of our visit."

Hollis sat down and wrote up her notes while Chappell prowled around the room. He looked at pictures of Frederick Southpool meeting local and national dignitaries. Southpool was a short man who wore tortoise shell framed spectacles. His brown hair was cut long and flopped over his brow.

Other pictures showed Southpool on holiday in various locations. He was dressed in scuba diving gear and accompanied by a younger version of himself. This had to be his son, Robert. In one photograph both of them were holding conch shells, in another they were holding harpoons. In a third picture they were displaying a large swordfish, one was at the tail and the other at the sword. Father and son were happy, tanned and smiling for the camera.

Chappell turned and sat at the head of the table, "Hollis, what we have here is a puzzle." Chappell played idly with a coin that was on the table. "Jennifer was fired and a few days later she is having a picnic on the land of the man who just fired her. Why? What is it that we do not yet know?"

"A lot sir." Hollis could have pulled her tongue out. Chappell shot her a look of disbelief. "Sorry sir, it's just that I'm reviewing my notes. I have more questions than answers. Everyone we speak to adds to my list of questions."

"I feel the same way. Was Jennifer murdered by someone she knew or a stranger? A stranger would not have taken the time to stage that picnic. Why stage it at all? I keep coming back to that."

Chappell would have said more but he was interrupted by a knock at the door. Hollis stood up, opened the door and admitted Marie Clarke.

Marie was probably not even five feet tall. She wore a faded black Star Wars t-shirt featuring Han Solo and Princess Leia, a short black denim skirt, ripped black tights and red Converse boots with purple laces. Marie's make up consisted of chalk white foundation, black kohl eyeliner, black lipstick and chipped black nail varnish.

Marie had a soft quiet voice, "Hello, Samuel said you wanted to see me. He said that you are police officers?"

"Please come in, take a seat. I'm Detective Chief

Inspector Chappell and this is Detective Sergeant Hollis." Chappell indicated the empty chair. Marie sat down and looked apprehensively at both the police officers.

Chappell began the questioning, "When we came in just now, I heard you call Frederick Southpool a lying, cheating bastard. You said that he had gambled and lost. Is that what you think has happened?"

"Hey, what's going on here?" Marie became agitated. "I just said that. I didn't mean anything by it. We all think that."

Chappell took the time to put Marie at her ease. He said, "Marie, we are not here to upset you but to carry out an investigation. Unfortunately, Jennifer Lindsay died yesterday."

"She what? She what?" Marie hung her head and started to rock in her chair. "No, no, she can't be dead. She's my friend. No, no, she just can't be. She just can't be." Marie paused, shaking her head as if she could refuse to accept what she had just been told. "And what was she doing with Mr Southpool? She hated him. He just fired her. No, it can't be." Marie started to cry.

Hollis spoke up. "Is there anything I can get you? A cup of tea, coffee?" Hollis handed a tissue. Marie blew her nose loudly and dried her eyes, smearing her black make up over her face.

Marie's voice was even quieter and more tremulous, "No, no thank you. It's just the shock. Sorry."

Chappell resumed. "There's absolutely no need to be sorry. I just wish that we were not the ones to break the news to you. I understand that you were good friends with Jennifer. I wonder if you could fill us in on her background and perhaps tell us why she may have been out with Mr Southpool."

Marie sniffed and dabbed at her eyes, "Why she was out with him, I have absolutely no idea. He fired her last week. The walls in this place are not the thickest so when she went to see him, we all heard about it. That man can swear I can tell you. If he said to me what he said to her you can bet, I'd just walk out and that is exactly what she did.

"In terms of working with her, she was a laugh. We all knew that she was way better than us at coding and software. She wasn't cocky about it though. If you had a problem, she would help you. She would help anyone. She got through her work far quicker than anyone else and she would just help people. She loved doing that." Marie paused, blinking back tears that threatened to fall. Hollis handed her some fresh tissues. Marie ignored the tissues and just let the tears fall. They traced grey rivulets on the black and white canvas of her face. The tears dripped unheeded from her cheeks onto her t-shirt.

Marie took a deep breath and continued in a soft low voice, "One thing I do know is, that Mr Southpool wanted her to work on some project with him. He wanted her to start it off and then the rest of us would have had to write some peripheral stuff. I know that she started working with him. He wanted her to come in at weekends and even go to his house. She wasn't keen on that, but she did want the project to succeed. That was until he fired her. After that she told him to stuff it and that the program was mainly hers anyway. He was ready to sue her for copyright, he told her that it was his intellectual property, she laughed and said how could he sue her for something

281

that was in her head and that she hadn't written down anywhere?"

"How do you know this?" asked Hollis.

Marie replied, "On the day he fired her, Jennifer just left. She rang me and asked that I clear her desk and bring everything over to her house. I did that. When I saw her later, she said that Mr Southpool had been on the phone to her several times. In the end she just blocked his number and refused to answer the phone to any number she didn't know."

Chappell asked, "Do you think that he could have apologised to her and she accepted it?"

Marie shook her head vehemently. With a slightly stronger voice she said, "Mr Southpool does not apologise to people. There was no way back after what he said to Jennifer. Let me give you an example of what Mr Southpool is like. He stopped Samuel from going to a funeral for his uncle. He was really close to his uncle. Mr Southpool said to Samuel that his uncle was dead already, so he really wouldn't miss him at the funeral. It wasn't like Samuel had any big meetings or anything major to do that day, Frederick Southpool was just being bloody minded and nasty as usual."

Chappell asked, "What did Samuel do?"

"He called in sick and took a week off." Marie continued, "He came back with a doctor's note so there was nothing Mr Southpool could do about it."

Chappell said, "I guess you're happy Samuel is taking over here at the business?"

Marie nodded, "Yes, we all are. Samuel is really fair. He's a nice man. If the new owners will just let us get on, I think this company could grow and become something major. We'll need to get a new chief programmer though."

Chappell smiled and asked, "You don't want to go for the job?"

Marie shut her eyes and screwed her face up.

Chappell apologised, "I'm sorry, in the circumstances I should not have said that." Marie's vulnerability and pain at her friend's death was hard to watch. Chappell berated himself for his misplaced comment.

Marie nodded. "It's OK. I would never have gone for the job I'm not good enough." Marie wrapped her arms around her waist and sobbed. Her body was wracked by emotion. "Jennifer was my dearest friend, I'm going to miss her. This hurts so much."

Chappell and Hollis took their leave of Marie and Samuel and went back to the police station. Chappell massaged his temples; a headache was beginning to make its presence felt. It was a sure sign that he needed some coffee and the problem of Jennifer Lindsay's death was becoming more complex. He sat in his office with a fresh cup of bitter coffee and a clean sheet of paper. He thought about Jennifer Lindsay's death and started making notes.

He needed the coroner's report, but his personal opinion was that the young woman had been killed. Jennifer had been found in shallow water, if she had been conscious or alive she would have been able to move. He also needed the location of the primary crime scene. Was Jennifer killed beside the lake or elsewhere? Why was she moved? Would the location help to find the killer?

Chappell reviewed the information collected from the interviews he had carried out that day. Jack Danvers had seemed to be truthful and keen to move on with his life. His comments about Peter and Elle worried Chappell. Peter Riggs had appeared to be nothing except an extremely concerned friend. If Danvers was correct Peter had turned into the exact opposite. Could Peter have attacked Jennifer? Perhaps sick of Jennifer taking advantage of him, Peter could have snapped and decided to be a little more forceful with Jennifer. Perhaps she had fought him off, they struggled she fell, hit her head and died. Peter could then have bought some food and staged the scene by the lake.

Chappell ran a hand over his face as if washing it. Elle Latimer had lied about not knowing Lisa Blaine. Elle had lied about when she had returned home. What was she trying to cover up? If she had returned on Tuesday instead of Friday, she may well have had an argument with the unpredictable Jennifer. Jennifer's flirtation with Elle's colleague may not have gone down well, especially if Jennifer had done the same thing with a previous acquaintance of Elle's. Had Elle lied about the day she had returned home to cover for something Peter had done or to distance herself from something Peter had done? He looked at the notes he had made and added the name of Lisa Blaine. He wanted to interview the ex-girlfriend and find out just exactly why she had left Jennifer.

Leaving his office Chappell called over to Hollis, "I'd like to see Lisa Blaine. Do you have her details?" Hollis who had been chatting with Detective Lee Hudson at his desk returned to her own and picked up a sheet bearing the woman's details.

"Let's go Hollis. You can ring Ms Blaine on the way and tell her to expect us."

Chappell ran down the stairs, Hudson remarked,

"It looks like action man is on to something, you'd better go."

Hollis nodded and ran after Chappell. The car was started and pointing out the police station car park by the time Hollis reached it. She gave Chappell the address and rang Lisa Blaine.

The door opened, "What are you doing in my room?" The hotel guest Rick Seers asked.

The duty manager said, "I'm sorry sir, I was just checking that your room was cleaned to our highest standard. We carry out spot checks just to make sure that guests have no complaints. I also came to place these in your room." The duty manager showed Mr Seers the small box of chocolates he was holding and placed them on the bedside table. The manager moved in such a way that his leg closed the drawer of the table he had been rifling through.

"Oh, ok thanks. Yes, you do have high standards in this hotel. I always enjoy staying here. Funny how I've never met one of you inspectors before though."

"We pride ourselves on not intruding on our guests. I try to do this when the hotel is quiet. I'll let myself out."

The duty manager was disappointed. A search of the room proved that Mr Seers was everything that he claimed to be; a businessman attending a conference where he was giving a few training sessions. No matter, there were a few other guests who would prove to be excellent targets. Henry Spires and Miranda Holland had added to his nest egg.

Lisa Blaine lived in a quiet cobbled street. Her home was in a converted warehouse which housed six large apartments.

"This is an expensive part of town." Hollis looked around and back at the building where Lisa Blaine lived. "What on earth did Lisa and Jennifer have in common?"

Chappell walked up to the entry door, pushed a button, explained who he was and waited for the door to be opened. Chappell and Hollis took the lift to the third floor and walked along until they were met by a smiling woman, dressed in a navy blue suit with short bobbed hair.

"You're the police? I'm Lisa's sister, Louise. Don't ask, everyone in our family has a name beginning with an 'L'. Do come in Lisa will be along shortly."

The apartment was cavernous. There was no hall way, one simply entered into a large open plan space. Along one wall was a staircase which connected to a mezzanine floor. On the ground floor were a kitchen, dining area and a space with sofas and two high backed chairs. On the other side of the kitchen was a door which Louise explained led to a small bathroom and second bedroom. Chappell went off to use the bathroom and left Louise Blaine explaining the design features of the apartment to Hollis.

Chappell returned just in time to hear Louise explain that Lisa was an architect who worked in the same practice as Elle Latimer.

Hollis said, "I bet that could be awkward with Jennifer living in the same house as Elle."

Louise replied, "I don't really know. I don't live here. I only drop in when I have meetings in the area."

Chappell asked, "What do you do?"

"I'm a project manager. If I've work up in this part

of the world I stay with my accommodating baby sister."

Louise directed the police officers to sit down whilst they waited for Lisa. Chappell and Hollis did not have to wait long before Lisa Blaine returned home. The resemblance between the sisters was striking. They could have been twins. Lisa was dressed in a chunky cream coloured jumper which was tucked into a brown skirt covered with a flower design. She finished the look with a pair of high heeled brown suede boots. She had the same bobbed hair cut as her sister. The haircut accented the sharp cheekbones that both women possessed.

Louise laughed easily as she saw the looks of confusion on the police officers' faces. "No, we are not twins, there is three years between us."

Louise turned to her sister, "Are you going to be alright? Do you want me to stay?"

"No Louise, you go. You've got to catch your train. I'll ring you later."

Louise Blaine nodded to Hollis and Chappell picked up her bag and coat that had been draped over a chair and left the flat.

Lisa turned to the police officers, "Would you like some tea or coffee."

"Coffee would be just fine," Chappell volunteered.

"Some tea for me please," Hollis replied.

Lisa busied herself filling the two requests, "Can you tell me why you have come to see me?"

Chappell spoke up, "I understand that you recently split up with Jennifer Lindsay. I wanted to ask you about that and about your movements in the past few days."

Lisa called out to Hollis, "Do you take milk and

sugar in your tea?"

"Just milk, no sugar." Lisa finished making the drink and handed a mug to Hollis.

"And you, Detective Chief Inspector, how do you take your coffee?"

"No sugar and just a dash of milk."

"Good man, that's how I drink it myself."

Lisa handed Chappell his drink. He sipped it, "This is good." He took another sip, "This is really good. You'll have to tell which beans you use. I'm impressed."

Lisa smiled, "I certainly will. As to your questions, I'll answer the easiest one first. I've been in Denmark for the past few days. I got back yesterday. If you need any proof my airline ticket is on the table." She sorted through a pile of papers on her dining table and gave her boarding card stub to Chappell. He looked at it and smiled. Lisa sat down.

Hollis asked, "Did Elle Latimer travel with you?"

"No, she should have been here in town at the office. She shouldn't have been travelling anywhere. She's had a few meetings with clients and contractors but nothing that would have required her to stay away from home on business matters.

"Now, I guess you want to know about Jennifer and myself." Lisa sighed deeply and took a gulp of her coffee. "What can I say, it was a mistake. I fell for Jennifer and she fell for me. I spent the last few months trying to extricate myself from the relationship and I told her quite a few times that everything was over, but she would not take no for an answer. I know that Peter, if you ask him will say that he and Jennifer caught me sneaking about having dinner with someone else. The thing is I wasn't sneaking or cheating or doing anything underhand. I had told Jennifer that things were over and that I had moved on. She just didn't believe me."

Chappell asked, "What did she do when she saw you together?"

Lisa spoke with a sad resigned tone, "At first, she walked out of the restaurant and then rang me to rant and swear at me. After that she bombarded me with text messages all accusing me of cheating on her. When she calmed down she sent me pleading messages and left voice mails asking to meet up and just have one last meeting."

Chappell asked, "Did you meet her?"

Lisa nodded, "Yes, out by the lake at Forge Tarn. She had a really ugly black eye. I asked her about how she got it. She mistook my concern for her injury and assumed that I wanted to get back together with her. I just had to walk away from her. I feel so sorry. I walked away from her and I understand that she was found drowned in the lake. The trouble is Jennifer could be so clingy and insecure. I was fed up of having to be the strong one."

Chappell asked, "Was that the last time that you saw or heard from her?

Lisa nodded, "The last time I saw her definitely, I had a few more text messages from her."

Chappell moved the questioning onto a different topic, "How did Jennifer's behaviour affect your new relationship?"

Lisa raised her eyebrows and said, "It hasn't. Or perhaps I should say that I decided that I ought to take some time for myself, so I called things off and I'm enjoying the single life right now."

Chappell asked, "You seem so much older than

Jennifer, how did the two of you get together in the first place?"

Lisa shrugged, "I have no idea. Truly, it's something that I have thought long and hard about over the past few months. I think that we had something that should have remained as a quick fling. It turned into something else and Jennifer put far more effort into the relationship than I was prepared to do."

Hollis asked, "Did the relationship cause friction between you and Elle Latimer?"

Lisa shook her head, "I shouldn't have thought so. I'm Elle's boss. I think for a while she thought that Jennifer was going to tell me everything that she got up to. Jennifer didn't and I didn't ask Jennifer about Elle either."

Chappell said, "Well, thank you. Great coffee."

Lisa stood up, grabbed a pen and wrote something down on a sheet of paper. She gave it to Chappell. "That's the name of the coffee and where you can buy it. Not many places sell it I'm afraid."

The sun set, colouring the sky muted shades of red and purple. Chappell and Hollis were soon back at the squat red brick police station. It provided Chappell with a sense of solidity in this otherwise confusing case. His headache was back, almost blinding him with its intensity. He was thankful for the dull uninspiring décor of the police station. The municipal greys and browns relaxed him even if normally, he wondered why more cheerful colours could not be used.

The police team tucked into the pizzas Chappell had provided for them. The team, like Chappell, were feeling stumped.

"Everyone, I think that you should take a break, go to the gym or get some sleep or do both." Chappell paused, "Of course, I do need a volunteer to stay behind and cover the office."

Chappell looked around, making eye contact with each team member. "No volunteers? I'll have to pick someone, you know that, right?"

"I'll do it." Hollis spoke up. "I'll do it."

Lee Hudson shouted out, "Well done Hollis."

After her colleagues left, Hollis sent a message to her boyfriend cancelling yet another date. She then walked over to the whiteboard and stared at the photographs and reports that had been pinned up. She looked at the timeline that started with the reporting of the death and ended with their current interviews and investigations. She unpinned a large photograph of Jennifer. She spoke aloud.

"Who are you? What happened to you? Why did someone kill you?"

Taking his own advice, Mike Chappell had visited the gym and had gone home. He too spent the evening reviewing the information collected so far on the death of Jennifer Lindsay. Something dark lay at the heart of Jennifer Lindsay's death, he had no evidence for this, and it frustrated him. He just needed one loose thread to pull and thereby unravel the case.

He read the pathology report. It indicated that Jennifer had been strangled and she was dead before she went into the water. The time of death could not be specified but it had probably taken place within a six hour window. There was no water in her lungs. There was also no food in her stomach apart from the remains of a partially digested croissant. Jennifer had not engaged in any consensual sexual activity neither had she been the subject of a sexual attack. Perhaps the most important point was that Jennifer Lindsay had no alcohol in her system.

It was murder. Jennifer Lindsay was now the victim of murder. The team would need to investigate deeper into the people who had been questioned. They would also have to question people who had been tangential to the investigation. What was Jennifer's relationship with Frederick Southpool? Who else had Jennifer angered over the past few weeks?

The photos of Jennifer revealed nothing surprising. Apart from the ugly bruises around her neck, she bore no other wounds or marks. Jennifer had been dressed in a purple sweatshirt and black jeans. She had worn black boots with flat heels and large buckles on the ankles. Her other personal effects included her telephone and purse. These had been jammed into the back pockets of her jeans and had therefore remained in place when thrown into the water. The phone was water logged and unusable. A request had been put in for the phone records, but they had yet to arrive.

Chappell reviewed the rest of the photos especially the ones of the food laid out on the bank of the lake, resting on a plastic bag. There was a packet of six sausage rolls, there were six sausage rolls evident. Another packet contained four pork and cranberry pies, there were two pies lying on the grass on top of a slip of paper. He studied the food packets and the label on the wine bottle. All of the food came from a well-known supermarket. Chappell recalled that there was a branch not too far from the lake.

It was nearly midnight. Chappell headed for his bed but not to sleep. From experience, he knew that he would not rest properly until the case was solved.

At midnight Hollis was still at her desk focusing on Jennifer's murder. Her phone buzzed yet again. A text message flashed up. It was from Simon, her boyfriend. He had sent five messages telling her how angry he was that she kept cancelling on him. Laura had not replied to a single one. This last message, the sixth was to tell her that he was finishing with her. To this message she replied, "Fine. Goodbye. Have a nice life."

Nothing in her life meant more to her than her job. She enjoyed looking for evidence, making connections and catching suspects. No relationship brought her that much of a thrill. Simon was better off without her.

Chappell strode into his office with his obligatory cup of coffee in hand. He set about finding the answers to his questions. He read over the initial report that Frederick Southpool had made and compared it with the information given to him by Officer Barnes. Frederick Southpool had not started to give his report until 3.40 pm. Why did he wait so long? The information from Samuel Adesinsi was quite damming about Southpool's character. Frederick Southpool was definitely a line of investigation that needed to be followed up. There were quite a few questions that needed to be asked of that man. Chappell also wanted to get to the bottom of the evasiveness shown by Elle Latimer and Peter Riggs.

Hollis walked into the Chappell's office with a

sheaf of papers, "The IT guys have started work on Jennifer Lindsay's computer. Apparently they agree that she is a genius. They couldn't make much sense of some of the programs that she was writing but looking at all the other information on her hard drive she seemed to have normal preoccupations. It looks like she looked up shopping sites, emailed a few people and had been working on find a new job. She does not appear to have wanted to blackmail anyone nor was she keeping any secret information."

"Take a seat Hollis. Let's discuss this case. I take it you spent some time reviewing the notes last night?"

Hollis sat down, "Yes. I did."

Chappell asked, "So why was she killed Hollis? Is this an accidental death and if so why not just leave her where she died? Who would move the body, place it in the water where it was bound to be found and then stage that picnic?"

"For my money, I'd say it was Peter Riggs. One minute he's acting like some lovesick fool and the next he's practically abandoning her, leaving her to make her own way home. What if he told her how he felt about her, and she just laughs in his face? He snaps, grabs her and strangles her. Now she's dead he bundles her into his car drives over to the lake and dumps her body."

"But Hollis, we've already established that dumping the body would be difficult. There were no tyre tracks there before the forensic team arrived. Peter would have needed to have parked in the car park at the other end of the lake and carried the body to where it was found. There was only one rowing boat and that was chained up."

"It could have floated over to the other side."

Hollis knew her point was weak, but she felt that Peter Riggs was responsible for the death. She continued her argument, "So alright, I don't know why someone apart from Peter would care enough to make out that she was having a picnic? Jack's moved out and has several witnesses as to his whereabouts. That leaves Elle. She could have killed Jennifer and moved the body, but I think it highly unlikely. In either case, if they were going to commit a murder I don't see them setting the scene so meticulously."

Chappell nodded and said, "It's this scene setting that we keep coming back to." Chappell held his hand out for the documents Hollis was holding. "Find out where the architectural practice is. I am not happy that Elle Latimer lied to us. I think we will pay her a visit and speak to her colleague Andy at the same time. First though, I think we should see Mr Southpool."

The bar of the Twelve Kings Hotel was the same as could be found in many mid-priced hotels. There were a lot of tinted mirrors and spotlights. The tables were of brown flecked glass accompanied by chairs covered in rough brown fabric. The few windows that there were looked out over the hotel's carpark. The bar was empty except for the Frederick Southpool and the duty manager who was currently doubling up as the barman.

Frederick Southpool was talking with a young man when Chappell and Hollis arrived. As soon as he noticed the police officers Southpool patted the young man on the back and they parted company. Southpool walked towards the police officers whilst the young man headed towards an exit at the rear of the bar leading to the carpark. He was wearing what seemed to be his normal attire; black top and jeans.

Southpool's manner was calm and polite. He made no mention of the man with whom he had been speaking. Before reaching the exit, the young man glanced around. Hollis caught a brief look at him in one of the many mirrors. The young man resembled Southpool so, it was probably his son.

Southpool said, "You are Detective Chief Inspector Chappell and Detective Sergeant Hollis? I've been expecting you. Is there anything I can get you? Tea, coffee, anything?"

"Was that your son, who just left, Mr Southpool?"

"Yes, yes it is." Southpool turned around and looked at the far exit through which his son had left. A faint smile on his face.

Chappell said, "Mr Southpool, I'll have a coffee, but we will have to pay for our own drinks. Thank you all the same." Southpool crossed to the bar counter and placed the order and returned to sit down.

He assessed Frederick Southpool. There was nothing about the man before him that bore any similarity to the man described to them back at Southpool Computing. Once the beverages were on the table, Chappell began his questioning.

Chappell started with the question that had been troubling him the most. "Mr Southpool, I have to say I am struck by the fact that you found a body in a lake on your land and drove all the way over here to tell us. Why did you not ring?"

Southpool raised his hands palms up, "My mobile was flat, completely out of juice. I put myself through a punishing running schedule, I did ten miles on

Sunday morning. The only thing that kept me going was the playlist on my phone. I had my earphones in and off I went."

Chappell continued his questioning, "I can understand that, I'm exactly like that but why didn't you ring from your house phone. You ran home why not go and use your landline?"

Southpool shrugged, "I don't know. I think I was on automatic. I just kept thinking I must tell the police; I must tell the police. I know that your police station is the largest in the area, so I just drove over here."

"And then you sat down and waited your turn. Why not just go up to the desk and announce your problem?"

Southpool looked from Chappell to Hollis and back to Chappell. He said, "I've thought about all of this. I really don't know. I had just seen a dead body. A dead body in a lake near my home. I mean that is the place that I live. I think that I was just trying to process all of that and the fact that it was someone I knew. I just knew it had to be Jennifer. I was thinking about that focusing on only that."

Hollis said, "I was going to ask you about that. We understand that you fired her and then tried to get her to come back. When that didn't work you threatened her with a lawsuit. Could you tell us about that?"

"Wow, you have been doing your digging."

Chappell frowned at Southpool and said, "This is a murder inquiry Mr Southpool, we will investigate, and we will do so thoroughly. So, please tell us."

"You probably know by now that I have been ousted from the company that I set up." Chappell nodded. "I can't say that my temperament was at its best over the last few months. I look back now and I realise that I must have been a monster to work with. Well Jennifer was toying with the idea of leaving and asked me for a raise. The business didn't have any money. I was actively searching for more capital. When she asked for more money I just told her to leave." Southpool gave a rueful smile, "I admit that my language was not the best and I probably used every swear word I knew but I couldn't believe that she was ready to jump ship.

"Anyway, she walked out. When I realised what I had done I tried to apologise and get her to come back. She didn't want to have anything to do with me. I'm not surprised really but I just wanted to say sorry. As for the lawsuit, we were working on a project developing a new program that would have been revolutionary. I will admit that her programming skills are far better than mine and that is why I had her working on it. The trouble is the program was mostly in her head and you can't sue a person for what is contained within their brain and not written down anywhere. So, at the moment I'm here trying to drum up some capital to start a new business. I'll have to hire some new staff and see if I can't get my idea off the ground."

Chappell nodded, he said, "Why was your son visiting you here?"

Both Chappell and Hollis had been watching Southpool intently throughout the interview. They saw annoyance race across Southpool's face just before he cleared his throat and swallowed.

Southpool said, "He came to see how I was."

Keeping to a conversational tone, Hollis asked, "What does he do?"

Southpool smiled again. The smile did not reach his eyes. He said, "Oh, he works in marketing, he has a small agency. He has done some work for me in the past and now I want him to join me with my new venture." Southpool shifted in his seat and cleared his throat.

Chappell nodded, and said, "What was Jennifer doing on your land?"

The abrupt changes in questioning left Southpool confused. He stammered his answer, "I.. I let her. She loved the pub and the lake. She said that she found it really peaceful out by the lake and that she got some of her best ideas just sitting by the water. I'm all for good ideas and if sitting beside a lake was all it took to get the program I wanted out of her, so much the better."

Hollis asked, "Why do you think she still continued to do so even after you fired her?"

Southpool gave another of his practiced smiles, looked Hollis full in the face and said, "My secret hope is that she was working on the program and that she would have come back to talk to me when it needed to be run in a lab. I hoped that I had piqued her interest. It's all well and good having an idea and running it on one computer but she would have needed access to more facilities in order to test it and to debug it. That was my hope. Now I'll never know."

Chappell sat back in his chair and looked at Frederick Southpool. The policeman was quite open about his observation. Hollis remained silent.

Needing to fill the silence, Southpool said, "Is there anything else?"

Chappell asked, "Did your son ever have anything to do with Jennifer Lindsay?"

Southpool's cheeks flushed. "No, I mean yes. I mean he didn't have that much to do with her, but he did stop by the office every so often to see me. There were a few times when Jennifer and I were working at my home and he'd be there, but I think that that was all. Are you suggesting that Robert could be involved? I mean really you can't believe that..."

With another change of direction, Chappell asked "Is there anything you can tell us that you think might be relevant to this investigation?"

Southpool regained his composure and replied, "No sorry I don't think so. Believe me, I have been thinking. At the end of the day, one of my ex-employees is found by me in a lake on my land. I know that it doesn't look good for me, but I had absolutely no reason to kill her. I needed her alive and working for me. I'm sorry, is there anything else? I have a meeting in a few minutes."

Hollis asked yet another unrelated question, "Mr Southpool why are you staying here?"

"That's easy, the company has an account here. We keep a few rooms for those people who have meetings and don't want to travel home. I'm staying here because I didn't want to go back to my house. I've been in and out of here for the past week, but I've stayed here continuously since I came to report the death of Jennifer."

There was a crash of smashed glass. The barman now back behind the bar had dropped a wine glass he had been polishing onto the brown marble countertop.

"I'm sorry for the disturbance," said the barman.

Chappell said, "Thank you for your time Mr Southpool. One last question, you no longer work for the company, how is it that you are using the company account?"

"I think that it is a courtesy. They are letting me use the hotel as a base while I sort myself out and find my feet again. You must excuse me; I need to get ready for my meeting."

Frederick Southpool rose from the table and walked quickly out of the bar. Chappell and Hollis followed him out of the bar, walked out of the hotel and back to the police station.

Chappell frowned and sighed. He sighed again and shook his head.

"You don't seem happy, sir. What is it about him that troubles you? He gave a plausible account of himself."

"That's just it Hollis, he gave a plausible account." Chappell answered, speaking his thoughts out aloud. "Was it true? He said all the right things, but they don't feel right. There is something about that man that isn't right. I understand exactly what Officer Barnes meant about him. The man is too controlled and too happy to help. The picture we have of him from the people at Southpool Computing does not match the impression that he just gave us."

Hollis agreed. She added, "Yes, especially when you asked him those unexpected questions. He just became flustered. I would add him to our list of possible suspects, apart from the fact that he needed Jennifer alive so that she could work on his program."

The duty manager took a long drag on his cigarette. He let the nicotine fill his lungs. He held his breath for a few moments and expelled the smoke through his nose. He took another drag and repeated the action. He would be back on duty in thirty minutes, just enough time to check up on the new guests.

Being an unobtrusive member of staff in a hotel meant that people ignored you. They carried on their conversations believing that they could not be heard, or at least the polite staff member would be discreet. They were wrong. There were a few things that he had heard earlier that day that he knew could not be true. Where there was a lie, there was money to be made.

Blue, Williams and Orell Architects was a medium sized business housed in a modern tower block in Bristol. Chappell approached the reception desk, introduced himself and asked to see Ms Elle Latimer. He was told that Ms Latimer was in a meeting and could not be disturbed. Chappell looked stony faced at the receptionist.

He leant forward slightly, narrowed his eyes and spoke in a slow even tone, "Young lady, Ms Latimer can be disturbed, and she will be disturbed. I wish to speak with her now. Is Ms Blaine in?"

The receptionist blanched. "Ah…yes she is".

"Please tell Ms Blaine that we are here, and we wish to speak with Ms Latimer."

The receptionist picked up her telephone and mumbled into it.

The receptionist said, "Ms Blaine will see you now Detective Chief Inspector Chappell. Please take the lifts over there."

Lisa Blaine was standing by an open office when Chappell and Hollis exited from the lift.

"Chief Inspector, Sergeant what is this about?"

Chappell answered, "Ms Blaine it's about gaining some clarity in the investigation of Jennifer's death. May we go into the office?"

Lisa stood aside and let the police officers enter.

"Ms Blaine, please take a seat." Lisa did so. Chappell continued, "Unfortunately I must report that there is no doubt that Jennifer was murdered on Sunday. Right now, all we can say is by person or persons unknown."

Lisa's face hardened, her eyelids closed, and her hands clenched into fists. "And you suspect me, is that it?"

"No Lisa, we do not suspect you. You say you were not in the country and I am sure that the Danish police will verify that fact. I'm here to question Elle Latimer and you have someone on your staff called Andy. We'd like to question him too."

Lisa sat stunned, head lowered, mouth opening and closing silently.

"Detective Chappell, is this all because I split up with Jennifer? Would she still be alive if we…if I had walked away?"

Chappell replied, "Lisa, I do not know but I doubt it. I don't wish to be blunt, but someone killed her and whether accidently or on purpose remains to be seen but I doubt that the state of your relationship had anything to do with it."

Lisa nodded, "She was a good person. I just didn't want to be with her. My feelings had changed." She swallowed a sob and looked up glassy eyed at Chappell and Hollis. "I will do whatever I can to help you. I'll take you to one of the meeting rooms and send Elle and Andrew along."

Hollis asked, "What is Andrew's surname?"

"Grinner. Andrew Grinner."

Lisa stood and left the office. She walked along a grey carpeted hall whose walls were decorated with abstract prints of architectural features. Some were of the struts of bridges while others were of the roofs of buildings. Chappell looked at them momentarily, they reminded of the mountains he had climbed.

"If you wait in here, I'll go and get Elle and Andrew. Do you want to see both together or separately?"

"Together to begin with. Thank you."

The meeting room contained a round table with four chairs, telephone conferencing equipment and a television screen. In the corner was a scale model of an office block designed and built by the firm. Hollis studied this while Chappell took a seat at the table and read through his notebook. They did not have to wait long for Elle and Andrew to arrive.

Hollis deliberately took a seat directly opposite Chappell. It of course meant, that Elle and Andrew would be sat between the two police officers and opposite each other.

Chappell began the questioning, "Ms Latimer and Mr Grinner. Unfortunately, I have the sad task of telling you that Jennifer Lindsay was murdered. She was deliberately killed. You two may be among the last people to see her alive. Mr Grinner, may I call you Andy?"

The young man nodded. He looked ill. His Adam's apple bobbed up and down his throat several times.

"So, Andy you were at Ms Latimer's home on which day last week?"

"Ah...it was Tuesday. Yes, Tuesday. Elle had a meeting in Bath, and she had left a drawing which we needed to show a client on Wednesday. I said I'd go around and collect the drawing and do some work on it on Tuesday evening."

"Who did meet when you got to the house?"

"Well that guy Jack. He was packing to move, and we got talking. He asked me to help him move a few things into his van. I helped him do that." Andy swallowed nervously.

"And then?"

"And then, I...I met Jennifer. She was there and chatted to Jack and me about stuff really. She made me a cup of tea and we had a good chat and I lost track of time. Next thing I know Elle had returned home and I had spent several hours talking to Jennifer. That was the first and last time I met Jennifer."

"What did you talk about?"

"I dunno. I mean which pubs and clubs we went to, best place to get a kebab after a night out and things like that. Nothing serious."

As Andy spoke, Hollis watched Elle's expression. Elle was staring intently at Andy. It seemed as if she wanted him to stop talking but Andy was suffering from that volubility that some people suffer from when being questioned by the police. Elle moved her legs and would have kicked Andy under the table if Hollis had not caught her eye.

Chappell continued with his questions, "About what time would you say Ms Latimer returned home that evening?"

"Oh, I would say about seven. That's about right wouldn't you say Elle, seven?" Elle nodded and looked up at the ceiling. Andy continued, "Yes about seven. I don't think that Elle expected me to still be there, so I just took the drawing off the table and left."

"Well thank you Andy you have been extremely helpful. I think that's all. Detective Sergeant Hollis do you have any further questions?"

"No, I don't. Let me see you out." Hollis rose, walked over to the door and held it open for Andy Grinner. She closed the door behind him and retook her seat.

Chappell stared at Elle, placed his elbows on the table and steepled his hands. He rested his chin on his hands. He sat in silence, allowing the silence to make Elle Latimer uncomfortable. She shifted in her seat and pressed her lips together. She began to pluck at her top and to look around the room. She looked anywhere but at Chappell and Hollis.

"Elle, I would like some clarity from you." Chappell looked at his notebook and up at Elle. "When we spoke to you earlier you said that you returned home on Friday and gave the impression that you had been traveling on business. Mr Grinner and Ms Blaine tell us that you may have had to travel to business meetings but none of them required overnight stays or foreign travel. Please can you explain yourself?"

Elle tried to shrug but her haunted look belied the movement. "Did I say that? It must have been a mistake."

"No, I don't think so. At first you said Thursday and you corrected yourself and said Friday. You wanted to give the impression that you had not been at home last week and now your housemate is dead. What do you know about her murder? Maybe you murdered her yourself?"

"Now look here." Elle jumped out of her chair. "You can't say that to me!"

"Sit down." Chappell spoke. His voice was cold and unforgiving. "Sit down and stop being so melodramatic. Lying to the police and wasting our time is an offence. Would you like to be led out of this building in handcuffs and arrested?"

Elle returned to her seat. Her face now bore a fearful expression. Hollis permitted herself a small smile. Hollis enjoyed watching Chappell cut witnesses down to size.

"Ms Latimer I will start again. You made a point in telling us that you had not returned home until Friday. Andy tells us that you were at home on Tuesday when Jennifer was present. Mr Danvers tells us that you were expected back that day. Ms Blaine tells us that there was no reason for you to have been travelling any long distances for business. Explain yourself, otherwise we will have to arrest you."

Elle looked at Chappell then Hollis and back to Chappell.

"I won't say a thing. My movements are my own. Yes, I came back on Tuesday and then I left again almost immediately. I came back on Friday as I said."

"What did you do on the intervening two days?"

Elle shook her head and looked at the table.

Chappell let out a snort of exasperation, "Hollis, arrest Ms Latimer, charge her with obstruction of justice and for aiding and abetting a criminal."

Hollis stood behind Elle, "Ms Latimer please stand up and place your hands out in front of you." Hollis removed a set of plastic cuffs from a pocket, "Ms Elle Latimer, you are being arrested on the charge of....."

Hollis unfurled the restraint and slowly began to

slide it around Elle's wrists.

"This can't be happening. You can't be doing this."

Hollis paused in doing up the handcuffs.

Elle's eyes started to water, "No, no wait. I'll tell you. I can't believe this is happening." Elle burst into tears, she took a number of deep breaths and continued to sob. "How can this be happening to me? I have been going to work and I did have some meetings."

Hollis gently guided Elle back into her seat.

"The thing is that I'm having an affair with Mr Orell, one of the partners of this firm. I have been for some time now. Nobody knows. I spend some evenings at the house and some evenings with him. He has separated from his wife and they are getting divorced, but we just didn't want anyone to know about it. Adam, Mr Orell has an apartment in Bristol, and I spent Tuesday, Wednesday and Thursday evenings there. I have been coming to work as normal. We don't see each other during the day and we just meet up at night."

Chappell nodded, "And the weekend, last weekend when Jennifer died?"

"I came back to the house on Friday like I said but I didn't see Jennifer. I don't know if she was in or not. I came back, had a drink with Peter in the lounge and had a bath. On Saturday I met up with some friends and didn't come back until the early hours. Yes, I can give you their names if you want. On Sunday I stayed in bed late, got up, did some laundry and not much else."

Chappell was remorseless in his questioning. He looked at Elle Latimer with disdain. He asked, "Why did you say that you did not know who Jennifer's girlfriend was?"

Elle shook her head and said, "I didn't want to get involved. How could I say that Jennifer's girlfriend was my boss? I thought that if I didn't say anything, you'd go away."

Chappell said, "But here we are again with more questions, treating you as a person of interest. Detective Sergeant Hollis, please go and see if Mr Orell is on the premises. Please tell him that we wish to question him immediately." Hollis acknowledged the order and went off in search of the man.

Elle took several deep breaths and said, "Detective Chief Inspector Chappell do you really need to do this. I've told you everything now."

"Ms Latimer, your housemate is dead. You have not shown an ounce of concern. Instead you are more interested in keeping your secrets."

A note of pleading crept into Elle's voice as she said, "I'm not a hypocrite. Jennifer made a point of flirting with my friends, both male and female. She made me feel uncomfortable and she knew it. I didn't like her. I didn't want her dead, but I just wanted her to leave my friends and myself alone. You don't need to speak to Adam."

Hollis returned followed by a slim muscular man of medium height, wearing a turquoise coloured polo shirt and black jeans. His dark curly hair was greying at the temples. Hollis introduced him to Chappell, "Mr Adam Orell this is Detective Chief Inspector Chappell."

Chappell stood and pointed to a chair, "Please be seated Mr Orell. Ms Latimer you can go."

"Oh but..." Elle looked helplessly at Adam Orell

as she was escorted from the room by Hollis.

Adam twisted in his chair to look at Elle and would have risen if Chappell had not said, "Please remain in your chair Mr Orell."

"Now see here Detective, I really don't see what this has got to do with Elle or me. What's the point of all this?" Adam curled his hands into fists and rested them on the table. His face reddened as he stared at Chappell.

Hollis re-entered and took a seat.

Ignoring Orell, Chappell asked, "Everything alright out there Hollis?"

Hollis nodded, "Yes sir, I told Ms Latimer not to leave the building in case we needed to speak to her again."

Orell uncurled his hands and began drumming his fingers on the table top. He said, "I've already asked you, what is this to do with us?"

"Mr Orell, we are investigating the death of Jennifer Lindsay. Ms Lindsay was a housemate of Ms Latimer's. Please can you tell me what you know of Ms Latimer's movements over the last week? I would appreciate candour and truthfulness. We have a lot to do and not a lot of time?"

"What can I tell you? Elle and I are seeing each other. I have separated from my wife and am waiting for the divorce to be finalised. Elle spends some evenings with me and some back at her own home. I'd like her to move in full-time but she's not ready for that yet."

Hollis asked, "Where is your wife? What does she think of Elle?"

Orell shrugged, "Oh, she's back in the States. When I moved over here she didn't want to come. I tried the whole transatlantic thing for a while, but it didn't work out. Elle has nothing to do with my divorce. I got to know her over the last few years and I really love being around her. Look I'm sorry that her housemate is dead, but Elle had nothing to do with it. I'm sure of that."

Chappell said, "Mr Orell, I find it a stretch of coincidence to find out that Ms Blaine had a relationship with Jennifer Lindsay, and you are having a relationship with Elle Latimer. How is it that both women lived in the same house?"

"I think that's a bit cart before the horse. Their house is where I met Elle socially for the first time. I mean Lisa was dating Jennifer and I dropped her off at Jennifer's home. I was there when Elle came home and all four of us went out for a drink. Things just developed from there. Is it possible to keep this quiet? The only person who knows anything about this is Lisa. Could we keep it that way?"

Chappell looked at his notes and back at Adam Orell.

Orell said, "Well, you wanted candour, I'm being candid."

Chappell frowned, "If it has no bearing on the case then yes, we will try to keep it quiet. Thank you Mr Orell."

After Orell left, Chappell remained at the table. He made some notes, threw his pen down and massaged his temples.

"You probably need some coffee, sir." Hollis stood, "I noticed a coffee shop next door. We could go and sit in there?"

"Good thinking Hollis. It's not really the caffeine, I need to try to find a loose end. If Elle Latimer didn't do it, who did?"

"Sir, I have a theory that it was Peter Riggs."

"Why? Why him? I need evidence Hollis, not a theory or a gut instinct. What evidence do we have that it was any one of the people that we have interviewed so far?"

"None, sir."

Chappell continued massaging his temples as he said, "There's some intelligence behind this death. Come on, let's get that coffee and then we can visit your chief suspect. You can interview him."

Peter Riggs opened the front door and took a seat in the lounge. His eyes were still red, and his nose was streaming from a cold.

Hollis was straight to the point with her questioning, "Peter, the last time we spoke you led us to believe that you were Jennifer's best friend and that you cared deeply for her. Wouldn't it be fair to say that over the last few weeks Jennifer cared very little for you and you were becoming obsessed with her?"

"Yes." Peter whispered his answer, his mouth barely opened. "Yes, it's true."

Hollis warmed to her theme as she said, "Is that true enough for you to have killed her?"

"But I didn't. Oh, I don't know perhaps I did. I don't know. I don't know. Is it my fault she's dead? Did I kill her?"

Hollis did not expect Peter to admit anything so quickly and even Chappell was caught off-guard. Chappell signalled to Hollis that he would take over the questioning. He used a low gentle tone, conscious as he was that Peter seemed close to another bout of crying.

"Peter, could you explain yourself. Why are you blaming yourself for Jennifer's death? What did you do?"

"Nothing, that's just it. I did absolutely nothing and now she's dead. Perhaps if I had done something she would still be alive."

Chappell asked, "What is it you think you should have done but didn't do?"

"I didn't go and collect her. She wanted a lift from somewhere and asked me to collect her. When she asked I didn't particularly listen and all I said was "I'll see." I wasn't busy or anything I was just sick and tired of her asking me for lifts to go to places. It wasn't that she wanted to spend time with me just wanted me to do her shopping and drive her about. I finally realised that she was just using me, and I wasn't going to do it any longer."

Chappell asked, "So, do you remember where she wanted you to collect her from and when?"

Peter shook his head. Tears ran down his cheeks. "No, that's it, I just told you I didn't listen, and I didn't care."

Chappell spoke slowly as if trying to calm an upset child, "Peter was she here on Saturday?"

Peter wiped at his face as he said, "At some point. I think that she came back late on Saturday, had some breakfast on Sunday morning and went out to meet someone. I don't know who or where. I didn't listen. I told her to catch a bus and I'd see if I was free in the afternoon to collect her. The thing is, I totally forgot and didn't care. She even called me a few times. As soon as I saw it was her I didn't answer the phone and I deleted her voice messages without listening to them. I didn't even remember anything about her needing to come home until the policeman came and said she was dead.

"So, can't you understand?" Peter continued, "Maybe I killed her. If I had gone to get her. If I had remembered or even listened to her I might be able to tell you who it was that she went to meet. She just made me so angry." Peter wiped his nose with his hand and started weeping.

Back in the incident room, Chappell called the team together to review their investigation. Jennifer Lindsay had a tidy sum of money in both her current and savings accounts. She was not extravagant in her spending, but she did like expensive clothes, shoes and bags. Clothing and accessories which she could well afford. She also spent money on top of the range computer equipment, again she could afford to do so. She was not in debt and her credit card was paid up. If she kept a diary it was neither electronic nor written down. The last email she had sent was to accept a job offer from a computing firm in California and she had said that she could start work in six weeks.

"Poor girl," Detective Hudson commented. "She had all that going for her and someone ups and kills her. One thing I have found out though, is that although she didn't use an organised diary system, she did note down people's initials, times and date on tiny little post-it notes and stick them up everywhere. Her work bag is full of them. It will take a while to organise them but that may point to who else was in her life or any appointments she might have had."

"I still favour Peter Riggs for this." Hollis was determined to arrest Riggs for the crime.

Chappell shook his head and said, "Hollis, you saw

him. He was practically on the edge of a nervous breakdown. He had turned his back on his best friend and because of that she is dead. It would really have helped us if he could remember who she went to meet and where but since he didn't care he didn't pay any attention. The memory of that will haunt him."

Hollis was adamant. She didn't care if she argued with Chappell in front of the team. "Sir, all I see is someone who is a pretty good actor. You mark my words when we get to the bottom of this Peter Riggs will be there. We've been told that he was seen wandering around her room when she wasn't there, touching her things sitting on her bed. That is definitely obsessive. Jack Danvers said he moved out because, amongst other things, Peter had turned into a creep guy. I think we have to hold him as a firm suspect."

As Hollis spoke Chappell massaged his temples and exhaled loudly. He stared at her. Two bright spots coloured his cheeks while the colour drained from the rest of his face.

Hollis stopped speaking, as she became aware that Chappell was staring at her with fury etched on his face and her colleagues were looking at her in horror.

Chappell let the silence continue for a few seconds before saying, "Need I remind you all and especially you Detective Sergeant Hollis, we operate on evidence. I've said that once already today.

"I want everyone to retrace their steps, do a deeper canvas of the area around Forge Tarn and the lake. I think that we need to look at the character of Jennifer Lindsay more closely. Various people have said that she is an inveterate flirt. We need to look at the implications of that.

315

"Hollis, get in touch with Marie, Jennifer's friend and question her about that. Find out who Jennifer was seeing, who she was flirting with and who if anyone she was annoying. Did Jennifer go on a date where one thing led to another and she ended up dying?"

Chappell paused, looked at a handful of notes and said, "Jennifer herself complained that she was being pestered by people so, it could be someone we know nothing about at the moment. Lee can you get started on organising those notes with the dates and initials and see how far you get with them. Just remember she knew her killer."

The police officers looked at their desks and began sifting through the information they had so far collected.

"Hollis, a word. In my office. Now."

Chappell stalked through the incident room back to his office. He threw his notes on the desk, stood behind it and crossed his arms.

Hollis got up from her seat and followed him. Hudson whispered "Good luck Hollis" as she passed him.

"Close the door." Chappell barked as soon as Hollis entered. His voice was cold and his face devoid of any emotion.

"Hollis, what do you think you were doing out there? I've already told you that I want evidence not intuition. I don't expect to have to repeat myself to the people in my team. If I have to, then maybe, you aren't ready for the job you have." A muscle in one of Chappell's cheek twitched.

Hollis stood stiffly shuffling from foot to foot. "But sir, I…"

"I haven't finished." Chappell leaned forward and placed his hands on his desk. "Are you ready to be in this team Hollis?" Chappell stared at her. Hollis was silent.

"That was not a rhetorical question. I want an answer. Are you ready to be in this team?"

Hollis bristled, "Yes, yes I am. What I am doing is my job, sir. I am pointing out a person of interest. We may not have any evidence, but we do have the opinion of Jack Danvers."

"Hearsay Hollis. From just one person. You are so fixated on Peter Riggs I want to know why?"

"He reminds me of someone from a case I worked on. A woman accidently killed her boyfriend and pleaded guilty to manslaughter in the end. The victim's best friend had been having an affair with the girlfriend and helped her to cover up the death.

"So, this is just a case of history repeating itself is it? Are you suggesting that Lisa Blaine and Peter Riggs accidently killed Jennifer?"

"No sir, but then again who knows?" Jennifer shrugged and raised her hands. "Sir, I am sorry. I got carried away. Next time I will…"

Chappell interrupted her, "There won't be a next time Hollis. If you have something to say, you will make sure that you have some evidence before you start suspecting people. You certainly won't undermine me in front of my team. Do you understand?"

Hollis nodded. She could feel her eyes watering. She blinked rapidly and looked at the floor.

Chappell sat down and picked up a sheaf of papers, "Make sure the door doesn't hit you on the way out."

Those members of the team who were still in the incident room pretended to ignore Hollis as she walked back to her desk.

Hudson made no such pretence. He came over to her, "Hey Laura, he's not that bad."

"It's bad enough Lee. It was just so clear that he was having second thoughts about my being here."

Lee chuckled, "When he starts shouting at someone so loudly that you can hear his voice downstairs that's when you need to worry. Did he shout at you?"

"No but.." Hollis slumped over her desk covered her face with her hands and placed her elbows on the table.

"Then don't worry. Well, I mean you should but, he's not going to kick you off the team, not just yet anyway."

Hollis sat up abruptly and looked at Hudson.

"You'll be fine Laura. Chappell's shouted at me a few times and look at me, I'm still here. So is he." Hudson tapped Sampson on the shoulder.

Sampson turned around to face Laura, "Chappell has torn so many strips off me I'm surprised I've got any skin left. Everyone gets shouted at once in a while. If he didn't think you could do it he would have sacked you after the first month. Take on board what he says and just do your best."

Marie chose a vegan coffee bar in which to meet, she was waiting for Hollis when she arrived.

"Marie, hi. I must admit it took me a while to find this place. Is it new?"

Marie nodded, "Aren't you supposed to ask a policeman if you're lost?"

"True but, there wasn't a policeman around."

Marie smiled briefly then her face resumed its grief stricken expression.

Marie said, "Why did she have to die? I don't understand."

Hollis looked apologetic and said, "That's what I'm hoping you can help me with. A few people have said that after splitting up with Lisa, Jennifer's behaviour became unpredictable. They have also said that she flirted with people all the time. Do you know of anyone she was flirting with or beginning to date?"

Marie thought for a few minutes and sipped at her drink. "It's hard to say, I think that Jennifer knew that things were over with Lisa long before she saw Lisa with someone else. Jennifer was always flirting with people even when she was with Lisa. After their break-up, I'd say she went into overdrive. She was just out socialising all the time. She said that she didn't want to stay at home."

Marie paused and said, "I don't think that Jennifer went out looking for people, but she met them in bars, pubs and clubs. She attracted people and they were attracted to her. I know that someone called Rick rang her a few times and she also spoke with Guy. She agreed to meet up with both."

Hollis asked, "How do you know?"

"She took the calls at work. I don't know if she actually met up with them. She'd been fired by then."

"Didn't she talk to you about these things?"

Marie shook her head, "After she'd been fired she just complained that Mr Southpool kept ringing her up all the time and she was talking about finding a new job."

Hollis said, "Think very carefully. Do remember

hearing where she was going to meet up with them?"

Marie answered immediately, "Yes, one in a pub in Bristol and another in a pub at Forge Tarn. That was a few weeks ago, there could have been others. She wanted me to go on a girls' night out. I did once or twice after she was sacked, but she wasn't good company."

Hollis asked, "What do you mean?"

"Her topics of conversation were Mr Southpool, Lisa and how much she could drink before she got drunk. I know that she was miserable, but I wasn't going to sit around and wait for her to pass out through drink."

"When was the last time you spoke with Jennifer?"

"Just a few days ago, she rang me and said that she was thinking of moving to America. I was happy for her, sad for myself but happy for her. Now though, I really have lost a friend."

Hollis asked, "Do you know how things were between her and Peter?"

Marie snorted her disgust and said, "That doormat. Look Peter's a nice person but he just needed to show a bit of backbone. I think that Jennifer liked him well enough. They were schoolfriends, but he seemed to think if he hung around long enough Jennifer would go out with him. He just wasn't her type and he didn't understand that."

Hollis asked, "What was her type?"

"Interesting and passionate. Jennifer wanted to be with someone who had a passion in their lives. Peter is probably the most passionless person you could ever hope to meet.

"I got the impression that they had fallen out. I think that's another reason why she didn't want to stay in at the house on her own with him."

"Thanks Marie, I really appreciate the fact that you've come to talk to me. If you think of anything else please contact me."

Marie nodded, smiled sadly and stood. "Please find out who did this, Detective Hollis. Please."

Chappell sat behind his desk, drinking a glass of water. Hollis had reported back on her interview with Marie and was now giving yet another impassioned appeal as to why she thought Peter Riggs should be brought in for questioning.

"Sir, I know what you said earlier, but now I have two different people saying essentially the same thing about Peter. I know it still isn't hard and fast physical evidence but, I really think that he killed her and if he didn't there's still something that he's not telling us. I cannot believe that he did not know where she was going. You can't help but listen when someone is talking to you. I think he knows. If he does know, why isn't he telling us? And sir, he hasn't exactly been clear about what he did over the weekend."

Hollis paused for breath and watched Chappell consider her suggestion. His brown eyes although looking in her direction were not focused on her. He drank some more water and looked at his picture of the Matterhorn.

"OK, Hollis. Do it. Take Hudson and Sampson and frighten the life out of him. I'll meet you in the interview room when you come back with him. Just make sure you are right about this. I don't want him complaining about police heavy handedness. Are you sure?"

"Yes I am. There's something he's holding back."

The smoke billowed from the corner of the hotel. It rolled in thick clouds over the surrounding area. The first fire engine roared into the car park. The driver executed an emergency stop. The rest of the crew were thrown violently forward.

One of the firemen shouted, "What the hell? The fire's over there, not in the carpark."

The driver replied, "I know but look." He pointed out of the engine's windscreen at the crumpled heap lying directly in his path. On the ground, lay the body of a man. He was unmoving with his limbs sprawled at unnatural angles. The second fire engine stopped behind the first and sounded its alarm. The driver of the first engine left his vehicle and inspected the body. His passengers went to inform the second driver of the problem. With careful manoeuvring the two engines were able to skirt round the corpse and begin to attend to the fire. One of the firemen called the police and informed them of the find.

Peter Riggs shook with fright as he sat in the interview room. Detective Chief Inspector Chappell and Detective Sergeant Hollis sat opposite him. They were grim faced.

Detective Inspector Chappell's eyes drilled into Peter's. Peter started to cry, this time however, neither police officer was sympathetic to his tears. He placed his head in his hands and shook his head.

"No, I didn't kill her. I didn't. You have to believe me. I didn't do it."

Chappell said, "If you wish us to believe you then you need to tell us the truth. All of the truth not just bits of it. I want to know what you did from last

Friday to Monday. You have not told us everything have you?"

"I didn't do it!"

Chappell said, "You are currently the prime suspect in the murder of Jennifer Lindsay. Now is the time to start telling us what you know."

Peter raised his head and looked at the ceiling. "I...I haven't been as truthful as I could have been." Hollis leant forward. Peter continued, "It's just that, well my feelings for Jennifer have been confused for so long.

"I enjoyed being around her. Then she met Lisa and it was obvious that nothing between Jennifer and me would happen. I tried to get on with my own life and go out with my circle of friends, but I was always thinking about what Jennifer was doing. Listening to Jennifer, it became obvious that things with Lisa weren't working out and she was really troubled by it. At night a few times she was so upset that she would crawl into my bed. Nothing happened, she just wanted companionship and someone to talk to."

Peter paused, looked at both police officers and continued, "When we met Lisa and her new girlfriend that night in the restaurant Jennifer went to pieces. She went to the pub and tried to drink herself stupid. I got her back home and put her to bed in her own room. A few hours later there she was in my room, in my bed, wanting to have sex. I turned her down. She got angry and left. She didn't remember a thing the next morning and I didn't bring it up. After that Jennifer would flirt with people and stay out all night. It was worse when she lost her job since she really didn't have any structure to her day. She argued with Jack about using his bike, so she started asking me to

323

drive her about. I was happy to do so. It meant that I could keep an eye on her. I would drop her off, but I wouldn't leave. If she met someone in a coffee shop I would park outside if I could and wait for her. She didn't know. Sometimes she met people and went home with them, I would wait outside. She didn't know that I was there, but I just wanted to check up on her and make sure the she wasn't in trouble."

Peter was silent for a few minutes. Hollis wanted to question him further, but Chappell motioned that she should not speak. At last Peter continued speaking, "Eventually I questioned my motives and wondered if I was becoming a stalker. I cared about her and I could see that she would get herself into trouble. She was drinking a lot and becoming vicious with it. Last week I realised that I had to stop. I just had to cut thoughts of her out of my mind. Last weekend I tried to do that. I went out on Friday with some friends, I can give you their details if you want. On Saturday morning Jennifer shouted at me. She had to get home on her own on Friday and why didn't I come and collect her? I pointed out that I wasn't her taxi service. She calmed down and apologised. She said that she would be going to Forge Tarn on Sunday to meet someone for a date and would I help her out and give her a lift. She said that she wanted to have fun with this particular person. After everything I just said to her there she was asking me to be her chauffer again. I deliberately went out on Saturday and stayed out until Sunday night. I blocked her number and, well, the rest you know. No, I don't know his name or where he lives. All I know is that was where they were supposed to meet."

Hollis asked, "Peter, when you waited outside

during the night, can you give a description or the address of these places?"

"No, not really. I would follow her to the house or flat and then drive around the corner. I didn't park right outside their homes. I didn't want Jennifer to catch me. It was dark and I just wanted to catch a glimpse of her leaving."

Hollis was incredulous. She asked, "Peter are you really saying that you waited outside these places and have no idea where they were?"

"It was dark, and I was worried. I didn't take notes of the addresses, just the doors. Can't you see this is what I mean? I killed her. If I had given her the lift she wanted, if I had paid more attention then she'd be alive." Peter glanced hurriedly at his watch.

"Do you have somewhere to be Peter?" Chappell looked at Peter's face and back at his watch.

"No, I just wanted to know what the time was. Look, if you want I could drive around and try and identify the places I think I went to. I don't remember but I could try." Peter shrugged helplessly and wiped his nose on the same grey sweatshirt he had been wearing days earlier.

Chappell ended the interview, "Thank you Peter. It would have been extremely helpful to us if you had told us all of this to begin with."

Back in Chappell's office, Hollis sat feeling deflated.

Chappell said, "Well done, Hollis. You stuck with it. Well done."

"Thank you. But, sir, how can you say, "Well Done"? He did not do it. I've made a fool of myself."

Chappell said, "You stuck with it and you followed your instincts. I'm more convinced that Peter Riggs did not kill Jennifer Lindsay, but he has now given us far more information than he wanted to. His information and his actions point to her state of mind. Her chaotic life style over the past few weeks tends to suggest that she probably annoyed someone, and they snapped. I don't see how the picnic fits in, but we will discover that. Your tenacity is to be commended, don't be so hard on yourself. Now we need..."

He was interrupted by a knock at the door and Dave Sampson's head came into the room.

"Sir, the Twelve Kings Hotel down the road had a fire. It looks like arson. The bar manager, Tom Starkey, has been found dead in the hotel car park. He was found by the firemen; they nearly ran him over. The coroner won't give anything away, but it does look like the man died from manual strangulation. Fortunately, the fire was just in one small corner of the building. It caused a lot of smoke but no real damage, none of the guests or visitors was hurt. They're not doing anything until you get there. They were holding off because you were interviewing a suspect."

Chappell sprang up and dashed out of his office. He ran down the stairs, out of the police station and over to the hotel in a matter of minutes. Hollis had barely made it out of the station, when Chappell slowed down, ran a hand through his hair, straightened his clothes and walked in a professional manner over to the coroner.

"Mike." Chappell nodded

"Hazel."

"Well Mike, most of what I can tell you is that this man has probably been dead for over seven hours and he has bruising around his throat. I'll let you have my report in due course."

"Thanks, Hazel." The coroner walked away and left Mike Chappell to his thoughts.

Two strangulations within a matter of days. What were the odds of that? Chappell looked at the sky and sent up a silent prayer that this body did not represent the beginning of a spate of murders. He turned around at the sound of huffing and puffing. Hollis, Sampson and Hudson were bent over, their hands on their thighs gasping for breath.

Chappell shook his head, "So glad you could make it. It was only a gentle little jog. I thought you all worked out and kept fit."

Hollis looked up, took in Chappell's evil grin, "Yes but you were nought to sixty in one second."

Sampson and Hudson who had yet to regain the power of speech nodded.

"Well team, you are here now. I want to know what caused this fire, who the dead man is and whether or not he is connected with the fire. The coroner tells me that the victim was strangled. I need to know if this is a separate killing or if it is related to that of Jennifer Lindsay. Two strangulations in less than a week cannot be a coincidence."

Chappell strode over to the gurney bearing the dead man and looked at the corpse before he was entirely zipped up in a body bag. Not more than a day earlier this was the man who had served him coffee, and now he was dead. What had this man done to get himself killed? Had he done anything? Had the man finished work and was about to head home or was he having a quick cigarette in the car park? What was the motive for this death?

Back in the incident room, more whiteboards had been wheeled in and this time covered with photographs of the crime scene and of Tom Starkey's body. Chappell inspected each of the photographs that had been stuck up. In some cases, he unpinned the photographs, looked at them closely and put them back up.

He turned and faced his team, "For now, we need to investigate these as two separate deaths. There is nothing for now to suggest that the death of Tom Starkey is connected to the death of Jennifer Lindsay. I think we need to wait for the pathology and forensic reports before we draw conclusions or parallels between these two people.

"Sampson, what did you find out?"

Sampson looked at his notes and said, "Thomas Starkey, Tom for short was thirty-four years old. He was the bar manager and sometimes doubled as the night manager. He had just finished for the night, he was working in the bar, the night manager was elsewhere in the hotel sorting out a customer's problem. The hotel runs a skeleton staff between ten at night and seven in the morning. Tom closed the bar at twelve last night.

"It's hard to tell exactly how many people are registered at the hotel at the moment because the fire has affected the computer systems. It looks like it was an electrical fire that started in a store room. There was no strong smell of accelerants in the vicinity of the store room apart from the cleaning materials already in the room. The fire brigade say that the liquids are toxic and flammable. It seems that there was an adaptor plug which was overloaded and stuck into an extension cable. Due to this the fuse blew or there was a spark which set fire to the materials and the room. Now whether that was deliberate or not remains to be investigated. The cupboard door was opened by a customer service assistant who was looking for an iron. The fire and smoke escaped. She's alright by the way, she was able to raise the alarm."

Chappell addressed Hudson, "What have you found out about Tom Starkey?"

"Thomas Starkey lived on the edge of Bristol in a rented flat. Looking around his lodgings he had qualifications in hospitality and catering and was working his way up to be a hotel manager. At first look there is nothing suspicious about him. He had left a pile of textbooks on his dining room table and a half finished essay on his computer. His bedroom was tidy, all of his clothes were put away and he had a pile of dirty clothes which was already bundled up ready to be taken to a laundry. I think he lived as he worked, his kitchen and bathroom were clean. There does not seem to be anything in his house that would mark him out as a victim. I also looked for signs of a partner, he appears to be single. He has pictures of friends and family dotted around but there was no one in particular. Sampson asked about that at the hotel and his colleagues said that he was single. He had split up with a girlfriend a few years ago. He was driven and ambitious. We won't be able to gain access to his financial records until at least tomorrow."

The rest of the team sat in silence absorbing the information. Chappell turned back to the whiteboards, crossed his arms and stared at the photographs taken from both crime scenes.

"Carry on with both investigations, we are close to solving Jennifer Lindsay's death and we will do the same for Tom Starkey."

The report from the coroner was ready before he left for home.

For a second night that week, Chappell studied the reports from his team and the coroner. Tom Starkey died from strangulation. Chappell studied the pattern of bruising around the throat of the latest murder victim and that of Jennifer Lindsay. The patterns were different. The person who killed Starkey wore gloves, Jennifer's killer did not. Did that mean that Jennifer's death was not premeditated whilst Starkey's was? The weather was quite warm if not wet and foggy, so why would a person wear gloves?

Chappell did not know enough about Tom Starkey to know who might have wanted to kill him. The more Jennifer's death was investigated the more it seemed as if Jennifer had angered someone who lashed out, pushed her, causing her to fall, hit her head and had then been strangled. The trouble with that solution was that it did not explain the staging at the scene. Chappell made a note to ask if Jennifer's blow to the head would have caused her death without having to strangle her.

Reviewing the photographs and reports from both scenes, he made lists of the similarities and the differences. He also made a list of the facts that had yet to come to light. He brewed himself a large cafetière of coffee and worked through the night. He constructed hypotheses, fitted the facts together and thought about those that he would need to know in order to prove his suppositions correct. He continued to do this until he had constructed a list of the information that he needed. When the first rays of a weak sun brightened the sky, Mike Chappell showered, made himself a mug of coffee for the road and set off for work. He called a meeting for seven o'clock.

"Hudson, Sampson and Hollis, I need the following information. Telephone calls made by the victims, the places they frequented, the people they dated, their bank details, where they bought their groceries, which buses they caught, where they spent their spare time. Every inch of their lives will be put under a microscope. I'd also like to know why we haven't had Jennifer's phone records. Get onto it. We need to know. I do not think that Peter and Elle have told us everything they know. Light a fire under them. Make sure they understand that they are in the frame for Jennifer's murder. Speak to Tom Starkey's colleagues again, who was he, why did he want to be a hotelier? Divide the rest of the team between you and make sure that when we meet later today you have most of the answers. The more I think about it, I want you to treat these two murders as if they are connected in some way. I believe that two strangulations in a matter of days is not a coincidence. Either we come across the killer through finding the reason behind Tom Starkey's death or through investigating Jennifer's. Please bear in mind though, that I could be wrong to link these murders, but your investigations will provide the answers. There is a lot of ground to be covered today."

Chappell reserved one task for himself; investigating why Frederick Southpool was connected to both deaths. Jennifer Lindsay was found by Southpool on his land. Southpool was staying in the Twelve Kings Hotel when Tom Starkey was killed. Did Southpool have anything to do with the fire? Why was the computer server damaged? When was the last time there was a fire at the hotel? Mike was running on caffeine and adrenaline, just the way he liked it. He walked over to the hotel and was gratified to see a number of his team interviewing guests and staff.

Hollis was interviewing the hotel's General Manager. Chappell let himself into the manager's room unannounced, both Hollis and the manager Leah Bourdon turned to face him.

Hollis introduced him, "Ms Bourdon, this is Detective Chief Inspector Chappell. Sir, this is Ms Leah Bourdon, the hotel General Manager." Both nodded to each other, Chappell took a seat.

Chappell said, "Forgive me if Detective Sergeant Hollis has already asked you this question, but when was the last time there was a fire at the hotel?"

Ms Bourdon nodded and said, "In fact, she just did. I was about to answer. The last fire we had here that needed the fire crews was over twenty years ago. The hotel was a wreck. It had to be gutted and a major rebuilding programme took place. We've had little fires since, in the kitchen normally, but even so we've only had three of those in the past few years since I've been here."

Chappell smiled at her wanting her to expand on her answer, "And how long has that been?"

"Six years. I came as an assistant manager and became General Manager two years ago. Nothing like this has happened before. I just hope it doesn't affect the reputation of the hotel." Leah Bourdon, paused, her cheeks paled, "I'm sorry, what with Tom's death that sounds terrible. I didn't mean to sound uncaring."

Chappell asked, "Whose decision was it for the computer back-up system to be located in that storeroom?"

"Mine or Tom's. We just needed it to be somewhere out of the way. The storeroom seemed like the obvious place. It was cool and apart from spare cleaning materials there was nothing else in there."

Hollis asked, "Is there anything that you can tell us about Tom Starkey? What did he do outside of work?"

Leah Bourdon replied, "No, not really. Tom kept himself to himself. He was keen to do well in his job and to learn about all aspects of the role. He had really mastered the new computer system that we had put in. I think that we are going to have to go back to the previous version of it because I really don't know what he used to do. It was a brilliant system though."

Hollis asked, "Why was it so good?"

"Well, not only did it take all the automated bookings, but it logged the drinks and the extra services that guests required with no more than a touch of a button. Then at the end of the stay, we were able to provide guests with detailed bills. Our previous system was not as thorough as the new one."

Chappell asked, "Was Tom the only one able to use it?"

"Oh no, everyone could use it but there are some sections that only managers can access. I must admit that I have so much to do that I let him deal with things such as the payments and refunds. Tom is...I mean was so charming and good with the guests. Some would complain that they had been overcharged and Tom would step in, speak with the angry person and they would leave completely reassured that the bill was correct. I must admit that in the past month or so there were quite a few customers saying that their bills were wrong. With a calm voice and a few key strokes, the money was refunded to their accounts and all was well. He was a great help, I can tell you."

Chappell asked, "Are these refunds automatically returned to the customers' accounts?"

"Yes, yes, I believe they are. Like I said there have been a few problems in the past month. Someone from the IT department was going to have a look at the system and carry out an audit. Now, I guess they will be giving us a completely new system." She hunched her shoulders and drummed her fingers on her thighs.

Hollis asked, "Is there anything else that you can tell us?"

Leah Bourdon shook her head, "I really do not know what he did outside of work. Whilst he was here he showed a lot of initiative. He would make a point of going to the guests' rooms with towels and chocolates. Tom made sure that their rooms were perfect. He definitely helped to set the high level of service I want us to offer and maintain."

Chappell asked, "I was wondering if you knew if your guest Mr Southpool was still here. I would like to talk to him."

"Oh, I'm sorry. He left this morning." Leah

Bourdon rose to her feet. "You must excuse me; I really have to get on."

Chappell asked, "Did Mr Southpool say where he was going?"

"I think that he was going home and then he was going travelling. With everything that has been going on, I must admit that I did not give him my full attention. I am sorry, but if there are no other questions, I must attend to a few things."

On the walk back to the police station, Chappell rang Detective Constable Hudson and asked him to chase up Tom Starkey's financial records. He stopped at a coffee shop close to the police station and asked Hollis to join him. It acted as an outpost of the police station. The owner of the shop was a retired policeman who had decorated the coffee shop with memorabilia and pictures from the Keystone Cops television series and was called 'Keystone'.

Most of the patrons were officers taking a break. Chappell urged Hollis to take a seat and queued up to buy their drinks.

"There you go Hollis." Chappell looked around, recognising staff from the police station. He looked at the pictures and memorabilia. He remarked, "The Keystone Cops were a bunch of inept and incompetent policemen. I always wonder if Roy, the owner is having a little joke with us. I certainly feel like one of those cops." He sipped his drink," How's your coffee?"

"Fine, thank you sir. What was it that you wanted to discuss, sir?"

"I have a theory. Based on the evidence or lack of evidence that we have, I think that either one person killed both Jennifer and Tom, or it was a pair of people. The likelihood of two deaths by strangulation being a coincidence would have astronomical odds. We still need to figure out why. I'd like to know how Tom Starkey could afford to live where he did. I also find it strange that there was a higher than average spate of overcharged customers. I think that Ms Bourdon delegated a lot of her job to Tom Starkey. What if he was able to speak to the customers, apply some pressure and they caved in. Instead of the overcharged amounts being refunded to the customer, what if Starkey redirected the money to himself? Does that sound feasible? It is a theory for which I believe evidence will be forthcoming shortly. I may be building castles in the sky but there must have been a lot overcharged customers if Ms Bourdon felt the need to tell us. I wonder if Mr Southpool has anything to do with this?"

"Frederick Southpool? But what does he have to do with this? He found a dead person that he knew on his land. He moved out for a few days just to get away from everything. What with the fire at the hotel he probably decided that it was time to move back home? We've nearly finished at the lake and let's face it his house is not close to the lake."

"That's my point. Two deaths by strangulation, days and miles apart. How is it that Frederick Southpool is present or at least in the vicinity of both?"

"Just unlucky, I guess."

"Hollis, think." Chappell gave her a sharp disapproving look. "I know that behind all of this you want Peter Riggs to be Jennifer Lindsay's killer, he may yet be, but I doubt it. Open your mind and review the facts as they are."

Hollis lowered her head and gazed into her drink. "I'm sorry, sir. You are right, I guess that I am locked into that idea."

"Yes, well you need to be flexible. There's nothing wrong with having a hunch but you need to change your mind as new facts come to you. And, you definitely need evidence if you plan on arresting someone."

Hollis said, "What I would ask though, is what motive does Frederick Southpool have to kill Jennifer?" Hollis took a sip from her drink and gave Chappell an appraising look over the top of her coffee cup. "Sir, Frederick Southpool should want her to stay alive especially if he wanted her to help him. Alright, he lost his temper with her but he's not going to want to kill her if he thinks that she can help him."

"That is the question, what does Southpool have to do with these deaths? To get the answer to that we are going to do one thing, I've made appointments to see Samuel Adesinsi later. At the end of the day Hollis, I'm playing a hunch too. I could be wrong."

"Sir, I still want to stick with Peter Riggs." Hollis held a hand up, "Please, listen." Chappell who had been about to speak nodded and drank his coffee.

"Go ahead Hollis. I won't interrupt you."

"I think that if Peter Riggs did not kill Jennifer, I bet he knows who did. There is something he is not saying. I just can't believe that he could wait outside a house and not know the area he was in. If he followed a bus home he should have been able to give us the number of it." Hollis' face glowed with enthusiasm as she warmed to her topic.

"Hollis, if you feel so strongly about this perhaps

you should do something. Do you think that you can get anything else from him?" Chappell looked doubtful but said nothing else.

"I don't want to pull him in again. I want to watch him. I wonder if he will return to the places that he waited for Jennifer. If he does, we might be able to catch someone out."

"What, all day? We don't have the manpower for that."

"No, I'll follow him, and I'll do it at night. If that is alright?" Hollis shifted in her chair, leant forward and continued, "I don't know if you noticed but when we questioned him about waiting outside the properties at night, I just got the impression that there was one last thing he hadn't told us."

Chappell narrowed his eyes and looked towards the ceiling. He thought about Hollis' suggestion, blew out a breath and nodded.

He said, "Yes do it Hollis. We've got nothing to lose. There is not a lot for us to go on at this point. Do it. Hudson and Sampson can work on the Starkey murder. Yes, do it Hollis."

Chappell stood, drained his mug and placed it back on the table. He nodded to Hollis and strode out of the coffee shop. Hollis sat at the table staring into space planning her next move. She looked at her watch. It was afternoon. She had no idea of Peter Riggs' daily routine. Where to start? What did she know about Peter Riggs?

Peter Riggs was a trainee psychologist. He was undertaking a work placement with a clinic. She would drive over to his lodgings and wait for him to return home. It was a long shot, but she wanted to know if she could learn anything else about him by carrying out some surveillance.

Scaffolding had been erected at the front entrance of Southpool Computing. The windows were being cleaned and a new sign was being hung. Mike Chappell dodged around the cleaners and made his way to the reception desk. Samuel Adesinsi who was speaking with a receptionist looked up when he saw Chappell.

"Detective Chief Inspector Chappell. Hello again. Please follow me."

Once again Samuel led the way to the boardroom, opening the door, he said, "Please take a seat, I just have to finish talking to the receptionist." Samuel left swiftly.

Chappell entered the room and glanced around. The pictures of Frederick Southpool and his son Robert were still stacked against a wall. Chappell crouched down and combed through the photographs once again. He covered his mouth with a hand. An idea was forming in his mind. No, it couldn't be. Could it? But why? What was the motive? Chappell ran his hand over his face as if washing it. Had he just stumbled on the 'how' of the murder of Jennifer Lindsay? He did not trust himself to consider the idea any further.

Samuel Adesinsi returned. He looked enquiringly at Chappell, "Detective Chief Inspector are you feeling alright? You look as if you have seen a ghost."

"A ghost of an idea, perhaps. Mr Adesini, please do not remove these pictures from this room. They are very important and must be kept."

"Yes, certainly. As you wish."

"Mr Adesini, I have to leave now. In fact, I think I

have the information that I need. Thank you for your help."

"But I haven't done anything."

"You have. More than you will ever know. Thank you." Chappell turned to leave, "Oh, does Frederick Southpool have permission to use the company account at the Twelve Kings Hotel?"

"Yes, he does. Anything to keep him from setting foot on the premises. We need to sort that out actually."

"Why?"

"Frederick doesn't actually own any property. The farm, his house, the properties in town they are all owned by the company. When the business became a limited company, he was able to say that he did not own anything. However, now that he has lost control of the business he either needs to buy the property back or walk away."

Chappell nodded, "So it was effectively a dodge then?"

"You could say so." Samuel spread his hands, palms up and shrugged.

"Samuel, can you send the information about the properties, Frederick Southpool does, or rather does not own to me. I would be very interested to see."

"Is Frederick under investigation?"

"Not at the moment. Please just send the information. I would appreciate it very much if you could do so as speedily as possible."

"Of course. I will make sure that it is emailed to you by the end of the day."

Chappell ran from the building, out to his car and tore out of the car park. He gunned his car in the direction of Forge Tarn. He had to visit the lake again. Parts of the jigsaw puzzle were beginning to take shape. He had a thread that he could pull on and unravel the mystery at last. Raindrops spattered the car windscreen. The dark gloomy clouds which had hung threateningly above for the last few days, shed their load. Within seconds the rain fell so heavily that Chappell's visibility was reduced to just a few feet ahead of him. The rain was torrential. Deep puddles formed on the road. Pedestrians had been caught unaware. Some were already drenched. People were scurrying for cover in shops and doorways. Chappell continued to drive as quickly and as carefully as he could. There was something that he needed to see at the crime scene. With the rain lashing down it was now doubtful that it was preserved but he had to see for himself.

Chappell parked in the car park at the far end of the lake and ran along its perimeter, choosing the side where the rotted rowing boat was chained up. He did not stop to look at it but instead ran further still to the crime scene itself. He ducked under the police tape and stared about him. The rain had created rivulets in the mud. There was nothing to show that a murder had been committed and a body found. Chappell was disappointed that he could not find what he had wanted to see. He was certain that a picture of it existed when SOCA had photographed the area. He hoped and prayed that this was the case. Mike Chappell stood exactly where the picnic had once been laid out and looked towards the other end of the lake. He smiled. Yes, this was definitely how the body of Jennifer Lindsay had ended up at this end of the lake. Where she had been killed was another matter. He had made progress of a kind. Now to follow the thread wherever it took him.

Hollis was parked around the corner from the lodging house. She had seen Elle Latimer return and let herself into the house. There was no sign of Peter. Hollis had researched the type of car and the number plate of the car that he drove. It was a blue, seven-year-old Fiat 500. This was parked directly outside the house. Hollis had no way of knowing if he was at home, but she would take the chance and believe that Peter Riggs had yet to return.

She had been parked outside the house for two hours already. She was prepared to wait the whole night through, if it would help her to find out more about her chief suspect. He arrived home an hour later. Peter was carrying a bag of groceries. Before he could open the door, Elle Latimer opened it from her side and stepped out. Peter and Elle had a short conversation. Hollis was not close enough to overhear what was being said. Elle was carrying a large black holdall and a handbag. Elle scanned the road as if looking for someone. Hollis slid down behind the wheel in her car. It was unlikely that Elle could see her, but if Hollis could see Elle anything was possible. A few moments later, a sleek navy blue saloon car drew up beside Elle. With a wave to Peter, Elle walked over to the car, opened the front passenger door and slid in. The door had barely closed before the car pulled off. Peter stood outside the house and looked at the car as it disappeared into the distance. At last, he walked into the house and closed the door.

Hollis sat in her car waiting for Peter Riggs to come out again. He did not. She watched the house as lights went on and went off. She saw heavy drapes being drawn across the windows. The hallway light, which could be seen through the glass window at the top of the front door, went off at eleven o'clock. As far as Hollis could tell the house was in darkness, from the front at least. She waited until three o'clock and decided to go home. Hollis knew that she was not wrong. One night very soon, Peter Riggs would retrace the drive he took when he dropped off Jennifer and when he did, she would be waiting for him. It was an instinct, but she was sure he would do it.

Tom Starkey's financial information was sent through to the detectives. Hudson and Sampson visited Chappell in his office.

Hudson spoke first, "Sir, you're not going to believe this"

"Try me."

"Well sir, I ran the dead man's fingerprints. It turns out that Thomas Starkey is a Swiss national called Thomaz Strenzi. He was a hotel employee who demanded money with menaces. He's wanted for assault and for actual bodily harm. He absconded from the hotel where he worked with the weekly takings. Let's see," Hudson flicked through his notes. "Yes, he absconded with the equivalent of £50,000 right after some fancy ball. He had programmed the hotel's computer to pay some of the money into his account and he took some cash and paid that in over the counter."

Sampson handed Chappell the financial documents he had been holding. "Read through that sir, what do you see? That's his current account."

Chappell did as asked and commented, "I see payments for his rent and utilities and nothing else. He has not made a single withdrawal. So, what is he living on?"

Hudson and Sampson smiled broadly at Chappell as he spoke his thoughts out aloud. "Tom Starkey, let's call him that, has a Swiss bank account. He pulls the same trick over here that he pulled in Switzerland. He diverts money to his account, an account which no one knew about. I wonder if he demanded money with menaces over here too."

Sampson commented, "I bet Starkey set the fire at the hotel as soon as he heard that an audit was going to be carried out."

Chappell said, "Very definitely. Good work you two. The computer system might have been destroyed but I wonder if he destroyed the central records. See if you find evidence of money from the hotel being diverted to a Swiss account. I have a feeling that he may have been blackmailing guests, overcharging them and paying the extra money into this account. We just need to find out who took exception to his scheme and killed him."

Chappell had spent the previous night poring over the photographs from the crime scene. More than ever, he was certain that he knew how Jennifer's body could have been placed in the lake. He had suspicions about Frederick Southpool but why would he have killed her?

Mike turned from looking at the whiteboards and faced Hollis as she entered the incident room. She looked tired and deflated.

"No joy, Hollis?"

"No sir, afraid not?"

"Stick with it. This is your hunch, play it and see where it takes you."

Hollis looked doubtful. She threw herself into her chair and surveyed the mountain of paperwork that had accumulated on her desk.

Chappell called out to the other members of his team, "Hudson, Sampson, what have you found out about Starkey's movements?"

Sampson spoke up, "Starkey seems to have just gone to work and then gone home. His neighbours barely saw him. When they did, he normally arrived home when they left for work. His phone has hardly been used. He probably made any phone calls he needed to from work."

Chappell nodded and said, "So on the surface we have two unrelated deaths. They appear motiveless because we don't know what motivated the killer or killers to commit the crimes. We are closer to find a motive for Thomas Starkey's death than Jennifer's. I want you to start to concentrate your efforts on Frederick Southpool. He was at the Twelve Kings and Jennifer's corpse was found on his land. I don't know why these murders were committed but I feel that Southpool will be connected."

Hollis started to speak "But sir, what about…"

Chappell interrupted her, "Stick with Riggs, Hollis. I am not discounting anything or anyone. If you are right about Peter Riggs he may well lead us to some further valuable information. At this stage, I wonder if he might turn into a vigilante and solve the murder for us." Chappell grimaced whilst the rest of the team grinned.

It was rare for Chappell to indulge in humour,

dark or otherwise. It was a sign of the desperate state of the case.

Chappell continued, "Seriously though, I think that we are in the end game. If the murders are connected the killer will want to get away. Again, I point to Southpool deciding to go home and then to go travelling. Why would he do that when he is trying to set up a new company to market his new, as yet unwritten program? He checked out of the hotel after the death of Starkey. Could Southpool have said or done something that Starkey was blackmailing him about? Now there is something else I want to bring to your attention."

Chappell walked back to the whiteboard and pulled a photograph of the crime scene where Jennifer was found from it. He passed it around the team. "What do you see?"

Hudson answered first, "The crime scene which we know is staged." Sampson and Hollis nodded.

"Have another look?"

Each of the detectives pored over the photograph in turn. Hollis said, "What should we be looking at sir?"

"When you see it, you will not be able to miss it. Have one more look."

Hollis, Hudson and Sampson tried but failed to find anything. All that they saw was a picnic set out on the grass. The mud beside the lake had a few indentations but no footprints. A fact which had caused the initial mystery of how the body appeared beside the lake. There were no footprints anywhere.

Chappell walked into his office and came back with a larger blow-up of the photograph he had passed around.

Hollis gave an exasperated sigh, "Sir, can you just tell us?"

Chappell held up the large photograph, "Those indentations you can see are footprints." He pointed to the prints in the mud of the picture he was holding. "They are the footprints of a person wearing flippers." The team gazed at the smaller picture and then the larger version.

Chappell continued, "I've looked at the picture so often and then I looked at the pictures back at Southpool Computing. Southpool can scuba dive. What if he somehow used his equipment to deposit the body of Jennifer Lindsay on the far side of the lake. He wouldn't be seen. He could also take the food in a waterproof bag and lay it out on the bank."

His team greeted his suggestion with silence.

Chappell felt the need to justify himself, "I know it sounds farfetched, but it is the only option that fits the facts. A woman's body is found beside a lake with no footprints at the scene. Food is laid out for a picnic which she does not eat. Nobody sees her there and more importantly there is no evidence apart from the footprints made by the flippers."

"So, sir, why am I following Peter Riggs?"

"I think that Riggs may have some part to play. I believe that there may be an accomplice. I have no evidence for this just a feeling. The murders, although similar are different. Don't forget Jennifer was killed by someone using their bare hands. The coroner tells me that the blow to the back of the head may have rendered Jennifer Lindsay unconscious, but it would not have killed her. Tom Starkey was killed by someone wearing gloves. In this weather you need an umbrella but not gloves. One murder may have been impulsive and the other premeditated.

Hollis and Hudson, this evening I want you to follow Peter Riggs. You have convinced me that he might try to retrace the route he drove when he followed Jennifer. Hopefully his interview with us has planted a seed. Sampson, Samuel Adesini should be sending over a list of the properties that Southpool 'owns' in and around town. I want to know who lives in them and if there is any personal connection with Southpool. In the meantime, Hollis I want you to accompany me to see Southpool at home. We need to interview him one last time. It may encourage some action on his part."

Frederick Southpool's house was located a mile from the lake. The road from the village of Forge Tarn was dotted with 'private property' signs. Chappell wondered if Southpool would have the money to buy back his property. A narrow road led from the main road to the farmhouse itself. From the outside the house looked in good condition. It was built from pale Cotswold stone and was a two storey building. Hollis who had driven, parked the car next to a gleaming black Mercedes sportscar. She made a point of feeling the bonnet of the car.

"The engine is still warm. Maybe Mr Southpool is at home."

Chappell made to walk to the front door of the house but was challenged by a ferocious chicken who squawked and pecked at his feet. More chickens joined the first and he was soon surrounded. A short, rotund woman left the house and shooed the birds away.

"Can I help you?"

"Yes, I hope so. I am Detective Chief Inspector Chappell, and this is Detective Sergeant Hollis. I wondered is Mr Southpool at home?"

"No, I'm afraid he's not. He left not more than fifteen minutes ago."

"Can I help you? Why don't you come in? I'm sure it's going to rain again."

Much like his business headquarters, the inside of Frederick Southpool's house comprised of mirrored glass and steel. In keeping with his tastes, the wooden floors were of bleached oak. The furniture was of a minimalist design giving the impression that one had walked into a show home. Sculptures and paintings adorned walls, tables, shelves and display plinths. The artworks were undoubtedly expensive but certainly not appealing to Chappell. He wondered if he was in a home or an art gallery.

On one carved wooden plinth were a number of photographs. Some were of Frederick Southpool shaking hands with business dignitaries and others were of Frederick and his son Robert. Here again, were photographs of the pair holidaying in exotic parts of the world. They were dressed in wetsuits and holding harpoons.

Edith Shorely, the housekeeper waddled through the lower floor rooms and took them to the kitchen. The farmhouse was large and rambling. Chappell and Hollis walked past a few rooms as they walked through the house. The kitchen was the warmest and the most welcoming place. There was an Aga range and a large oak table with accompanying chairs.

"Edith what can you tell us about Frederick Southpool?" Chappell smiled encouragingly at her.

349

Edith bustled about her domain preparing tea and fetching biscuits. She seemed to like the attention.

Once seated, she was ready to regale the police officers with everything she knew about Frederick Southpool. She touched on his loss of the company and the finding of Jennifer's body.

Hollis asked, "Edith do you have any idea why Mr Southpool would want to live out here?"

"Well, I think it's because he liked the idea of being a farmer. It massaged his ego. I remember he went to the shops and bought a lot of what he called his farming clothes. Sometimes he would say, "Edith, I'm a farmer" then he would laugh. I think really, he was looking for a big house in the area and this came up. Dave, the farmer who sold it to him, had made quite a bit of money from the sale."

"Does he take any interest in the farm?"

"No not really. There is a tenant farmer, Phil, living in one of the smaller houses not far away. Phil runs the farm, Frederick Southpool just owns it."

"What is life like here in this house?"

"Well Robert, Mr Southpool's son, has his own place in town so it is really just Mr Southpool and me. I make sure that the meals are cooked, the laundry is done, and I vacuum and dust. He's not here enough to make a mess. To be honest with you, I don't like this place much. It leaves me cold."

Chappell asked, "Is Mr Southpool divorced or widowed?"

"He's divorced. A long time ago. I've been working here for eight years and I know that he was divorced before then."

Hollis asked, "Did you know Jennifer Lindsay, the young woman who died by the lake?"

"Oh yes, I did. That was absolutely dreadful. I really liked her. She was helping Mr Southpool with a special project of his. Something happened, I don't know what and then she was sacked from the company. Is that right? I can't think what she could have done, Mr Southpool really depended on her. Do you know what happened?"

Keen to keep Edith on the topic, Chappell asked, "Were you here when Mr Southpool found Jennifer?"

"No, no I wasn't. That was Sunday wasn't it? I don't live here. I live in the village. Mr Southpool had said that he might not be staying here and that he might just stay at the Twelve Kings, so he gave me the weekend off."

Hollis doubled checked, "So, you don't know for certain if he was actually here on Sunday?"

"Well not for certain but, I'm sure that he would probably have been here over the weekend. It's not like he would have any business meetings. He does like to go for a jog around the grounds on a Sunday morning. He said it clears his head."

"Edith, does Mr Southpool have his own scuba diving equipment? I've noticed quite a few pictures of him in wet suits."

"Yes, he does."

"Can we have a look at it?"

Edith looked at him warily, "I'm not sure. Are you here to search the house? Don't you need a warrant for that?"

Chappell gave an easy disarming smile, "No, I don't want to conduct a search. I just wondered if you would be able to tell me if Mr Southpool possesses scuba diving equipment and if he does, where might it be kept? That's just a question, I don't want to look in any dark corners. Would you be able to answer that question for me?"

"Well, yes he does. Normally it would be in the shed out the back by the chicken coop. Just before you came I saw him putting luggage into his Range Rover. I don't know if he packed the equipment. He told me that he was about to go on holiday."

Chappell asked, "Do you know where he was going?"

"He was going to collect his son, Robert and then they were going travelling. That's all he said to me. I'm really sorry I can't be any more helpful."

"No, that is alright Edith. I think that you have been very helpful. Would you mind going into the shed and having a look for the equipment?"

The housekeeper looked doubtfully at Hollis, who in return gave her a beaming smile. Edith struggled to her feet and gazed at the two police officers.

"I'll go and have a look. You two stay here though. Don't move a muscle."

"We won't," Chappell replied.

A few moments later, Edith returned, ashen faced and slumped into a chair. Her mouth opened and closed a few times before she was able to make a sound.

"There's blood in there. There's blood in the shed."

Chappell said, "Show me."

Chappell was on his feet and striding out of the kitchen in the direction of the shed. Hollis helped Edith to her feet and allowed the woman to lean on her as they walked at a slower pace. By the time they reached the large, wooden shed, Chappell was looking into the dim interior of the building. A range of gardening and D-I-Y tools were arranged either on the floor or hanging from hooks attached to the rafters or walls. Leaning against one wall beside the doorway was a metal spade. It was resting on its handle while the blade was uppermost. On the edge of the blade was congealed blood. On closer inspection hairs were trapped in the mess of blood. On the ground beside the spade was a large dirty rag. This too, was covered in blood. It appeared to have been used to clean the spade. Instead, whoever had attempted to clean the spade had smeared the blood over the tool.

Hollis commented, "That's a lot of blood."

"That wound on the back of Jennifer's head was substantial and it probably led to her being rendered unconscious."

The officers had forgotten about the presence of Edith. The housekeeper whimpered, more frightened of the conversation taking place than at the evidence of a crime.

"Hollis, you take Edith back to the house. I'll ring SOCA. I want this area sealed off. This could be the primary crime scene. We need to find Frederick Southpool. He is now our chief suspect."

The processing of the scene was expedited as quickly as possible, as was the issuing of a search warrant. Chappell sat behind his desk, studying photographs of the scene at the lake and of the inside the shed. There was no doubt in his mind that Frederick Southpool was guilty of Jennifer's murder. He thought about how it might have happened. Both Jennifer and Southpool had had violent outbursts over the past few weeks. Had Southpool managed to lure Jennifer to his home? Southpool would have needed Jennifer's expertise if he was to set up a new company. She may have agreed to visit. Once with him, their conversation descended into a violent argument and he strangled her? As she fell she hit her head causing her to bleed. Perhaps he had worn his wetsuit and transported her body underwater to the other side of the lake. The circumstantial evidence against Southpool was mounting up. Chappell was sure that Southpool was probably also guilty of killing Tom Starkey, but as of yet there was not a shred of evidence to prove this supposition. There were a few pieces of the puzzle missing and Chappell did not know what they were or where to look for them.

A knock at the open office door was followed by Dave Sampson stepping into the room.

"Sir, Southpool's vehicle has not been seen. We've been looking at traffic cameras, but we can't find it on any major roads. We've had a look at the three properties he has. The apartments are located within two tower blocks. He has two properties in the same block. All apartments have been let. The trouble is the two blocks are located in town and have underground parking. There were no maintenance people or security guards when we called. We've rung the property management agents and they are sending people over to meet us, after they find their keys.

Sir, I'm just popping downstairs to get a drink. Can I get you one?"

"Yes please. I'll pay for both."

Chappell reached into his jacket pocket and withdrew a bundle of receipts and some crumpled ten pound notes. He laid the receipts on his desk and handed two ten pound notes to Sampson.

"Buy the drinks and food for the team from this." Sampson advanced and took the money. He glanced down at the receipts on the desk.

"Mind you sir, that's a lot of coffee you've been drinking." The coffee shop's logo was clearly visible of the receipts.

"Coffee makes the world go 'round Dave." Sampson nodded and left.

As a way to momentarily distract himself, Chappell smoothed out the receipts and looked at how much coffee he had actually drunk over the past few days. He looked at how many times a day he had bought the coffee. He stopped. He sped outside and looked at the evidence boards laden with photographs.

"No, no it can't be, can it?" Chappell muttered to himself as he searched for a particular series of pictures. Ideas were coming thick and fast to him, he needed time to process what he had just realised.

"Hollis, Hudson, drop what you are doing. Hudson go downstairs and find officer Barnes. If he's not on duty, find him and drag him in here if you have to. Hollis where are your notes from when we interviewed Southpool at the hotel? Find them. Both of you get going now."

Chappell found the photograph he was looking for. At the supposed picnic he remembered that some food had been laid out on a slip of paper. The piece of paper had been a receipt. Hollis found her notes, Hudson came back accompanied by a somewhat flustered Officer Barnes whilst Sampson came back laden with drinks and pastries.

Chappell paced up and down the incident room, "Toby, can you remind me again when Frederick

Southpool came to make his report."

"Well sir, he came in about three o'clock in the afternoon and just waited. I didn't speak to him until forty minutes later. He just sat and waited and then told me about the drowning."

"You're sure he was there at three and you didn't speak to him until three-forty?"

"Yes sir. There are cameras and I wrote the time and date down when he spoke to me."

"Good man. Thank you Toby. Well done. You can go."

Toby Barnes left the room hurriedly he had no desire to be questioned by Detective Chief Inspector Chappell again. Being pulled up the stairs by Detective Sergeant Hudson was bad enough.

Chappell looked at his team, "You just heard him. Southpool came in at three and didn't make his report until three-forty. My question is why was the food laid out for the picnic accompanied by a receipt that was printed at three-twenty?" Chappell waved the picture of the receipt around before handing it to the team.

Hollis exclaimed, "That means that Southpool was not acting alone. He had an accomplice. He comes here to make the report and the accomplice buys the food and sets the scene. This isn't about anyone caring enough about Jennifer to make it seem like she was having a picnic. This is about giving Frederick Southpool an alibi."

"Yes Hollis. Read your notes, what did Southpool say about his whereabouts on Sunday?"

Hollis flicked through her notebook.

"Southpool said that he was at home on Sunday, went for a jog and put himself through a punishing schedule. He moved back to the hotel after Jennifer's death."

Chappell grinned, "And then what happened?"

"Nothing sir, nothing."

"No Hollis. Something did. What happened was the barman dropped a glass. That barman was Tom Starkey. Starkey had just heard Southpool give us a barefaced lie and he dropped the glass. He probably couldn't believe what he had heard. I suspect that Starkey confronted Southpool about it and was killed.

"What I think is that Southpool wasn't at home at all. He had given Edith the weekend off and had stayed at the hotel. What if his accomplice, and at this stage I am willing to bet that it was his son, was the one who killed Jennifer? What if the son kills Jennifer, rings his father and his father tells him what to do? That's why Southpool is in no hurry to make his report. He has to wait until his son Robert has set the scene. That's also why he gave the reason that he acted on automatic and drove over here to the police station instead of ringing us."

Hollis, Hudson and Sampson nodded in agreement.

Chappell stopped his pacing, "So this is what I want done, notify the airports about Frederick and Robert Southpool. Go and check on the properties. I bet that the vehicle was left in one of the underground carparks while the Southpools took a taxi to the airport."

Hollis asked, "Why an airport? They could have driven straight to London or anywhere, Wales or just kept going up to Scotland."

"With two murders under their belts, I think that they would want to leave the country as soon as possible. Hollis don't bother with following Peter

Riggs. Put him in a car and drive him to both the apartment buildings, something might jog his memory. I have a feeling that Jennifer may have had a date with Robert Southpool."

Sampson asked, "One question sir, what were Jennifer and the son doing up at the house?"

Chappell responded, giving as full an answer as he could, "That's a question we can ask later. We know that Jennifer liked going to the lake. It might be that she had met Robert Southpool previously and was happy to accompany him to the house. We already know that she was moody and unpredictable. Something happened, and it was Robert who placed her in the lake.

"I think that this is a case of a father trying to cover up his son's crime and the second death was because he lied in the presence of someone who knew the truth. If Starkey had come to us instead of trying to blackmail Southpool he'd be alive. Notify the airports and check the properties. We should be able to clear this up shortly.

"Frederick Southpool clearly loves his son. That is one of the first things that Samuel Adesini told us. A loving parent would do anything to protect their child." Chappell gave Hollis, Hudson and Samson deep penetrating stares, "Including murder and covering up a murder."

Peter Riggs was waiting outside his lodgings when Hollis drove up beside him. She had already explained the purpose of the exercise during her earlier phone call. Peter had agreed to help.

He opened the front passenger door and slid into the seat.

Hollis said, "Peter I need you to concentrate and think. We have two possible addresses where Jennifer's killer might be. I need you to help me to identify which one is the most likely."

"I'll try. I hope I can do this."

Hollis replied, "Not to worry Peter, just do your best. Let's go to the first address and see if you recognise it."

Both occupants of the car were quiet. Laura Hollis concentrated on driving while Peter looked out for any roads and landmarks that he recognised. Hollis arrived at the first of the properties. The roads were busy, Hollis was forced to drive far slower than she would have liked.

She explained what she wanted Peter to do, "There are two possible properties in this tower block that Jennifer could have visited. Does this area look familiar?"

Peter shook his head, "No not at all. I don't recognise anything."

"Ok Peter, why don't you get out and walk around like you did when you were following Jennifer. Things are going to look different in daylight."

Peter did as suggested and wandered about.

Returning to the car he said, "Detective, I really don't recognise this place." Peter was genuinely disappointed. "There is nothing about this place that I've seen before."

Hollis spoke with more optimism than she felt, "Well there is one other location."

Starting the car, she headed off towards it.

Chappell who was seated at his desk, looked at the pages of information Samuel had sent him. Southpool owned three apartments which had been rented out.

Mike could sense that there was something he was missing. In their haste the team had looked only at the apartments that Southpool had once owned. More information had been provided than just naming the three properties. Adesini knew that Chappell had only been interested in the properties once owned by Southpool, so why had he sent so much information?

Chappell tried to put himself in the place of Frederick Southpool. If he were a rich doting father what would he do? Would he let his son rent a flat from him or the company or would he buy a property and give it to his son outright? Chappell would just give his child a deposit towards a property but what would Southpool do? The list of information he was reading showed all the properties that Southpool Computing had owned, bought and sold over the past ten years. Chappell needed to make sense of it. Somewhere buried in this list was the possible location of where the Southpools were hiding.

Hollis was now parked outside the second property. Peter had wandered around the area. There was nothing about this location that he recognised either. There were a few landmarks such as a large modern church on one street corner and a cinema on another.

Peter said, "Detective, I think I would remember if I had sat outside that church or that cinema. No, wherever I was it wasn't here."

Hollis was deflated. She had been so sure that she would be proved correct. Three buses drove past her, stopped at their designated stops and disgorged their passengers. Hollis looked at the number of people who had lined up at the buses.

An idea came to her, "Peter didn't you say that

there was a bus route near where Jennifer was? You waited until she caught a bus. Could this be the bus route?"

"Yes," Peter said as he looked out of the windscreen and looked at the buses as they drove further along the road. "This road is on the bus route I followed."

Hollis suggested, "Do you think if we follow the bus route you might recognise something."

Hollis started the car, the three buses, although bearing different destinations, were following each other. She followed the buses. The traffic had built up along the road. There were a series of road works and accompanying temporary traffic lights. The delays were becoming frustrating.

After ten minutes, she asked, "Do you recognise anything yet?"

"No, but this is the bus route I know that for sure. I'm hoping I will recognise the block of flats."

Hollis continued driving. As she did so she asked Peter to describe what he remembered of the last property he followed Jennifer to.

"It's coming back to me now; it was a dark night though. I remember I was parked opposite a kebab shop. Jennifer went into a block of flats that wasn't that modern. It was well-kept though. It probably only had three floors. The flats at the front had large windows. I do remember that. One flat had a really unique lampshade. It wasn't exactly a lampshade, maybe it was more of a chandelier. I remember it was such a big thing that you couldn't miss it. It was like a work of art."

"Well, that is something for us to keep our eyes open for," Hollis said doubtfully. She continued driving. Hollis looked for the kebab shop while Peter looked out for the flat with the chandelier. The pavement was so crowded that Hollis had trouble identifying the type of food outlets they were passing.

After reading through several pages of information Chappell came to a page that was headed, 'Gifts and Loans'. Only one property was listed. The property had been disposed of as a gift to Robert Southpool. This had to be the address and where the Southpools were hiding.

Walking into the incident room Chappell called out to Hudson and Sampson, "I think I know where the Southpools might be. Is Hollis back yet?"

Hudson replied, "No, sir. She rang to say that Peter Riggs hadn't recognised the two properties and now they were following a bus route but that was about ten minutes ago."

Chappell grimaced, "Both of you come with me. Hollis might be lucky and find the Southpools. I'm a little concerned about what will happen if they see her and what might happen if she sees them. Southpool will know who she is." Chappell turned and raced down the stairs to the car park. Hudson and Sampson were at his heels.

Hollis had been driving for twenty minutes and was beginning to feel as if she was on a wild goose chase. Peter was also becoming disheartened. Hollis carried on driving trying to keep their hopes up.

"There, there it is." Peter bounced up and down in his seat. He pointed to the block of flats. Hollis scanned the area. Yes, there was the kebab shop and opposite that was the block of flats. With no curtains covering the window, a huge unlit chandelier could clearly be seen in one of the front windows. Hollis stopped abruptly. The driver behind her honked his horn in rebuke. Hollis pulled over to the kerb.

"Looks like you've done it Peter." Hollis smiled at him. She sat staring at the building. She looked around. In addition to the kebab shop there was a coffee shop and a pub. Either would make an ideal vantage point for her to start her surveillance.

Hollis said, "Thank you Peter. This is great. I need to stay here. Will it be alright if you take the bus back home?"

"That's fine. In fact, there's a bus coming now." Peter was out of the car and running towards the nearest bus stop before Hollis had a chance to say goodbye to him. Hollis had no way of knowing where the Southpools were, or even if they could see her. She had to work on the assumption that they were not expecting to be found and would not be looking out for the police. She sat in the car for a few minutes longer. Even if the Southpools were looking out for her, there were such a large mass of people she might easily be overlooked.

Frederick Southpool had indeed spotted the car parked opposite the block of flats. His flat was the one which possessed the elaborate chandelier. He had been peering periodically out of the front window as he waited for his son to pack a few items and find his passport. He had kept a note of any vehicle which parked close by and did not move off soon after. The driver of the navy blue car was just sitting in it. Southpool kept to one side of the large bay window and looked down on Hollis' car. The angle of the sunlight was such that he had no difficulty in identifying the driver. Detective Sergeant Hollis was a striking looking woman. With her shoulder length curly hair, she was easily recognisable. Southpool looked up and down the road, making sure to keep behind the long drapes covering the window. He had no way of knowing if the police woman was on her own. Damn. How had the police tracked him down so quickly? He thought that he would have had enough time to make it to an airport. He walked away to find his son and to decide what to do.

Hollis looked longingly at the coffee shop. She definitely needed a drink and a break from driving. Stepping out of the car, intending to walk towards the coffee shop, she debated whether or not to ring in her location. Deciding to ring the team when settled in the coffee shop, she rolled her shoulders trying to ease her cramped muscles. A breeze ruffled her hair and blew it against her face. Pulling a hair band from her wrist she gathered her hair into a ponytail.

As she bent to retrieve her handbag from the car, she was aware that there was a man standing close to her on either side. A hand was placed on each of her arms above the elbow.

"Detective Sergeant Hollis, keep walking and don't make a sound. If you do, I'll break your arm." Hollis turned towards the speaker. It was Frederick Southpool. On the other side of her was his son Robert. She was being led along the street away from the block of flats. Her fellow pedestrians thought nothing of the three people walking abreast and taking up the pavement. The Southpools did not for one moment let go of her arms.

The change in Robert was striking. When she had seen him at the hotel he had looked presentable. Now, his hair was greasy and sticking to his forehead, he was pale and unshaven. He appeared to be wearing the same clothes she had seen him in before.

Hollis tried to slow her pace. Neither man slackened theirs.

"Sergeant Hollis don't walk any slower. If we have to drag you along the road and pretend that you're drunk we will. Speed up!"

Hollis sped up slightly. She cursed herself. Why hadn't she rung in and said where she was before leaving the car? She had to think of a way to get away from the Southpools. Both men had a firm grip on her arms. There was nothing that she could do.

Hollis stilled the panic in her voice and said, "Threatening a police officer is a criminal offence. What are you going to do? Do anything to me and you will be looking at a long custodial sentence."

Robert Southpool laughed. He said, "You think we care about that?"

Hollis turned and looked at him. Robert Southpool wore a vicious expression; his eyes were ice cold and his lips were thin and colourless. Laura could well believe that this was the person who had killed Jennifer Lindsay. Robert dragged her into a walkway between two buildings. He quickened his pace. Hollis had no option other than to speed up. The compact driveway was silent. It was between two office blocks. No-one was following them, and no-one was coming towards them.

They were walking along a drive way that was leading to a parking area at the back of the flats. No-one was going to know where she was. She looked up at the buildings. There were very few windows. Those that were there were covered in frosted panels or blinds. There were a few cars in the open parking bays. Frederick Southpool's was one of them. Robert walked towards the car.

Frederick Southpool said, "No, I have a better idea. Let's take her upstairs."

Chappell raced his car along the road. Seeing Hollis' abandoned car, he screeched to a halt behind it. All three policemen piled out of the vehicle. Chappell tried the driver's door of Hollis' car. It was unlocked. Her handbag was in full view. Breathing in deeply he placed a hand on the side of the car. The implications of Hollis' disappearance sprang immediately to his mind.

"Hudson and Sampson, we need to find her. She didn't leave this area willingly. If she is with the Southpools, she could be in extreme danger."

Hudson asked, "Would they really do anything to her?"

Chappell nodded, "Think about it for a moment. Each of these men has killed someone. They will have no compunction about killing Hollis. The way I see it they have two options. Either way they kill Hollis and then leave her body in their flat or else in the boot of a car. They would be long gone before she was found. Sampson call for back up. We need more people. Now!"

Chappell and Hudson ran along the road as Sampson put in a call to the police station. Since Hollis had not passed them as they had driven up she must have been taken in the opposite direction. It would be difficult to make her out. There were shoppers, officer workers, students and pensioners all taking up the pavement. Chappell and Hudson dodged past them hoping to see a trace of her.

Chappell asked, "Hudson, you were talking to

Hollis this morning, what was she wearing the last time you saw her?"

"Sir, I don't remember. I know she was wearing jeans and maybe a dark sweatshirt."

Chappell nodded and they continued running along the road, looking through shop windows and scanning the pavement ahead of them.

Sampson caught up with them, he said "Back-up is on the way."

Chappell, the desperation, sounding in his voice said, "We have to find her." His height was no advantage to him. He could not see through the crowd in front of him.

"There, there she is between those two men. See them?" Chappell pointed to the trio who had just turned into the walkway. The three policemen dashed down the street and into the walkway.

Hollis focused on thinking about how to escape. With one man she might have been able to overpower him but, with two men gripping her arms there was little she could do. She would have to wait for her chance. It came shortly after. The back door to the block of flats needed to be opened by a key. Frederick Southpool let go of her arm so that he could search his pockets for his keys and then select the right one. Robert Southpool pulled her to one side. This was her chance. She turned, kicked Robert in the groin and punched him in the stomach. He grunted and bent over. Frederick Southpool dropped his keys and moved towards her.

Hollis ran back towards the main road. She did not make it. She ran straight into the arms of Dave Sampson. Chappell and Hudson raced past her and tackled the Southpools. It was a short fight. Robert

Southpool put his hands up. He was still in pain from Hollis' powerful kick. His father attempted to land a punch on Hudson. It was an ill-judged move. Hudson punched him twice. Once in the stomach and once to a shoulder.. Southpool didn't attempt to dodge. When Hudson's fist connected with his shoulder Frederick Southpool fell straight to the ground.

The wail of police sirens could be heard in the distance. Chappell walked back to Hollis, while Sampson and Hudson handcuffed the Southpools and led them away to the waiting police vehicles.

Chappell looked at Hollis, ensuring that she was not injured. "They didn't hurt you did they?"

"No, sir. Just my pride." Hollis looked embarrassed.

Chappell laughed, "That will heal Laura. It will heal."

Chappell walked into his office, tidied his desk, and threw the coffee receipts and empty coffee cups into his dustbin. He picked up his latest cup of coffee, leant back in his chair and looked at the picture of the Matterhorn. Another mountain climbed; another mountain conquered. He silently toasted the picture and took a deep draught of his drink.

Outside in the incident room, his team tidied their desks and wrote up their reports.

Hollis asked Sampson and Hudson, "but how did you know?"

Hudson replied, "Hollis you know our boss. Detective Chief Inspector Chappell is always in at the kill."

THE END

MILDRED PIERCE

The Film
The 1945 American film noir crime-drama, was based on a novel by James M Cain.

The Storyline
The film, which is based in Glendale, California, starts with a murder. Monte Beragon (Zachary Scott), the second husband of Mildred Pierce (Joan Crawford), is shot dead. The police believe the killer is Bert Pierce (Bruce Bennett), her first husband who confesses to the crime. Mildred Pierce says otherwise and reveals her life story to the investigating officers in flashback.

The dominating personality is Mildred Pierce's daughter, Veda, (Ann Blyth), a bratty social climber. Her mother is dedicated to providing her with material possessions. The film focuses on the convoluted relationships between her second husband (Monte Beragon), a Pasadena society playboy, Mildred and Veda.

In the end, the detectives reveal that they have known all along who committed the murder. Mildred Pierce leaves the police station to meet with a further surprise.

The Production
The director was Hungarian born Michael Curtiz whose Hollywood breakthrough came in 1935 with the casting of an unknown Errol Flynn in the swashbuckling action drama, 'Captain Blood' followed by the 1936 film, 'The Charge of the Light Brigade'. He wanted Bette Davis for the role of Mildred Pierce and had a tense relationship with Joan

369

Crawford throughout the filming. He went on to become one of Hollywood's most prolific directors.

The producer was Jerry Wald who, despite dying at the age of fifty, made a staggering number of films as writer/producer including Key Largo (1948) and Peyton Place (1957). He was a close friend of Joan Greenwood.

The Stars

The film is dominated by Joan Crawford's Oscar winning performance: she became a Hollywood legend and often played the role of the hard-working young woman who would find romance and success. In 1999, the American Film Institute voted her the tenth greatest female star of classic American cinema. At times a controversial figure, she once said: "I never go outside unless I look like Joan Crawford, the movie star. If you want to look like the girl next door, go next door." She died in 1977 aged seventy-two.

Zackary Scott, an American of Greek descent, played Monte Beragon early in his career (being his fourth film). He made many more but never really achieved genuine fame. He was subject to bouts of depression and died at the age of 51 of a brain tumour.

American Anne Marie Blyth, who played the key role of Veda, has had a rather varied life as a cinema/television actress, a mother of five children, a devout Catholic and an active Republican supporter. She was nominated for an Oscar for her role in 'Mildred Pierce'. She is ninety years old.

The Book

The author, James Mallahan Cain (1.7.1892 –

27.10.1977), was an American journalist and author. He wrote over twenty-five novels, novellas and many screenplays. He is credited with being one of the creators of 'hardboiled fiction' (sometimes called 'roman noir') whose heyday was 1930 - 50s America. It featured detectives dealing with violent crime within a corrupt legal system. It often featured tough, perhaps cynical, attitudes towards emotions triggered by violence. His first novel, 'The Postman Always Rings Twice' was published in 1934 and was followed, two years later, by 'Double Indemnity', both becoming successful films. 'Mildred Pierce' was written in 1941.

ABOUT THE AUTHOR

Billie-Jean has worked in education for over twenty years as a teacher and developer of educational materials. She has been an elected councillor of the 'Economics and Business Association' working to ensure that business economics materials met the needs of teachers and students.

She has mentored young adults and teenagers to motivate them to succeed in education and to achieve their career goals. She lives in Kent.

Taking note of her own motivational advice, she has written her first novella, 'DS Laura Hollis: Time of Death' as the start of a series based on the work, life and loves of a policewoman.

She is writing her first full DS Hollis novel which will be published later this year.